# There is Love

Jo Guasasco Meador

abbott press

Copyright © 2012, 2017 Jo Guasasco Meador.

Interior Graphics/Art Credit: Author photo by Edward J. Meador

All rights reserved. No part of this book may be used or reproduced by any means, graphic, electronic, or mechanical, including photocopying, recording, taping or by any information storage retrieval system without the written permission of the author except in the case of brief quotations embodied in critical articles and reviews.

Abbott Press books may be ordered through booksellers or by contacting:

Abbott Press
1663 Liberty Drive
Bloomington, IN 47403
www.abbottpress.com
Phone: 1 (866) 697-5310

Because of the dynamic nature of the Internet, any web addresses or links contained in this book may have changed since publication and may no longer be valid. The views expressed in this work are solely those of the author and do not necessarily reflect the views of the publisher, and the publisher hereby disclaims any responsibility for them.

Any people depicted in stock imagery provided by Thinkstock are models, and such images are being used for illustrative purposes only.
Certain stock imagery © Thinkstock.

ISBN: 978-1-4582-2107-0 (sc)
ISBN: 978-1-4582-2109-4 (hc)
ISBN: 978-1-4582-2108-7 (e)

Library of Congress Control Number: 2017907792

Print information available on the last page.

Abbott Press rev. date: 06/29/2017

*In loving memory of Charlene—
sister extraordinaire
kindred spirit
—with Laughter, Love and Joy*

Acknowledgements

I wish to thank the board of Northwest Institute of Literary Arts for offering the opportunity and facility to pursue my dreams of writing this novel, and to the capable staff who have assisted me over the years. I especially appreciate the patience and support of this team as I struggled to find my story.

To the faculty of Whidbey Writers Workshop I owe a debt of gratitude for their continued belief in this project, for the persistence of Director Wayne Ude and his mighty tow rope that hauled me out of the rut, for the patience and endurance of advisor Bruce Holland Rogers, and the incisive remark of David Wagoner who in workshop expressed the hope that someday I might move out of the way of my characters. I am grateful for the many adjunct teachers like Elizabeth George who, on more than one occasion, appeared before me, pointing to signposts along the way.

To my fellow students in the fiction workshop I have appreciated the time taken to read and comment on my work, and to all those who were willing to endure my earliest efforts to find character and story: Loren Cooper, Stefanie Freele, Lois Brandt, Ann Gonzales, Nina

Bayer, Nancy Cluts, Judy Dailey and Terry Bergren. A special thanks to the poets, Tanya Chernov, Caleb Barber and Rachel who walked down that other path with me, along with Carolyne Wright, a poet and teacher most passionate.

A special debt of gratitude is owed to two of my fellow students in the writing workshop. With everything else going on in her professional and personal life, Nancy Boutin shared her talents freely with good cheer, and coached me through difficult times. To Helen Sears I owe the deepest gratitude, for staying through the long haul, to the end of a hard and transitional journey.

I am grateful for many teachers who have inspired me, in particular, Marian Blue—who helped me rediscover a lost inner voice of poetry—and Norm Siringer, my first Creative Writing teacher, who taught me how one examines a life worth living.

For this project I owe a debt of gratitude to Frances Grant, who opened the edges of Idaho to me in many visits to her homes in Idaho Falls and Sun Valley. Thanks to Lary and Judy Croom who further introduced me to the cultures of Pocatello and Nampa, and the wide spaces in between. For an insight into the rural expanse of western Virginia I owe much to the hospitality of Doris and Otis Turner. Finally, I am indebted to Dick and Pamela Freytag for introducing me to northern Delaware and the Brandywine Valley, the perfect backdrop for my character's early years.

I am thankful for early inspirations. My mother, Dot Mudd encouraged my early reading and introduced me to the magical universe of the San Mateo Public Library. Elsie Kilpack, a formidable and voracious reader, who helped me explore the wonderful world of the arts and books, from City Lights of the sixties to Powell's today.

My final acknowledgement—the last and first—is to my husband Edward, constant companion and spiritual anchor for twenty-nine years, a frank but gentle editor and a relentless proofreader; co-author of my private love story.

*If I have... all knowledge... but have not loved, I am nothing.
If I give away all I have... but have not love, I gain nothing.*

I Corinthians 13:2-3 RSV

*For now we see through a glass, darkly;
but then face to face: now I know in part;
but then shall I know, even as also I am known.*

I Corinthians 13:12 KJV

One

*E*mery Truitt crossed the expanse of lawn bordering St. Clements College with a certain spring to his step. The distant mountain peaks—always jagged and raw— now seemed radiant in the wash of light from the rising sun. He had won—and on his own terms. All that nonsense of moving with the herd, of "going along" in order to advance himself in the academic chain of being, had proven to be nothing at all. The promotion had come without surrender of his ideals.

The mid-May sun rose quickly, dissipating the cold air—orange and gold hues streaked across a sky giving way to the softening yellows, and then turned to blue. Truitt spied one of the great rusted hawks circling above, in search of a morning meal. Not a herd animal, but a singular icon of strength and intelligence, the hawk was going it alone—and succeeding, Truitt noted, as the bird dropped into the field and wrenched the life from its fuzzy prey.

Herd mentality led to mediocrity and complacency, a sure road to slaughter. There was little glory in that. Truitt had won his promotion without compromise, without surrendering his time or his will to the fly-fishing, rock hunting, and backcountry mindsets of his peers. With attention to scholarship and education, on his own, he had moved from the rank of Assistant, a mere instructor, to Associate Professor. He had gained the prestige and entitlements endowed on that position.

As he approached the limestone block Admin Building, Truitt recalled his earliest response to the place, *Abandon every hope*.... With steep bluffs surrounding the small campus, it resembled something out of Dante's inferno, a hot place devoid of soul. Over time, the vision was justified as he had come to see it as a soulless place, leeching the very spirit from his dreams.

The college town of Hawkes Ferry in southwestern Idaho was smaller than his hometown in the Brandywine Valley of Delaware—and far more desolate, hugging a two-lane road that wound up the sagebrush steppe, eventually ending on a bluff above a narrow river gorge. Everyone wore cowboy boots, jeans and ten-gallon hats in the shops, in the diner, and even to church. The whole place might have been a backdrop for a B-rated movie whose denizens rambled along in a haze of cowboy-think. Every day that he passed in this outland pulled him further and further from the realization of his goal. Or so he had believed, but now he was back on track.

Truitt had always been an academic star, from his earliest recollections. His superior intelligence had been honed in the town library of Sycamore Falls where his aunt served as librarian, caretaker and guardian. From a nook tucked behind her desk, he had watched as she stocked shelves, checked out books, and exchanged niceties with town folk as well as members of the town council and directors from the state board. Truitt's young life had been swaddled in the leather bindings and stitched pages of Knowledge.

His first scholarship allowed him to attend the elite Priory at St. John's Academy where, at the age of six, he found a seat among the sons of the privileged. It had been a rough go at first. His being the only day student, he had been relegated to the bottom rung of society, like a bastard stepson in the family attic. There's herd mentality for you.

Yet by the time he was in the third level, he had won the favor of key fourth and fifth levels, by sharing the fruit of his adept skill at research. His love of learning, of erudition and books, had served to raise his status. When he graduated from the Academy, he had secured a prestigious, four-year scholarship to Columbia University. Truitt had tied his proverbial wagon to a scholarly star, and it had rarely failed him.

In the Admin Building, he passed two students who greeted him with reserve. After collecting his mail, Truitt climbed the stairs to his office on the second floor, in the Humanities Department. He made short business of the memos, meeting schedules and administrative proclamations that had been shoved into his box. He was disappointed to find no mention of staff changes or promotions, until he reasoned that the news would hardly have had time to make the press by this morning. The last memo, a reminder of Saturday's year-end barbecue, had been addressed to "All Hands." Truitt frowned at the notion that there was no distinction between professional faculty and unschooled administrative staff, and both were collectively on par with farmers and cowboys. He tossed the memo into his waste bin.

It was true that he had expected much more from this first position. He had anticipated a rural atmosphere, of course, something a bit more provincial than the old-world college towns of New England. But he had not foreseen the stark wilderness of the country he had landed in. The arid, desolate terrain that surrounded St. Clements yielded little to nurture his aspirations. Yet considering the promotion, he had in the end carved out a singular niche of opportunity for himself. Few Columbia fellows had yet to run the gauntlet from Assistant to Associate Professor in the six short years since graduation. And Truitt himself had no confidence that he would make the grade either, or that the College Board of St. Clements would approve his promotion given his faltering association with its president.

The call from his department chair on the previous evening had surprised Truitt. Even more astonishing to him was his own response to the news. He listened to the news with a tacit joy, then responded to Dr. Mudd with reserved gratitude. Before the phone hit the cradle,

Truitt was already rearranging his plans, for he had been expecting another result. To that end, he had already set things in motion to make a move the following year. Yet, he had not been encouraged by the responses from a dozen applications he had made. Only one position held any possibility at all and, for Truitt, the small college in West Virginia was hardly his idea of progress. He had only applied there as a last ditch effort, enticed only by its proximity to the northeast and home.

The promotion would enhance his appeal when he sought a more favorable position in the future. He would, of course, stay the ground now, and gain experience and exposure to a wider body of colleagues. For the new position came with a grant for professional enrichment such as membership in the national congress of medievalists and its summer conference.

Truitt set about the morning's work with elation. Even the drollest papers from his medieval lit class could not dampen his mood. He sorted through the themes that he had read and graded over the weekend, ordering them by grades from top to bottom. Being as conscientious and thorough as he was, he set about to review every comment and finalize the grade in pen, considering the work of the individual student in terms of the class as a group.

The task made for a long morning. Truitt was already anticipating the hiring of a teaching assistant—another benefit of his new position—who would be addressing the less savory administrative tasks that went with teaching undergraduates. With the right person, he could surrender discussion groups from his core classes of English composition and introductory lit. That would leave Truitt time to focus on the upper level courses, on his responsibilities as advisor to a group of English majors, and to further develop his body of work on the Calabrian monk. In particular, Truitt wanted Thomas Martin for the job, a noteworthy student, who had followed Truitt from his freshman comp class to the medieval lit course.

Martin's paper sat at the top of the pile, just as the student stood above the rest of them, with insight and intelligence of a doctoral candidate. In the batch of fair-to-middling essays, Martin had selected the most serious and difficult topic, "Divine Intellect and Divine Illumination." He had exhibited a mature grasp on key arguments differentiating the work of Aquinas from Augustine with an exacting interpretation of both source texts. His argumentation was concise and clear, albeit delivered in the casual style of students arguing in the commons. Truitt had praised the work in a note on the front page under the *A* grade, which he now confirmed in red ink. He flipped to the back page to assure that he had been equitable in noting the student's disparity between subject and style. It was a gaffe that would be corrected with experience, but could not override the excellence of his topic.

The class had done tolerably well as a third year group. The ladies—there were four of them in the class—had predictably chosen themes regarding chivalry and romance. And the next paper was one of these, "*Noblesse Oblige* and the Medieval Knight" The topic was sentimental, nowhere near matching the elevated nature of Martin's theme. The student had a good opinion of her work and her person, something he hesitated to reward. Still, it had been thoroughly researched, appropriately annotated, and well written. Truitt could assign Miss Day nothing less than an *A-minus*, considering the leniency he had extended on Martin's style. In truth, he also needed to demonstrate fairness to prove that he was not favoring the male students as he had been recently accused of.

He confirmed the grade in red ink, yet when it came to writing the usual comment below the grade, he found he could not do it. Conflicted by a need to be seen as unbiased on the one side and a higher value for truth, he found he could make no comment at all. He turned the paper aside, assuring himself that he would fix this in the future by clearly denoting A-level topics from the others. He was, after all, nothing, if not fair and just.

It was nearly ten o'clock by the time he was done with the medieval term papers. He thought of taking a breather, but was just as anxious to be done with the sophomore essays on Romantic Literature. Spreading the papers on his desk, he was ordering them from bottom to top, hoping to save the best for last.

A sharp rap on the door commanded his attention.

Before Truitt was able to utter a word the door opened, and the janitor's head popped through.

"Yes?" Truitt asked with little interest as he returned to his work.

The janitor pushed the door open, standing full form in the office, armed with a tool. "Sorry to disturb ya', perfesser... Got the news, did you…about the system repairs and all?"

Truitt glanced at the discarded mail, unable to recall such a notice. "Perhaps—just this morning, though." He continued to work.

"Glad to hear it…" was the response, but the door didn't close.

Truitt looked up at the man.

The janitor wasn't budging. "Need to check the radiator. You're first on the list."

Truitt was first because of his junior position in the department, he had little doubt about that. Yet, things were about to change. He needed to take a stand with the staff, and start acting the part of an Associate, by responding as any of the others would in this situation. "As you can see, I'm busy at the moment. Come back at two. I have a class then." He readdressed the work in front of him, and by the tone of his voice, dismissed the man's expectations.

"Oh sure…I see…but I got to be outta here by noon myself. Taking the missus to town, you see. Doctors and all."

No, Truitt did not see. "Then start somewhere else…Like the second floor."

"Gotta work down from the top, you see. Boiler's in the basement. Steam rises…"

"Yes. Yes, but in someone else's office," Truitt urged. Did he have to plan out the man's schedule to get him to return to this office later?

The janitor shook his head, bouncing the tool gently against his hand. "No can do. Everyone's busy right now... students... finals. With year-end to-dos. Dr. Mudd says start right here. 'Perfesser Truitt won't mind' he says."

Truitt sighed impulsively, then restrained any outward show of irritation. He'd been trumped by the department chair. "Fine." Recalling his improved position, Truitt resigned himself to the interruption. *Noblesse oblige* and all that.

"Just be quick about it." Truitt said, trying to concentrate on his work.

"That's the spirit, perfesser. Be done in no time. Just checking a valve or two..."

"Quietly." Truitt said.

"Sure thing," the janitor muttered. Attacking the radiator with aplomb, he tapped and twisted metal upon metal, causing an erratic tattoo that jolted Truitt's concentration.

A rattling clank ended in a clunk followed by the human utterance, "*Whoops!*"

Truitt was determined not to look up.

Steam hissed, followed by another interjection, "*Aw jeez!*" Then a noxious odor filled the room.

Truitt scooped up the papers, shoved them into his bag, and left through the door with all the dignity he could muster.

"Be done in just a sec, perfesser!" The janitor called after him.

Truitt was already headed down the stairs and toward the Faculty House.

Two

Against the distant sounds of silverware on pottery and the aroma of roasting beef in the faculty dining hall, Truitt continued grading the papers. At this hour—wedged between breakfast service and lunch—he would be able to work in relative peace with minimal interruptions. There were only two other teachers in the building, both hovering over grading tasks. The lobby was busy, though, with College Board members scuttling about, disappearing into the executive dining room.

Reading papers of the underclassmen was Truitt's least favorite task. The sophomores were not only wanting in rational thought, but had also lost any sense of grammar they might have picked up in Freshman Comp. In complete abdication of the essay form they, in toto, favored the rambling commentary of the pop mags found in the Sunday paper.

Scarcely a decent paper in the bunch. Still, Truitt pulled out four passable essays. Putting these on the bottom of the pile, he hoped to finish up the batch with some sense of satisfaction from the exercise. He wanted to complete the job this morning. That would leave him free to work on more important things this evening, like finishing his second article for The Medieval Journal.

Spotting Leif Sanders out the window, Truitt knew he was heading for the dining hall, and would, no doubt, want to join him for lunch. Truitt did not want the interruption. As the geology professor paused at the door to extinguish a cigarette, Truitt shifted his chair to position his back toward the entrance. He picked up the next paper and allowed himself to be engrossed in it, a rather poor interpretation of Wordsworth's Ode.

It didn't matter. As he set the paper on the table to grade it, Sanders stood lurking over him like a raptor ready to pounce.

"Well, well, well, Dr. Truitt." The man was actually smirking as he tossed his satchel on the table. "What shall become of you, I wonder?"

Truitt surrendered, setting aside the rest of the work. "And why should you be wasting your time and energy worrying about me?"

"Rumors aflying," Sanders said plopping into the chair across the table from his friend. "And here I thought you had big plans for your life that didn't include sticking around this wasteland."

The fierceness of his hazel eyes melted into the warmth of a grin.

Truitt smiled, stashing the papers into his bag.

"Yet, old man, somehow, I can't picture you fading quietly away from this place, in your dotage," Sanders said.

"Dotage? You? Hardly. And why should you be thinking of me at all?" Truitt said, already knowing what the answer would be.

"Promotions. It seems you've made Associate—congratulations." He clapped Truitt soundly on the shoulder. "And you thought they'd pass you over, once again."

"I was a little surprised when Mudd told me that I'd made the cut, actually. I thought the political winds were still against me."

"Christian Day, you mean? You should listen to your elders, you young whippersnapper. I told you not to put too much into all that. You forget that Day and his cohorts were once pleading passing grades from me in Earth Science."

Truitt sighed in relief. "I'm just glad it's over."

"Egad!" Sanders said with some concern. "What would I have done here without you?"

"Seems to me that you're jumping ship, in any case."

"Yes, but only to Salmon River. Two hundred miles, maybe—not two thousand." Sanders stood to survey the flux of teachers filling the room. "Shall we celebrate your victory over lunch? Or should I go away and leave you to the uninspired notions of underclassmen?"

"I could use a hearty meal," Truitt said. He followed Sanders to the serving bar. For all the aromas promised the palate, only plates of assorted sandwiches, salads and fruit desserts were offered at the bar—not even a hamburger in sight. Apparently, the hot lunches had been prepared for the sequestered board.

"I hope the board enjoys my steak," Sanders said, picking up a brown wedge of bread stuffed with cheese.

The two men ate in companionable silence while Sanders occasionally remarked on the human condition as it applied to his peers, a topic that entertained him unceasingly. He speculated on the business which might be commanding the board's attention, guessing that it probably had to do with the school's sports program and the ultimatum that had been issued by the athletic league.

Sanders leaned forward and squinted. "You think so? Then what might that have to do with our comely language professor?" He nodded toward the lobby.

"Sofia Avila?" Truitt turned, only to catch a flash of red disappearing in the direction of the dining room.

Sanders laughed at his marked interest. Truitt frowned, once again regretting the bottle of scotch they had shared one evening last fall, when he had confessed feelings of envy about her advance to Associate. It went without saying that Truitt had been the worthier candidate, having already published half a dozen papers.

"Coffee?" Sanders asked.

He returned with two cups. "I'll miss you, you know. Of all the men who have wandered through my life, you've been one of the most interesting. Probably because you talk less than I do."

Truitt piled the dishes and Sanders took them to the sideboard.

"You're a loner, Truitt, like me," Sanders said on his return. "If you don't watch it, you'll be spending the rest of your days in a bachelor's bungalow somewhere, waiting to be put out to pasture."

Truitt grinned, sipping the hot coffee.

Sanders considered another angle. "I wonder—do they have pastures in those Ivy League schools of yours?"

When Truitt didn't make Associate the prior year, he had claimed to Sanders that his eye was set on greener pastures in the northeastern region of his roots. The geology professor was seeing him now as a dissembler, no doubt. The truth is, Truitt had been sending out letters to improve his position for the past year. Out of seventeen letters, he had received only four responses, all negative.

"Pasture? Your cabin is in the middle of a forest."

"Forest land and a rapid river brimming with fish in the fall. A veritable Eden," Sanders responded. "Me with my rod and reel, and a lifetime supply of line. At least what's left of my life."

After a few moments of reflection, he added, "It's too bad, Truitt, that you have no interests outside of this place. Nothing to pull you out of yourself and connect with something real."

"The mind is the only reality, Sanders. Everything else is an illusion. The world lies in the mind."

"That's the illusion, man, that what lies in our heads is real. It's what we've made up from the lies and deceits we have hoarded about ourselves. To make us feel good, when things start to crumble. Tell me, what is it that you love?"

Sanders had ignited the old debate. He already knew that, in Truitt's view of the universe, the terms real and love were not linked. He knew full well what Truitt's position in the argument would be.

What Truitt loved was easy enough. From his earliest memories, cradled in the small room behind the librarian's desk in Sycamore Falls,

Truitt's world was encompassed by books. The library had been his hearth and home, and the little cottage merely a second place.

"My academic work. Teaching. Publishing."

"And when the books pan out, and the pages shred to dust, where will you be then?" Sanders reflected. "Real work is in the field. Digging with your hands to reveal the mysteries of the earth. Feeling the power of the ages rise with the dust."

Truitt shook his head. "History lies in the archives of man, not in latter day speculations on shards and bones. Besides, if you don't write about your work and your discoveries, how could future generations know what your work is all about?"

Sanders listened with fading interest.

Truitt went on. "Think of it, without the written summation from men who preceded you into the field, you would be clueless. Without your accounting, students would be encouraged to believe in their own undisciplined thoughts and follow their whims chaotically. Idle thought would replace academic curiosity, random hunches would displace theory. And there would be no rigorous testing for truth."

"En garde!" Laughing heartily, Sanders raised his fist in mock battle. "Publishing—what rubbish!"

Truitt nodded his head in acceptance of where they would leave these matters between them—unsolved.

Reflecting on the world passing outside the window, Sanders shifted into melancholy. Truitt looked around to see a group of girls from his afternoon class passing by, chatting excitedly.

"What do you dream about Truitt?" Sanders asked.

"Dreams are wasted bits of energy, the idle occupation of schoolboys and lovers."

"I was thinking more directly of the female race."

"Female students—an oxymoron. School is wasted on them, for the most part. They disrupt the class with private discussions, yet rarely contribute to the conversation. And their essays are abysmal."

"You can always dream of getting better students," Sanders smiled.

"I don't dream, Sanders. I pin my hopes on my knowledge, experience, and the successful outcome of my goals. Then I aim my efforts and my plans toward achieving those goals."

"The problem with you, Professor, is that you are too damned logical. You see what you have trained yourself to see, and little else."

"The girls, you mean?"

"That yes. But the boys, as well. Our students haven't been cut and polished by the lathe of Ivy League mentality, which instills certain sophistication, I agree. Yet because this is missing you don't see what is there."

"What is there?"

"Heart. These kids know the smell of the earth and what's brought on by changes in the wind. They know the language of cattle and sheep and horses. They understand the rocks and arid plains."

"Of what use is that in teaching Chaucer or Shakespeare?"

"They live with their hearts instead of their minds, old boy. They navigate with hunches, not theories, and let their intuition guide them."

"Yet, they come to St. Clements for a degree, of all things."

Sanders grinned, as he picked up his satchel. "Now that I've planted the seed for a new direction, our post-retirement dialogues can take on a grander feel—avoiding, at least, discussions about me and publishing."

Truitt stood up and gathered his books. "Still, how do you plan to face life day after day without purpose? What will you do?"

"Nothing. That's the point. Life without a goal—ahh."

"I'd rather curl up and die."

"Come up to the river, Truitt, and I'll make a believer out of you."

The two men parted outside the hall, Truitt trudging up toward the Admin Building and Sanders following the easier path of the service road toward the Science center.

As Truitt headed for his Medieval Studies class, Thomas Martin was climbing the staircase ahead of him.

"Martin! I'm glad to catch you. The term paper was excellent.

Most graduate students would find Aquinas too dry, and Augustine hopeless."

Martin was pleased. "Actually, it wasn't too difficult. We had studied some of Aquinas in Philosophy class last fall. Dr. Haug said Aquinas sets the foundation for studying argumentation."

"And so he may... after the Classics." Truitt agreed, walking in a conversational pace with his student.

Martin stopped. "You don't think he sets the standard?"

"Perhaps not all of it," Truitt did not want to appear as if he were criticizing the philosophy teacher. "Anyhow, I enjoyed your take on Augustine, in light of Aquinas's argument. You didn't read the works in Latin, did you?"

"No, sir. I have enough trouble with English. I took Spanish for the requirement, though," Martin said with some levity. Then he seemed concerned. "I put all my sources in the bibliography. Didn't I?"

"Yes. I had wondered because Augustine's notion of Divine Illumination is often muddled in translation. It's often inferred as some sort of grace, which is not Augustine's intent. Your paper demonstrated that you understood the difference. Well done."

When they reached the classroom, it was empty, with twelve minutes to spare before the session started. Truitt emptied his satchel on the front table, next to the lectern, and sorted his lecture notes.

Martin took the front row seat by the window, unloading his own sack. After a quiet moment, he said, "I have to give credit to Reverend Smythe, though, for helping me with the Augustine. The City of God was a bit foggy, even in English."

"You read the whole thing during this term?" Truitt asked.

"Oh, no. We were reading an excerpt for Theology class—the stuff about the soul." Martin paused unsure of what he might have given away. "That's not cheating, is it?"

Truitt laid out the papers for students to retrieve as they entered the class. He knew that Haug and Smythe had every right to teach the medievalists in their respective disciplines of philosophy and theology, yet it still felt like an impingement on his territory. The school was small and classes few. There was so much material that couldn't be covered that it seemed a waste for all three of them to cover the same ground.

"Dr. Smythe didn't know I was writing a term paper, you see. We'd been looking at the Confessions—the nature of sin, and all that. When we were done, I kind of read more on my own. I asked him about the City of God. Actually, I picked this topic specifically because I thought I could write something useful about it."

"You have used your resources well. The question of cheating would only arise if Smythe had actually written the material for you—or if you had blatantly copied his work without any due consideration on your own part."

Truitt handed him his paper." I think I can tell the tone of Smythe's rather dull sermons, from your work. You'll note I had an issue with your tone. Sounded as if you'd picked up some jargon from television. But you've done a terrific job reasoning out your position. An excellent job, in fact."

"Maybe I should have copied some of Dr. Smythe's explanations, just for tone? He surely is the model of sobriety." Martin smiled, taking his seat.

As the rest of the class trickled in, picking up their papers, Truitt moved toward Martin's desk. With a lowered voice he said, "I'd like you to drop by my office today, if you can." He wanted to give Martin a heads-up on the new position, to let him know that the job was his. Truitt had no doubt that he'd jump at the chance—the position would be an asset on his application to graduate school. Truitt had no intention of mentioning the opening to the others, avoiding undesirable inquiries. It was a short-term tactic. He could only hold the other applicants off for a week until the administration would insist that the job be posted.

"Can it wait until next week, sir? I have some business to take care of after class."

Truitt reluctantly agreed.

On the lectern, he opened the class by inviting questions of a general nature. He encouraged the students to limit their queries to "topics of interest to the class as a whole—for instance, something that might appear on the final exam."

"I don't get this grade, Dr. Truitt." Orville Parker took no time to involve the entire class in his personal problem. He brandished his C paper in a way no self-respecting scholar would do. He habitually inhabited the back of the classroom, when he came at all, and paid as little attention as he could get away with.

"Mr. Parker."

"I mean, we all know the university started in Paris. I think I really showed that in this paper."

"You merely cloaked my lecture in a travelogue from the trip to Paris you took two summers ago."

The students chuckled.

"Yes, sir. My graduation trip. Saw Napoleon's tomb, the obelisk and everything."

"In a paper entitled, The Rise of the University, I expected something a little more, such as an exposition of events leading up to the establishment of the institution or perhaps a comparison between Paris and Bologna which, you remember, rivaled each other for the seat of scholastic power. Or perhaps you could have offered a discussion on the art of argument and Scholasticism. Shall I go on?"

Parker dropped into his chair. "Jeez. I thought sure I'd get an A this time. All these pages."

"Professor? Is this on the test?" Emily Turner, who always had more interest in what Truitt was testing than in what he might actually teach her.

Truitt took aim at the bigger issue. "Mr. Parker, you have confused quantity with quality. To earn a grade of B, one would have referenced at least two secondary sources beyond the primary work. An A level would have required at least five secondary sources."

"Why didn't you tell us that on the handout?" Several students demanded.

"That will be on the test," Miss Turner said gleefully, jotting in her notebook.

"You might have started with Abelard, Mr. Parker, and moved on to Aquinas, comparing the advancement of the method through the late Middle Ages. In translation, of course."

"I could have lent you my Abelard," Miss Turner said in a wistful way.

"Twenty pages for nothing," Parker groaned.

"Professor?" James Macdonald spoke up. "I had five secondary sources in my paper. Two books on the church, one on the Protestant Reformation. A book on the Crusades and one on Francis of Assisi."

Truitt had some sympathy for Macdonald, whose paper aimed at defining the role of the church in society. Yet it had lacked a central thesis, the topic jumping from one subject to another, making no connections between each of them beyond a limited chronology.

"In itself that is commendable. However, your paper suffered from lack of focus. I was hoping for a thesis-based one of the topics we've covered this term. Your paper addressed a broad perspective over a much wider expanse of time. If you want to talk specifics…"

"Dr. Truitt." Parker jumped in, with rising agitation. "You just said I used your lectures too much. Now Mac here didn't do enough? What's up with that?"

If Parker had hoped to lead a bandwagon of malcontents to undermine Truitt's authority, he was mistaken by the sharp retort from Macdonald.

"That's enough, Orv. You're not being helpful. Thanks, Professor. I got it."

Truitt might have felt victorious to some degree, had not the rising tension among the others begun to wear on him. They had diverted far from the course he had planned, and he wanted to wrap this up quickly. A disturbance arose from the group of girls sitting behind Macdonald, whom they quickly recruited. Macdonald seemed helpless in avoiding them, especially since his girlfriend, Amy Gaites was, at that moment, having trouble expressing her thoughts.

Truitt gave her a little shove. "Miss Gaites, do you have an issue for us?"

She looked up at him in alarm. "I'm not sure if this applies to anyone else?"

"Just ask him," Macdonald whispered.

The other girls chimed in, to encourage her. They acted as if Truitt were the ogre in some fairy tale of innocent babes lost in the woods. Her timidity bothered him, if truth be told. Even if she had chosen ill for her topic, he was still capable of seeing her effort. In fact, he had done just that. She had made an unfortunate choice. A work well known for its obscurities and ambivalence, The Romance of the Rose was an obscure work whose meaning scholars had argued over for centuries. It offered few teaching opportunities for the average undergrad. Truitt certainly couldn't blame Miss Gaites for failing to grasp its deeper meanings. He did express his dissatisfaction, however, with her casual treatment of the work, putting it on par with modern romance novels.

Miss Gaites waved the paper, as if to remind him of her work. "I don't get what you're saying here... in this comment." The red C+ beaming like a beacon of her worth.

She hadn't gotten anything at all about it, he explained. "The work is an extended allegory. Characters represent ideas—they are symbols of deeper abstractions—and the story itself works on both the superficial plane as well as the deeper levels."

Truitt had to remind himself to show some sympathy in taking the girl to task. "Miss Gaites chose to write about a thirteenth century poem, a rather difficult task. It's an allegory...."

"A parable?" One of the other girls announced in the form of a question.

"I thought it was a love story," Miss Gaites groaned.

"It's about love," Truitt said. Then realizing his opportunity to teach, he added without pause, "As understood in the 13th century, which is to say, a heated topic disputed widely across the span of society. Agents of the church accepted no other ideal of love but that of sacred devotion. Nobles, on the other hand, fostered an ideal of secular love, which had nothing to do with marriage, by the way. Marriage was a business arrangement, binding states to each other and building alliances among nobles. Marriage was the vehicle to impose Church authority on power of the state, as defined by the doctrines of the Divine rights of kings and primogeniture...."

"That's where only the oldest son wins, isn't it? The rest of them get kicked out of the castle." The student seemed to hold a personal grudge against history.

"Not all royals agreed with the Church, mind you. In Southern France, for instance, daughters were not barred from inheritance if they were the sole heirs to the estate. And remember, the Church itself was split into multiple factions all bidding for control of Europe's souls. This is the background against which the Romance was written."

For once, the class seemed interested in the lecture. Unfortunately, it was not a work that he had chosen to cover in the course.

"So, to answer your question, Miss Gaites, the work is an extended allegory. The characters represent medieval ideals, which the author is presumably examining—or even, perhaps, parodying. Its intent has not yet been settled by scholars in the last seven centuries."

"Okay," Miss Gaites interjected. "I did get all that, Professor. But it is a story. The Lover character enters the kingdom and falls in love with the Rose. He desires her all through the story. He gets lectured by all sorts of people—ideals, as you say. All of them talking in essays. Yet when he finally reaches the rose, through all their objections and obstacles, he plucks her from the bush. She'll be dead in two days!"

"Another example of a maiden's exploitation at the hands of uncaring men." The unwelcome observation came from one of the girls.

Truitt overlooked the remark. "So what does the story say in allegorical terms, then? Lover represents an aristocrat, a knight indeed, but one without fortune and property, a lesser son who must pursue his fortune through marriage. Rose is the heiress in want of a husband that can raise her social status. According to the social mores of the time, she is sequestered from public life. The locked garden in which she dwells can be understood as the impregnable castle in which the lord keeps his daughter. The lord will also gain prestige when his daughter marries well. The characters, to a greater or lesser degree, each weigh in on the behaviors and actions of the lover. As you noted, the characters make their cases, in essay form."

As Truitt warmed up to the topic, most of the students were losing interest. The girls seemed to hang on longer than the men, with Macdonald and Martin still attentive to the game. He acknowledged to himself that he shouldn't have delved so deeply into a work that had been read by only one person in the class, and a female at that.

"Isn't Love about the heart, Professor, and not the mind?" Kristina Day asked.

"I agree with Kristi." Miss Gaites said. "There's nothing in that book about real love. It's all words—definitions and arguments. It doesn't even feel like love."

"I can appreciate your position, Miss Gaites. Your task was a difficult one, and your effort has been courageous." He needed to move on to the day's lecture.

"Will this be on the test?" It was Bob Patterson, this time, who asked.

"No, it will not." Truitt said with some annoyance "The Romance of the Rose, has not been covered in this course, and is unlikely to be in any course that I teach."

"Then why did you put it on the list of term paper topics?" Birdie Caldwell asked with an edge in her voice.

"Why is the work so important, Professor?" Martin asked.

"A much better question, Mr. Martin. I'll answer it briefly. To some degree, Western civilization today is still remarkably influenced by the romans courtier, the courtly romance. Our notions of love and marriage, of the role of the church, are still very much tied to the notions of this age. In terms of literature, the Rose introduced to its 13th century readers the notion of sentimentality, a product of the imagination—not the mind. The troubadours in Eleanor's court, as they transcribed oral tradition from the sagas of Arthur and Charlemagne, refashioned the tales into the contemporary rage for sentimentality. This imaginative flair took hold, opening the body of western literature to work less rational than the classical canon. From these romances, as they were called, our study of literature lay along two paths, one serious, serving the mind, and the other... Well, the other is based on sensation—what Miss Day refers to as the heart."

The term romance itself was highly sensational, finding its roots in Ovid, which Truitt would never teach, especially in this school. And as for matters of the heart, he was in no mood for taking on that battle.

"Professor." It was Martin again. "From what you've described, it sounds as if reading this work would reveal a lot about the world of the Middle Ages. Social mores and ethical thought. That kind of stuff. Why wouldn't you ever want to teach it?"

Truitt granted the question from Martin. "The poem is eleven-thousand lines, constructed by two poets over a fifty-year period. The form itself has little appeal to the twentieth-century student. The process of teaching would be an uphill battle. Wouldn't you agree, Miss Gaites?"

She nodded.

"The allegorical form offers a level of complexity that would be hard to deal with in the brief time that we have to dedicate to the work. In graduate school, one devotes at least a month to its study. Finally, the literary tradition of the work rises out of Ovid, a Roman poet who would require much more attention than the Rose itself, necessarily expanding the time needed to teach it." Not to mention its erotic nature, which would most certainly be taboo at St. Clements. Then there was the whole saga of Eleanor of Aquitaine that he had no desire to dip into. Leave that to Professor Avila and her Advanced French students.

In the remaining time, Truitt turned to Aquinas and Scholasticism. The students nodded off in the rising heat, trying to snatch a phrase or two in their notebooks. Had anyone besides Martin connected to his ideas, as Truitt himself had connected to his own mentors at Columbia?

The thought occurred to him just then that he might be as irrelevant to his students as Rumbag had been for him in his post-graduate years. There was the chance that even Martin might be placating him, that they all might view him as a fraud, the professor who had been pushed ahead for political expediency, rather than academic superiority.

By the end of class, the heat had done its work on him, as well. He was worn out, glad to see the backs of his students, every one of them, as they shot from the room. No one lingered to inquire about his judgment on an individual paper. Truitt erased the board to the rhythm of footsteps fading down the hallway and the labored sound of the lobby door opening and closing. He was grateful, though, that Martin stopped to thank him for new insights on Aquinas.

As Truitt organized the notes scattered across the table and dais, he thought about the effectiveness of his teachers. Of course, he had experienced the advantage of a classical education rooted as it was in the ivied halls of New England, a place where knowledge and literacy both were held in high esteem. He considered how he might fare among the other teachers at St. Clements—a group of slackers, for the most part, Sanders notwithstanding. Scholarship took a back seat to rodeo, fly-fishing, skiing, and trail riding. Again Truitt stood out, spending his days expanding the body of medieval literature and thought with his continued scholarship and writings.

He placed his notes into the satchel, considering how much he had deserved this promotion. He summoned the mass of his knowledge and effort when he stood at the lectern. If he had failed to interest his students today, it was their own shortcoming and not his. The girls, in particular, had no respect for history or its lessons. If arguments on love and marriage did not suit them, they devised their own reasoning. The male bias they claimed he held toward the subject, was merely a reflection of the medieval mind. Like the male rational process, the medieval mind was bent toward logic and argumentation.

"Professor Truitt?"

Kristina Day had come back through the door. Something in her manner grated deeply in him—though he could not say what it was. Some inborn joie de vivre, some sense of entitlement bestowed upon her with a most fortunate birth.

In her hand, she grasped her paper with its prominent A minus.

"I am done with papers and grades today, Miss Day. Office hours in the morning." He made a beeline for the door.

"Oh! It's not that..." She said, following him out of the room. "I won't be on campus anyway tomorrow. I'm helping Grandmother with Saturday's barbecue."

What Kristina Day lacked in intellectual curiosity, she made up for in her exaggerated sense of duty to family and community. Truitt did not admire her for it—even as all his peers did. He merely observed that her involvement had the effect of drawing attention to her charitable deeds, and thus to herself.

"Tuesday next, then," he said dismissively.

"Well, it's just that... I've heard you made Associate Professor. I genuinely think you deserve it."

He accepted her words gracefully, although he knew it was merely another duty fulfilled, a check mark on her roster of polite things to do. He excused himself abruptly. "I'm developing a splitting headache from all this heat." He rushed out of the room.

Crossing the shaded green toward his bungalow, he wondered how many students knew of his promotion. Had she tapped into some special line at the family table? Certainly it must be the latter for Martin, of all his students, would have been the first to acknowledge it.

Anyway, it was certain that he had earned the position, if only for putting up with the board president—and his daughter—for the past six years.

Three

*K*risti left the classroom on the heels of the professor and watched him leave the building. It was odd that he had not returned to his office. She turned toward the lobby and found Birdie waiting for her.

"What did he say?" Birdie asked as soon as they were together.

"Nothing." Kristi headed toward the glass doors that marked the entrance to the building from the quad. "He had a headache."

"He is a headache," Birdie quipped, following Kristi out into the hot sun.

"He really did look ill," Kristi said.

"Whatever you want to believe, Kristi. The man is a regular pain. I don't know how you can defend him after all..."

"That's not fair, Birdie. I don't at all believe that he hates females as much as you think he does. He's just uncomfortable around them—us, I mean. It's all those boys' schools and monasteries."

"Whatever," Birdie waved her hand, as much to dissipate Kristi's defense as to point toward the student union. "Let's get a soda. I'm dying."

On the first floor of the Business Admin building, the student union housed a snack bar, a bookstore, a study room and the student lounge. By four o'clock, the place was nearly empty. They got their drinks right away and took a seat in the lounge.

"If we're still planning to meet at Jake's we'd better get moving," Birdie said after downing her drink.

Kristi agreed and collected her books and bag. Birdie hadn't budged.

"Look, Kristi, I'd hate to have your drive to be a TA interfere with our plans to go to Vegas this month."

"Why do you think that it will?"

"I mean Aunt Joni has asked for time off and all, just to show us around. She has a special trip into the desert planned for us."

Kristi had not known that Joni planned to spend some time with them. She liked Joni, who was not more than a few years older than they were. Yet, she was worried that she might not be able to accompany Birdie as she had promised. Not if she were hired as Professor Truitt's teaching assistant.

"I don't know what you want to be a TA for, anyhow—especially his TA."

"I think it will be fun. Like your internship next fall."

"This summer, actually. Which is why we need to go to Vegas right after finals. But—it's not the same thing at all. Working at the paper is my future, Kristi. Teaching is not your future."

"I can see myself teaching."

"See yourself…? Your future is set out till kingdom come. Your future is being Mrs. Si—excuse me, Mrs. Josiah—Befford II. The heiress of Day Enterprises creating heirs to Befford Ranches. Dreamer!"

"Don't be cruel, Birdie. It's just that someday…"

"I'm not being cruel. If I were, I would point out how totally unsuitable for you Si Befford is—for any self-respecting female, in fact."

Kristi smiled. "Oh, so now I'm not self-respecting? My, Birdie, how you do go on. I know you don't hold much favor for Si, but he truly is the right man for me."

"Boy, you mean. Okay, okay. I'll back off. But believe me, Kristi some day you will see the wisdom of my words. You need to find yourself first before you can help others find their way—even your own kids."

"Yes, Mother. I will keep that in mind."

Birdie ignored her remark. "A teacher. When did all this come about, anyhow? And why not go after somebody who could really help you, like Professor Avila?"

Kristi considered the advantages of helping Professor Truitt. Perhaps she could prove to him once and for all how capable she was, and despite all the problems between them for the past three years, that she was a decent human being. And she thought he was one too.

"It wouldn't be fair to ask Sofia. Besides, Jennifer Flores wants that job."

"Always thinking of what's good and right for others, aren't you? Think about yourself! You're hopeless. But you are right about Jennifer. And she will be taking a teaching position when she graduates."

Kristi nodded, feeling a little saddened by the fact that, in another year, she would become distant from her once close friends, who were all taking jobs so far from home. She loved Hawkes Ferry and never wanted to leave. Her family and her heritage were bound in the very foundation of the town. She agreed with her father that Si Befford was the right man to marry because Befford roots were also bound to this land. They had common visions for the future. Although she would never tell Birdie, she secretly agreed with her on the suitability of Si for marriage at the moment. Her father said that all men needed to sow a few wild oats before they settled down. Grandmother said that the boy needed to grow up.

"Were you expecting Si to pick you up?" Birdie asked a little annoyed.

The car rumbled and bounced as Si called out, "Hop in Kristi!"

"I can't right now." She shook her head and pointed to Birdie.

Si revved up the motor and cut the volume, speaking with impatience. "We need to talk."

"Can't right now," Kristi repeated, glancing back to Birdie, who seemed to resign herself to having their plans hijacked. Kristi was determined not to let that happen. "We're taking the horses out on the canyon trail...."

"At least I can drive you home, then. It's a bit out of the way if Birdie saddles up at Jake's." He looked at Birdie. "You don't mind, do you Birdie, if I talk to my gal here about some personal business? It's important."

Birdie smirked.

"I'll see you at five," Kristi assured her, as she climbed into the Corvette.

She didn't like riding in it at all. With its low-slung seat, and chassis low to the ground, she felt every bump and rut in the paved road. Soon enough, Si turned onto Stage Coach Road, a gravel route that led toward the fish camp in Murphy's gulch— away from her place and toward a den of trouble. Si had turned up the volume on the stereo, letting his hand grace her knee in a sign of affection.

Kristi tried to object to his route, but she could scarcely hear her own words, competing as they were with the stereo and the wind rushing past. She reached across the console and turned down the volume.

"What did you do that for?"

"Where are you going?"

"Slick's place at Fish Camp. He said we could use it..."

"Home. I need to go home."

"What?" The surprise in his voice told her that he had no intention of taking her home.

"Now," She insisted, her voice had taken a much firmer edge that she had intended, still competing as she was against wind and motor and Si's desires.

He didn't respond, but eventually he slowed the car and pulled over in the gravel lot near the Way Station, a dilapidated settlement built by her family in the time of the territory, now given way to neglect and ruin.

The car rolled to a stop. Si cut the motor.

"Now what are you doing?" Kristi asked. "I need to get along home."

"I know. So's you can meet Birdie at her uncle's place? Where are your priorities, woman?" He was loud and belligerent, but smiled as he pulled her close. "I need a little lovin'."

He'd been drinking, so it was no use to resist his attentions. She played along hoping to improve his mood. After all, she belonged here in his arms. It was the one place where something true might happen between them, besides the swaggering bravado and his need to prove himself to her and his family. His kiss was tinged with the vile sweetness of chew blended with beer and sweat. She wanted to push him away, but restrained herself until his lips opened and his tongue pressed against her lips. She tensed then pushed him off with a gentle shove.

"No tongue wrestling, I told you." She was glad he had crossed the line, glad for the opportunity to push back, but not in a way he would see as rejection. He would not like that at all.

"Sure," he said, almost pleased with the prospect of her being indebted to him.

She laid her back against his chest, enduring the bulge of the console jabbing into her hip.

"You really do need to grow up, Kristina," he said with some authority. He took her hand. "We're not kids anymore. It's time we made love like grown-ups."

"You know I don't care for kissing when you've been drinking." And chewing she could add but what would be the use?

"Is this how you'll be after we're married?" The belligerence returned momentarily, then he seemed to remember what he had come for. "Ah, let's forget about that. Look, I need to ask you a favor. I need you to come to Elko with me tomorrow afternoon. It's for our future. See, I'm supposed to meet this guy who's all about a new-fangled breeding operation. Wants to bring me in on the ground floor."

"What for?"

He ignored her question, so Kristi listened without speaking further. She appreciated his interest in being a part of the future, following new technologies in cattle rearing and breeding. She liked that about him, always an eye on the future and what it meant to him, and to her by extension. But he could be reckless, too, playing the odds without any real sense of the risk.

"How does your father feel about it?"

"Not telling him. I got my own reserves, anyhow."

Kristi frowned.

"Aw jeez, Kristi! You know him. He won't like this innovation in breeding. He'll try to stop me."

"Now who's not acting grown up?" She smiled. He wasn't focused on the past like so many others. He saw the opportunities out there. It was something her father liked in him as well.

But as she considered his propensity for taking risks, especially the rash nature of the current enterprise, she didn't want to encourage him. "How do you figure I fit in?"

"This fellow, a breeder out in California—Sacramento. Says he knows your father. Worked with him, or maybe for him, I don't actually know. Anyhow, he hears we're an item, and he wants to meet you. So I figure we make a showing in Elko—talk a little business and be back in time for Saturday's bash."

"But I can't, Si."

"You can skip school for one day. It's for us, for our future."

"I'm skipping class tomorrow, anyhow. I promised Grandmother I'd go with her, to shop for the barbeque." He was about to object, but she cut him off. "And what about your Econ class—the last class before finals, isn't it? With your grades…"

"Crap. Now you sound just like my mother. They'll graduate me.

Don't worry." His mood was turning again. They had been talking a long time, and Kristi was anxious to end the discussion.

"I've got to go, Si. I'll be late as it is."

Si grumbled as he revved up the engine, and spun out onto the road, tires spitting gravel in every direction. He raced down the road still headed toward the fish camp in defiance of her wishes. She held her tongue and reckoned he would loop back to the highway along Salmon Creek. "I'll tell you something, Kristina. There are plenty of women who know how to please a man—a smoking, chewing, drinking kind of man. Plenty of them, too, who'd like a piece of Si Befford. I don't have to marry you at all, you know."

"Yes, Si, I know, and I don't have to marry you either." She understood him. It was the same weight she had lived under her whole life, the expectation of fulfilling her father's dream. It was Joe Befford's dream as well, to unite the cattle ranches with the agricultural industries to form the largest empire in the state, a tribute to the Hawke's blood that ran through both their veins. Kristi knew how corny that would sound to Birdie, how unacceptable it was to her friend, but she felt it was right for her. And Si Befford was the right man.

"Yeah. I do want you, Kristi." Si answered. "I just wish you weren't such a damn prude is all."

Kristi was amused, if put off by his tone. "Is this about the fish camp, or about the other?"

"It's about you and me getting away somewheres. Where there's no family, no friends, no social obligations."

"Like Saturday, you mean."

"Yeah, like Saturday. I just wish we could take off and spend a weekend in Elko. Go to the party Saturday night. This guy's got the whole casino booked." As Si's energy picked up, his foot pressed on the gas as if they could be set free at the moment.

"The cattle breeder?"

His eyes gleamed as his voice ramped up with excitement. He grabbed her hand. "Yeah, lots of big dudes from Chicago to Stockton coming round to talk about new breeding techniques. Imagine. I could get real connected with you at my side. Later we could have our own little private party in a suite upstairs."

The idea was ludicrous on so many levels. A spontaneous trip to Elko to spend time with people claiming acquaintance. A party with drinks, and who-knows-what other substances and amenities. An all-nighter, no doubt. The possibilities raised every red flag in Kristi's arsenal—not to mention that little private suite.

"It's unreasonable, Si. We committed to helping at the faculty barbeque months ago. We both have work crews reporting directly to us, made up of our friends, no less. All our professors will be there, the school administration and board. Our families expect us to be there. No, it's not possible at all."

"That figures. You always put everyone else before me—before us, I mean."

His mood downshifted with the gears as he turned onto the highway heading back toward the Double Circle Ranch. He was like that, euphoric at one moment when he could see the whole world working around his needs, then deflated as he realized he wouldn't be getting his own way. His family created that in him, never denying him anything—even his two sisters had to work around his needs—but when the rest of the world didn't agree, he caved in to a sort of despair. Sometimes Kristi could see the years laid out before her like an endless trail crossing the desert. Trying to meet Si's never-ending needs seemed a joyless prospect. Maybe those 14th century scholars were on to something after all. Marriage was looking more and more like a trial of endurance. She wondered if her father—or even her mother—had come to see that. As it was, though, morose didn't suit Kristi's world view. She was determined to be better than others before her, she was determined to exemplify the biblical Good Wife.

"I know you want this to happen, Si. We can go down to Elko Sunday morning." She couldn't believe she was giving up the last precious hours she would have to study for her finals. An all day trip south would cut into her holiday as well. Monday was the time she had set aside to pander her mare, with a proper grooming and a fair run up the rangeland. Still, Si was her future and he must be groomed and nurtured as well.

"Sure. It's better than nothing." He wasn't pleased. He offered her the standard comeback reserved for Mary when he didn't agree with her but knew there was no argument. Kristi feared she had become his mother.

He slowed the car and took the sharp turn into the ranch. In the front drive under the kitchen portico, he braked suddenly, leaned across the seat, and popped open the passenger door. "See you Saturday, then," he sniped.

When she kissed his cheek, he didn't respond. Kristi stepped onto the drive, the heavy door swinging shut. Before she could say goodbye, he spun the car onto the gravel road, clipping a fragile purple blossom from her grandmother's giant rhododendron.

Kristi eyed the apple biscuit she had perched on the top of the fence post as she readied Nikki for the ride up to Jackson's Bench, keeping a keen sense of the other horse. It was the third day in a row that the bay gelding had directly snubbed her in the stable yard, despite the yummies that she carried. Nikki was all too eager to down the rejected treats when Common Dancer would not yield to Kristi's hand.

Common Dancer—the name was a mouthful, a nod to his thoroughbred blood three generations back. Royal blood appealed to Mary, Si's mother, who had bought the horse at auction two years ago meaning to show him in competition. Apparently, he was in good form that day and won second place handily, and turned out to be the height of his glory. Mary was no trainer and had little interest in the stables at Befford Ranch. It was no wonder that the horse never lived up to her aspirations for him. That's why he'd ended up in the Day stables—a birthday gift from Si, who disliked Kristi's mustang. In fact, he considered all mustangs as ugly and undesirable as his mother did.

Kristi rubbed Nikki's sweet spot, behind her right ear, as she fit the bridle and reins. The disarray of her color and form set the Befford bunch against her—A pale golden coat and paler mane, like a palomino, with a small cluster of freckles on her rump that revealed some appaloosa blood. Each feral horse off the central rangelands carried the genetic chaos of an equine mutt. However, what Nikki lacked in good looks, she made up by her loyalty and courage. They shared a secret language, horse and rider, and she knew Nikki didn't like Si much, either. His roustabout manner on her back, and harsh hand and spurs enforced absolute power over the filly, and a feral one at that.

Kristi settled the pad and blanket on the horse's bare back.

Christian Day came out of the stable and joined his daughter at the post. "You ever going to give that cutter a trial? You haven't given him a decent workout in a month."

She pointed to the biscuit still waiting for the gelding's submission. Nikki kept her eye on the treat as well, and when Kristi pulled back to talk to her father, her horse nudged her chest in anticipation of a second treat of her own.

Her father tossed the saddle on Nikki's back.

"I'm not taking him on the range until he lets me run the reins," she said.

Father cinched the saddle, then tugged the stirrup checking the pull. "You've got to work on him every day, Kristina, just like you do this filly." He patted Nikki's neck, then rewarded her with a scratch on the sweet spot under her mane.

"She's earned it."

"A fair trail horse, I'll give her that. But at the Beffords' you've got to be ready to cut and herd. Beffords don't trust the mustangs. See them as wild and untrainable."

Kristi finally granted the bay gelding a glance. To her frustration, he was ambling toward them friendly-like. Kristi had noticed that the horse would socialize as soon as John or her father were in the yard, and Si had no problem with him either. "He prefers males, I think."

"That's nonsense, Kristina. The horse senses a weak hand in you. Joe said Mary was too gentle with him too. You have to take command." Common Dancer had joined them at the rail after helping himself to the apple biscuit. Father rustled the black mane and was rewarded by a gentle nudge. "Why don't you take him out for a run in the corral right now?"

"I'm meeting Birdie on the bench. I need to get going."

Kristi climbed onto the rail and hoisted herself into Nikki's saddle.

Father checked the cinch. "By the way, I saw young Befford today. He says you're off to Elko tomorrow on cattle business."

"Is that all he said?"

"Said you might spend the night. I was glad to hear it. You know you can push a man too far, Kristina. He don't like to be put off forever." His tone had fallen into that down-home folksy chant usually reserved for visiting politicos. The sound reasoning of the West contrived to get something in return for his support.

Kristi did not want to talk to her father about this subject. Her moral vows were her own, and she had legitimate reasons for her stand, but he wasn't going to know about that either. Si might be an exception, but crossing that threshold would not only break her vow to herself, it would put her future husband into a powerful bargaining position for almost any debate that might arise. She wasn't stupid enough to give it to him. And they weren't engaged yet.

"I promised Grandmother to be on call tomorrow. We're going down to Buhl for supplies. Anyhow, Si knows that Saturday is the barbeque, and he's signed on to lead a work crew for his dad." She headed across the corral to the gate that opened into the grazing lands.

"Be back by dark," he called after her. She waved in response.

The afternoon had cooled a bit, but the semi-arid sagebrush steppe held the heat long and hard into the night. Kristi stuck to the tree line—if you could call the scattered half-dead dogwood and cottonwood trees a proper tree line. The trail wound along the base of a small crag, then opened to a grassy plain that followed along to the top. Negotiating the trail alone gave her a feeling of freedom. A coyote—sleek and well nourished from the trove of hares and small varmints that populated the steppe—stood as a sentinel on a distant boulder, watching her progress.

The access to the top of the bluff was blocked by a rockslide, forming a talus slope. She urged Nikki to move forward, but the horse remained on the firm footing of the trail. Kristi trusted her instincts and did not push ahead like Si or her father would have done. She guessed this was the weaker hand her father spoke of. She continued down the trail toward the creek bed.

Everybody seemed to think she needed to grow up. Father was suggesting she give in a little to Si's demands for loving. It was Si who said she needed to grow up about love—he had already been talking to her father earlier in the day. Were they plotting her whole life for her, without her consent or presence? That's not what Birdie would say. She thought Kristi spent too much time listening to others and not her own heart. Well, out here, there's no one to hear, nothing, but the sound of Nikki's hooves.

A quarter mile down the trail, they crossed another open gap in the bluff where the rock face dipped to meet the trail, opening up the grasslands above them. She urged Nikki in that direction. The horse was glad for the open land, as she picked up her pace when Kristi loosened the reins. They passed an aging pronghorn that paused in his evening meal to watch horse and rider pass. With no sign of a herd nearby, Kristi thought of the coyote and its healthy coat. Yet, the pronghorn seemed content enough to have his own patch of sweet grass.

Birdie saw the oneness of nature and would see the pronghorn and the coyote in an unending circle of life. Kristi tried to see it that way too, but the image of the lone animal stayed with her. Another case of putting too much into others, she supposed, but it made her a decent person—she was sure. It wasn't that she didn't consider herself at all, anyhow, it was just that she respected and valued others more than herself. That was the opposite of being selfish and spoiled, as Professor Truitt saw her. Birdie thought she oughtn't to go for his TA position, but Kristi was of a much different mind.

She meant to prove him wrong about her nature and motivations. She also hoped to make amends for the slights her family—that is, her father—had issued to him in the past six years. She didn't know why her father disliked him so much, but she knew that the heresy charge against him in her sophomore year had been designed to chase him away. To his credit, Professor Truitt stood his ground and defeated the ill feelings building against him.

A ferruginous hawk momentarily cut off the sunlight above them. The victory call of the coyote was answered by a nearby pack on the trail behind them. A shadow crossed her heart as she thought again of the pronghorn. Kristi loosened the rein and urged Nikki across the steppe at full gallop. The horse gave up freely to the wild play of her unfettered youth. She had been captured in the annual round-up years before and trained to saddle, along with Birdie's gray pony, by Jake. Both horses were mustangs, both gentle and smart.

In Kristi's experience the feral horses could be dependable workers if trained right. And Jake Redtree was a terrific trainer. In the end, she might come to terms with Common Dancer, but she would never give up Nikki, not even if she moved to the ranch house Si had picked out for them on Befford Ranch.

Kristi considered that as others claimed her life, the professor didn't care about it at all. He devalued it, and for some reason that pleased her. She seemed to have so little control over her father or Si, over what her place in the world should be and would be, that Kristi was determined to make a stand on the TA position. It was a goal, a goal with a specific ending and a specific gain. Although Birdie couldn't see it, that position was the means to mark her territory of Self. Let everything else fall where it might, she would let go of the things she couldn't control—Si, Father, the natural world around her—and take control of what she could impact.

As she reached the edge of the wood at the top of the trail, Kristi caught sight of Birdie waiting for her on the ridge of the bench. She waved to her friend, and tucked away any concerns she had about the good opinion of her friend.

Four

Crossing the green the next morning, Truitt spotted Harrington Mudd, the Humanities Department Chair, waiting outside the back door to the Admin Building. He was chatting with his protégé, Mike Temple, a freshly minted MA from the university. Truitt found Temple to be a little too eager to make friends—and far too compromising. Slowing his pace, Truitt hoped they would move on, then quickened as he reasoned that Mudd had no doubt informed his protégé of Truitt's promotion.

"Professor Truitt, you remember, Mike Temple, I'm sure."

What Truitt remembered about Temple was his casual attitude toward scholarship, his unpolished mannerisms, and his pathetic little wife, Deb, who tagged along after him. They had married in haste, it was said, before her graduation from the high school where he taught English.

"Mike will be joining us in the fall." Mudd was revealing all this by way of introduction, since he had covered all these changes at the last department meeting in early May. He would also be relieving Miss

Garmin with the Advanced Placement students at the high school, but Mudd made no mention of that.

"I've asked him to come this morning, to get in the flow of things." Turning to his protégé, he added, "Mike, why don't you run along to the Board Dining Room. Check in with Miss Gramin, and feel free to help yourself to the coffee and donuts."

Temple smiled with the eagerness of the very young. "Sure thing. It's nice to be working with you, Professor. And congrats on that Associate." He made a mock salute, departing in the direction of the Faculty House.

As Truitt opened the door, Mudd suggested a walk in the morning sun instead. "If you don't mind."

Truitt did mind, preferring to spend the next thirty minutes preparing for a morning's absence from his office and his real work. He swallowed the impulse to rebel and instead followed Mudd along the gravel path that circled the building on the side of the sports fields, passing the gym, and ending in the central plaza, by the front door.

"No doubt you've heard all the rumors?" Mudd said as soon as they were out of earshot of any students or faculty passing by.

What on earth does this have to do with today's meeting, Truitt wondered. Mudd had requested the ad hoc meeting through a personal call from his secretary the day before, leaving no clue as to its purpose.

"Yes, I know what you think of rumors." Mudd was annoyed. "However, as I've told you often enough, it would serve you well to listen to these idle rumblings which often tell us the way the wind is blowing. These particular rumors concern the standing of the school in the Athletic Conference. We'll lose our division standing unless we manage to build up our numbers to qualify as A Division."

It was a subject in which Truitt had little interest. He didn't see what it had to do with him—or with Avila, for that matter. Unless it affected the funding for his new position, or the funds provided to him now for a new teaching assistant, he wasn't interested. "The department budget isn't affected is it?"

"No worry at this juncture," Mudd said, shaking his head, "however, we are affected in a different way. The opportunity has been laid at our feet, in a way, to be the heroes. Professor Avila has a scheme to help raise the numbers significantly, drawing from current demographics."

Truitt waited to hear him out, but Mudd stopped short of the nature of Avila's brainchild.

Instead, he zeroed in on his real purpose. "I want your active support for Professor Avila's proposal in today's meeting. Oh, I know you've had your differences, but this meeting is vital for the department, the whole school of arts and letters."

Truitt frowned.

"I don't need to remind you that Professor Avila was your most ardent supporter when you were running the gauntlet for your medieval course."

Truitt was annoyed by these sudden expectations. Professor Avila had pushed Truitt's proposal simply because it fit into the grand plan she was building for her Advanced Language classes. She wanted to include works from the romans courtier, especially The Romance of the Rose. Presenting the controversial and secular topic to the board five years ago would have undermined the favorable opinion she had enjoyed among its members. It was easier to wait until the two elderly members retired.

Truitt's proposal had offered the opportunity to reopen the case, and she had hoped to win him over as an ally for the effort. Yet, what she understood as collaboration, Truitt saw as annoying commitment—to have someone else profit from his efforts, his research, to establish inroads in his specialization. He never considered her suggestions seriously. Part myth, part fiction, with a heavy dose of religious dogma and abrasive secular parody, Truitt had found the material difficult to teach to students, especially the females. Professor Avila prevailed with them, using The Romance of the Rose in medieval French for her advanced classes.

When they reached the front door, Mudd indicated he was not done, and circled around the statue in the center of the plaza.

"You know, Truitt," Mudd lowered his voice, conspiratorially, "I think it's important that you understand how Professor Avila has actively advocated for your promotion. Using her influence among the board members."

Truitt was embarrassed as he recalled seeing the professor leaving the boardroom. "No. I didn't know that," he admitted.

"I don't have to remind you that some board members were set against you. Professor Avila helped them see your finer qualities."

Truitt knew of one board member in particular who stood against him, one that was rumored to hold Professor Avila's confidence in high esteem, Christian Day.

Glancing at his watch, Mudd ended the confab on a note of brightness. "Big changes are coming our way, Truitt. I am counting on your support."

They separated, Mudd heading toward the Faculty House while Truitt went up to his office with no more than ten minutes to spare. Mudd had said nothing of the problem Professor Avila's proposal was to address. Nor did he confirm or deny the rumors. How could he possibly promise to support something about which he knew nothing?

At five minutes to nine, Mudd stood in the alcove of the board dining room. He invited the staff to refill their cups and plates before taking their seats at the table. Built to seat twenty-four for dinner, the table handily fit Mudd's staff of twelve. The boat-shaped table sat in a room that might have seemed cavernous, were it not for the furnishings that added an intimate nuance. Small leaded windows with amber glass captured the northern light which gave a contemplative feel to the space, like chapel in late afternoon.

A buffet and cabinet with two sideboards lined the wall opposite the entry, equal in length and weight to the table. At the moment, one of the sideboards was occupied with coffee urns, tea service and platters of breads and fruit. Faculty meetings in this room were rare.

The offering of refreshment at a faculty meeting was even rarer. It was a credit to Professor Avila's influence with the board that the meeting could be so easily and happily accommodated here.

Darren Withers, the head of the Liberal Arts division, piled his plate with sweet rolls while others worked politely around his portly figure. The Reverend Dr. Smythe was finishing an emphatic point to two professors who held fast to his words, which discouraged Mudd. Smythe had shown utter disdain for Avila's proposal when Mudd was forced to brief him earlier in the week. Mudd suspected he was gathering men of like mind. Haug and Ralston were also busy gathering allies, but as friends of the court, Mudd mused with some comfort. Professor Avila had two strong collaborators in them.

As he stepped onto the dais, Mudd smiled at Professor Avila and Miss Gramine who had volunteered to assist Avila with the presentation.

"Let's get started, shall we?" Mudd called across the room, noticing with disappointment that Truitt was not among them. Sitting on the fringe of the group by the doorway, Temple offered his assistance by clanging a spoon against his water glass.

"Today's meeting is an important step toward the future of our department, and I am appreciative that you could take the time this week."

Just then Truitt slipped through the door. "Good. We are all here." Mudd was glad to note that Truitt had taken the seat behind Temple. He wanted Truitt to take an active interest in the new teacher. Seated next to each other, they would likely exchange words during the session, expanding into ideas that could help knit a friendship. It was Mudd's hope that two men so close in age—Mike was twenty-six and Truitt thirty—they would form a mutually beneficial bond. Mike was still green in his scholarship, wanting for some improvement in that department, while Truitt needed to spend a little more time socializing with his peers.

Mudd made his opening remarks amidst general confusion of rustling papers, hushed whispers and the clinking of silverware against china. In short order, he called Dean Withers to the podium. Only then, did the group settle into respectful silence.

Always glad of an occasion to address gatherings at the college, whether student or faculty, Withers opened with his usual self-deprecating humor, about his love of food.

"But enough of that. Our first order of business today is of a congratulatory nature. We wish to recognize the achievement of Professor Brooks and Professor Truitt on attaining Associate Professorships. Your combined knowledge and scholarly merits further enrich the scholarly traditions of St. Clements. Well deserved, Gentlemen. Well done."

Truitt shifted uncomfortably at public recognition, but in the end seemed remarkably pleased. A rare grin crossed his face, and he actually responded to Wolfe Haug's vociferous accolade with a perceptible nod.

The dean launched into the day's agenda as Mudd had instructed. But rather than tie Avila's proposal to board support he rattled on about the role of the university in society, and the demands made on the university in the twentieth century, Mudd got the clear notion that he was not going to address the situation at all. "What's good for Saint Clements," he summed up, "is good for all of us. Thank-you for your time. Professor Mudd."

"So what's this all about, Dean?" Brooks demanded, no doubt emboldened by the earlier recognition.

"Best to leave the details to Dr. Mudd." Withers responded on his way to the door.

A discouraged Mudd picked up the reins. It was left up to him to provide the background necessary for Professor Avila's proposal to be presented in the right light, to disarm her naysayers. A light better appreciated when delivered by the executive level.

"Most of you have heard about the decision of the Athletic Conference to change our status. The association has grown robust over the past fifteen years with the addition of thirty-two new schools, greatly expanding the conference." He went on to explain that, since its charter in 1950, the association had been inclusive of all four-year colleges dedicated to the Christian faith. A sound athletic program—with a body of athletes to compete—and financial support from the College Board were the sole qualifications of acceptance. In the ensuing decades, the conference had expanded beyond the ability of the association to manage the competitions. Large metropolitan schools were pressing to create a system where schools competed in divisions, the assumption being that smaller schools were not able to compete with the larger ones.

Individuals were beginning to flip restlessly through papers held discreetly out of view, one or two getting up to refill their cups. Cecil Durham left the room entirely, only to return a good while later.

"So the rumors we've been hearing are true, then?" Brooks asked.

Mudd welcomed the interruption.

Brooks continued, "We need to boost enrollment then. Makes sense."

"And how is the Humanities Department expected to resolve..." Sims asked in his quiet voice, only to be cut off by Smythe.

"Why not share the exact nature of the problem, Dr. Mudd?" Smythe goaded.

"Yes. The board wants to increase the student population thirty percent over the next five years, meeting a deadline issued by the Association—if we wish to remain an A Division school."

"Thirty percent?"

Complaints issued from both sides of the table.

"In the dwindling population base of the region?"

"With the state schools cutting into our student base?"

Beyond meeting the needs of an athletic program, Mudd saw other benefits arising from a larger student base, his own private aspirations that he need not share with anyone. An increased number of students, especially in the Humanities Department, meant more teachers. The department itself would grow and change, finally dissolving into specialized departments such as English. Then at long last, Mudd would be able to embrace his dream of heading a small department of literary-minded souls, leaving the administrivia of cross-disciplines to politicos like Withers and his ilk.

"We'll have many discussions on the subject, I'm sure. Today we're here to consider how the Humanities Department might address this problem. I'd like to have Professor Avila share some ideas with you about a course on Women's Issues."

"What?" Durham blurted out, abandoning his usual self-restraint.

"He's joking," Brooks said with confidence, smiling.

"I'm afraid he is not," Smythe responded gravely.

Brooks frowned, while others vented with ridicule or sat in stunned silence. Mudd was disappointed to notice that Truitt was among those who seemed to disapprove.

"Don't women have enough of their own issues?" Gordon Sims said good-naturedly while a few of the others poked fun about the devoted wife and three active daughters that provided enough issues at home.

Mudd would have laughed too, if he hadn't spied the reaction of Viola Peck, who had emerged from the kitchen at that inconvenient moment to refresh the coffee urns. The cook blushed furiously then frowned, hastening to dispatch her task before rushing out of the room. Across from him, Adele Gramine was harboring the same insult.

"And just how does this help the sports program?" Durham demanded to know.

"Women's softball," Brooks ventured.

"Who cares about women's sports?" Someone asked, his voice buried in a cluster of bantering salvos.

"Gentlemen!" Mudd said, raising his hand and voice. "Why don't we hear directly from Professor Avila?"

Sofia Avila stood on the lectern in front of the group. She briefly wondered if Dr. Mudd had been successful in his quest to bring Professor Truitt on board with their plans. But even without that support, she was not concerned. Like Mudd, Truitt had little interest in becoming a formidable foe, in being the one to stop the train on the tracks. At worst, Avila would lose an ally of potential value. She was not one of those who believed that Professor Truitt disliked women in general. Rather, he was a man of deep conviction. He would support the proposal, if he believed, in his heart, that it was the right thing to do. And that was the problem, no? For Professor Truitt rarely listened to his inner spirit, the voice of his heart.

The meeting with Mudd had occurred the previous day in order to put the pretty touches on her pitch and to prepare her for what Mudd believed to be the pack of wolves. Avila did not think it necessary to go into such detail with them. In fact, she had hoped that the pressures of finals and year-end tasks would delay any announcement of her plans until the start of the fall term. Alas, La Fortuna was not in her cards.

Mudd felt that the way to win over the Administration was to gain the backing of her peers in the Humanities Department. Such support would stand as proof that a course in women's issues was not only relevant, but also of academic merit. She had agreed to his guidance, of course. But the approval of her peers was not necessary. Neither did she require the magnificent words of Dean Withers or President Gerhard, if it came down to that. She had already attained the blessing of the board through the person of Christian Day. In fact, Christian had been actively encouraging her to pursue her dreams. In all matters at St. Clements College, the endorsement of the board president carried implicit approval of the board. And where the board fell, so followed the Administration.

Avila understood that attaining "buy-in," as Mudd called it, would appease him, flatter his need to mentor younger staff, as well as win allies, and expose the fallacious arguments of adversaries. To Professor Avila, the battle was best fought under the open sky.

Now in the faculty meeting, as she mounted the podium, the mocking continued to percolate around the room on the wings of Brooks' little joke. Avila smiled with the group, allowing the laughter to fade like little ripples in the pond, until the mirth faded. Then she spoke.

"Who in this room does not know what keen intelligence must be applied to the racing of stock ponies around the fixed points of barrels? The mathematics of speed and wind mixed with the incalculable single will of horse and rider. Sparking the win with nothing more than the language of touch."

The busy rumblings in the room ceased. Avila enjoyed taking command of this group of well-honed men, keenly aware of the impression she made, her dark eyes accentuated when her raven hair was drawn into a chignon at the back of her neck, the somber black of her suit electrified by the fiery red of a silk blouse, the color echoed by Fire and Ice painted on the tips of her fingers and glossed over her lips.

"Which among us would not like to see these urban elites in the Athletic Conference compete in such sports? Or challenge them to breaking the Mustangs?" Only two of the professors in the room could be classified as urbanites, having no knowledge of such things. But even they were all ears now, not to the feminista, but to the vaquera from Buenos Aires.

"Today we find ourselves in an era where too many girls are not taking advantage of our education at St. Clements. They pass through our secondary education and vanish into the world around us, not considering other options for their futures."

The men tacitly agreed.

"While women make up nearly half the population of the region, less than one fourth of our incoming freshmen are female. We ask ourselves, why must this be? Then we understand. The girls of today look for value only in those things that serve their future needs—as wives and mothers. Most of you will agree that this is their shared destiny."

"Too busy working on the MRS to think about any real future," Sims tossed out with his usual levity. The others encouraged him.

"Sí. That is the case. Yet for most girls, the Prince Charming, he does not come. The pursuit of happiness eludes those girls who marry in ignorance of what life can offer otherwise. They make contracts on a whim and pay for them over a lifetime. These young women will commit to being responsible for new families, but still do not know how to be responsible for themselves."

"Come, now. Not all the girls see their salvation in men," Philips countered.

Avila privately agreed with him, but it would not serve her case to yield the point. The best offense was a measured defense. She aimed to identify the need for the new course in terms of women's deficiencies, rather than the more likely causes that lay in the shortcomings of men.

"I hear men say always that the wife has no sense of responsibility. She has no training. No education. These girls—and sí, not all of them—are committed to nothing except waiting for their prince. They fail to see that the cost of this inaction, this passive waiting, has been at the cost of their future freedom."

"Aren't you being a little dramatic, Professor?" Smythe said with rancor.

"I do not think so, Reverend. These girls see no connection between higher education at St. Clements and the roles they will take on as wife and as mother. Yet we know they are wrong, for the health and welfare of their families, and of our community, depends on the choices they make today, no? It is here in college that they will discover the usefulness of rational thought, to think critically and thus to comprehend the world—and thus to gain it. Education is illumination."

"No one disagrees with you," Phillips said thoughtfully glancing around the room.

"So what's your point?" Durham asked with no expectation of an answer.

She answered it anyway. "In one respect the girls are right. Our current curriculum offers little appeal to the female gender. As educators, we offer them little encouragement to stay in school. We assume they only wish to find husbands. Our financial incentives are also targeted at the male students."

"And why should girls be offered special incentives?" Brooks said. "What's good enough for the boys...."

"Not that many women are expected to bring home the bacon," Sims added. "Especially the ones at this school."

Avila pressed her point, "For the girls who do enroll here we offer an education tailored to the male sensitivity. A history written by men about men. A philosophy that examines only the rationalizations of men in Western thought. Where do we find the role models for our women?"

"Are you saying that we purposely cut out contributions by women?" Durham was incensed. "There are precious few, you know."

"Only too true," Haug responded to Durham. "History is written by the man left standing."

As Avila was enjoying the dialogue between competing disciplines, Truitt spoke with impatience. "This whole conversation totally ignores the fact that few females want to be educated, here or elsewhere." So Mudd had failed.

Sims responded to this remark with rancor. "Some of them might experience it more as mutually exclusive, Truitt, education or marriage, career or family."

"Woman was created to be the companion of man. Not his rival." Smythe summed up his position. The rest of the group shifted uncomfortably, not wanting to confront the reverend on the lack of rational thought in his fundamentalism.

"How do we know, Gentlemen, that there aren't hundreds of local women who would attend St. Clements, if they had the chance? Not all unmarried, and not all young, but all flesh and blood students hungry for better opportunities. We do not."

Sofia turned to the easel on which Adele Gramine had written a list of issues driving women toward the quest for equity. "By focusing on these women's issues, we can shape the dialogue that females young and old—Women—will find relevant and compelling. It is a view that reflects the trials and persistent problems that have shaped the lives of their mothers and grandmothers, impacting their own families, and surely affecting the lives of their unborn children—boys as well as girls."

"Women's lib," Durham complained. "I've been through this before."

Avila ticked off the bulleted items. "The persistence of poverty—something which keeps women and children in the cycle of economic depression. Superiority of the male—which leaves women politically vulnerable, an underdog in society. Inequity of women—legally, politically, and in matters of wages and opportunity."

"This is hardly the Dark Ages, Professor," Sims pointed out.

"Yet the promise of liberty and equality has continued to elude women, who are considered unequal to man in all aspects of life. Even now, in the last decades of the 20th century, we find the general attitude toward woman is as an inferior to her male counterpart."

"I'm sorry, Professor, but I fail to see what this has to do with us. Especially now, this week when my plate is full, along with everyone else in this room," Philips said.

Smythe smiled at him indulgently. "These issues are grist for our charities and social workers. It is hardly appropriate material for the Humanities Department."

"Yet, has it not everything to do with humanity, and thus the Humanities that we teach. From history to philosophy to literature to language, everything touches upon the nature of being human. And it is this right to be equal in humanity that these girls need to consider before they can become the women who take control of their lives."

"I haven't seen any dissatisfied females around here," Philips said.

"Sí," Avila agreed. "Yet, why wait to cross the stream until the water has already risen to sweep you away?" And sweep them away it will, Sofia thought. This rising stream of women inundating universities across the country from New England to Chicago to California. Sofia revealed her second chart, goals for a class on Women's Issues.

"These are our initial thoughts only. Nothing is carved in marble. The best classes will be done in collaboration with those of you who will participate. Then we all win."

The primary organization of the course covered the milestones of Western civilization from ancient times to the mid-20th century, highlighting women's contributions from the infamy of Helen of Troy to the exemplary figures in the suffrage movement.

Avila stopped short of revealing her full plan, one that covered women's accomplishments into the current decade, thus saving today's topic from a major derailment. The attitudes and social mores of each era would be studied through the words of contemporary writers, philosophers, and poets. Rather than treat whole works, she planned to make use of several anthologies in history, philosophy, and literature. As she came to the end of her key points a lively discussion ensued as individual conversations erupted in evoking passion, laughter and disdain. Avila didn't mind as she had done what she came to do.

"I can offer you an example of collaboration from our current term. Three of the advanced French students, who are also in professor Truitt's Medieval Studies course, have written term papers based on lectures in both classes. The romans courtier of the French court in the 12th century—which my students translated—was widely read in the twelfth and thirteenth centuries. We worked last term to identify the overlaps in our two courses, cooperating on how the topic should be presented, for the students' optimal learning experience."

Avila avoided looking in Truitt's direction while she spoke, stretching the truth with the term "collaboration." She was almost sorry for the exaggeration when Durham and Brooks shot spiteful looks across the table to her named collaborator. She pressed on with her case, but allowed her gaze to fall briefly on Truitt, who remained silent, his lips pursed under flushed cheeks, glaring at the director. The imperturbable Smythe amused himself, as always, with the papers in front of him, paying little attention to anything else in the room.

There was a general restlessness growing in the room. Lunch was approaching and the aromas coming to them from the kitchen left little consideration for anything else. Clearly they were done. Avila made a few summary remarks before turning the meeting back to Mudd, who wisely closed the meeting without further comment, a full five minutes before the hour.

That evening, as the old air conditioner labored noisily without succeeding to refresh the stuffy air in his den, Truitt sat at his desk revising the final exam for his Sophomore Lit class. The front door stood ajar and, on the opposite side of the house, the kitchen window was propped open waiting for the temperature to drop and the evening chill to set in. The test was easily revised from the meticulous notes Truitt kept on class discussions and student progress. Most of his colleagues were satisfied in reusing tests from previous sections of their classes. It was Truitt's opinion that the quality and variety of students in the class formed part of the equation of test preparation.

Doing the right thing often came at the expense of working on the things one wanted, like working on the article that languished on the top of his desk, buried under a pile of reference books and notes made last month. He had little hope of returning to it before the end of the term when his final grades were submitted. It was a pivotal work, a critical review of the treatise on the New Age written by an 11th century monk. This was the second of two parts he had offered The Medieval Journal. The first part had been in the mail at the end of spring break.

Regrettably, the delay on his writing would push his return home till the end of June, a great disappointment to Aunt Nell who anxiously awaited his return every year, counting the days from Easter Sunday. This year she had seemed particularly impatient for his return. He suspected she was trying for another go at convincing him to take a position at St. John's Academy as head of the English department and housemaster of the upper-class boys. She had probably arranged another dinner with the headmaster to follow-up the discussion he had begun with Truitt last Christmas. At that time a promotion had seemed unlikely. He dreaded the prospects of another year in the scablands of the west, so remote from any sense he held of civilized society and culture. But everything had changed yesterday. Now he needed to muster up the courage to call and reset her expectations.

It was six-thirty, a little late in her day to be delivering the unpleasant news. What was a boon to him would surely be her disappointment. As her only living kin, Truitt knew that taking a position in the west had cost her more than it had him. Yet, as disappointed as she would be about his delay, she would still want to share in his moment of triumph.

Just then, Sanders rapped on the screen door. "Yo! Anyone home?"

"In here," Truitt called out as he headed toward the door, meeting the geology professor who had let himself in.

"Going down to get some grub at the watering hole. You game?" Sanders said.

"Not tonight, I'm afraid. I've got to finish up some work." Truitt indicated the papers stacked and ready for his attention.

"Another article, eh? Well, too bad, old man. I wanted to find out about your big meeting today. Lots of flack in the faculty lounge this afternoon. Wanted to get the right perspective."

"Sit down. I can use a breather," Truitt was already sweeping a pile of papers to the floor. "Still have some of that scotch."

Sanders hesitated before taking a seat on the sofa. "You're sure it's all right? Good. Then I won't turn down the drink."

Retrieving his chair from the den, Truitt positioned it near the sofa, then poured two generous glasses of the scotch he had stashed in the cabinet of his sitting room.

"Sims and Durham were in a huddle when I walked into the lounge, spewing venom—at least Durham was—riled up about something concerning Sofia Avila. Brooks came in just then and said to me in passing that they were still ticked off about the proposal. But he didn't explain. I guess he thought you had clued me in. He expected it would blow over soon enough."

"Did he? That was tidy of him—not to be the teller of tales."

Sanders laughed. "Yes, that would be in character. So what's up? Why did Mudd call a critical meeting at this time of year? And what's with this proposal? I don't think I ever saw Sims rise to the bait before. I didn't think he could, quite frankly."

Truitt did not relish reliving the details of the meeting, nor did he want to reveal his own thoughts about the proceedings, even to Sanders. "I don't know what Mudd is all about with this. Sofia Avila has proposed a course on women's issues for the Humanities Department."

"Oh my," Saunders said in a voice full of glee. "What a pretty mess that must have been, among all those old boys. And Mudd was behind her, I guess."

"He worked the group before the meeting. He got to me just before it started. I'm not sure how committed he is to the idea. But you know him, always trying to build team consensus. This was no different. She had her detractors, for sure." Truitt took a swallow of the scotch.

"Sims?" Sanders asked, then sipped his drink as if to prolong his visit.

"Not that I could see. It's hard to tell with him. He was his usual jolly self, taking a shot at the wife and kids when it could get him a laugh." The meeting had consumed enough of Truitt's day. He wanted to be done with it.

"For all the resistance put up in the meeting against the proposal, everyone was pleasant enough afterwards. Even Smythe had joined the group for lunch."

"Did he now?" Sanders' tone exposed his own surprise that the reverend would take lunch in the faculty lounge instead of at the Chapel House with his wife.

"Yes, he had decided by then that Avila's plan wasn't going anywhere. It would die in the boardroom. Everyone seemed to agree that the social costs were too high. Too much risk."

"The precious reputation of dear old SC!" Sanders found great fun in that idea. When his laughter subsided, he mused, "I wonder what prompted this spark of genius from our fair colleague?"

"You know as much as I do, probably a great deal more. It's something to do with this athletic association business."

"Ah," Sanders digested the idea, then his eyes lit. "But that's brilliant!"

"You can't mean that you agree with the idea?"

"Oh, but I do!"

The naked delight in Sanders' voice was unsettling to Truitt. "The board won't agree to it. Surely you can see that? Even Withers, who had been corralled by Mudd, wouldn't claim any connection to the proposal. He bolted from the room after his usual glib nonsense about working for the good of the school. He bolted out of the room before Mudd could even introduce the topic."

"Women are making waves across the land, old man. A movement, they call it. Demanding their civil rights. Equity with men in society. An irresistible force, as the song goes, meeting the immoveable object of tradition. The sacred bastion of male superiority." Sanders laughed anew, unaware of the effect his words had on Truitt.

"You sound just like Sofia Avila. You might want to join her cause." Truitt's tone was more acerbic than he wanted it to be.

Sanders took a swallow of his drink, then responded evenly. "I find her charming, is all. She's a dynamic woman, Truitt, even if you resist her success. And she's not bad-looking, either. You must see that."

"I didn't know you were so besotted with the professor."

"I'm too old for that. Besides, Sofia Avila is way out of my league. I never had the imagination for a woman like that." Sanders slipped into quiet reflection. He pulled a cigarette from his shirt pocket and stuck it in his mouth, unlit.

Truitt, who was deep in his own thoughts, finally said, "Even if she were to win over the board—Mudd pretty much admitted that she had—I doubt if she'd ever gain the approval of Christian Day. He's the one she needs to convince."

Sanders stared at his friend. "You've got to be kidding me!" Suddenly energized he jumped to his feet, laughing. "Don't you know, man? No, I guess you wouldn't, denying all rumors as you do. Avila and Day have been an item since Easter. Certainly you've seen them at chapel together?" Sanders dislodged the cigarette long enough to down his drink then set the glass on the kitchen counter.

Truitt followed him, emptying his own glass.

"No sir," Sanders added, "I wouldn't count on his quashing the effort any time soon. Most likely he's backing her."

The thought of this bit of news disheartened Truitt in a way he could not name.

Pushing open the screen, Sanders stopped to light his cigarette. "Sure you won't come? Brooks is actually buying the first round—celebrating. You ought to be celebrating too, you know."

"How about I buy you a drink tomorrow afternoon?" Truitt smirked.

"Sure, on Day's tab." Sanders crossed the stoop, then paused and turned. "You know, old man, you can't keep denying yourself the small pleasures of the day waiting for some hoped-for future that may never come."

"Goodnight, Sanders."

"One of these days you'll find out that those hopes of yours were rooted in sedimentary rock and have all eroded into sand."

"Washed away by that wave of women rising, I suppose?"

"Don't know," Sanders waved him off, "But something's got to give."

Sanders words lingered in the air too long after he had disappeared. Truitt struggled to finish the changes with the exam, disturbed in part by growing hunger, and random images of professor Avila flashing across his mind, her command of the group as she pitched her proposal, those surreptitious trips to the board room at lunch hour. And now the seemingly friendly banter at church between her and the Day family was imbued with a deeper meaning. As if he did not have enough to worry about. And why should it bother him so much? He didn't know.

In the kitchen, he fixed a plate of dried cheese and days-old bread. He washed it down with a tumbler of milk. Certainly he felt no obligation to support Avila's proposal, which he found to be a ridiculous idea. She would attempt to revise history and pander education to girls who otherwise had neither the interest nor the will for academic standards. The faculty was being asked to curry the interest of potential female students, to take them seriously without any regard for the teaching profession.

And what was Mudd about? Even if Avila did support his promotion, there was no reason for Truitt to be obligated to her. Mostly others must have supported him too, or he wouldn't have succeeded. In fact, the further removed he was from the meeting, the more he realized the absurdity of what Mudd was asking him to do. The director was probably offering a sympathetic ear to Avila's ambitions, and in his usual manner of building consensus, supplied her with the venue to put out her ideas. After all, Mudd was interested in probabilities, not dreams. He was a practical man—not a believer in Avila's world of magical reality.

Truitt finally finished the sophomore exam and set about reviewing the exam he had built for the medieval studies class last summer. He had stuck pretty close to the syllabus, but there was that irritating digression into the romans literature that he was obligated to address in the final exam. Collaboration, indeed! The professor had communicated a desire to merge the term paper exercises, wanting to influence what Truitt might deem "acceptable." When he refused her offer, she worked through the students who were only too willing to pressure him. He finally yielded only after extracting a promise from each girl that two papers would be written, one focused on the subject matter of his class, and one for professor Avila's class. From her comments at the meeting, he had only to assume that she had accepted for her class the papers submitted to his.

Professor Avila represented everything that Truitt distrusted in women. While she appeared to have no need for men, she managed to gain her will by exerting her influence over them with flashing eyes, a charming smile and a personal energy that sucked them in like the sirens drawing ships to their fate on rocky shores. Those fools saw only the outer show, what Avila wanted them to see. Alas, Truitt had believed that Sanders had better sense than the rest of them.

Twice in his life Truitt had fallen prey to the bewitching eyes of a female, falling victim to the hidden wiles of some unknown game. The first time he was fifteen with a big crush on the mayor's thirteen-year-old daughter. An episode in the park outside the library, concerning kisses and rivals ended that crush. The second time he was a fool. He was at Columbia, in graduate school when the lithesome Caroline drifted into the graduate stacks without a pass. Aunt Nell had cautioned him early on about letting love bring shame to their door. The affair ended poorly in his humiliation. Never again, not for him. The only woman he needed in his life was Nell, strong in mind and spirit and body, with a directness that belied her gender. To Truitt, she was the paragon of womanhood.

By ten o'clock, Truitt gave up, still unsatisfied with the revisions to the Medieval final. The incandescent light of his study cast dim shadows on his mind. The optimism with which he had designed his course seemed a long-ago memory, especially in light of Avila's proposal. Fixing a warm Brandy, he lounged on the sofa, allowing his mind to fall into random reflection, which seemed to settle on the topic of females and education. He didn't understand why girls needed special classes for literature or anything else. Avila's reasoning ran along the all too familiar lines that Willema Rutherton had used when she denounced his doctoral dissertation. How unfair she had been in criticizing his innovative work on the 11th century monk, Joachim, just because he had chosen not to pursue her line of inquiry on the letters of Eleanor's Confessor at Poitiers.

Truitt twirled the Brandy around the glass, thinking of Dr. Rutherton, a woman who still held judgment over his work from her position as chief editor of The Medieval Journal. After years of having his work rejected, Truitt had begun to see signs of hope that the editor was coming round, the encouragement he had received to submit the first part of his article, for instance. There was no tangible proof of what had changed. His writing had only improved over the years, and he was becoming recognized in the secondary press, but his topic was still as had always been, the Calabrian monk, Joachim. There was no accounting for the fickleness of women's minds.

Swallowing the last of the brandy, Truitt swiped the glass clean and replaced it on the shelf. He wondered how the others would see him—as Avila's collaborator, no doubt, someone who caved in to pressure from the Admin. Did they think he had sold out?

Switching off the lights, Truitt retreated to his bed, resolved that no one had reason to accuse him of collaboration. If Sanders were right about Avila and Day, board approval would be a fait d'accompli, and Smythe's hope for failure would be lost. Still, Day's interest in Avila did not guarantee her success either. So let the professor play with her lists and charts. Nothing she could conjure up would affect the content of Truitt's classes. For the moment, he could live with the professor's cause as long as it served his own. He would neither resist her efforts nor go out of his way to assist her. He certainly would not be adding The Romance of the Rose to his course syllabus.

Five

By the time the sun rose behind the silhouette of the Sawtooth Range on Saturday morning, the household at Day Ranch was abuzz with activity. The women were assembled around the breakfast table finishing their meal. The matron of the house, Anne Day, was checking over the list of tasks to be accomplished before the morning was over. Stooped over her shoulder, was the housekeeper, who took a keen, almost possessive, interest in the task assignments. Kristi listened respectfully to her grandmother, as did her two friends, Birdie and Amy, who had spent the night in order to start work before the first light of day.

"Amy, you'll do us proud with these florals," Anne said.

Amy reddened at the attention, but her smile betrayed a delight in the compliment. The cartons of greenery and cut flowers that surrounded the table had been fetched the previous day from the wholesaler, and she was delighted at her assignment.

Anne continued down the list. "Tessa will be working with the caterers in the kitchen, and setting up the dining hall. Oh, and the living room! Tessa, can you get those boxes removed from the front salon? And be sure we've cleared Christian's den."

"Where do I put the boxes?" Tessa asked with some disgruntlement.

"You can use the guestroom on the other side of my bath," Kristi offered.

"Okay, then, coats and wraps in the big room, I guess," Tessa said.

"Kristi, you take charge of the cleaning upstairs," Anne continued. "Be sure your father's bed is made. Tessa has far too much to do this morning to look after that. Then, make sure the sitting room is presentable, as I'm certain the ladies—especially the wives—will want to see the quilt we've been making for Cousin Sarah's wedding."

"And talk about something besides the school," Tessa added. "Better make sure there's a table for tea up there, too. Mrs. Smythe is likely to sit out the day up there."

"With Mrs. Sims," Amy added helpfully.

"Which reminds me. I'll open my room, for another powder room," Kristi offered. "And my sitting room will make a nice retreat for a more private chat, don't you think?"

"If you are sure," her grandmother responded.

"Be sure you don't leave anything lying around," Birdie said. "Like your unfinished essay for Professor Avila's class."

"She wouldn't read your private stuff," Amy said, defending her favorite teacher. "But we'd better get our stuff out of your way."

Kristi's room was currently holding the girls' school backpacks and overnight bags.

"I can stow your stuff in the adjoining guest room, along with the boxes. Then everything will be secured with lock and key," Kristi said.

"Birdie," Anne said moving on through the list, "I was hoping you'd help move the boxes since they are packed with porcelains and pictures off the mantle."

Birdie was the heftiest and most sure-footed of the three girls. "Sure thing, Mrs. D. Getting things out of harm's way. I understand."

"Well, that's it!" Tessa straightened up and circled the table to collect the dirty dishes left earlier by the men, who were now outside tending to the picnic grounds and barbecue pits. She motioned to the girls to finish up with their plates. "Be sure you've all had plenty to eat. There won't be nothing else till the barbecue, and Lord knows when that will happen."

"It'll be fine, Tessa," Anne smiled. "The catering crew comes at nine. Just be sure there's room in the kitchen when they arrive."

"Anyways... I'd better get to this lot," Tessa said, taking the dirty dishes to the kitchen.

Birdie picked up a handful of silver and napkins and followed her to the sink. "I can do these, Tessa, while you set up for the restaurant crew."

"You are such a dear, Birdie, always pitching in where you're needed," Anne said.

"I don't mind, Mrs. D. I like to keep busy. I can help Tessa move the boxes from the living room, too, when we're finished with the salon."

"Mac will be here pretty soon," Amy said. "He'll help too."

"Si will no doubt keep Mac busy outside," Kristi warned.

They had all seen the Steakhouse van arrive while they were eating. Birdie half-expected Si to make a good show, but he hadn't, and now Kristi was out of sorts. She was right, though, he'd probably waylay Mac to help with the barbecue pits. She carried an armload of dishes into the kitchen.

"And if I'm done super early, I'll come back and bug Amy with the flowers." Birdie laughed carting another load of dishes to the sink.

In truth, Birdie had little patience for sitting pretty, playing with flowers or papers or paints. She didn't relish standing around upstairs, either, waiting for Kristi to choose just the right soaps–lavender or lemon? rose or mint?—for powder room ambience.

Birdie needed to move, and move she did. By the time Mac arrived, she had finished with the kitchen and had already carried some of the boxes upstairs, afraid that his gridiron sensibilities would be too hard on the antique tea sets. As he helped her move the rest, Mac surprised her with a cautious delicacy that was unknown among Si's rough and tough friends. With Mac's help, she was done quickly and available to help Amy with the floral assemblies.

Meanwhile, Kristi fussed over her selections of soap and lotion, choosing lavender for the powder room and summer rose for her own bath, with matching linens and scented candles. The only clue Kristi had of Si's presence that morning was the sound of his voice, shouting orders across the yard. As she worked, Kristi admitted to herself a twinge of jealousy toward Amy, especially in the way that Mac treated her. On his arrival, for instance, Mac had come straight away into the house to see Amy. He offered his services there, before joining Si and the crew outside.

Assessing her room, Kristi deemed it ready for any white glove inspection, particularly the scrutiny of Si's mother, Mary Befford, who always met Kristi with a critical eye. Leaving the door to her suite invitingly open, she left through the bathroom, tossing the privacy lock as she had promised Amy. She locked the guest room from the hall as well, mindful that she needed to let Amy and Birdie in later to fetch their bags. All the upstairs rooms were now ready for powdering noses, holding private chats or not, and for the admiration of quilting projects and photos of shared memories.

She thought of Mac and the way he included Amy as part of his world. Kristi could almost find fault with Si on that matter, but then, the lock worked both ways, didn't it? Maybe she should go outside to greet Si, making him part of her world.

As she headed down the back stairs toward the kitchen door, she was distracted by the sound of Amy and Birdie arguing. She made a beeline for the breakfast room and found her two friends standing over the remnants of a floral spray scattered across the table.

Birdie raised her arms in frustration. "I'm not an artist! Everything I touch is ruined!"

"What's going on?" Kristi asked, standing at the door.

"Nothing. I lost it." Amy said. "Never mind, Birdie. It wasn't your fault. I didn't tie the knot strong enough. But now I'm afraid nothing will be done on time. It's already eleven. I've got four more to make."

"Well, Amy, they don't all have to be made," Kristi consoled her.

"But we bought all the materials, and the flowers are cut. We can't put them back. We can't waste them!" Amy wailed, near tears.

"Here, now. What's this?" Anne bustled into the room. "We can get these all done in no time if we work together. You've already shown us how, Amy. Just look at these beautiful sprays." No one was admiring the finished arrangements.

"I wanted the centerpiece higher," Amy explained, "But the container just didn't support the height…"

"Still these are lovely, don't you think so, girls?" Anne seated herself next to Amy and began to separate the strands from the fronds and grouped the plants into packets for assembly. "You have such a stylish touch for making elegance out of the ordinary, Amy. It's a gift."

With scissors in hand, Birdie continued to cut the remaining fronds to the shorter size while Kristi cleaned up the mess on the table. Amy had nothing to do but continue assembling the sprays with accents of bows and bonbons and trailing ribbons.

"I remember the first faculty barbecue we ever gave. My cousin Sarah and I had hiked up to the bluff to fill our baskets with wildflowers. Our arrangements were a meager collection of prairie brush and sagebrush shoots, with a few Indian paintbrush in the center of each bowl."

"A few?" Birdie was scandalized to hear Mrs. D. admit to picking the protected species.

Anne laughed. "There were only two bowls. And, no one thought about preservation then. The bounty of summer seemed so unending."

"Wasn't it too early in the season for paintbrush?" Amy asked.

Anne shook her head. "Fourth of July. Poppa had been planning a more formal event at school in June, but I convinced him to sponsor a barbecue."

"People weren't so mobile then," Kristi said. "Today the campus empties right after finals." Kristi had moved to help cut the ribbons for Amy's bow making.

"It probably wasn't so easy to get away from here back then," Amy said.

"Oh, we had roads, but gasoline was hard to come by. Most folks depended on the train. It's true, though, that most of the teachers tended to stay put as long as they held their position."

"That was a terrific idea you had, Mrs. Day," Amy said, admiring the spray she had just finished. "To give a barbecue. Why hadn't they done that before?"

Anne handed Amy the last of the floral ephemera. "I expect it wasn't dignified enough for a college event. They were always trying to emulate the culture of the eastern schools, but that's exactly why we needed a western barbecue, to showcase our own culture, in our unique way of celebrating."

Amy worked deftly to assemble the last bowl as Anne continued. "Actually, I got the idea from our science teacher, a recent graduate from Pennsylvania who had a new bride. A city gal—Philadelphia, I think. He had spent several summers here during his student years working with the Army Corps. He liked to share the memories of which he was fond. There were many of them, but his wife did not enjoy the place or his memories. He was particularly drawn to his memories of those early days in the field, where he shared the camaraderie of the range, with meals round the chuck wagon under the open sky. Gave him a taste for what we were about, I expect. Well, anyone knows that a barbecue in the right attitude can be as gala and grand as any ballroom party. If there were a will in that bride of his, an old-fashioned barbecue would have opened her heart to the bounty of what the west had to offer."

Amy tied off the last bow.

Anne rose from the table. "There now, Amy, our task is done." She left the room, her list firmly in hand.

"I wonder what happened to the bride?" Amy asked.

Kristi shook her head. "I've never heard that story before. Well now, we'd better get these arrangements out to Tessa."

"John don't much like strangers messing around his turf," Joe Befford grinned, making his observation on the Day Ranch foreman to Christian. "Can't say as I blame him."

Joe Befford was leaning on the mobile bar on the patio outside the front salon, talking to Christian Day. His dialect had slipped into folksy cowboy talk, as it always did between two men who had grown up in each other's company under the shadow of shared heritage. The subject of comment was John Navarre, foreman of the Day Ranch, who was not taking well to Joe's crew setting up the canopy on the meadow which he had worried into a semblance of rolling lawn like the one Tessa had pulled out from the magazines. Finally, John seemed resigned to the ordeal and headed back to worry over the fire pits and the spits where the cook, another of Joe's staff, had set meat roasting before the rooster crowed. Already the aromas of beef and lamb whet the appetite, with chicken soon to be added.

"I reckon we got to start moving with the times, Joe," Christian finally said, returning to a topic they had begun earlier.

"Nothing wrong with the old ways, in my mind. Traditional values, like the Reverend says, are the mortar of civil society."

Christian grunted. He did not much cotton to the Reverend's sermons, especially when they were aimed at countering his own goals, like Sofia's proposal for a course in women's studies, an idea he supported.

Just then, four comely females with stringed instruments strolled by, heading toward the bandstand. A member of the set-up crew redirected them to the house. They smiled then blushed, scurrying past the two board directors into the living room.

"Now there's tradition for you," Christian noted. "Sofia's idea."

"Seeing a lot of her lately, I've heard" Joe said.

"It just might do to attract a few more girls to the college, Joe. She's got a solid plan, you know. Nothing too radical."

"I don't know, Christian. Too quick a change, in my estimate."

Christian laughed. "Why, I do believe you are becoming an old lady, Joe."

"Respecting tradition is not a bad thing, Christian."

Christian thought darkly of some of his father's traditions. "Depends on whose tradition it is, I guess." He signaled Turk, who had been stocking the bar, for a shot of whiskey and filled a second glass with water. "Coffee done yet?"

"I'll have one of those," Joe said pointing to the cup of coffee.

"We've made quite a few changes, in our time," Christian continued, "Can't say it's all been bad."

"Changing feed or feeding ground is one thing. Introducing a whole new breed, well, that's another matter altogether."

"You didn't do too bad with the Angus in '62, as I recall."

"You know what I mean. This business of inviting discord among the women. Well, I don't know. With two daughters to consider, and a wife who would fight this every step of the way... And what about you? Aren't you afraid of outright rebellion if Kristina gets on this horse?"

"Kristina?" Christian was a little surprised at the connection of his daughter with this future program. Why would she care? She'd be out of school before the thing ever became an issue.

"I see you cowboys are called to spirit a little early," Sofia Avila came through the door behind them, stepping up to the bar with an air of entitlement that annoyed Joe. She placated him with a disarming smile, then asked Turk for a silver fizz.

"What is so serious today that the clouds keep the sun from your eyes?"

She aimed the question at Joe, but Christian responded, opening the circle to include her. "Just a little cow business."

"Angus bulls," Joe added without adding the epithet for manure, but his tone said it all. He had recently developed a distaste for the company of the lovely señorita. Few circumstances in their lives had put a wedge between Joe and his closest friend. They weathered the storm that had erupted when Christian snatched the state title for roping right when Joe needed most to win his father's approval.

"Darling, here you are!" Mary called out, approaching the patio bar from the direction of the front salon, her son following close behind. "You two getting an early start, I see."

Mary frowned at the sight of Sofia Avila, then smirked as she considered the rumors about her and Christian. She shot a knowing glance towards Joe, in confirmation that what she had told him was true.

Getting up, Christian pressed the shoulder of his friend, and murmured, "Think more about it, Joe." He put his arm through Sofia's and attempted to escort her out of the room.

"Please stay, Christian," Mary said. "I just want a few words with my husband... Darling, is there any real need for Si to stay on today? The boys are gathering at the lake house, for a last weekend celebration."

Mary's gaze swept the room to fix on Christian. She had a honey-sweet voice that could pacify a stampeding herd. "You two ought to appreciate Si's predicament. It's the last time these friends will be together. They'll all scatter after graduation."

Christian paused at her request, and regarded her lukewarm hospitality. "Except for next month, when the gang of six plans to invade Sonora for a few weeks."

"I'll go help Anne with the platters," Sofia said as she escaped from the room.

Joe regarded his son with some rancor, wondering at what age he might abandon using his mother to plea bargain his cause, when he would become a man. It was easy to see that Christian disapprove of his son's behavior as much as he did.

Si kept an eye on his mother, ignoring his father's stern brow. Wisely remaining silent, he avoided eye contact with Christian, who knew more of his plans than Si had admitted to either parent.

Christian realized, in the moment, just how easily deceit came to the boy. Joe would be angry if he guessed what his son was up to.

But with Joe, anger was expressed in terms of disappointment, not fury. Si was lucky to never bear the scars of his father's displeasure, as Christian had born from Justin Day. Joe would simply not allow the boy to leave—he would, that is, if Mary weren't insisting on her son's freedom. At that moment, Christian was reminded of his own desire to break free of his old man's control—and the silence of his own mother in such matters of authority.

Joe addressed Si, with Mary looking on hopefully. "What do you say, Son? You didn't have to tell Turk you'd work today."

"I forgot about this gig at the lake this weekend."

"Yet you've committed to work," Joe argued, "and now you want to back out at the last minute, when others are counting on your help."

"There's plenty of guys here to help," Si countered.

Intervening in her persuasive way, Mary reminded Joe that this particular event was not Si's type of thing, implying that it had little to do with herding and wrassling steers. "Si had committed to this job before he realized he'd lose the weekend. It's not like he needs the money, Joe, or you need the help."

Mary's excuses for the boy were always innovative but happened far too often. Joe wanted to put his foot down, but considered the exertion of handling a row with Mary while they entertained a notable guest at the ranch, the beau of his eldest daughter. Instead, he reminded Si of yet another commitment. "You promised Elena that you'd show Ross Delaney around the stables, show him the stallion you gave to Kristina. Elena's counting you."

Mary laughed. "Why, Joe, Elena has no such expectation. She'll want to show Ross off to the company herself. Besides, Christian is a much better guide of his own stables than you are." Turning to Christian, she added, "I have a hunch you'll want to meet Ross yourself. Harvard Law School, he's headed for corporate law. His father's a senator. Elena's got her bonnet set on him." Mary was grinning from ear to ear.

Joe was still regarding his grown son. Finally, he sighed. "All right, son. But someday you're going to have to stand by your word."

Mary smiled in triumph, pecking her husband's cheek. She started to lead Si away, but her son held ground.

"What about Kristi?" Now he made direct eye contact with Christian.

Mary frowned, not willing to argue the case for Kristina Day.

"What about her?" Christian asked.

"Well, we're supposed to go together—they expect it, you know."

The boy was gutsy too, Christian judged, switching the subject to his intended purpose without giving his parents any clue as to his real game. Christian thought to have some fun. "Kristina's said nothing to me about the lake. You might have assumed that she would stay at her Grandmother's place. But my mother is here for the weekend."

The boy frowned in confusion. Yet, the fun was short-lived, for even as he teased young Befford, Christian saw it would not be long before Kristina would be out of his life, and running Si's.

"Kristi says she can stay at Mrs. Day's lodge even if she's gone. The caretaker can let her in." Si had recovered.

Christian had to give it to the boy, he could think on his feet.

"Well, Christian," Mary said, not a sign of sweetness left, "I think you can spare her for one weekend."

"Let's ask her," Christian said, sending one of the crew to fetch her from the house.

When Kristina appeared, Si hurried to greet her. "Come on, Kristi. Get your things. We're going."

"I told you that I was working today, Si," Kristi said, joining her father at the bar.

"It's okay," Si replied. "We don't have to work. I made it good with the folks."

"I am glad for you. I know that's what you wanted," Kristi said. "But as for me, I'm not free. I've committed to Grandmother and Tessa to help with the party. And I have recruited my friends to help as well."

"Certainly those girls can help the housekeeper run things without you." Mary's voice harbored a smirk. Her girls would never be caught serving guests. Then she glanced at Christian. "Your father hardly expects you to be in service."

"Grandmother expects me to stand by my word," Kristi offered her a pleasant but firm smile.

Si was steaming. "All you really want to do is kiss up to those professors of yours."

"Son," Joe warned with a hint of displeasure in his tone.

Kristi reddened at the accusation, then took leave of the room. "If you will excuse me, I have some tables to set up."

At her departure, Mary said, "That girl has a lot to learn about loving," speaking to no one in particular.

Kristi headed upstairs to hide from Si, who was sure to come after her in order to pursue his case—that is, as soon as he was done with his family. From the hall, she spied Amy primping at the mirror in her bathroom, talking to someone—probably Birdie—behind the door. Before she could be spotted, Kristi headed toward the adjoining guest room and shut herself behind the locked door.

Her heart was pounding with fury at Si, at the scene he had made in front of the family. He had not told his parents where he planned to go, she was sure, or his father would not have agreed to let him go. But Father knew, didn't he? Things were happening that Kristi did not understand—yet she had no interest in understanding them any further.

The voices of her two friends, though muffled by the heavy door, could be distinguished clearly. Amy was talking about her plans for the summer with Mac. When Birdie made her usual remarks about a girl giving up her freedom for a boyfriend, Kristi was glad they hadn't caught sight of her, for Birdie would have guessed her problem in a heartbeat.

Another voice chimed in then. It was Si, asking if they had seen her. Kristi held her breath as if it would make her invisible. Her friends chased him off, in the direction of the kitchen. Then, gradually, all three voices faded, and Kristi was alone.

She lay on the bed for a long while, listening to pleasant vibrations of the string quartet warming up in the foyer on the first floor, directly beneath her room.

True to its reputation, the Humanities Department had won first place in the full-staff-present award, bestowing bragging rights for all faculty gatherings until September. Humanities had just barely beaten out Business Admin, however, owing to the very late arrival of Professor Truitt, who was justly castigated by his peers.

Taking his jibes in good humor, Truitt ducked into the front salon. There he found Sanders leaning against the bar, nursing his favorite scotch, watching people come and go. Truitt ordered the same drink for himself, and joined his friend in mute observation of the human condition. They watched together, each lost in his own world.

Truitt's attention was fixed on Kristina Day, who was in the hall greeting folks as they arrived at the front door. He was glad that he had slipped through the front patio unnoticed, able to avoid the embarrassment and pretense of these felicitations. The faux smiles and superficial niceties accompanied by a half-hearted female handshake with its faint hug. It was reminiscent of the library open houses in his youth, when his aunt played hostess to the town and its officials, opening her home and heart to them, only to have them patronize her. She was a servant of the community, to be treated as a child not quite responsible enough to handle the budget or other important matters. She and her nephew were not of the ilk to be invited into their homes.

Aunt Nell treated all with an easy grace, making her guests feel comfortable whether or not they harbored her ill. Truitt hated the pretence of others who were pleasant to her on those occasions only to snub her the following day in church. Of course, Aunt Nell hadn't seen it that way at all. She would always feel satisfied that she had fulfilled her duty, and would take pleasure from the obligation.

Miss Day seemed to enjoy her role in a similar fashion. In her foyer, she exhibited a gracious confidence that she lacked at school. Yet, she could hardly be fulfilled by waiting on her teachers, and serving the school admin staff. No doubt, she had been pressured into the job by her father. Or, perhaps she had volunteered with a secret desire to watch them make fools of themselves, with too much to drink and the promise of summer and freedom looming.

"Looks just like her mother." Sanders was observing him with a half-ironic smile. "She was a beauty."

"Really?" Truitt saw no beauty, only willfulness in the girlish face, supported as it was by a pedestrian mind. At that moment, she was engaged by the janitor's stout wife.

"Don't sound so interested," Sanders jibed.

"Interested in what?"

"Honestly, old man, your lack of interest in your fellow humans astonishes me at times. How did you ever come to choose teaching as a career?"

"I didn't. I chose scholarship, and teaching is part of the package. But what am I supposed to be interested in?"

Sanders signaled the bartender and indicated the two empty glasses that needed refilling.

Truitt started to object but didn't.

Handing Truitt the refilled glass, Sanders sipped from his own, then asked, "Ever been with a woman, Tru?"

Truitt cringed—not only at the truncation of his name. It was a little late to be sharing peccadilloes about their past lives. Truitt had nothing to share and Sanders was soon retreating to a cabin in the mountains. There was no need to further fuel the acquaintance.

"I didn't think so, "Sanders responded to the silence.

Truitt ignored the man's conclusion, allowing his mind to drift with the movement in the room. A little drama was unfolding in the hallway where Si Befford, senior jock and class jerk, was wresting Miss Day away from two middle-aged ladies. To her credit, Miss Day politely ended the conversation before letting Befford whisk her away.

Sanders was watching the scene as well.

"I would say that Miss Day has definite designs on Befford," Truitt commented.

Sanders shook his head. "You would be wrong. That young buck always has designs on her. And by the look of it, her resistance is wearing thin. Poor old Meyer."

"Meyer?" Truitt retorted. "Your replacement? What's he got to do with it?"

"Oh, Truitt. You are carelessly wading into the waters of the rumor mill."

"Never mind, then," Truitt said with some annoyance.

Sanders chuckled. "I suspect that Kristina Day had a lot to do with Geoff's desire to return to his roots. Let's face it—even if he had been released by Berkeley, there are plenty of schools who would want his expertise and his connections."

"And you didn't warn him off by letting him know of her current attachment to Befford?" It seemed an unworthy gesture, one Truitt thought as being beneath Sanders' dignity.

"What? And pass along campus rumors? Really, Truitt, what do you take me for? An old gossip?" Then Sanders let out a hearty laugh as he slapped his friend on the shoulder. "I'm going to miss you, Truitt. I really am."

On the patio, with the jazz band bouncing through a set of Glenn Miller arrangements, Elena was introducing her new beau, Ross Delaney, to the gathering. The son of an influential senator and a recent graduate of Harvard Law School, Delaney commanded the attention of the faculty. The Business Admin teachers were keen to elicit his views on the current deregulation of the banking industry. Reverend Smythe wasted no time in turning the discussion from corporate law to the topic uppermost in the minds of the Humanities professors, the current status of women's studies in the Ivy League.

Delaney was affable, testing the sensitivity of the crowd as his father might, answering with neutral responses about the small number of women he actually had to deal with in school. There was tacit agreement, among the law students and professors, that women did not really belong there—and the less said about the subject, the better. However, as a true son to the popular Senator, Delaney kept that information to himself.

"You mean the schools aren't integrated by now. Surely I've read somewhere...." Gordon Sims seemed bothered by the prospect, and was joined in suit by Smythe and Brooks.

Delaney, who was still flanked by Elena, squeezed the arm she held under his and replied, "Let's just say that ladies of my personal acquaintance," and here he squeezed Elena's arm affectionately, "prefer the niceties offered at the sister schools. After all, what decent woman wants to be thrown on the playing field competing against their betters?"

"I thought those feminists were running the place by now," Cecil Durham weighed in with his usual scorn.

Delaney laughed. "No, they just think they are!"

Some of the men hooted.

Then Delaney quickly switched his tune as he picked up on the unhappy faces on the ladies gathered around him, He added gently, "Oh, but don't get me wrong. We welcome women students, of course. There are a number of women enrolled in the law school. They just aren't the kind of woman a man would attach himself to." This comment won Elena another squeeze.

"By niceties, do you mean facilities like a proper woman's room?" Sofia Avila stepped forward, her smile beaming with her dark eyes full of mischief.

Delaney reddened while Elena made the introduction. Sofia enjoyed the young man's discomfort.

Jenny Brooks was right on Avila's heels. "Mr. Delaney, I've read where women have not been able to find work after law school..."

"...Or they work for free," Avila added, "advocating for women's rights."

Delaney frowned at the women, at a loss as how to continue. He was saved by Mrs. Day who descended on the group like a guardian angel, calling the women to appreciate needlecraft and home arts in the upper regions of the house. The women drifted from the men, even Elena who reluctantly left Delaney's side and joined her mother heading up the stairs.

Only Deb Temple remained, not quite attached to Mike, but feeling more comfort next to him even in a field of men than she did in a group of women unknown to her. In a moment, Sofia Avila returned to the group and ushered Deb upstairs with much encouragement.

With the ladies gone, the men turned a sharper knife on the subject of women in school.

"Thing is, Delaney," Reverend Smythe explained, "St. Clements is going through a little challenge concerning this matter."

"And that woman is central to the discourse, I'll bet," Delaney said, indicating Sofia Avila.

"These women are just taking seats that a man could use." Tom Parker, the registrar's husband, a rancher, added his two cents.

"A man's got to work, to earn a living. These gals are just hunting for husbands to snag, is all." This comment emanated from one of the servers, a high school senior on the brink of manhood with no college in his future. Joe Befford reminded him of what he was there to do.

Christian stepped in to take charge of the group. "Luckily, Ross, we have no feminists here, clamoring at the gate. Only teachers trying to help the school move forward into the new century. There's plenty of beef and brew left, boys. And my foreman's a little concerned about the lamb that hasn't yet been carved. Come on, Haug, Reverend, you guys can always be counted on for the lamb."

The crowd dispersed toward the barbecue pits.

Amy came into the butler's pantry where Birdie and Kristi were busy shuffling left over appetizers onto smaller platters, in order to make the larger plates available for the cornucopia of fruits, cakes and pies offered for dessert. "Kristi, your grandmother is looking for you. She's up in the sitting room with the rest of the ladies."

"Oh, I'd better go and leave you to the dessert platters. I promised I'd be there to help show off the quilt." Kristi shed her soiled apron. "I'll be back shortly."

"Since you're going upstairs anyway, would you mind putting this into my overnight case? I caught the clasp in the dishwasher, and I'm afraid it's going to break." Amy had removed her charm bracelet and handed it to Kristi.

"Sure thing," Kristi said.

"Told you it would get in the way," Birdie was saying as Kristi left the room.

The sitting room on the second floor was formed by joining two smaller guest rooms which had been built in the days when a trip from Boise took the better part of eight hours, and visitors were prone to spend the night. As such, the room had two doors, both of which were opened up to accommodate the flow of guests. As Kristi passed by the room to stow Amy's bracelet, Professor Avila and Mrs. Mudd both called out to her. They had been waiting for Kristi to show off her handiwork which was prominently mounted on the large quilting frame in the center of the room. Kristi and Anne explained the stitching and fabrics they had used. Everyone agreed on the stunning quality of their effort.

Kristi was proud of her work, but embarrassed at the accolade which she certainly deserved no more than any of the cousins who worked on the pieces. Mary Befford was quick to include her own two daughters among the quilters, but Elena denied her talents and pulled her mother from the room, while her sister tried to bask in what little attention was left. Noting that Harriette Befford was about her own age, Deb Temple tried a little harder to fit into the group. Filling the void left by the departing Beffords, she moved to center stage, declaring that the quilt was pretty enough, but she could never waste that kind of time making one for herself.

"Perhaps you'll join our quilters guild next year?" Liz Ralston said hesitantly.

Why would she, the young wife retorted, when they had enough blankets already.

"Maybe you'd prefer embroidery work," Helen Mudd suggested, showing her a pretty piece, silk thread on linen, that Kristi had done the previous summer, of the county fair and rodeo.

"It's nice," Deb said, "but what's the purpose? I mean, spending all that time on something you can't eat or wear. Seems silly."

Kristi stayed only a few minutes longer, quietly withdrawing to finish her errand.

Sofia Avila watched Professor Temple's young wife, half-amused, and somewhat more perturbed, at the girl's lack of interest in the world around her.

As if Deb sensed the criticism, she reassessed the silk embroidery, then shrugged her shoulders. "I don't know. Horses and bulls. It's kind of ugly, don't you think? All that red and brown."

She finally joined Harriette, who was circling the room looking at the art and photos on display in the glass cases, while the other ladies talked animatedly about shared talents, unfinished projects and the memories that linked them together.

"Deb. Look at this beautiful layette," Harriette said. "Those little pink rosebuds. My great-great-grand-aunt made those for her son. How precious they are."

Next to the sophisticated Harriette Befford, Deb Temple seemed callow and seemed so very young to Sofia. She felt the tension rise among the other faculty wives as they failed one by one to arrest her interest. It would eventually fall on Helen Mudd's shoulders to distract the girl, once her husband was occupied with school.

"Ooh. These little booties are so precious. Look at that little cap," Deb cooed.

"Perhaps we could teach you to crochet," Helen suggested anew.

Deb turned away from the case, her face pale. "I don't think Mikey would like that at all. He doesn't even want to think about babies until he has a lot more money."

In the guest room, Kristi looked glumly at the piles of boxes and papers stacked on the bed and surrounding floor. She finally spotted Amy's overnight bag buried under a pile of knitted throws. As she unzipped the pockets, digging through the variety of contents in search of the red pouch, she heard two ladies talking in the adjoining bathroom. Mary Befford's dialect was clear, but the words were blurred by water running in the sink. As the tap shut off, she heard Elena's response clearly enough. They were talking about marriage, Ross Delaney, and then Si—when the conversation suddenly broke off, and the door handle jiggled sharply.

Kristi jumped, Amy's bracelet still in hand.

"It's locked from the outside too," Mary said moving away from the door.

Elena continued, her voice ebbing and flowing as if she were pacing the floor. "I don't know why he keeps after her. There's plenty of fish in the ocean, better than...He needs to get around. My friend..." The words fell away.

Kristi could hear mumbled responses from Mary, then Elena's voice amplified. "...Her cousin. Well, you know the Winslows, don't you? Do you think she's good enough for him?"

Mary guffawed. "Good enough? That's not the issue here. You should consider whether they are suitable... Hand me that eyeliner, dear. Ash blue? Well, it'll do." Mary paused for a moment. "Your brother's no fool, Elena. Christian Day's fortune is seven times that of the Befford clan altogether. Besides, your father's got his heart set on the match."

Kristi couldn't catch Elena's response. But Mary's voice was quite clear.

"Worthy of my son? Don't make me laugh. Any offspring of that wench Christian married would never be worthy of an Evans, nor a Befford. Blood will out, I tell you. Blood will always show itself, breeding never lies. Not good enough for you when you were tots, not good enough to be Si's wife, by a long shot. But there's no turning your father on the subject. Well, there now. We'd better get below stairs before...." Mary's tone brightened as the voices faded from the room.

Nothing good comes from eavesdropping, Grandmother would say, and Kristi had just gotten an earful of why. For a long while, she sat on the bed to compose herself. She found the red pouch tucked into a pocket at the bottom of the bag, and slipped the bracelet into it. Her heart beat wildly as she recalled the ugliness of Elena's tone and Mary's words. How duplicitous the Befford women were, and how disingenuous Elena had grown in her privileged education.

At least now Kristi understood the cause of Mary's disregard for her. Beyond a sense of natural superiority derived from her Boston origins, Mary Befford harbored contempt for Kristi's mother, Marlyss Day.

Kristi managed to contain her own harsh feelings against Mary, and headed back to her guests. At least she would demonstrate the sense of responsibility that Mary's son failed to do. And Kristi would live up to her commitments with the same grace and elegance as her grandmother.

Truitt had talked to Sanders before strolling out to the patio where platters of meat and bowls of salad lay for the taking. The fire pits in the back of the house still burned under turning spits. Truitt helped himself to a modest plateful then wandered around to the front garden where a fountain spilled water into a small pond, and several benches surrounded the arced pathway. He ate his lunch in peace, listening to the strains of old warhorses from the Jazz Age, spiced up, as it were, with the honks and squeals of student enthusiasts.

He had a filtered view of both the front salon, the doors of which spilled onto the garden lawn, and the back patio situated around the corner from the salon. The Humanities Department was doing its best to empty bottles in the salon bar, while the Science and Business Departments worked on the patio bar. With rounds of scotch, Sanders was bidding a farewell of sorts to his cronies, no doubt praising the worthiness of their fine hostess.

Sanders' good humor and praise of the ladies had put Truitt into a mood more generous than usual amid the school crowd. But then, President Gearhart had acknowledged him along with the other Associates, dispensing gifts in the way of congratulations. The professors had received gold-trimmed pens with the school insignia on one side and the professors' initials on the other. Truitt was especially pleased that someone had taken the trouble to learn his preference, for he had received the only fountain pen in the group.

Sanders had also opened Truitt's eyes to the usefulness of Kristina Day. Seeing her here in her natural habitat, so to speak, sharing the duties of hostess with her grandmother, gave Truitt another side of the girl. He could feel genuine sympathy for anyone whose mother had abandoned her, in the lap of privilege or otherwise—although he conceded that the lap of luxury was much preferable to impoverishment. Not that he had been dealt a poor hand entirely, thanks to the hard work and ingenuity of his aunt.

When Kristi emerged from the patio door carrying platters to the barbecue tables, he realized that she had not allowed herself to be pulled away by Befford, after all. He liked her better for that decision. She wasn't really a bad sort, and seemed to have a brain about her, but too much influenced by romance novels and Avila's romantic notions of knights in shining armor to suit him. Even if she did not have the ability to pursue serious scholarship, still, she was skilled in handling people, in working a crowd.

Not an exacting one, this skill that women had, the desire to please others. Miss Day seemed to have this trait in excess. To Truitt that showed an unexacting mind, one that could flitter from person to person and topic to topic without much focus on anything at all. That tasting of a wide range of subjects hampers the disciplined mind from serious pursuit. Finishing his dinner, he was ready to leave. Yet he felt a singular emptiness in just quitting the crowd, an incompletion. Inexplicably, he had the urge to acknowledge Miss Day upon leaving. Depositing his empty plate in the trash bin outside the kitchen door, he walked through the house, to see if he could catch her in a quiet spot. By the time he reached the foyer, he had been unsuccessful, and so headed for the front door.

"Professor, are you leaving?" Kristina Day came down the staircase, her dress billowing in colors of summer, like one of those floral shirtwaists favored by his aunt. Her face was somber and sad, he thought, until her foot lit upon the bottom step. Then the warm smile of the hostess reappeared.

"I wanted to talk to you…" she said.

"Professor Truitt!" Christian Day bellowed, coming at him from seemingly nowhere. "Leaving before supper? Kristi, go fetch the professor a box lunch."

Kristi disappeared into the pantry while Professor Avila came through the salon with four box lunches to leave by the front door for those early departures.

Setting three of the boxes on the table, she handed the last to Truitt. "Professor, you must take one. Tessa has been fussing with these since noon. We shouldn't disappoint her, no?"

Truitt grimaced and accepted the box reluctantly. He was forced to make his goodbye to the two people for whom he held no warm regard at all. He left.

When the door closed, Sofia turned on Christian with curiosity. "You don't seem to like Professor Truitt a great deal."

"Not much," Christian responded, and escorted her back into the crowd.

Six

Truitt wished he had skipped church as he had planned. Reverend Smythe was still on his soapbox about women's place in the world, a campaign he had started with his Easter sermon on the pieta, the Christian icon of mother and child, or rather, the holy Mother embracing her son at the foot of the cross. The bond of mother and child was that day's focus, the birth, not the death. Then, on Mother's Day, he had embraced the ideal of Mother as the mainstay of home and family, no matter that some of the reverend's faithful flock had been denied the loving comfort of Mother for one reason or another.

Now, this morning, the righteous reverend was rhapsodizing about St. Paul's message against women speaking from the pulpit, somehow wrapping it all around the biblical idea of the good wife. His whole talk seemed aimed at Sofia Avila who was perched in the midst of the Day clan—evidence that Sanders' rumors might be true. As the pastor carried on, a tedium settled through the congregation. After all, most of them agreed with him. There was no need to set out deliberately irritating the ladies. They were trouble enough without his provocation.

Truitt discovered that he was growing defensive on behalf of his aunt, neither a mother nor a wife, but a virtuous woman who lived in Christ, and dedicated herself to rearing an orphaned nephew. Considering this, he was glad he had called her before leaving the bungalow. He wanted to manage her expectations about his arrival back home, which was to be delayed two weeks.

The initial cheeriness in her tone faded. "I hope you won't be delayed too long." She sounded weary.

"You sound tired," Truitt said. "Did I wake you?"

"Goodness, no. I have just returned from church."

"I need to get the second part of my article to Willema before I leave. It's almost done, but I have finals first and grades to get in."

"Of course, Dear. I don't want to take away from your duties. I just need to talk to you."

"We can talk now. It's an hour before I need to get to the chapel."

"Well, it's only two weeks. I can wait till then. But come home straight away, will you?"

"Yes. Well, don't sit around counting the hours and minutes, though. It's still a four day trip. Don't forget I'll be driving back."

"Of course. It would be so lovely to take that trip with you some day."

Truitt had suspected that his aunt was going for another salvo in her campaign, to bring him home at any cost. The previous Christmas, during his holiday, she had invited the colonel over to dinner. He was headmaster at St. John's Academy where Truitt had attended prep school, and spent the whole evening crusading for Truitt to join his staff as housemaster for the upper class students. From there, both Nell and the colonel had argued, Truitt could launch a campaign to find a decent position at the right university. He had reluctantly agreed to consider the plan, when his prospects for an Associate at St. Clements looked dim.

Truitt's promotion, however, had changed everything. He couldn't possibly compromise the progress of his career now. He was already out of the starting gate. Telling her over the phone seemed unreasonably cruel. He would wait until he was home.

The chapel was growing warm in response to the sun's arc rising overhead. Already a few of the ladies were fanning themselves vigorously with the Sunday reader, as if to send the reverend a message. Foremost among them was his Mrs. Smythe, who seemed as peeved as everyone else about his message. With a grand gesture, he finished his sermon, closed the portfolio and descended from the pulpit like a king from his throne.

In upstate New York, at the Rutherton family estate, Willema retreated on the weekend, to finish up the work to be included in the next issue of The Medieval Journal. She sat at a generous table in the midst of the magnificent tomes of the Rutherton family library—collected over three centuries by statesmen, judges like her father, and educators such as herself. Her own body of work was meager, filling less than one shelf. In this room, Willema humbled herself before the wisdom of her forebears, playing judge and jury of young and seasoned scholars alike. She was devoted to the cause of opening the medieval canon to new work and newly formed theories once banned by the publisher.

The number of submissions to the journal had increased by threefold during her tenure at the helm, giving fresh views of what had become a claustrophobic body of work. In her day, most of the material was sanctioned by the Church, with all outside material considered suspect. The tight hold, that religious schools once held on historical interpretation of what was in their mind church history, had eroded with a half century of war and chaos. This, along with the rising power of state universities, produced a wide range of secular-minded scholars, who had emerged outside traditional theories of prestigious medieval programs.

These new submissions that she now considered were expanding the body of knowledge of what was now being called "the Middle Ages." Archaeological research in the past fifty years had debunked fallacious theories that had been accepted for centuries. Strong evidence had emerged to prove that history had been written by the victors.

Obscure manuscripts, once discredited by Church authority, were now being reconsidered in light of archeological digs conducted under the secular authority of science and scholarship.

Oral histories, too, were finding new ground among the champions of the common man. Those disinherited from history had discovered their voices. What most pleased Willema, was that medieval scholarship had finally become relevant. Finally, she was able to accept an article on Queen Eleanor at Champagne and the literary efforts associated with that court.

Willema had a full weekend ahead of her, with eighty-seven manuscripts to read, of which only nine would be selected for the next issue. She expected that another three to six papers would be ready for publication, and these would be put aside for future issues. A handful would be sent back to the author for rework with editorial notes hastily scratched on note paper. Caroline Chatham, her niece and a protégé of sorts, would type up those comments on official stationary from the editor. The majority of the submissions would receive a form letter of rejection.

Rejections came with the territory, and Willema gave as much attention to these submissions as they deserved, which was a quick scan and move to the rejection pile. Some did cause her to reflect, though, such as the paper she now considered. Some were still submitting hackneyed work from research conducted during their doctoral dissertation, with no update on research or the ideas.

Such was the work of Emery Truitt. She scanned the paper, seeing nothing new in his half-developed approach about a twelfth century monk. Although he suggested a connection between the monk and the new age of the thirteenth century and its effects in the fourteenth and fifteenth, he did not extend the argument to include newer research, such as Eleanor's proclamation of a new kind of knight, or how the seeds of the reformation might have been fomented from his effort. She would have given up on Truitt long ago if not for the particular regard she had for Nell. She tossed the paper into the reject pile.

A quiet rap on the door offered a welcome break. Caroline entered with a tray of tea and sandwiches, a job she took responsibility for once she learned that the cook was gone for the day. "I hope ham is okay." Caroline set the tray on the table next to the rejection pile, moving the papers aside to make room for the service.

Pulling a chair for herself up to the table, Caroline said, "I'll get to these letters after this."

Willema thanked her, taking some tea.

"And you've selected only one for the journal? It will be a long weekend. Still, I have nothing better to do." She noticed the name on the first rejections. "Emery Truitt? You're not serious, Willa, a flat rejection? A cold form letter?"

"I am most serious about it," Willa responded, her mouth set.

"Surely he deserves more than that from you. He has tried so hard."

Willema considered her niece's complaint and thought about her former student while she ate her sandwich. Willema was indeed tired of rejecting his work, but even more weary of dealing with his single-minded obsession on his doctoral dissertation.

She took a sip of tea, then finally said, "He tries hard to please himself, I agree—but he shows a total disregard for any suggestions we have offered so far. Yet another rehashing of the Trinity theory of Brother Joachim—and now he promises a second part to follow. The thought is unbearable."

"Oh, Auntie." Caroline took the rejection personally. "Surely, you must have some compassion for the poor boy."

"I've run out. But I see your interest in him has not dissipated, as I would have expected."

Caroline toyed with the half sandwich on her plate, calling to mind the student she had once dated. "He was sweet."

"He had his head in the clouds." Willema said dismissively. "I do recall a time when you found him equally aloof—awkward, you said, and lacking in social graces."

Caroline finished her tea and wiped her mouth. "What I meant was, there's something innocent about him, so untouched by the reality of life. Naïve, in a word."

"Immature, I'd call it. With his biggest problem being his ego. He can't quite accept that someone else might be as knowledgeable as he is—or wiser."

Caroline raised her eyebrows to the determination set in her aunt's voice. Then added meekly, half in jest, "Maybe he just needs the right woman. You know, someone he can grow with."

Willema frowned at her niece. "I hope you're not considering yourself as a candidate. You've grown way beyond him."

Caroline stacked the plates onto the empty tray. "At least Emery had ethics. He would have suited me far better than Lionel Chatham did."

"You would have eaten him alive." Willema smiled drily.

"He was naïve," Caroline reflected.

"Don't be absurd. Your father would never have allowed you to throw yourself away on a man without name or fortune to recommend him to the family."

"You would have," Caroline grinned. "I'll clean these up, then return."

In the shadows of the great library, Willema considered her niece as she closed the door. While Willema did indeed root for the upsurge of the common man, Truitt's beginnings were far too humble, not to mention controversial, for anyone in her family to warm up to. Yet for just this reason, she felt that Emery Truitt, of all people, should be able to embrace the rise of the common man. But his prep school education had thrown him a curve. While Nell never lied to him about his beginnings, she had certainly deceived him, all the same. She should have told him long ago, so that his grand experiences and his life could be shaped in the context of his birth.

Later, when Caroline returned to collect the rejections, Willema saw her slip Truitt's paper under the stack slated for the author's rework. She said nothing. If her niece had a mind to give further encouragement to the poor boy, Willema wouldn't interfere. Maybe Caroline could succeed where she had failed.

Back at Saint Clements, Professor Avila handed out the final exam, which was comprised of three questions on translation and meaning, to her Advanced French students. She had decided on an oral exam in French. The three students in that class were amiable girls, a close knit group who had been together since grade school. Yet, they varied as much in academic excellence as they did in personality. Amy Gaites was a mediocre student, with little sense of academic inquiry, but with an almost preternatural inclination toward language and conversation. It was for her benefit that Avila had decided to offer an oral exam.

Birdie Caldwell, on the other hand, flew through her French texts, having no patience for standing still, or for untangling the dense meanings of nuance and idiomatic phrases. She exercised her curiosity only when pushed to do so, usually through some incorrect assumptions that led her to a wrong conclusion. Then she would go to her two friends for discussion and clarification, as the girls formed a long lasting study group.

Kristina Day—or Kristi as she was called at school—was neither as fluent in language as Amy nor as curious as Birdie, but she was by far the best student because of her persistence and dedication to her academic standing. She was the most apt of the three to reference the dictionary, or the phrase books until a particular translation made sense.

The work under question was Madame Bovary. Avila hoped that it would naturally lead into the discussion of women's issues. Kristi had, by far, the deepest understanding of the work. Yet, her conclusion about the effect of its message lacked compassion for the plight of the heroine, shaped by a preconscious notion of woman, a view carefully honed at home and church. Instead of seeing the author as antipathetic to women's plight, Kristi had agreed with Flaubert's condemnation of Emma Bovary.

Birdie was adamantly opposed to Kristi's view, and argued in increasingly awkward French, trying to grasp abstractions beyond her capability in that language. Finally, no longer able to contain her frustration, she burst into English. Instead of reining in the students, Avila let them carry on, seeing more value in the discussion of women's issues, than in the execution of the final exam for French.

"Emma Bovary is the victim of Gustav Flaubert, that male chauvinist...His view of women is flawed, I tell you," Birdie asserted in an agitated voice.

Avila nodded indulgently and looked toward Kristi for her response.

"Why? She is the most despicable woman. She doesn't appreciate her husband. She makes a fool of him, lying, cheating. She deserves to be ruined."

"Flaubert paints this pretty picture of her doesn't he?" Birdie countered. "A woman with no conscience at all. A device of fiction, his fantasies so we will all despise her."

"I guess he has a right to create the fiction he wants," Kristi noted.

"Come on, Kristi! What woman would desert her child like that with no feeling at all? At all?"

Avila felt the stirring of something personal in the argument. She realized with some discomfort that Kristi's mother might be the type of woman described by Flaubert. As much as she had been in the Day household of recent months, the mother was never spoken of, at least in front of her.

Birdie hadn't finished. "Look at the ending! Not only does he make Emma pay for her sins, but he punishes the daughter, too. I tell you, he's a misogynist."

Kristi never flinched from her friend's attack, giving Avila the sense that the girl's mother was not an issue between them. But something was brewing between them.

"He's simply pointing out that a married woman should be faithful to her husband..." Kristi began.

"Charles Bovary is a dolt," Birdie intruded.

"...no matter how tedious he might turn out to be. It's her job to love and comfort him, not chase around the countryside for a thrill." Kristi sat erect, pen poised, making eye contact with her friend.

Dios mio! How naïve she is! The girl was worse than Professor Truitt in her innocent view of the world. Yet, Kristi's openness put to rest Avila's assumptions about her mother. Whatever reason the woman had for leaving her house and home, the daughter did not see it as desertion. As an exchange student, years ago, Avila had lived for a short while in the Day home. Mrs. Day did not seem the siren type of woman to string men along. In her, Avila saw only love and devotion she gave to her family. Quiet and unassuming she was, like Amy.

The comparison drew Avila back to the present discussion. "Well, we've heard two of you. Amy. What do you think about the author's intentions?"

"Emma is desperate for love. It doesn't matter what the author intended. It's what we see in her from one mistake to another."

"She already has a husband—she just needs to learn how to love him." Kristi countered.

Birdie rolled her eyes. "Yeah, just like you'll learn to love Si Befford."

The remark surprised Avila, it was more than she had bargained for, but didn't seem to affect any of the girls. She followed Kristi's lead and ignored the remark as well. Birdie's insight that Si was totally unsuited for Kristina was something Avila had considered often in the past few months. He was a cowboy version of Rodolphe, the villainous nobleman who exploits Emma Bovary and brings her to ruin.

"Mac wouldn't see her husband as respectable at all." Amy was talking now, seeing the book through her boyfriend's eyes. "The way he leads her on and he's married to the old lady. I don't think he'd like Flaubert, either. I agree with Birdie that Emma's treated badly."

"That's an excellent take on the book, through men's eyes. What do you other ladies think men would see?"

Birdie shook her head. "Not knowing any males personally, up-close like, I'd just say that the guys I know—and you know them too—would label Emma Bovary a slut and not care, except to take advantage of her on Friday nights."

Kristi responded in terms of her own father. "Grandmother would have us all not be judgmental. She'd pity Emma. My father would judge, of course, condemn her actions. But in the long run, he'd try to help. It's sad that there's no one to help her."

Avila was pleased with the way the discussion had turned from translation to meaning. Amy had earned a B for her fluency in French conversation. Each of the girls offered a valued view of women's issues from her unique interpretation of the novel. Avila would use this session as a starting point when, in the fall, she would solicit the help of these competent ladies in developing the course on women's issues. She was also pleased to learn more of Kristi's take on her family life, and especially on the motivations of her father. The discussion might have been heated, but it maintained an academic tone. The students revealed a solid understanding of the work, however imperfect their reading of Flaubert.

Finals week had been a harrowing one for Professor Truitt, full of interruptions and surprises, few of them pleasant. Department meetings had been called, at the last minute, to cover issues uncovered by negligent planning. Students competed for his attention in hallways or after class, in an attempt to change grades, get a preview of the final, or seek counseling for course offerings in the fall.

Truitt dodged and deferred as best as he could but with limited success, resulting in the loss of time that could have been better spent on his article. There would be no hope of getting back to Delaware before the end of the month, if he were to meet his publishing goal. He was glad now that he had been successful in discouraging Nell's hopes for his earlier return. Still he did not like to disappoint her. She was a good sport about it, though.

At three-thirty Friday afternoon, he was seated in the classroom proctoring his final exam for Medieval Studies, hopefully the last time he would have to monitor his students for the exam. In the fall, he had every expectation that his teaching assistant would take over the proctoring duties for all exams. He had received a nasty turn earlier in the week regarding his open position for a teaching assistant. He had yet to secure Martin's application. In fact, Martin had yet to contact him. In the meantime, Kristina Day had actually applied for the position. Kristina Day, of all people.

In fact, Miss Day had been dogging him all week, trying to find time on his schedule. With a new sense of urgency, he cornered Martin before anyone else had arrived in class, and extracted a promise from him to meet in the morning. When Miss Day entered the room one minute before the hour with her gang of friends, she demonstrated no desire to talk with Truitt. She picked up the exam off his desk and settled into her own, blue book and pen in hand, diving into the test with fervor.

At three-forty Miss Day stood before him, her blue book placed on the table before him. He looked at the book, hardly believing it was finished, doubting the quality of work inside, but said nothing. He returned to his reading.

"Professor," she whispered softly. "Professor, I'd like to speak with you."

He finally was obliged to look up. "It will have to wait."

"Did you get my application?" She was bending near his ear now.

A couple of students, distracted by the whispering, glanced back in annoyance. Truitt had no ready excuse to put her off again. He dared not openly discourage her, considering who she was, who her father was. Still it was with some effort that he agreed to meet her in his office later, when the finals session was over.

By the time Truitt arrived at his office, he had devised a plan for discouraging Miss Day from pursuing her application. With gentle dissuasion, he would simply tell her that she just wouldn't do. The job required at times long hours working together, and it would be an impossible situation with a female student. In his mind, the conversation was amicable, pleasant, with Miss Day coming to understand why the whole scenario was impossible.

But Miss Day did not play to script. "What do you mean, I'm not suitable? It says here, 'Requirements: Assist professor with administrative tasks; Help tutor students in lower class English; Assist with selective research. ' I can do that."

"On the surface, yes, you can do those things. But I am looking for someone who can work longer hours. Evenings and weekends will be included," he said gently, hoping to warn her off.

"I can do that," she settled into the chair in front of his desk. She was getting too comfortable.

"But would you be willing to give up a year of evenings and weekends?" He did not want to deny her the job outright. It would be much better if she elected to drop the application.

He gave her a rough estimate of what he would expect from his TA, exaggerating to some degree the length of time and hours. To each point he made, she matched with qualifications. She worked long hours for the Rodeo Queen Association, doing much heftier work. She was as familiar with the school at night as anyone having spent a considerable chunk of her childhood running through the empty halls. She offered her references, which he hadn't asked for and certainly didn't need.

Truitt was frustrated. She just didn't see the inappropriateness of a female student, sequestered for long hours with a male professor, in his office alone, at night. All sorts of misunderstandings could occur. He certainly wasn't going to lay out the problem, fearing she might interpret that as his intentions. He was perplexed, having come to the end of any logical argument that was not charged with sexual overtones—and that would be the primary reason to avoid the whole situation altogether.

"Look, Miss Day, the truth is that I want someone to help me with some research I am doing for a series of articles." She started to speak, but he held up his hand. "Wait. Hear me out. Research is exceedingly difficult to do for someone else—I am looking for someone who is more in sync with my own thinking. I'm sure you understand."

"In what way?"

He leaned back in his chair. "Rational. Logical progression. A process of thought based on rationalization."

"And you're saying I'm not rational? Would you mind explaining that?"

She seemed to be making an earnest inquiry, one that he didn't mind answering judiciously.

"For one thing, you're more emotional in your responses."

"I do feel things, yes. But I don't think I act out in a dramatic fashion, do you?"

"Of course not. I meant more a sense of jumping to hunches about things rather than taking logical steps to discovery."

"Like you?"

"Of course. But also—and you must admit this as a shortcoming—you are too timid about speaking up. In fact, you don't speak out in class, unless your friends call on you to defend some point."

"I see. And this couldn't be out of respect for you, the professor, out of deference to your authority?"

"Well, it might be. Yes, it probably is. But that hardly makes a case for you to take on the task of directing others in their studies, does it?"

"Look, professor. I've gotten A's from you for three years. I have written papers for you, and you know my abilities there. If I am asked to take control, I have no problem with that. I am qualified to do this job."

He might have asked her why she thought she wanted the job, but he did not want to encourage her application. She didn't discourage easily. He couldn't tell her that Martin already had the job because technically he had yet to apply for it. But Martin was his man, and he had no need to carry the interview on any longer.

"Frankly, Miss Day, I have a problem with the way you think."

"The way I think?"

"Your thought process, which is not logical by any means."

"And my way of thinking is different from, say, the way you think?" A tone of irritation slipped into her rising voice.

Truitt had meant to relay the unadorned truth of the situation in order to free her from any fanciful notions she was entertaining about getting the position, but the discussion had gone awry. He had little patience for her annoyance and no strategy to combat a face-to-face conflict. "You know what I mean. The way your mind runs in circles."

"Circles? Like, I don't know what I'm doing?"

"Yes. No. Jumping to conclusions like now. Arguing with hunches instead of sound reasoning, as I said."

"Oh. You mean my intuition." She stood up clearly annoyed.

He was glad to see her retreating. "Call it what you will. It's not logical or orderly it's so ...so...."

"It's so like a woman?" She was baiting him, turning the discussion into something altogether different.

"I didn't say that," Truitt responded.

"You didn't have to. So I get it that even though you have a job open for TA, the job is not for me. Is that correct?"

Truitt pursed his lips but denied her a verbal confirmation.

"We're done here, I think," she quipped, as she stormed from his office.

Truitt sat a long while in the silence of his office. He wanted to feel elated that he had won the battle without losing his cool, even in the face of Miss Day's rising irritation. But on reconsideration, he had to acknowledge that, from another point of view, the interview had gone badly. How did it get so far out of hand? But then, if she were upset, it couldn't be helped. He wasn't obliged to hire anyone at all, much less someone so ill-adapted to his way of thinking. In the end, he was glad the whole situation had taken place in the privacy of his office with no one as witness. It wouldn't have done for Martin to witness the meeting. It might put him off from applying.

Studying the shut door, reconsidering the soundness of its closure, Truitt wondered who had been in charge of the meeting. Had she dismissed him?

Seven

*B*illy Reilly pulled his old Ford truck up to the back door of the Steakhouse, figuring he'd park on his usual stool at the end of the bar till closing time, or till Willie called to apologize. Then he'd go home, if he could rightly call it home, what with her tossing him out every Saturday night so's she could watch that goldarned sissy bubble-man on the TV, the leader—My-stro, she says. That's what comes of educating women. He said so to Turk, too. Why, he had half a mind just to keep traveling on down ninety-three to the state line, and lay his week's wages on the table, instead of surrendering it all to her. He might have told the bartender that too, but he couldn't remember.

"Give me another one, Turk." He shoved the glass down the bar.

"Now you take it easy, Billy." Turk warned him. Billy knew Turk Boone was a good man, a drover once, like himself, working for Befford down to the Jarbidge range. Lucky, too, that old man Befford had taken him on in the restaurant, after that nasty fall he had taken moving cattle up to the bluff, leaving his leg useless for any work on the trail. Turk was a good man, yes sir, but that didn't give him no call to tell Billy Reilly how much liquor he could hold.

"Hey Billy! You get tossed out again?" Rufus Gibson came through the door, all prettied up. "Yeah, my old lady's invited the whole town over for a stitch and bitch—you know, they stitch and they bitch about everyone who's not there." He sniggered.

"How's about you and me going on down to Porkey's for a game or two?" Reilly asked, scowling at Turk who had yet to refill his glass. "Maybe something else, as well. Come on, buddy. You know you want to."

Billy tossed a handful of coins on the bar and the two cowboys left out the back.

Nora Caldwell was coming through the door as they left. Billy bowed in a great gesture, removing his hat, and Rufus just giggled.

"Those two don't need anything else to drink," Nora Caldwell commented to Turk as she grabbed a starched apron from the closet and tied it over her black dress.

"Just happy they took their trouble someplace else," Turk grumbled.

"Mr. Befford call in? I expected to see the place all lit up, the front doors open."

"He's stuck in Boise with the missus. Says Carlos is in charge of the restaurant, excepting you're supposed to run the front."

Nora frowned. To Carlos Vasquez the restaurant began and ended at the kitchen door. Nora didn't want to be in charge of anything, especially new busboys and junior waitresses; she noted both on the schedule. And, she surely didn't want to be playing referee between Carlos and the rest of the world all evening.

"Two tables came in, asked to be seated. Hope you don't mind," Turk was telling her. Noting her rising objection, he added defensively, "A family with kids. They can't sit in here."

"And I supposed they couldn't wait outside?" Nora asked.

Turk shrugged his shoulders, "The guy wanted a beer."

"And the second table?"

"You'll see him—one of the professors."

Nora spotted the family right off, calling out to them, "Be right with you, folks." In the kitchen, she reported to Carlos and wrote down the night's specials, strip steak with mushrooms and barbecued ribs.

"Where's Mr. Befford?" Molly came into the kitchen, tying on an apron. Nora let Carlos deliver the news on the pecking order, so as to avoid making waves herself if the girl objected to the way things were run. The girl was new, and Nora had worked only one shift with her, not long enough to size up her temperament.

"The tables in back haven't been set up," Molly said. "Who's bussing?"

"Get on them, then." Nora told her. "Mr. Befford likes things to be spiffy when we open. Right now I got to get those lights on and open the front."

Unlocking the front door, Nora took in the warmth of the early evening sun as it dropped to the ridge, bringing a golden glow to the sandstone bluffs that teemed with hues of orange then pink. The shadows were already cast along the rock, the first sign of the long twilight of summer. Flipping on the switch for the sign in the parking lot, she watched the light bleed into the dining room, in waves of blue, green and red.

Nora spotted the occupant at table seven, a semi-private booth on the backside of the fireplace. It was that professor who Birdie had so much trouble with. No matter, he wasn't much trouble to her anyway. scotch and water, steak dinner, a little rude, but not much bother as he spent the evening reading. Since Turk had served him his first round, he was set for a while.

Nora set up the coffee machines, and was preparing the regular, when Molly came into the galley. "Need a cup of decaf," she said, pointing to an elderly couple whom she had just seated. "Bergens. They asked for you special."

"Oh, my. It's their anniversary today," Nora said in an unusual display of sentimentality. She reflected on the small wedding in the chapel, when she and Bea were just six, all prettied up in their twin jumpers, black and white with large red bows. "My first wedding."

Molly issued a curt smile, then said, "And you'd better check the reservations. There's a problem."

"Day – 2" had been entered in the childish hand of the hostess who did the lunch service. Carlos had added in a heavy pencil "#7." Great! How was she supposed to free up Table 7 with the professor taking his time over drinks and reading college papers? She didn't want to rush him, especially as he might be working on one of Birdie's papers, maybe her final. Not that he'd know Birdie belonged to her or anything. Not so much as a how-dee-doo in all the years he's been eating here. Nora doubted he even knew her name as he'd never used it, even though it was clearly written on her name tag. Still, it wouldn't do to rush any man who'd just settled down to his evening meal.

Not her business, really, who sat where. No one expected her to settle disputes over tables. On the other hand, Nora felt that she needed to do right by Mr. Day, a man who had always been kind to her and her sister, especially after Papa died, helping them keep the farm, getting her this job with Mr. Befford. Everybody knew they were boyhood pals. Not to mention, his generosity to Birdie—even if she was Kristina Day's best friend. Well, Nora just needed to do right by him, that's all.

It put her in a mind to help things along. She approached Table Seven. "Ready to order, sir?"

"Not yet. I'll let you know when I'm ready." He didn't look up at her.

"Another scotch, then?" She pressed, hoping this would do the trick.

He looked up at her, then at his near-full drink, considering what she might be thinking. She retreated, worrying about the lineup waiting for Carlos, already dinners for a foursome, a threesome and the Bergens. There was little hope for Mr. Day and Table Seven at seven o'clock, unless the professor gulped down a sixteen-ounce porterhouse in thirty-seven minutes, clean up and table reset included.

Truitt was, in fact, not terribly pleased with anything at the moment, the least of which included his sorry treatment at the hands of the restaurant wait staff. Finding the front door locked, he went to the back door which led into the bar. He asked to be seated in the dining room, a request that miffed the bartender, although he was able to wrestle a scotch from him. Then to be accosted every ten minutes by the waitress trying to hurry him through dinner. It was not to be tolerated. He planned on a leisurely dinner, finishing the article he had started in the Journal, and being on his way home by seven, long before the Saturday night patrons turned into a rowdy crowd.

The entire progress of his life at the moment was moving in a direction contrary to his aspirations. Starting with his argument with Kristina Day the previous afternoon over his opening for a teaching assistant. Whatever gave her the idea that he would even consider her for the job? Fortunately, Truitt kept his wits about him, even as the student grew increasingly emotional and unreasonable. Her departure was unsettling as they had not come to a rational conclusion.

Truitt had suffered a much greater blow to his plans when Martin turned down his offer. After agreeing yesterday to meet in Truitt's office that morning, Martin didn't show until two in the afternoon. Truitt had finished nearly the whole stack of final exams from Friday's class when Martin finally showed up. Their meeting was brief as Martin had no interest in the job. Upon graduation, he had no plans to continue his education, so he had no need to "play at teaching," those were Martin's very words. His career lay with learning the ins and outs of his family's dry goods business, not in more education.

Truitt tried to be objective, but he felt the insult nonetheless. Worse, he now had no idea who might be able to replace his chosen candidate. Martin was so perfect, his methods and processes so aligned to Truitt's own. Dismayed that Martin, with his extraordinary mind, would choose to throw his life away selling hardware to farmers, Truitt diverted his attention by finishing up the tests and then filling out the grade forms for all three sections of his classes.

Truitt's one consolation for the day was getting his grades in that afternoon, two days earlier than expected, freeing him to begin work on his article. In his mail box, Truitt was glad to find a thick manila envelope from the Journal, the size and weight of which could only mean that his manuscript was being returned for final revision, having passed muster with the senior editor, Willema Rutherton. Finally, something was going right. He stashed the envelope into his valise, along with the latest issue of the Journal, and headed toward the Steakhouse.

In the darkened alcove of the restaurant, a table that he coveted for its privacy, Truitt spied the waitress approaching once again. After satisfying her by ordering another scotch and a salad, he turned his attention to the brown envelope that held the balm to lift his spirits. As he pulled the manuscript from the package, he was confused by what seemed to be a rejection letter tacked to the front of his manuscript. The note was not in Willema's familiar hand, but another, signed Caroline. The name jolted him, evoking a certain dread mixed with confusion. He couldn't accept that it was Carolyn Walsh, the siren in his post-graduate year, his room-mate's cousin, who had made such a fool of him. His room-mate's cousin, but also Willema Rutherton's niece.

After making a ludicrous suggestion as to how he might proceed—by tying his work on Joachim to the courtiers of Champagne—she let him know of her new job as editor's assistant, and the excitement of seeing her own name in the editor's box under her aunt's. Was she patronizing him? Or, was she just rubbing his nose in his failure? He flipped through the manuscript looking for any sign that Willema had read the piece, but nothing more was written on his pages. In anger and disappointment, he shoved the manuscript and rejection letter back into the envelope. Then stuffed the lot into his valise.

It was ironic, in a glum way. The moment he was free to start writing the second installment of his article, thanks to Martin's desertion, he was freed from that obligation as well. The days ahead, which had promised so much, now seemed to offer the tedium of uncertainty. There being no audience for the first part, robbed him of incentive to rush into completion of the second part. At that moment, Truitt realized there was nothing to keep him any longer in town, that he could begin his journey home the next day. At least Nell would be pleased.

That settled, he was now ready to eat, but the waitress seemed to have disappeared. Where was the wretched woman?

Nora was busy working out her dilemma since the professor was clearly not going to cooperate by ordering his dinner in a timely manner. It wasn't for her to ask why Mr. Day wanted that particular table, but she did think it odd. The Days usually liked to see and be seen, and if they wanted privacy, well, they could have it in that nice big house of theirs. It was none of her business anyhow, excepting that she needed to solve her dilemma.

By the time the busboy had arrived Molly had finished most of the table set-ups, excepting sixteen, which was not in the books, on account of its being permanently reserved for the Beffords. Nora used number sixteen to show him the ropes. It was the best table in the house, overlooking the river canyon as it did. The space tucked into the far side of the fireplace making another quiet nook for private dining. As she explained this to the new boy, Nora knew she had finally solved her problem, for Christian Day was as close to being a Befford as you could get—them both being Hawkes and all. Mr. Befford wouldn't mind at all letting the Days take number sixteen.

At five minutes to seven, when Mr. Day came into the restaurant, it was Professor Avila who was draped on his arm. Nora took the news in stride, her taciturn manner hiding any surprise. Professor Avila was Birdie's favorite professor, and a favorite among most folk in town, having come to Hawkes Ferry as an exchange student at the college. Mr. Day and his wife had brought her up from South America, where she was the daughter of some business connection. That was when Marlyss Day, God bless her, was still the lady of the house, and before Miss Anne moved back to raise Kristi.

Nora wondered how Kristi felt about the two of them together like that. But that was none of her concern. For the moment, she had an expectation to tend to. She explained her dilemma to Mr. Day, who listened politely. He then stepped to the back of the restaurant to check out table seven for himself. When he caught sight of the occupant, Nora saw him scowl, and thought he might make a ruckus.

He returned to the desk, and patted Professor Avila's hand as she slipped it through his arm. He grinned at Nora, "That is too bad."

She felt relieved. At least he wasn't of a mind to blame her for the mix-up.

"The Beffords won't be in tonight," Nora said suggestively.

His face lit up. "A splendid idea, Nora. That will suit us fine. Just fine."

For Christian, this date with Sofia Avila was a test run. Increasingly, he had been seeking her company in social settings, taking time to chat when she appeared at Sunday services, and taking advantage of chance meetings at the college. In recent months, he had included her in several key dinners at the house, to see how she worked a room when business was on the table.

He was trying her on, so to speak, to determine how she might play a bigger role in his life. She had returned to St. Clements after completing graduate school in Texas, by invitation of the board. Already of noble blood, Christian had watched her grow into a fine woman since she had begun teaching at St. Clements, a woman worthy of his name and his influence. He thought she might be just the person who would pick up the reins when Kristina graduated in another year and married Si Befford.

Drinks were served, and a bottle of wine was opened. Christian then ordered the chateaubriand for two—a specialty of the house, prime cut beef from one of Befford's prize steers. As the meal was being prepared, he entertained Sofia with stories about himself. He impressed her with the important work of his business and the extent of his influence. Day Enterprises was the fastest growing agri-business in the country. Its connections to Argentina and Brazil were already well known to her family through the business of her father and brothers, but he told her of things she was not likely to learn from her family. To his own ears, his words sounded like an extended sales pitch. Maybe it was. He wanted to move the relationship up a level, from the mentor-protégé model to a place where they might be on a more equitable footing, where they might explore the idea of a more intimate relationship. Exactly what he wanted from her, he was not ready to declare. The astute questions she asked demonstrated more than a casual interest in the game on her part, and the authenticity of her responses to his questions satisfied him.

Sofia enjoyed listening to Christian tell his stories, and watched with pleasure as he negotiated around landmines of ego. He was a man who shied away from talking about himself, avoiding any semblance of boasting or narcissism. He was not showing off or flattering her with his attention, but rather laying out for her what he had to offer. Sofia liked what she saw. He was a man of action like her father, with a strong sense of himself but a constrained ego, which made him a formidable foe to one who would cross him. He had personal power and knew how to wield it to get what he wanted. In most cases, though, he was a just man.

Yet, like her father, Christian was overly protective of his family and his property, sometimes not seeing the difference between the two. Kristi's affection for Si Befford, for example, was not unlike her sister Bela's affection for Volante, an attachment forged by the dream of two fathers for the future of their children. For Bela, her father's need to merge Avila and Volante was the tragedy of Bela's life. Sofia did not wish this for Kristi.

Unlike her father, Christian had demonstrated the desire to grow beyond traditional views of life and family. After all, he had championed her ideas for advancing the cause of women. In his enthusiasm for her work, Sofia saw a regret he held for his estrangement from Marlyss, a wound to his heart that changed him, as her father had changed from her mother's death.

The man across the table from her was as noble and upright a man as Sofia had ever known outside her father and brothers. If she were ever to decide to marry, and she was still uncertain about this, it must be to a man like this.

Exhausted and defeated, Truitt trudged back to the bungalow. He felt his world spinning, spiraling downward. The finals were over, and the grades turned in. Yet he felt no sense of relief, no sense of accomplishment. Finding that note from Caroline added a surreal horror to the building tension of the day. The lingering twilight made fearsome shadows of mundane things.

At home, he distracted himself by gathering his things into piles to pack for the trip to Delaware. There were few things to pack, since his clothes were scarcely suitable for the hot, humid summer of Delaware and points east. He needed to cart along his fall textbooks since he would work on his lectures and course materials over the summer. His research on Joachim already filled three boxes, too much to carry back and forth for what would essentially be eight weeks. In the end, the material and personal items he chose amounted to one suit case and three boxes, all of which would fit neatly into the back of his Civic. He would finish packing in the morning. After a decent night's sleep, he would be on the road by eleven.

A railroad trammeled through his head, the bell ringing insistently on the other side. Truitt pulled himself awake, the darkness of night surrounding him. The phone still pealed tenaciously.

"Emery Truitt?"

"Yes." It was pitch dark. The clock that Truitt was reaching for was hidden in one of the piles in the front room.

"This is Bill Wahl. I have some bad news, I'm afraid. I'm sorry to tell you like this."

Truitt shook his head to clear the tunnel. The bell stopped ringing. But the darkness held tight.

"Emery?"

"Yes. Yes," Truitt stammered, pulling himself out of a deep sleep. "I'm here."

"This is Bill Wahl. Your aunt's had a heart attack."

"Wait. What?" To clear his head, Truitt switched on the light. "What do you mean? Where is she?"

"She's dead, son. She had a massive heart attack. Died in the emergency room.

Eight

The church was full. It could have been any Sunday morning, but with Bill at his side instead of Nell. An odd idea, but not impossible. However, it was Monday. Bill Wahl was standing at the pulpit, instead of the pastor, delivering a quiet eulogy for the woman whose casket lay in front of him. Nell's presence filled the church dispersed in the scent of flowers in the dozen bouquets and sprays that surrounded her coffin. She was buried in a small cemetery north of town, where the road wound through deciduous forests and along green rolling hills. It was a place of treasured memory, where they would picnic in the summers at a nearby park.

The reception was held in the town hall which sat in the middle of the square. The mayor said a few words with the council beside him. Coffee and tea were offered on a table filled with tea-sized sandwiches and cookies. It was a simple affair, in keeping with the ascetic nature of the town's librarian.

Truitt received condolences and sympathy—phrases echoing "so sorry," with frequent exclamations of "so you're the nephew," and the tiresome, "she was so proud of you." Truitt took his role in stride, knowing what he needed to do. He stood as he always did in church by her side, and accepted the remarks with cordiality. He watched others expel their grief, yet he felt nothing. Even thought seemed to desert him, and he floated through the day like flotsam on a stormy sea.

Colonel Cleary approached him with some deference. Truitt had only met the man once, the previous Christmas when he came to Nell's for dinner. He was the headmaster at St. John's Academy the prep school Truitt attended before Columbia.

The colonel took Truitt's hand with warmth, conveying deep sympathy. "I never realized she had a heart condition. Perhaps that's why she pressed so hard..."

"No one did," Truitt responded with crispness that he hoped would discourage any further pursuit of the open position for housemaster.

"Yes. Of course," the colonel stepped back. "I expect you'll be calling soon? There are several other applicants, you see..."

"It won't be necessary, sir." Truitt cut him off. To the colonel's protestations, he said in a neutral tone, "Things have changed now, haven't they?"

"Why, yes. I suppose they have." The colonel wished him well.

Truitt happened across one or two old school mates who claimed varying degrees of acquaintance with his aunt. Chas Greenstone had tagged along with his father, who owned the only bank in Sycamore Falls, where Nell maintained her modest checking account and what she called her "rainy day" fund. The other fellow was Trevor Steed, although Truitt hardly recognized him, as transfixed as he was by the man's missing arm, his right arm.

"Sorry about your aunt, Tru."

Truitt cringed from the name that to him was more an epithet than a nickname between friends. It was a label, a daily reminder of his place at the bottom of the heap, having neither name nor wealth to be their equal, even as he yearned to belong, to be one of them.

"Say, you don't have a brother, Truitt, do you?" Chas asked.

"Things haven't changed that much, Chas."

"No, I suppose they haven't. But you hear about all these cases of adopted kids turning up." Chas said.

"There was a fellow that could have been your double." Steed clarified.

"He left when the casket was lowered," Chas said.

Truitt was not interested in what the boys considered an anomaly. He looked around the room for an escape. In a far corner of the room, he spied someone who could double for Willema Rutherton. It was an incongruous sight, for the woman, who was sipping a cup of coffee, seemed to be staring at him. Then she saluted him with her cup.

"If you'll excuse me...." Truitt said to his former schoolfellows.

"Say," Chas shook his hand. "Come round to see us, same old address."

Steed offered his own left hand. Truitt had nothing to do but accept it in all its awkwardness. Steed regarded Truitt for a moment with an earnest assessment that belied Truitt's recollections of him. "Nell was a kind woman. Sympathetic. I'm truly sorry for your loss."

Truitt muttered his thanks and crossed the room to find out what brought Willema to this corner of the world.

"Apparently you are surprised to see me," Willema said. "Why should that be? You knew that we were friends long ago."

"I knew you worked together at the Library of Congress, but that was before she moved here.

"Before you came into her life?" She said. "Nell and I were more than acquaintances. She was a friend. One has few enough of those in one's life."

"But you haven't seen her for years?"

"Not in the past few years, but we get together from time to time. Or did so. Still, I will miss her. A lot." Her gaze fell into a past she did not share with him. Finally, she said, "You and I have much to talk about. Come up to New York and see me. When you're ready, of course. But soon."

Truitt absorbed her words but could find no curiosity to pursue them. She left with some urgency, needing to catch a train back to Manhattan. In her wake, Truitt decided that she must be done with her game of lobbing his manuscripts back to him, that she was ready to recognize their worthiness and start publishing them. It was a shame to think of his work laying neglected on his desk back in Hawkes Ferry. There was no question of retrieving them simply to curry her favor.

Although it was barely two o'clock in the afternoon, Truitt breached house rules with a glass of scotch, adding ice to dilute the effects of wanton indulgence. He sat on the wooden armchair in the corner of the living room, afraid to surrender to the familiar comfort of the past. The room was an eclectic collection of furnishings, accumulated by rule of economy over art, each piece holding its own ineradicable memory, the overstuffed sofa, the wooden rocking chair, the small bookcase with its well-loved volumes, and a stack of new books waiting to be read. By whom, he wondered from afar.

The railway desk, battered and worn, loomed over the room, formidable and forbidding to the small boy who wondered at its inner secrets. In what seemed like an unnatural state, its top yawned wide, as if frozen into a permanent scream, it stood as a sharp reminder of the speed of her unexpected departure. Truitt slammed the lid shut, cutting off memories that began to roil inside.

Around five Bill called and invited Truitt to dine with him at his club, a private country club in the hills beyond the cemetery. It was the first time Truitt had visited the place, and he was surprised at the modesty in which the members dined. Dinner tables were set out in a large open space with a tiled floor and windows open to a vista of forest and lawn. The maitre d' ushered Truitt into the bar where Bill sat at a small table.

"Ah. There you are," he said, pushing his papers into a waiting briefcase. "I'm sorry I didn't get by the house after the reception. How'd it go?"

Truitt ordered a drink from the waiter, then turned his attention to Bill.

"The task is a bit overwhelming, I'm afraid. The house. The car. I just don't know what I'm going to do with everything. I can't take it back to Idaho. My place isn't big enough."

"And you don't know how long you're going to be there?" Bill shook his head in sympathy. "But look, you needn't be concerned about it for now. Everything's likely to be tied up in probate at least nine months. Or longer. You need to go see her lawyer."

The waiter delivered Truitt's drink, and there was an awkward moment where a tip was offered and refused. Later, when the waiter left, Bill explained the way in which things were handled at the club. "You are my guest here."

Truitt shuffled uncomfortably and checked the knot in his tie.

"You need to see a probate lawyer," Bill advised.

"I thought you would do that."

"I'm a financial adviser. Law is not my thing. You should call up Ferd Ridell, he's the one who handled the trust."

Lost in thought Truitt was gazing into the amber whirlpool created in his glass as he rolled it in small circles.

Bill signaled the waiter for another round. "I met your aunt through Ridell years ago. He called me in to answer some questions Nell had about setting up a fund."

"So you're her financial advisor?" Truitt asked with some irritation.

"Not in recent years, you understand. Our business was finished years ago. But that's how we met. I liked your aunt—I admired her. Still do. She was an admirable woman. Good values. A rare find these days." Bill said with a hitch in his voice.

"Where can I find the lawyer Ridell?" Truitt asked coolly, trying to nip a bud of regret before it blossomed into melancholy.

"There should be something among her papers. A business card. In any case, Ridell has an office downtown. The same building as my office, in fact. If you want, I can have my girl call you tomorrow with his number."

Truitt said that he'd done enough. In truth, he wanted to unfetter himself from the old man's assistance as soon as possible. In a short time, the maitre d' summoned them to dinner.

The next morning Truitt set about the daunting task of finding a business card in the accumulation of papers in Nell's desk. There was a stack of unopened mail on top of the desk hutch, collected from the box and left there by Bill, no doubt, before Truitt had arrived. He lifted the roll top, still averse to prying into his aunt's personal affairs. As with everything in her life, her current papers were stacked in neat piles—receipts, bills, and bank statements, none of which he was willing to examine closely. He checked the contents of the desk drawers, discovering a bundle of business cards secured by a rubber band. They were ordered alphabetically, of course. He found the lawyer's card, F. P. Ridell, Attorney at Law—Estate Planning, Probate and Wills.

When he dialed the number, a woman answered the phone in a cheery voice. "The office of F. P. Ridell. How may I help you?"

"I'd like to speak to Mr. Ridell."

"I'm sorry, Mr. Ridell is unavailable at the moment. Would you care to make an appointment? Next Monday at..."

"I'm not sure I want an appointment. Bill Wahl suggested I call Ridell." Truitt wasn't sure what he was calling for. He just needed to talk to the man, ask a few questions. He didn't see the need of explaining his uncertainty to anyone. "He thought that Ridell might be of some help. My aunt recently passed..."

"And your name is?" To his annoyance, she cut him off.

Still, he surrendered his name. She jumped on it. "Mr. Truitt! You were at the top of my list this morning. When could you be available to see Mr. Ridell?"

"Sooner than next week, I hope."

"Certainly. Tomorrow morning at ten?"

"Not this afternoon?"

"No, I am sorry. Mr. Ridell is in court in Dover today."

Truitt agreed reluctantly.

"Oh, and Mr. Ridell has requested that you bring all Miss Truitt's current paperwork, her bills, bank records, insurance papers. Anything that..."

"I just want some information. I don't even know if I need his services."

"Oh, but he's already been retained."

"By whose authority?" Truitt demanded, feeling a loss of control. Bill Wahl was certainly exceeding his authority here.

"Miss Truitt, of course," was the cheerful answer.

By the end of the afternoon, Truitt had accumulated a current record of his aunt's business matters. It was no surprise to him that her bills were current, and that the records from all the prior months—going back for years—were filed tidily in the bottom drawers of her desk.

There were some surprises, as well. The "rainy day" fund she kept at Greenstone's bank had grown into forty-eight thousand dollars. She lived sparsely. Yet, he wondered if he had been on his own long enough for her to accumulate that much money. He wondered, too why Bill wouldn't have encouraged her to invest it in something better than a bank savings account. Did Bill not know about this account?

Truitt was also surprised to discover a deed for the house, dated the year he was born. She had owned the house outright, for all those years? Even as she watched every penny from their use of fuel to the purchase of her clothing? He did not know how to rectify this image of her with the frugal, austere upbringing he had in her household. He felt he was entering dangerous waters, and backed away from projecting his current values into those memories. It would not serve any purpose to furrow along the seams of the past to unearth memories that she could no longer answer to.

That night, when he met up with Bill for dinner, he said nothing about his findings but told him about the appointment the next morning with the lawyer.

"Good. I'm sure he'll be able to provide you with some answers. And advice on how to move forward. If you need any assistance financially, you can count on my help. These guys want to be paid up front."

So he didn't know. "She retained him."

"Good God. Tidy to the end. A truly exceptional woman."

F. P. Ridell was a small man with a large mustache and an open sense of humor that he didn't mind sharing frequently through little jibes and jokes. Truitt could not see why his aunt had selected such a fellow, one who so contradicted her own nature. Once they settled down to business, Ridell revealed yet another surprise. Nell was the recipient of an annuity paid to her quarterly through a trust fund. "Not a great sum," Ridell said, "But a tidy sum which saw her through the little niceties of life."

"She lived austerely," Truitt objected to his optimism.

"True enough. True enough." He cleared his throat, then spent the rest of his allotted time apprising Truitt of the nature and conditions surrounding probate in the state of Delaware. Truitt found most of his ramblings dense and arcane, bordering on ambiguous, and certainly beyond the understanding of a mere layman like himself.

Finally, tamping the papers on his desk, he drew to a close. "There you are. The long and short of it, probate takes at least six months—more like nine. But, depending on complications, could take up to a year or two. So don't go spending it before you have it in hand. Can't tell you how many lads, like you, I've warned, only to find my good counsel falling on deaf ears. Now then, Mr. Truitt...Any questions?"

Overwhelmed with the enormity of this lie that was his life, Truitt said nothing.

"Yes, well then. Miss Truitt kept me on retainer. Can't say she ever drew down the thousand she'd put up. Course that was a few years back. That should do the job. Unless you expect complications?"

"Of course not. I expected nothing."

"Still, the fees are pretty much covered for now. Any run-overs will be settled by the court before distribution." Looking at his watch, the lawyer stood up. "Call me, then, if you think of any more questions. Otherwise, we're done here, I think."

Truitt followed suit, and shook the hand that was offered.

"Oh! One more thing."

Ridell handed him an envelope addressed to Truitt in Nell's familiar script.

Truitt did not open the letter until he was back in the cottage and settled into the sofa. The letter was written on a sheet of typing paper, folded with two inserts, a birth certificate for one Anna Bella born to Winifred and Ezekiel Truitt. The document didn't make any sense. Anna Bella was his mother. It was Joshua, his father, who must have been born to the Truitts, not Anna. The letter was dated the year he went abroad for study.

Dearest Emery,

If you receive this letter from a lawyer, then the unthinkable has happened, and I have passed on, without telling you what you deserve to know.

Shame breeds treachery, and for my shame, you have been deprived of your proper place in the world, and robbed of your true name.

Because I wanted a father worthy of you, I gave you my brother for a father. He was everything that I have ever told you about him, kind, loving and so good to his kid sister. He was everything, except that he died years before you were born. He was not your father.

Enclosed is my birth certificate and yours. I am your mother. I only hope that someday you will forgive me these trespasses. I am free at last to claim you as my own son.

Mother

Truitt sat on the sofa for a long while trying to understand what the letter said so plainly. When the phone rang, he ignored it. There was no escape. No place could divert him, nor any person distract him from the crushing confusion. Deprived of a birthright? The fancies of his young imagination not a myth but truth?

The phone rang several times during the evening, but Truitt had no will to answer it. His world was spinning away from its anchor. He needed to pull himself together before he saw Bill or anyone else. The answers must be in Nell's papers, either in her desk or her room, the door of which had remained shut since his arrival. Hours later he fell asleep on his bed, having discovered little more than an address book—a gift to her that he brought back from France—and an unstamped passport, issued to Nell Truitt the year he was born.

Nine

Kristi and Birdie cruised down fifty-one headed toward Elko. With the windows down, they took in the refreshing cool of the morning. The chatter of the radio filled their ears and heads. They had left the reservation early, with only a cornmeal pancake with their morning coffee. In Elko, they planned to eat a substantial breakfast before trekking down the seven hours to Las Vegas on ninety-three, a long drive through semi-arid land with few amenities along the way.

Birdie had spent the past few days with her Gran in Duck Valley. Kristi had come in the night before so the girls could set out early. Always generous with her house and her time Gran had welcomed Kristi like another granddaughter, and presented her with a box of blankets and winter woolens for the mission in Las Vegas.

After breakfast, Kristi filled the gas tank, and they set out under the searing sun. The windows were shut tight, and the air conditioning was on full blast. Birdie was taking a well-deserved vacation to spend a week with her Aunt Joni, a blackjack dealer in Sin City and Kristi was tagging along. She had told Birdie that she wanted to get her mother's commitment to attend her engagement party. Kristi's real purpose, though, was to find out what bad blood lay between Mary Befford and her mother, Marlyss Day.

Birdie leaned back in the seat settling into her ride. "So you never said what happened with the professor. How'd your interview go?" Birdie had left Kristi right after class to leave for her Gran's place.

Kristi frowned, still angry about the meeting with Professor Truitt. "He turned me down."

"Because you're a woman."

On the one hand, Kristi hated feeding fuel to Birdie's campaign against their teacher, on the other hand, she had to admit to herself that Birdie was half-right about him. "He made a big deal about how much time he would need from his teaching assistant, nights and weekends."

"What? He's afraid you'll jump his bones?" Suddenly she shrieked with delight at some inner image. "Maybe he's afraid of losing himself to you."

As she laughed, Kristi frowned, wondering if she should continue the subject.

"Oh, come on. You've got to see the humor in it. Can you imagine Professor Truitt? Or how about Durham?" She laughed again.

"What was in your coffee?" Kristi asked. "He does seem to be afraid to show his feelings toward things. He said that he wanted his TA to help with some research. His rationalization was that my method of thinking was not suitable for his task."

"Thinking? What?" Birdie snapped, then she blurted out, "Yes! Because you think like a woman."

A hearty laughter followed down several miles of road. Kristi allowed Birdie to have her moment ridiculing the professor, and she confirmed her friend's suspicions.

"Basically, that's what he said. Not logical, or something like that, just, 'the way you think'. However, I don't accept your misguided premise that the professor is some kind of misogynist. He doesn't despise women so much as he fears them."

"Fears? Sure. Sure." The laughter subsided as Birdie tossed off the old argument between them. "And I suppose that you can't be rational, in his way of the world, because logic is distorted by your belief in intuition?"

Kristi mutely assented.

"Well, don't be too discouraged, girl. I overheard a conversation he had with Tad Martin just before class the other day. I think he's already selected Tad for the job."

"I'm pretty sure Tad said he was working in the store this summer," Kristi said.

"Can't he do both?"

"Sure he could, but then, you'd think the professor would have just told me that the position was filled, without going into details about my inadequacies."

Birdie was frowning. "Don't you see the bigger problem here? Because you think like a woman, you don't qualify for a TA position. If all of them feel that way, then we don't have a chance at all to be TA's."

"I'm sure Professor Avila doesn't. Besides, you already have an internship at the paper. Hey! Did you get initiated in your summer work this week?"

For the next hour, Birdie talked about her new position, which was to begin the day they returned from Las Vegas. She would spend most of the summer on the reservation and surrounding communities digging up story material, as well as selling ads. Kristi was glad for her friend but disheartened to acknowledge that she would not be working toward any worthy goals herself. Besides that, she would miss the lighthearted lens that Birdie brought to her life.

At Caliente, an oasis in the semi-arid basin, they took a break. Parking their car under the lush canopy of trees, they grabbed a sandwich at a small diner. Then Birdie took her turn at the wheel, from the low scrub grass plains to the scrabble and rock of the desert. They listened to local radio until the signal grew weak and the broadcast was as scabby as the land.

Birdie cut off the noise. "Say. I just heard that Geoff Meyer is coming back to town. He's taking over for Dr. Sanders. But I suppose you knew that already."

The news surprised Kristi. She hadn't heard anything about it. "When did all this come about?"

"I think I heard something at the barbecue. Dr. Sanders was telling some of the professors about his replacement. Then Jake mentioned it Saturday night at dinner. He's looking forward to having Geoff around again."

The two men were buddies when Geoff was in school at Saint Clements. Although Jake never stood for a higher education, he had always enjoyed rock hunting, as much as Geoff enjoyed playing cowboy on Jake's ranch.

"I wonder if he's still the stud, or if teaching has made him as dull as the rest of them? Remember how we used to hang out at the pens waiting for a glimpse of him?"

"We were fourteen."

"Yeah, I know." Birdie sighed. "Say, you were quite smitten with him too. But I guess Si Befford knocked all that silliness out of you. Although, I don't see how you could favor that boy over a hunk like Geoff."

The truth was that Kristi didn't. Geoff Meyer was as alive in her heart today as he had been the summer of her seventeenth year. The image of another love, as deep and real to her as her mother's yet sweeter, drawing in her a yearning to blend and merge in the swirling waters. It had been a year since her mother had left, and Kristi could not yet fill the emptiness she felt at the loss of her mother's love. Then Geoff was there, accompanying his mother to the ranch. When the parents left for the stock sale, a two-day event, Geoff stayed behind, visiting his old haunts with Jake. One evening, Kristi trailed along and took him up toward Jackson's Bench and Indian Spring. A careless moment, his hand reaching out to pull her into the spring, the gentleness of his touch, the yearning of her heart, his voice as soft as the twilight breeze. Geoff was the noble Romeo to her Juliet, and she gave to him of her own free will. The secret lay deep in her heart. Not even Birdie knew. Her heart raced at the rise of memory.

"Do you? Earth to Kristi? Where are you? Hello!"

"Yes." Kristi uttered her habitual response.

"You always do that. Saying yes when you don't know what I'm talking about. Where were you, anyhow?"

"Thinking of Si, I guess."

"Trying to measure him up to Geoff Meyer? You know, Kristi, you should seriously rethink this engagement thing. You've got one year to finish school, and then you could be free. You should be free for a while, anyhow, to roam the world. See things. That's what I'm going to do…"

Birdie talked all the way to Las Vegas about what she intended to do as a reporter to the world. Kristi listened indulgently, offering suggestions when asked. Her mind was already at their destination, working through the conversation she planned to have with her mother about Mary Befford and the Day clan.

After a decent night's sleep at Joni's place on the outskirts of the city, the two girls followed Joni into the underbelly of the town where Marlyss Day ran a mission to save underage kids from the streets. The mission itself was a nomadic operation, spaces changing with the seasons and the rate of vacancies. Joni kept in touch with the mission and often delivered goods there. Today she was delivering a battered sofa, rejected by the thrift shop in town. They might not be welcome here, but Kristi knew that the box of goods from Mrs. Colson, and the food and clothing from the Hawkes Ferry ladies' society certainly would be.

The mission was in an abandoned building, single story with a cavernous room and a couple of offices in the back. The plate glass windows had been covered with plywood, the front marked by the itinerant sign declaring the mission as a safe haven.

Marlyss seemed annoyed at the sudden appearance of Kristi and Birdie, no doubt wanting to save them from the sordid nature of the place. Kristi was appalled, not realizing what squalor her mother was willing to work in. She stood frozen on the cement floor, taking in the makeshift beds of air mattresses, foam pads and spring mattresses strewn around the place. Birdie nudged her to snap out of it and help them unload the vehicles.

The place was devoid of other humans besides Marlyss and an assistant who disappeared on an errand shortly after their arrival. Marlyss was grateful for the donations She thanked Joni and the Colsons for their continuing generosity. She offered them a cup of coffee from the aluminum pot on the small stove in the kitchenette found against the back wall. They sat at a marred picnic table, among a jumble of mismatched benches and chairs, in the corner of the hall.

"How long did you take to drive down?" She half-listened to the answer. The volley of questions that followed seemed aimed at filling up the time. How their finals had gone. What their plans for the summer were. How things were at home. Marlyss tried to chat casually, but her attention was elsewhere, her eyes kept a nervous vigil in the direction of the door.

Joni talked about her plans over the next few days with the girls, visiting some old Indian ruins to the south. Birdie followed her aunt with a description of the internship at the newspaper and how excited she was to start in a week. Then Birdie tossed the ball into Kristi's court by mentioning her aspiration to be a TA in the fall.

Kristi scowled at Birdie as Marlyss turned her attention to her daughter's story. Kristi blew it off, explaining that while she had applied, that Professor Truitt had already picked someone else.

"He wouldn't hire her because she's female," Birdie said, finishing the topic.

Joni emptied her cup and stood up. "Birdie, I need some help back at the house with that bureau. Let's get it done. Then I'll take you by the casino, so you can say hi to everyone, and wow them with your internship. We'll be home by seven," Joni said to Kristi as she guided Birdie out of the building.

When they had left, Marlyss let out a frustrated sigh. "Why did you come here? You know it's not safe, and I've promised your father not to expose you to this."

"I'm sorry. I tried to call your folks but no one has gotten back to me. Birdie was coming down, so I came with her." Most of the time, Kristi visited her mother at her grandparents' pig farm, near Elko. They were a hard scrabble lot, suspicious of strangers. They were weird enough from Kristi's point of view, and she had never brought anyone else along, not even Birdie.

"They're in Arkansas at a hog show," Marlyss said. "What's so important it couldn't wait?"

As Marlyss spoke, a woman came into the shelter with a kid, no more than eleven or twelve years old. Kristi stared at the young girl in horror. Marlyss hurried over to the door to meet them.

"I found her at the..." the woman's voice dropped to a whisper. The girl was sniffling, her head bent down submissively, her body trembling.

"Sister Anna is coming in soon," Marlyss said to the woman. "Will you be okay for a while? I need to take care of some business this afternoon."

The woman agreed, looking over at Kristi. Marlyss had disappeared into one of the offices and emerged immediately with a lightweight jacket and purse.

She called to Kristi, "Let's get out of here."

Kristi offered to take her mother out for a meal. At first she declined, but when Kristi commented on how thin and worn she looked, Marlyss admitted that she could stand a bite or two to eat. Since she had given up wearing silk dresses and crepe tops with gabardine slacks, Marlyss always looked gaunt and thin to Kristi.

Kristi drove toward the strip, turning in at the oasis where Day Enterprises maintained a suite of rooms, a place where Kristi was well known. In the restaurant, she was seated at a private booth reserved for privileged guests. Kristi was grateful that Marlyss hadn't objected. In fact, she seemed to watch her daughter with a certain admiration.

"My, what a sophisticated lady you've become." The compliment was sincere.

"I hope you don't mind." Kristi blushed, thinking of how selfish she was being in not considering her mother's feelings for the place. "Is this place too painful for you? We can go..."

Marlyss laughed. "No, no. This is fine. I'm not a withering vine. This place causes me no more sorrow or joy than any other. It's your comfort that's pertinent. I assume you have a delicate matter to discuss."

"Well, yes. Maybe no. I don't know. Is it delicate?"

They ordered lunch and coffee. Kristi was hoping the maitre d' would remember her preference for leisurely service, and he did not disappoint, carefully spacing out the delivery of each dish, starting with the salad.

Kristi jumped into the story of Mary Befford, her continued assault against Kristi through small insurrections, culminating in the discussion she overheard between Mary and Elena.

Marlyss listened with detached interest. She showed compassion for the storyteller but remained utterly detached from the tale, and any relevance it held for her life. When Kristi was done, Marlyss had finished her salad. She laid her napkin on the table, then began to evaluate what effect the incident might have on Kristi's future.

"I know it must all seem so trivial to you," Kristi said, rushing to forestall the kind of advice she had witnessed that morning at the mission.

Marlyss read her statement correctly. "Kristina, my dear! You mustn't think that because my life's work deals with the downtrodden and exploited that I can no longer have an interest in your life. Erase the thought from your mind."

Kristi was relieved. She had yet to touch her salad. Noting the waiter hovering in the recess behind them, she picked up her fork, eating as her mother responded.

"You are my only daughter. What pains you, still pains me. Is it trivial compared to the horrors facing a young girl on the street? Yes. Is it trivial to a young woman considering a life commitment to that woman's son? Definitely not."

"It's more than considering, Mother. We're getting engaged this Christmas. I…I want you there." She hadn't meant to blurt it out like that.

Marlyss frowned, but didn't disrupt the line of conversation to address that revelation. "Mary Befford. Where should I begin? Mary Befford will never see anything of value in you, because you are my daughter. It's as straightforward as that. I was hoping she would rise above her pettiness by now, but…Well, there you have it—she hasn't."

"Why does she hate you so much? What happened between you?"

"Everything that happened between us was a direct response to her feelings for me. You see, she thought that she would be Mrs. Christian Day. She resented me for stealing her future. In her eyes, I hadn't lifted a finger to earn the privilege, whereas she had spent years kowtowing to his ego. Poor dear never saw what the problem was. She was kind enough to me at first, especially as she was out to win Joe's proposal of marriage. She treated me with charming contempt." Marlyss was painting a portrait of Mary that matched Kristi's experiences with the woman.

The waiter knew the precise moment in which to pick up the plates and deliver the entrée dishes. He did so without any fuss.

Marlyss continued her story. "You can bet that Mary was quick to notice my shortcomings in that crowd. I preferred to stay at home and learn the homely arts—as you can guess, I never learned these at my mother's knee. I didn't like mingling, especially in your father's world of multinationals and political influence. I hated that. The more I retreated from that world, the more Mary hated me and worked to diminish me in everyone's eyes. Even your father fell victim to her toxic interpretation of things."

"Is that why you argued? Why you left?"

Marlyss shook her head. "I simply never fit in there. Well, you know my folks. I had no tools to deal with the kind of people in Hawkes Ferry, church-going, decent folks."

A horrible idea emerged in Kristi's head. "She never met your parents, did she?"

"At our wedding, of course. But Christian made sure they were whisked out of town the same day. I doubt she ever demeaned herself to talk to them. You can imagine how Ma dressed." Marlyss raised her eyebrows.

Kristi pictured her maternal grandmother dressed in some tawdry costume assembled from the wardrobe at the nightclub where she had once danced.

"That would explain a lot. So I'm not good enough for the Boston blood Si carries in his veins, but, believe me, I am more Hawke than any of them," Kristi consoled herself.

"You know, Kristina, everyone is worthy of love. Everyone has value. We don't need to find it out there, because it lives in here. These kids that I work with every day are treated like trash, have always been, that's why they are on the streets. Every day we work to help them to find that ember inside, that spark that ignites the spirit, that burns in spite of all the horror and darkness that is their daily existence. From that single ember grows their connection to love, to God." She seemed to be far away, then suddenly woke. "We all have that glow, Kristina. We are all children of God."

Kristi pushed her half-eaten lunch aside. "So you have no advice on how to win over Si's mother?"

"You can't. Ask her, and she will undoubtedly say, blood will out."

"She did," Kristi said with surprise.

"There you have it. But are you sure that Si is so right for you? I know that he's your father's first pick—only pick, for that matter. But have you allowed yourself to wander through the field a little, unrestricted by everyone else's expectations?"

Kristi sat back in her chair. "Si is the perfect man for me in so many ways. We both love ranching and Hawkes Ferry, for one. Everybody else wants to escape' including Birdie."

"Maybe they just want to see the world. Your opportunities to travel have not been available to many others."

"What travel? I don't go anywhere. A shopping trip to San Francisco once with Grandmother and another one to New York with the Beffords is all."

"And Las Vegas whenever you want. All expenses paid." She gestured to include the current space. "You could go other places if you wanted to. Just ask."

"But Si doesn't want me to."

"And naturally, as a dutiful daughter and future wife, you do what is asked of you," Marlyss said.

"The thing is, Si is the right man for me, for my position in the world."

"Oh, my! Your position in the world. Now this is your father speaking. What does Kristina think? Can you honestly say you love him?"

"I can learn to love him. That's what a good woman does, isn't it? If the match is right, the love will come."

"Is that in the Bible?" Marlyss seemed amused by the notion.

"I don't know how I feel about Si right now, to be honest."

"Then why care what his mother says or thinks?"

"Because everyone expects me to love him."

"I don't expect it. I expect you to go out and embrace the world, to love a lot of men before you decide who to commit your life to. I expect you to grow into a reasonable and sound woman who does not need to depend on a man for your livelihood or your happiness. Your father expects Si Befford to be that man."

"There is no one else I can even consider."

"I always thought you might have an eye for Dove Meyer's boy."

"No!" Kristi said a little too quickly. Then added, "He was too old for me."

"At fifteen maybe, but not at twenty-one. You're an adult. Is he still around?"

"I heard rumors he might be teaching this fall at the school."

"There's an option. There must be some unmarried professors. How about this Dr. Truitt that Birdie mentioned? Is he still a bachelor?"

"I'm not building a shopping list for potential replacements, Mother."

"Pity."

As Kristi signed the bill, she asked Marlyss, "So will you come at Christmas?"

Marlyss looked at her with surprise. "For the engagement party? Certainly not. I will not help mount your sacrifice to the gods in exchange for fair winds."

Kristi was disappointed, but as they walked back to her car, she understood that Marlyss held no ill will toward her. She simply would not support an engagement that was lacking in true commitment of the heart. Kristi knew that would come later.

They parted mother and daughter, still bound in mutual love.

Ten

Truitt found parking just below the museum in a spot overlooking the Hudson River. Over the tree tops, he spied the boats and barges plying down the river below. The museum was built in the thirties specifically to house the art and architecture of medieval Europe. To that end, it purported to transport the ideals of the great monasteries of France and Spain to American shores.

The excavation of subway tunnels in the thirties had offered up enough island bedrock to build a medieval fortress here, on the northern tip of Manhattan. Its imposing stone edifice transported him back immediately to southern France, the Pyrenees, and the eighth-century monastery of St. Amadour in Rocamour. In contrast to the verdant setting of forest-on-the-Hudson, the monastery crowned a promontory near the top of a treeless mountain scoured by the constant wind sweeping up from the sea, thousands of feet below. The isolation of the place, its imposing ramparts and large wooden gates kept the Moors and Franks at bay. Pilgrims found their way up the winding, rocky trail to ring the bell at the foot of the gate. There they found welcome refuge from the world.

Today's pilgrims were of another sort, offered up in tour buses, which were unloading as Truitt followed the path toward the main entrance of The Cloisters. As he pressed through the throng of visitors, he wondered why he had come.

The house in Sycamore Falls had overwhelmed him with memory and loss, and had made him wonder at the meaning of life, his life, motherless and mothered at the same time. He had no idea, no way to respond to the enormity of her sin, or her salvation. What was to become of him? The walls seemed to close in on him and after three days he fled, taking her car into the countryside, then across the river heading toward Columbia University. The next morning, after a full night's rest, he set off for the museum to take up Willema's offer for a visit.

Just below the cobblestone drive, Truitt ducked into the side entrance and scaled the two flights of steps leading to the main hall. He wasn't sure what his advisor wanted from him, nor the reception he'd receive by popping up unannounced.

Thinking of the friendship that Dr. Rutherton had claimed with his Aunt Nell, Truitt wondered if it were reciprocated at all. He had rarely heard his aunt speak of the woman, and certainly not as a long-standing friend. He was led to believe that the woman was an old acquaintance from Nell's stint at the Library of Congress, before he had come into her life. He had made her acquaintance only briefly before enrolling in the doctoral program, where she became his advisor. It was a curious twist now, as his mind wrestled with snatches of memory scattered across years and memory. Had he met her before Columbia? Was she among the entourage of Nell's librarians and information professionals?

Perhaps she did know something about Nell's life before, but did she know about his birth? For a brief moment, he considered the possibility that the fact of his birth could be the reason she found his work as unworthy of publication in the Journal. He immediately dismissed the notion as sophomoric, yet had confusion as to her presence at the funeral and her request for his visit. And, what did Caroline have to do with any of it?

Opening the door to the main hall, he found it filled with visitors, mostly tourists, with individual patrons roaming from one gallery to the next. Truitt asked for Dr. Rutherton at the reception desk, only to learn that she would be in the workshop until eleven. Signing the visitor's register, he found his name was posted on a list of expected visitors. The receptionist invited him to visit the galleries until Dr. Rutherton was free. She would meet him in the tapestry hall at eleven.

Truitt wandered through the chapel and enclosed cloister leading down to the medieval herb garden. At the monastery at Rocamour, Frere Guillaume had tended such a herbarium, in which he raised the culinary delights and medicinal balm that served the brothers well. At the museum, the herb garden was surrounded on two sides by the French cloister from Bonnefort with a parapet opening on two sides to a broad vista of the park and riverscape below. Beyond the river, the forested slope of the Palisades on Jersey shore, added to the illusion of a medieval monastery isolated from the world. Here one could sense, if not fully understand, an earthly realm of ascetic devotion to the greater glory of God. As he stood at the edge of the walk, halfway between earth and heaven, peace settled on Truitt as did the cloister of St. Amadour a decade before.

At eleven, Truitt arrived in the hall where the unicorn tapestries were displayed. While waiting for Willema's arrival, he allowed himself the pleasure of viewing the works freely, pulling into them his biases against French courtly art and literature, as well as his appreciation for icons of medieval art. Such distraction kept his mind from returning to the weightier thoughts that had driven him away from the cottage.

The tapestries were woven in the Netherlands in the last years of the fifteenth century but designed for a French noble house. They depicted a fabled unicorn hunt. Other than his previous acquaintance with the tapestries, he knew little about this hunt, but thought it related closely to a Persian tale of Alexander the Great and his invincible mount, which was said to be a unicorn. Truitt knew little of Persian culture and less of bestiary, considering the topic suited for the fantasy-laden world of small children.

From his rare encounters with unicorns in medieval miscellany, he thought that the depiction of the white beast gouging two hunters—as shown in the second panel—at odds with ideals of purity, magic and healing that the unicorn was to represent. The hunters, coming upon the beast healing the waters in a stream, set to ensnare him. Presumably they want to capture his magical powers. As he charges, they take to the chase, finally killing him in the woods with their spears. Then, in the same panel, present the lifeless body with its detached horn to the liege Lord and Lady of the manor.

The last tapestry stood alone. The unicorn was enclosed in a garden of sacred herbs and flowers, a brocade collar around his neck. A golden chain shackled him to a large tree that sheltered the garden. Here, Truitt saw the greatest evidence of French design, in the colors and symbols of French courtesy, and in the fantasy of the contented bridegroom. The romans courtier, which preceded the tapestries by nearly three centuries, was alive and well in the fifteenth century, as if there had been no recriminations of Dante and no realism of Chaucer in between.

"What do you think? Sacred or profane?" Willema Rutherton stood behind him.

"I couldn't say." Truitt turned to face her. Catching the glint of mischief in her eye, he turned back to the tapestry, ready to play. "Beyond the secular fable of the unicorn hunt, there is a homage to Christian iconography, especially when one considers its placement in the series, the final panel showing the killing and presentation to the lord."

"How so?" Willema stood back, amused to consider his findings.

"At least in this venue, the panel concludes the topic of the hunt. Across the hall, the unicorn is sacrificed, and then offered to the liege lord and his bride—the Crucifixion and Deposition neatly packaged in one piece. The scene before us celebrates the Resurrection, the risen Christ..."

"Shackled by the Church?" Willema conjectured, almost to herself.

He turned to face her and smiled. "Did I pass?" She had a point. Christian symbology took it only so far.

She offered a gracious smile. "And the other—the profane—view?"

"Certainly romans courtier is prominent in every scene, the colors of the court, the symbols of love and courtship, the flowers and trees chosen to suggest erotic intentions. The golden chain of the contented groom trapped in the garden—the landless noble who has given up his freedom for wealth and land of a fortunate marriage."

"Yet what he wins, she loses. And what's her story?"

The game was moving beyond Truitt's skill, and he knew better than to offer her an ill-considered response.

"I'm playing with the tapestries this summer, Emery. I'm reconsidering the interpretations we scholars have made of them over the years, the conclusions we reach in our rush to fame."

Her voice took on the momentum of a building passion and Truitt felt the stir of some long dead promise. Willema was still capable of firing the light in her student. As much as he could denounce the editor, he was still not immune to the professor. Is this what she wanted him here for? He had no intention of moving into the realm of fantasy. "I wasn't aware of your interest in fable and myth."

She ignored the concern in his voice. "Did it ever occur to you that the unicorn might not symbolize man at all, but woman?"

This was her connection, not fantasy but woman. As ridiculous as her premise was, Truitt offered a willing ear to exercise her academic curiosity.

"Woman, that elusive creature of beauty and mystery." Willema crossed the hall to stand before the first scene, where the hunters stood beside the wood ready with spears and hounds. "Here, the men gather at the edge of the wood, half afraid of entering, yet unable to suppress their desire for the quarry. In Celtic lore, the women of the woods lived by the sacred streams and wells. They served the goddess of the land, offering aid and succor to passing knights."

In Truitt's earliest readings of Arthur, such creatures of the woods and sea lured the unwitting knights to their peril. Yet even the Arthurian tales were of ancient origin. The tapestries were not. "Medieval knights were duty bound to serve God and the king," he reminded her.

"And themselves, at the expense of others," she said sourly. "But you are right, of course, free love was dangerous to both king and church. To assure pure bloodlines, wives and daughters of the nobility were sequestered behind castle walls. The castle Keep, as it were."

"Or enclosed in a garden?" Truitt asked, objecting to her fanciful flight through the tapestries. "Tell me, if the maiden is useful to the knights—and presumably the king—then why kill her?"

"Captivity is the goal of society and social order, but too many resisted and escaped into the wood. They wanted to remain free."

"Why show death at all, then? And what is the meaning of this presentation to the Lord and Lady?" Truitt asked a bit annoyed.

"It is interesting to note that the church viewed them as wild creatures without grace," Willema said. "The Lady had been a captive herself. But she'd forgotten what freedom was."

The story was vaguely familiar to Truitt, perhaps one of those tales from his youth, before he discovered that Malory's Arthur was a fanciful reworking of oral tradition, and entirely unsuited for serious study.

Willema was studying the Lady's hand closely, pointing out to him, "Those rosary beads in her hand show her complete indoctrination by the Church. Her freedom cannot be endured."

"Why?" Truitt's tone was challenging now.

Willema turned to him, a look of wonder on her face. "Why to preserve the patriarchal line of inheritance, of course. To maintain the divine right of kings. To assure the sovereign authority of the church. Where there is an accumulation of wealth and land, bloodlines matter.

In the agrarian societies of the goddess, the offspring were raised in community, undistinguished by bloodline."

"Prehistoric, perhaps, but it's conjecture at best," Truitt said.

"Yet, there might be traces of it after all, if we are willing to look at these tales and fables in a different light. Percival's mother, for instance, might have been such a priestess, raising her son alone in the woods…"

"His father was identified as a knight, along with his brothers." Truitt was growing tired of the exercise and demonstrated his impatience.

Truitt frowned. The topic had strayed far from the story in the tapestries. He felt Willema edging closer to the heart of the disagreement that had lain between them for the past ten years. She had approached it from a strange angle. He felt the rising discomfort nonetheless.

Willema held up her hand, seeking his forbearance for a while longer.

"The unicorn here, dressed in her embroidered collar and gold chain and locked in a garden cut off from the world, she's isolated from her corrupters, from her kinswomen, and from the world she had once known as a maiden. The liege lord keeps her for himself. But, she's not always a bride. Here in captivity she withers without hope, robbed of her freedom, she dies in spirit."

"You are referring to Eleanor of Aquitaine, of her years in England."

"Perhaps, but there are others as well."

Truitt didn't agree with her portrayal of the queen as some helpless, captive maiden. "Eleanor exiled herself from England and managed to direct the whole courtesy movement from the court she established in Provence." Truitt pointed out, happy to have renewed the details of her antics in the past few months. "I would argue that she persisted in defeating her husband, by outliving him. She was powerful enough."

"True, but Eleanor was fleeing back into the metaphorical wood. Provence had been her world, and in her case, salvation lay with exile in France where she was able to live out a worthy and respectable life, a life away from the defamation and humiliation that she had in that other world." Suddenly, she turned. "Let's take a stroll, shall we?"

Truitt was glad for the change. He followed her through the Gothic chapel then to the Bonnefort cloister.

Standing at the parapet, both of them facing the river, Willema continued. "In our efforts to be accomplished scholars, we search for truth. Yet, we find only what we expect to find—or even worse, what we hope to find. By changing a single ambiguous element in our view—the meaning of the unicorn, for instance—, we find an entirely different truth. Does the unicorn stand for chastity, the maiden—or invincibility, the knight?"

"Or the resurrected Christ," Truitt said, reaffirming his own view.

Willema frowned, then countered, "Is it a tribal myth, or the story of an individual woman?"

"Like Percy's mother, I suppose?" Truitt found her insistence on combining the subject of the French courts to the tales in Arthur a little trying. There was no precedent for it, even though the troubadour who first recorded the tale of Percival was at Provence. Chretien was playing with oral myth. Percival's mother, who the poet did not name, had fled from the king's court after the death of her husband and sons to keep the young Percival from enlisting to be killed in battle, as well. Her purpose, as well as her person, was noble. Truitt used to fashion himself as a type of Percival when he was a young boy of six or eight, raised as he was in the remote woods of Delaware by a maiden aunt. The thought gave him pause, for she wasn't his aunt, was she? She never had been.

"And there were others..." Willema said, perhaps to coax his participation.

As if awakened to the beat of his own thoughts, Truitt stared at her in surprise. "Like my aunt, you mean? This whole contrivance of the unicorn is about Nell, isn't it? My mother."

"It's not a contrivance, Emery. It's an alternate way to weave the story, with the same images interpreted by the monks one way, and by the poets, another. And indeed as personal allegory it reveals the truth of your own creation myth."

Hours later, Truitt sat on the cold concrete bench in the gated garden of the cathedral of St. John the Divine, a few blocks from his inn, trying to assimilate the web of details threatening to dislodge the bedrock on which his life had been built. Even in this garden, though, there was disruption and instability, from the carelessly tended plant beds to the vagrants sleeping on stone benches. The chain link fencing was a disturbing reminder that even this place, dedicated though it might be to Heaven, was not saved from the ruinous hand of man.

Willema had woven a story of a young ward of a senator betrayed by her guardian. Rescued from a life of oppressive poverty, the girl was grateful, and naïve, too eager to repay the debt. While his wife was large with child, he took sordid advantage of the girl's gratitude. A pregnancy resulted, and he demanded she abort the life he had planted. The girl could not make such a sacrifice, one that would put her eternal soul in jeopardy. She confided her secret to her only friend, a graduate student working at the Library of Congress, where the girl was a youth volunteer.

The student offered to help the desperate girl find a situation in which she would be allowed to carry the baby to term. Instead of taking the trip abroad laid out by her guardian, the girl disappeared from the scene. With strong allies vested in her welfare—and the senator's restraint—the girl settled out of the spotlight in a quiet community of friends. There she raised the child in anonymity on the salary of a town librarian. The trust fund came later, thanks to the effort of her allies.

Truitt had listened to the story of the pathetic girl as if it had nothing to do with him. The heartfelt warmth of her storytelling told Truitt that the girl was indeed a friend, but it could have been someone else, not Nell, for this friend was a stranger to him. The austere and righteous aunt who had guided his life was not the pathetic naïf of her story.

Truitt pressed her for the senator's name, but she refused to surrender it. The conditions of the trust, she said, had prohibited Nell from ever revealing the true identity of his father. Willema would not betray her friend's trust, even in death. His identity would not help

Truitt connect with him now, since he had died shortly after Truitt's birth. He died serving the country on legislative business when his plane crashed in a remote jungle. He had been a hero to his public, and Truitt should choose to think of him that way, as well.

No good could come of raising the dead, thirty years after the fact, she had said. The lives and reputations of others had to be taken into consideration. Changing topics, she led Truitt back to the entrance.

Willema's rationalization was not credible to the boy that longed for name and family. Truitt considered the paternal name on his birth certificate, Joshua. A brother might also have spawned a throw-away boy. A storm brewed inside him, roiling unanswered questions and fomenting unspoken accusations that he was loathe to give air.

He fled the garden where no peace would settle. He walked through the forest of the nearby park, but gained little relief from the oppressive heat and memory. A scraggly band of students pounded vibrations from electric guitars and shouted inaudible words, breaking any peace that might find him there.

His creation myth, Willema had said. His misbegotten beginnings, in stark contrast to the legitimacy of the orphan, who came to live with his only surviving relation, a maiden aunt. A crash begins one story and ends the other. He wanted to ignore the fanciful imaginings of the professor, and simply accept what Nell had told him all along. There was no one to contradict her story now, except that letter written in her own hand.

As he stepped off the curb, a car honked urgently and a blue sedan whipped by, driving him back to the sidewalk. He retreated. Turning up the hill, he stayed on the safe path. If it was a lie, how elaborate the fabrication. The elopement and honeymoon at Niagara Falls, the picture of his young mother with blonde and stylish hair, his father in an army uniform. Nell telling him their story every year on his birthday until he knew it by heart.

Curious about this place of marvelous horseshoe-shaped falls, they read about it in picture books and travel books. Wanting to share what his parents had shared, he begged Nell to take him there. "Someday, Emery. And maybe you'll take me when you've grown into a fine young man." Over time, stories and yearnings fell away to serious study and achievements building toward great things to come.

Only when those great things started to come, he didn't tell her, did he? The thought startled him into a sense of hopelessness. The seat of Judgment frowned on him. He had never shared the good fortune of his promotion for fear she would be disappointed. Better, he had reasoned, to tell her in person. And now it was too late. Too, too late.

Truitt arrived back at the inn in the early evening. A visitor was waiting for him, sitting in one of the Victorian high back chairs in the small drawing room that formed the lobby. It was Caroline, as beautiful as he had ever seen her.

She stood as he approached her, offering a hand in greeting. "I wasn't sure you'd call me back if I left a card. Auntie told me you'd be here."

The reference to her aunt evoked a flood of memories of the earliest days at Columbia when she had barged into the peace of his existence and toyed with him for a complete summer when he worked in the stacks at the graduate library. He had suffered a great humiliation at her hands and was not eager to do so again. The opulent wedding set on her left hand told him all he needed to know about her. He wondered what she wanted from him.

"Can we go for a bite to eat? There's a little Italian place around the corner." She was as charming as he had remembered, and as difficult to turn down. With the clerk watching them with some interest—Truitt was sure he was admiring Caroline—he agreed to dinner, hoping the place was not too expensive.

The walk along Broadway reminded him of the spell he was under so many years ago, pleased to have this beautiful woman at his side, so unaware of her potential for treachery. She had played with him that summer, as a cat with a mouse, for the entertainment of her cousin, his roommate. They were determined that he should give up his virginity with Caroline the willing—priestess? He settled on Willema's word for the willing maidens of the well. Even now her actions seemed innocuous enough, but he could not forget the crushing humiliation he felt at the time—a devastation that forever shaped his dealings toward all of her gender.

Caroline pointed out a small storefront which used to be a nondescript diner serving home cooking. When they were seated, she asked Truitt to talk about himself. He told her about his courses and his preparations for the coming fall. Mindful of her new role with Willema's journal, he emphasized how his papers had been accepted in a few literary journals. The waiter brought the bottle of Chianti that Truitt had ordered, relieved to see prices targeted to student economies.

She asked about his experiences living in the west, and after his terse description, she said, "The place sounds dreadful. You're probably dying to move back here." She laughed.

"Actually my career is doing well. I'm an Associate now. With a few more years under my belt and the right exposure in publication... well..." He sipped at his wine, watching her reaction. What did she want from him?

"What a pity I was hoping you'd be coming back to the city."

Truitt wondered about her purpose and looking at her rings, asked, "So what have you been up to besides getting married? Any children?"

She pulled her hand off the table.

"No. none at all. Actually there won't be any. We are not living together anymore. I am filing for divorce." Her well-toned face reddened and she averted her eyes. When he said nothing, she continued, "Lionel Chatham. Did you know him? He was a literature major, then went into law. Great lawyer. Lousy husband."

Watching the waiter place the dishes on the table, spaghetti and meatballs for him and a cheesy penne for her, Truitt thought about what might make a great husband to the charming yet toxic Caroline.

During the meal, her tone changed. She was now her aunt's editorial assistant. "Auntie sees promise in your work, Emery, but it needs to be targeted toward a broader audience. The field is widening to include a wide range of scholars, not all of them educated in elite private schools or Catholic universities. There are other histories to consider besides the ones passed down by nobles and ecclesiastics, who preferred to downplay the contributions of women and heretics."

Truitt listened with respect to her position. He graciously poured her wine, as he had seen other men tend to their female companions, then filled his own glass. He wondered how long her little talk would last.

"The field is changing, Emery. Willa is aiming to broaden the scope of the Journal to include the rising interest in social and cultural history which appeals to the broadening base of academia. Your research is good—it's excellent—but you need to expand your view of it to accommodate this broader base."

"My work focuses on the work of Joachim regarding the trinity and the new age it predicts. Although my academic work confines itself to the Middle Ages, my scholarship takes the trajectory into the effects of work into the eighteenth century. The effects are limitless, carrying even into today's world—everybody's talking about this new age business, but few understand its origins. However, I must limit my aspirations to what I can reasonably hope to accomplish in my lifetime."

"Why must you limit your scope to cover the distant past? It's just this consideration of relevancy that Willema wants to foster. I believe she has sent you several notes regarding her opinions on your work."

"Yes. She expects me to toss off my life's ambition and support the ascendance of woman in history, unrecorded as it is," he said sharply.

"Not unrecorded, exactly, but unsourced in the scholastic papers, which were all accumulated by the Church and collected into ecclesiastical libraries. But there are other sources. The Welsh translations of Lady Grey, which examines…"

"Yes, yes and the voluminous exhortations of the courts at Poitiers and Champagne. Willema has made it abundantly clear that she will consider nothing less than the revision of medieval history to accommodate these women."

"This isn't going well at all." Caroline shook her head.

Truitt was embarrassed that he had let his guard down.

"Look, Emery, I made a grave error in judgment back then. Stephen had suggested a bit of fun. I was stupid and young and bored so took him up on it. You were attractive and sweet and I really enjoyed your company. You need to know that. Still, there is no excuse for my behavior. I was wrong. Stephen was wrong. You were better than either of us."

He wondered what she was up to. She was alluring and enchanting even now with a wedding set on her hand, and a promise of divorce, offering to be free for him when he moved back. She would humiliate him again if he let his guard down.

"I am sorry, Emery."

Caroline said goodbye at the restaurant and walked away—to where, he didn't know. Every bit the siren that she used to be, he was glad to be rid of her, of the temptation she wrought. The whole business of what he might do to make his writing worthy—of what now seemed to be a *woman's* Medieval Journal. It was just a ruse to lure him to the well. No matter how the business between Nell and his father had occurred, he knew that Nell would have never humiliated or demeaned anyone, even a man.

Eleven

Truitt found Siphered—the town mentioned on Nell's birth certificate—at the end of a rural county road in western Virginia. The town, nestled in a gully on the slope of the Blue Ridge Mountains, was a small community of four houses, a general store and a church propped in the middle of a grassy meadow. Only the church looked respectable, a clapboard structure on a cinder block foundation, freshly painted in white with a mossy trim. The store and houses were in various stages of decay. The faintly legible sign on the storefront declared the name of the town and the date 1907.

A sign outside the store announced a U. S. Post Office within. There Truitt inquired about any Truitt family in the area. He was directed toward the church and a path to a house, hidden behind a large, unruly hedgerow. He found a woman, wrinkled and tanned with time, sweeping the front porch in a faded floral dress and tattered apron.

"I'm looking for the Truitt family. Do they live here?"

The woman gave no signal that she heard him, continuing across the porch to its edge, then with a hearty swoop, sent the detritus into the wild grass and brambly bush to the side of the house. Then she turned toward the path he had come up. She shifted her eyes, squinting to take in his presence. She gave him a long hard look.

"Them's used to live here, sure." She said, her withered and tanned face working out some inner turmoil. "Elder Truitt it is, though, he ain't here no more."

Truitt considered the news. "He's a minister then? A preacher?"

"You ain't said what you looking for, young fellow." She gripped her broom in a menacing way.

"I'm bringing news of his daughter."

"No news is good." She was still squinting at him, assessing if she was acquainted and might give him what he wanted.

"This is the pastor's house, then?

She nodded.

"I should probably speak with him."

"Cain't. Gone off to Mount Airy for the day." She answered, adding immediately, "But seeing as how you're the cantankerous sort, I'll tell that no one sees Elder Pike without going through this old woman. And you ain't told me your name or your business yet."

She was tight-lipped with a stranger, but Truitt had known such old women to be gossipmongers of the worst sort. "My name is Emery." He was not ready to tie his person with a family he little understood.

"Do you know of any other Truitts in the area?" He asked after some moments while she assessed his worthiness to have the answer.

"I can tell you that they ain't none," she finally said, picking up her broom to sweep. "Them's a sad lot, if you want to know. The elder retired ten, say, fifteen year ago, and went off to that old folk's home in Roanoke."

The woman set her jaw in anger. "Wouldn't have had to, if'n they was family to look after him. Sad lot, those Truitts."

"No other family around here, then? I thought there might be children or next of kin." Truitt was disappointed.

She shook her head, sweeping the broom once or twice over the doorsill, as if she might ask him in. Stopping she bent forward to take a closer look at the man who now stood near her. "Say, you ain't one of them, is you?" She shook her head in pity and abandoned the door.

"Might have been kin still here, if he weren't so good at driving them all away. Nothing but meanness and spite in that old man. Kept himself a young wife. They all do that, you know, these mountaineers. Take a girl before she knows what's what."

She swept the porch again, talking in riddles and half sentences, as if her words took fuel from the work. "They take it, though, these girls. Married off for cold cash by their pappies and start bearing their progeny. Four before she dried up. But he wasn't happy. Wanted more, 'specially after the fever took the babies."

"There were four Truitt children?" Nell never mentioned but one, a brother. Truitt began to doubt the soundness of this quest he set for himself.

"They's son died in that conflict over there. Know that? Rightly kind boy, he was. Died in the war that wasn't a war."

"Korea." Truitt offered.

"Were only seventeen. Not even old enough to join up. Lied to the army, I suspect, to get away from his pa." She was momentarily lost in the shadows of the past. "Good boy. Would carry water for an old woman—my granny kept him hid when the old man got mean."

Truitt was impatient to follow his own story. "What happened to the wife? Her name was Winifred, wasn't it? Is she still around?"

"Hah! You could say that. Run off, she did, after her babies died. Run off and leave that poor girl to manage the rancid elder on her own. Vile man! Worked her to the bone. Whew, she was a scrawny little thing. Wouldn't let her finish school, neither. Warn't going let any boys at her, no way."

"The mother ran off? Where to?"

"Run off with that two-bit finagler, preaching to folks about their rights, getting them to sign up for this and that. Never trusted no one with wavy hair and a fancy suit."

"Did he have a name?"

"No name that I'd care to know or say. The devils own hand servant, you can bet. The road to perdition is served by many like him."

"And the daughter, do you know what happened to her? I mean—if she doesn't live around here..."

"Run off like her mother, eventually. That's when he went mad. Why, the night she took off, they was a-rowing like nobody's business..."

"Do you have a name for that place in Roanoke? I'd like to visit him." Truitt saw that every question was a chance for the gossip to dig deeper into her well of rumor, and he had little patience for the misbegotten tales of sordid life in this sorry town.

"Just a minute, then." She laid the broom against the jamb and disappeared inside. The summer heat was stoking up. Truitt was dry from thirst. He longed for a glass of water but refrained, wanting only to escape.

She returned to the porch, handing him a half-torn envelope from the rest home. "You tell Elder Truitt that Bernadean Barnes was asking after him. Don't say I miss him, though, 'cause I don't."

Truitt didn't stop until he had put twenty miles behind him. At a roadside gas stop, he looked at the map and found a more direct route to Roanoke, about fifty miles up the highway. He filled up the car and bought a couple of bottles of spring water. It was mid-afternoon when he found the facility, an aging building reminiscent of veteran's homes, a bit dilapidated with withering vines drooping from the brick walls.

At the front desk, Truitt asked to see the elder. As the receptionist took his name, she looked at him with surprise, then summoned the director.

A large man in a business suit came through the double door, behind the reception desk to greet him. He had a gentle face and a soft voice. He held out his hand in greeting. "Welcome, Mr. Truitt. I'm Dr. Thomason, the director."

"I must say, it's is odd to see you, Mr. Truitt," he said. "We were given to believe that Ezekial had no other living relatives. He's been here for eight years now, and we've seen only two, maybe three, visitors. Are you by any chance related to Anabel Truitt?"

Truitt hesitated. It was awkward. He didn't want to claim the unmarried woman as his mother, yet he didn't want to deny her, either. "She was my mother. I came to tell him that she died."

The director didn't seem to notice Truitt's discomfort, but clasped Truitt's hand in his own. "Oh, my dear boy, I'm sorry for your loss. For Ezekiel's loss as well." He paused respectfully before letting go of Truitt's hand, and continued on.

"She came only once, when he first arrived. There was a terrible row. She's never come back. I believe that the reverend cast her off. He's never asked about her or shown any interest in seeing her again. I would have liked to ask her back, to try to work with him, but she left no address."

Truitt didn't tell him that her name had changed, as well.

"So he probably won't want to see me?"

"Not at all. It's a different thing altogether between daughter and grandson. I should think he would find joy in meeting a grandson. I'm assuming you two have never met? That is if communication has been strained with your mother. At least, he has never spoken of any grandchildren."

"No, he probably knew nothing about me." Would she admit that she had a son? Was that what they argued about? He wondered if he still wanted to go through with this. "Perhaps I shouldn't push…"

"Don't see why he would mind you at all. Come this way, I'll show you to his room. These old folks need the company, anyway. Spend far too much time alone."

Truitt followed him down the hall to an elevator located at the far side of a community room of some sort. People watched them cross with varying interest, making Truitt self-conscious. As they waited for the car, Truitt ventured to ask, in a low tone, "Who was the other person that visited him, then? Do you remember?"

"Of course there was Mr. Pike, the pastor who replaced him. He'd come up quarterly, on church business. After any conceivable business was finished up between them I think the pastor felt duty-bound to visit. Finally, Ezekial turned him away for good."

They got off on a floor with narrow walls and empty beds overflowing into the corridor. "This is the older part of the facility. We haven't gotten around for a remodel. Ran out of funds, I'm sorry to say," Thompson apologized, then pointed out that the funds were spent on patient care.

"Facility upgrade can wait for another benefactor," he added, as they reached the end of the hall. "Ah, here we are."

Truitt stopped him from knocking on the door. "You said there was another visitor."

"Did I? Nothing you'd be interested in, I'm sure. But the senator's wife, Mrs. Dodson, came by. She does a lot of charity visits in this part of the country, mercy visits. Don't know why she chose to visit this one, though."

The director knocked on the door, then stepped back to let Truitt enter. "I'll let you handle this," he said and walked away.

"What do you want?" A craggy old voice shouted from the bed.

Truitt entered the door gingerly, afraid of coming face to face with the old man.

The small frame barked from his bed. "If you're another pill pusher come to save my life, you can leave. I want for nothing but to redeem my soul."

"Elder Truitt? I'm Emery, your grandson." He stopped half-way across the room.

The elder cast a glance filled with fire and vitriol. "Don't have no grandson. My progeny died with my boy in the government's war."

"I'm Anabel's son." Truitt said.

The man screwed up his face and peered at Truitt, a wild look flaring through his eyes. "Jezebel! Daughter of Satan! That heathen bride, bought with my very soul." His eyes rolled as if a seizure had gripped him.

Truitt was alarmed as the old man flung his arms to the heavens, then let them collapse on his chest.

Beating his breast like a penitent, the old man shook his head piteously. "'More bitter than death is the woman, whose heart is snares and nets, and whose hands are as bonds: whoso pleaseth the Lord shall escape from her; but the sinner shall be consumed by her.'"

The preacher paused for breath, then raged, "That Jezebel should've been tossed from the palace, with her body torn asunder by the trotting hooves of horses, that dogs could consume her."

"Sir, are you speaking of your daughter Anabel?" Truitt hesitated, "Of my mother?"

"That daughter of the Whore—no! 'Can a woman forget her sucking child, that she should not have compassion on the son of her womb? Yea, they may forget, yet will I not forget thee.'" His ranting seemed to consume him. He folded over in exhaustion.

Truitt was frozen to the floor, unable to move forward or backward. He was not sure if the preacher were expostulating Biblical passages as illuminations for his current life, or if his own dialogue had surrendered to Old Testament ravings.

"Dead, all dead to me. All these things the work of imperious, whorish women."

"Winifred, then? You speak of the mother?"

"'And if a woman shall put away her husband, and be married to another, she committeth adultery.'"

The old preacher was not speaking to Truitt. The room was filled with ghosts of his past, the damned souls of his religion. There was no family left here for Truitt, no trace of blood, or name. With despondency, he left as the old man wrestled with his demons, "How weak is thine heart, saith the Lord, seeing thou doest all these things, the work of an imperious whorish woman."

Twelve

Truitt was devastated after leaving the home in Roanoke. Nothing made him feel so alone and so isolated as that vitriolic old man, raging like the woman-hating priests of the late Middle Ages, those judges of the inquisition who damned women and heretics, and sent them to be burnt at the stake. The mess, he noted, growing out of the licentious teachings and practices of the courts of southern France. Even before Eleanor, though, church fathers, like St. Jerome, saw Woman as the gate of the devil, the path of wickedness.

Any sympathy that the old man had at all, he held toward his son—who had also run away, according to the old housekeeper. He held nothing but contempt for those women in his life who had stayed with him until he made life unbearable for them. These were his true fount of blessings. The image of the unicorn seeped through the darkness in Truitt's vision. Suddenly, he felt a strong surge of pity for the woman that was his mother. He wished to God he had taken time to know her, to know who she really was.

What it must have been like for her. And yet she passed none of this rancor onto him. She was a paragon of dignity, of respect, of integrity—those precious values that she had passed onto him, her son. The old preacher knew nothing about her, about the woman she had become. What was it like for the fourteen-year-old girl, abandoned by her mother and brother, to face the cruelty of her father alone?

Truitt stopped for the night at a motel outside Charlottesville, not sure of where to go from here. He was not hungry for food, but for renewed spirit. With none of his texts to comfort him, he turned to the bedside Bible. Oddly enough, he found solace there. He had been no great believer in Biblical rhetoric, especially the ilk of malevolent and toxic preachers like his grandfather. Yet in Job, he found a certain strength and forbearance to carry in the face of catastrophe, in the day's work that had robbed him of his mother's family. Later, as he contemplated the trust fund, he saw the implication of family, a name, waiting for him in the days ahead, he felt the stir of hope renewed. He found in Paul, the three great virtues, the greatest of which was Charity. Certainly he would find charity in his father's house.

Early the next morning he set out with a plan. He had to rely on the sketchy details and near-truths of his birth stories. Willema said his father had been a senator. He was killed in a plane crash. The crash was in a jungle sometime after Truitt's birth. Such a significant event would be reported in any daily newspaper. He headed for the public library.

Three hours and six indices into his search, he discovered an article in a news magazine, a one-page editorial on the loss of Senator Reese Dodson. The magazine page featured a photo of the senator and his family, but it was badly overexposed on the microfiche. Truitt read the article over and over, hoping that some word or phrase would reveal him as Son. He found four more articles and an obituary before he was done.

On the road, he stopped at a small diner, eating lunch while he scanned through the copies he had made of the articles. From the library material, Truitt sensed that the family had remained in Washington. He saw nothing to discourage taking up his search there.

Before setting off for the city, Truitt opened Nell's floral address book once again to match the newly discovered names against her entries, in the hope that an address would be written in there. The entries were marked by initials or single letters instead of names. The entry for his Idaho address was under E and identified by address only. This time he perused the book page by page, looking for Reese, Dodson, or simply an address that seemed to be in Washington D. C. He found it on the page tabbed M, a number followed by a letter with DC underneath.

With the use of a city map, the address was fairly easy to find, once Truitt oriented himself to the circular pattern of streets and crossroads. It was a well-kept townhouse in a trendy area of town, offset from the street by green hedges and wrought iron fencing, a quiet neighborhood near a university.

Parking was not as easily negotiated. He found a spot on the street several blocks past the house and had to hike back to the address. Standing on the sidewalk in front of the townhouse, he considered what he was going to say. A black wreath graced the front door, something he did not expect, since the senator had died a quarter of a century before. The idea of confronting the unknown past now unnerved him.

How would he feel if they rejected him, denied him as Ezekiel had?

A young mother pushing a pram past him scowled with suspicion. Truitt opened the gate and went up to the door and knocked.

An elderly woman dressed in black answered the door. She stared at Truitt, in surprise.

"Is this the residence of Senator Dodson?"

His voice broke whatever spell she was under. "My goodness, for a moment, I thought you were someone else."

Apologetically she said, "Please, forgive me. I'm not myself today. My daughter…"

"Mother, I'll take care of this." A man appeared behind her in the doorway.

"My son, Raif," the woman introduced him as she withdrew.

The son glared at Truitt, who was surprised to see a reflection of himself in the man's face. This was his doppelganger, the look-alike that Steed had seen at the funeral.

"What the hell are you doing here?" Raif hissed with a barely audible voice. His face showed disgust as if Truitt's mere existence offended him. Pulling the door closed behind him, Raif stepped onto the stoop.

He was mortified by the man's behavior, but the invective only fueled his resolve. "I'm looking for my family. I'm Nell's…"

"I know who you are!" Raif seethed. "I saw you there, didn't I? At her funeral?"

Truitt didn't respond. The two stared each other down until Truitt backed down a step.

Raif moved forward to gain ground, grabbing the porch railing with both hands. "You've been well taken care of. My brother has seen to that, the bleeding heart liberal. You've got no business coming around here making trouble. Just keep it up and it'll cost you dearly."

His threat fell on deaf ears. The trust fund was not what Truitt wanted. "I'm not trying to make trouble for anyone. I just want my…"

"No trouble?" Raif said in exacerbation.

It was the name Truitt wanted, the family. The connection.

"Ma doesn't know anything about you, okay? It would kill her to know what that wench did to her—her daughter, her own flesh and blood." The fire in his eyes flickered, momentarily then withered into fear. "Look, she's already had a stroke when she learned of Anabel's death. You'll kill her if you tell her."

Against his will, Truitt surrendered another step, then another, backing down off the stoop. It was his right to push forward, to demand his place among them, to have his true name bestowed upon him. Yet, to push forward would kill the very person who could give him what he wanted.

Truitt knew he had come face to face with Nell's great shame. His very existence had the power to wound, to destroy the old woman's memory of her daughter, to dishonor his own mother in the end. He knew he could never belong to this family.

"We'll do right by you when the time comes. That old lawyer will make sure of it." The rancor was spent, only pity and disgust remained.

Truitt retreated from the house in shock. The old woman was Nell's mother, his grandmother. The senator had been her husband, betrayer of a stepdaughter who had run to her mother's house for protection from the cruelty of a misogynist preacher.

She knows nothing about you, Raif had said.

Nothing about me. Nothing about Anabel with her husband. Nothing about the bastard child who should have been aborted, the boy who had both uncle and brother in her son Raif.

Nell's great shame had become Truitt's great degradation.

All hope of a name and family behind him, Truitt returned to the cottage in Delaware. The place seemed cramped now, dark and dull, full of the ghosts of his unknown past. The walls closed in on him, as he tried to sort through her things. He could not bear to touch them. Although he had entered her room only once, he couldn't linger among the things so deeply imbued with the confusion he had about her. He could not grieve—who would the grief be for? Not aunt, for that role had been eradicated. Not mother—for that grief had been spent many years before on the woman who died in a car crash beside the dead brother who wasn't a father.

He thought of the photo, and needed to see it, to look into the past that wasn't, and to see with his eyes what was true. The black cardboard photo album was tucked in the bookshelf, among mementos of the life they shared. He pulled it out and flipped through its pages.

There was no wedding photo, after all. The story began with three snapshots, smudged and torn, taken in the churchyard he had visited in Sipherd. Churchgoers whose faces were blighted out by overexposed film faced the camera. Next, a row of children dressed shabbily in their Sunday best, stood near the open door of the church, the old preacher scowling behind them. Then, a shot of the little house before it was fixed up for Elder Pike, shabby and run down, recognizable only by the large hedgerow that hid it from the road.

Two photos were mounted in the next two pages. A young soldier smiling for a photographer. Then a tinted postcard of Niagara Falls. Beyond that a collection of snapshots of Nell holding a baby bundled in blankets on a snowy day. They were by a small church that he didn't recognize. A baptism. And next to Nell now he saw the familiar form of Willema Rutherton playing the role of godmother.

He found no photo of his mother in blond and stylish hair on her wedding day with his father, the soldier. There never had been one. There was no place where missing photos might have been mounted, no empty spaces. Where had he gotten such an idea?

He pulled the postcard out of its mounting. There was nothing written on back. It was an aerial view of the cataract in a sepia tone, with the waters tinted blue, a souvenir from the healing waters of Niagara Falls.

Not healing, he corrected himself, but romantic. Wasn't that what drew people there? Honeymooners and lovers. Healing waters and women of the wells. The significance of Willema's words hit him.

Not a honeymoon at all, but a tryst. This too was part of his creation myth.

Truitt drove through the night straight north through Pennsylvania and New York, returning to the place from which he had begun. The place where all her dreams had risen and fallen in one careless moment. Recalling the stories—the lies—she made to weave him a cloak of honor, he now heard their unlived longings.

The falls were greater than anything he could have imagined. Their thunderous roar deafened all senses. The power of nature summoned him back to the sacred place of his creation. A bastard son with no name, no family. Of what use were his achievements when she could not share them? What purpose did his scholarship serve, if not to make her proud?

She's gone.

Who will bear witness to his glory?

Who will share his triumph?

Who will love him now?

Thirteen

Marlyss Day was already late as she headed toward the truck stop, where she had promised to meet Christian for dinner. The evening was stifling, made worse by the fact that her windows were rolled up to fend against the squalor and crime that littered this part of town. Her motor thumped sporadically, causing misgivings about not letting him pick her up. It was better to meet in a no-man's land, a neutral place that belonged to neither of them. He would have taken her back to the high-end hotel where the company kept a suite of rooms, evoking in her the dark memories of the schism between them. He had volunteered to meet in her end of town, but she didn't want that. The tenderloin was too cluttered with business of the mission's work for her to focus on anything else there.

The truck stop was mutual ground in every respect. The place had little ambience of the sort that he would find pleasing. Full of truckers and night people as the place was, Christian wouldn't have to pretend that her unkempt hair and thrift-store dress didn't embarrass him. The clerks and regulars who filled the place were her kind of people, real people, those who struggled and scrimped and lived from day to day.

It was the world she grew up in, the world that took her back easily enough when his world had failed her.

She spotted the large marquee far down the road, trembling with missing bulbs. It marked the entrance of an expansive lot strewn with big rigs, pick-ups and old beater cars like hers. The squat building, built in an earlier era, and expanded over the years, was a flat roofed oddity with no style or design. Marlyss parked in a spot between a two-trailer rig and a sheepherder's camper. When she passed a trucker, he tipped his hat. It was not a come-on, but a gesture of respect for her gender, these cowboys connected to the world of respectability and manners learned at a mother's knee. She smiled in return, something that would bring unwanted attentions on the strip where lizards and snakes crawled out of dark caves in search of high stakes games and easy sex.

As she opened the door, chatter and laughter poured out, accented by the pinging of pinball machines and red-hot sounds vibrating through speakers, all metal and twang, country-western style. The cashier's booth was placed strategically to provide a clear view of both the gas lanes outside and the food mart within. A deli counter served fast-food, and a coffee shop accommodated sit-downs, the place that she had suggested for dinner. The casino and bar were in the back of the amenities, which included restrooms and showers for the truckers. Everything was priced to accommodate the regulars, the stop being too far off the interstate to be of any interest to Angelinos trekking up from the coast for a weekend of pleasure seeking.

Christian was at the slots, a bottle of beer in hand, feeding three machines from a roll of coins. He had dressed to fit in, wearing faded work jeans and a clean plaid shirt with a bolo tie. At the end of a round, he glanced at the entry, then scanned the aisles of the mart.

When he caught sight of her, he glared and looked at his watch. "You're late—forty-five minutes late," he said brusquely. He checked the mouths of his machines and, finding nothing, walked toward her.

She offered no excuse for being late, but he hadn't really expected one. "I was running out of change, anyhow. You hungry? I could eat half a steer. I hope the chow here is decent."

Marlyss assured him that he wouldn't die from it, and led him to the coffee shop.

The waitress grabbed two menus and showed them to the first empty seat.

Christian surveyed the empty rear of the room. "Do you have something a little quieter? The lady and I need to talk, and we'd like to hear ourselves."

She seated them in a back corner at a table set up for six. "Won't no one bother you here. Tonight's kinder slow."

"I'll let you know when we're ready to order," Christian said, as she stood by, pen poised, to take their order.

"Sure thing."

"We'd like something to drink. I'd like some water, no ice."

"Put her ice in mine," Christian said. He spent some time studying the four-page menu, turning it from front to back several times in disgust. "I thought you said this was a restaurant. You ready to order?"

When the waitress finally arrived with the waters, he ordered sandwiches and coffee for both of them with fries on the side.

"Kristina's postponed her engagement. Cancelled the party at the end of the month. I assumed she invited you."

Marlyss nodded in response, more than pleased at the news, but restrained her feelings. "Did she tell you why?"

"She didn't say—didn't seem to think she owed an explanation to anybody. Not Befford. Not her Grandmother. Not me."

"I see." She wondered if her refusal to support the engagement had given wind to Kristi's doubts. She certainly hoped so.

"I thought you'd know." His tone was bitter. "Why did she do it?"

"I don't know. I haven't talked to her since early last month."

"You don't know, but you see." He adopted a sarcastic edge to his voice. "But she asked you to the party? So tell me what you talked about, when she came down last month. You must have said something."

Marlyss was caught off-guard by his demands. There was no way she was going to betray her daughter's trust by repeating their conversations to him or anyone else.

"Do you suppose they had an argument? Maybe he was pressuring her for sex."

"Did she say that?" His tone had changed, from peevishness to worry.

"No—I was merely fishing for possible reasons why a girl like Kristi might want to cool things for a while. If he was persistent and she wanted a white wedding, for instance."

"A white...?" Christian was frustrated. "No. I'm not aware of any argument."

The last words were spoken with a vitriol that Marlyss attributed to his hunger and the prospect of not satisfying his appetite by the limited menu of the coffee shop.

The waitress came then to deliver the sandwiches and coffee. Christian added a side salad and a second order of fries, bribing the girl with an extra tip if she would be prompt about it. Then he charged through his plate without another word.

The salad arrived immediately with apologies for fries that needed to be cooked first. "But I'll get them as soon as they're cooked."

Marlyss picked through her food at a leisurely pace, glad for the respite in their talk. She knew that Kristi had doubts about Si, if not the idea of their relationship. She knew that Kristi would never agree to sex until there was a feeling of love. She suspected Kristi was waiting for the love to grow.

As he ate, Christian thought about Befford's trip to Elko in May. He had asked Kristi to go and stay for the weekend. Christian had sanctioned the trip hoping the two kids would take the relationship to another level. He had counseled Kristi to be more accommodating to a man's needs. What else could he do? He couldn't replace the mother that wasn't there. He was disappointed when Kristina had stayed home. Had Befford pushed too hard? Or was Kristina still holding back? For the first time, he considered the politics that might lie between the two separate from the wishes of their fathers.

"So you're not going to tell me," Christian had finished the salad and was munching on the second plate of fries.

"What Kristi and I talked about? No." Marlyss had yet to finish half her sandwich. "It had nothing to do with you, I'll tell you that much. But beyond that would be a betrayal of her trust. I won't do that. Why don't you just ask her yourself?"

"What makes you think that I haven't?"

Marlyss raised her eyebrows. "Because you don't want her to know that you know. What does your mother say about it?"

"She doesn't want to be in the middle of it. She keeps her opinions to herself, to my detriment, as always."

Marlyss considered the truth behind his words, yet she believed that Anne believed in the good-for-all approach that denied Christian autocratic power over his family. "That's too bad. Kristi could use an ally."

"What do you mean? She's got me, for God's sake. I'm not the enemy."

"But you're the one who's pushing her to marry into the Befford clan. Do you know if she even loves him?"

"What kind of a stupid ass question is that? Of course she does. Always has. She's wanted this since they were kids."

Marlyss was annoyed at his convenient remaking of history. "I know she's always wanted to please you. And this is what you've always wanted. You and Joe. You never considered how the kids might feel..."

"That's not true!"

"Or how your wives might feel about it."

"I knew you'd jump at the chance to bring Mary into it," Christian said with more anger than the subject warranted. "You never did care for her. It kills you that Kristina is going to marry her son, doesn't it?"

"Not at all. In fact, you have it backwards. Mary has always had it out for me," and mine, she added silently. "I stole her prize bull, if you recall."

Christian finished off the last fry. "She doesn't see it that way."

"Look, this isn't about Mary and me—or Mary, or me. It isn't what I want or what you want. Kristi is twenty-one. She's an adult. It's time she makes up her own mind about people—me, you, your mother, Mary, or Si Befford."

"Nobody's telling her who to choose. She made that commitment on her own."

"And now she wants to reconsider it. We need to accept that."

"Is that what she said? That she wants to reconsider the engagement?"

The man's persistence was beginning to wear on her. "I was suggesting that whatever she is doing, we need to support her, not question her motives. I have to tell you, Christian, I firmly believe that these girls—fledglings jumping from the nest—ought to experience the sense of freedom before they commit themselves to a lifetime of responsibility."

"You're talking about me..."

"I'm thinking about both of us—what we didn't do. I've had a lot of time to consider how things might have gone, if I hadn't been so naïve and starry-eyed myself, when we met."

"What are you saying, that I tricked you into marrying me?"

"Why is everything about you?" Marlyss felt the heat rise to her head. She drank the last of her water.

"Damnation!" He thumped his hand on the table." So you told Kristina to go out and experience life before committing to Si Befford?"

"Why are you pushing her into this so quickly? What would it hurt, for either one of them, to postpone things a year or two? Let Si sow his wild oats, as you are so fond of saying. Kristi can gain a broader view of the world. Send her to Europe for the summer. You can afford it."

"Why? Send her away as if she's done something wrong? Besides, she's never indicated a desire to go abroad."

"And she won't ever because you want her to marry Si, the sooner the better."

"I want to see her graduate first. It's good for a wife to be educated."

"She needs to expand more than her intellect. She should be stretching her social circle as well, meeting different people, dating different boys. Getting a handle on men beyond what's she learned in the constricted world of St. Clements and Hawkes Ferry," which, by its very nature, was a Day-Befford world.

"What do you mean date other boys? Who? Nobody's more suitable for her, for what she brings to a marriage than a Befford. And Si's the only one qualified, being that he's male. You do agree that she should be looking at males, I hope." A mean edge crept into his voice.

Marlyss scowled at him. She didn't want Kristi to be looking at anyone. She was just emerging from that tightly wound cocoon of his control. And he knew it.

Christian signaled the waitress, who came hurrying back with fresh coffee. "What do you have for dessert? Any pies?" he asked her.

Marlyss accepted a refill, but declined the pie.

Christian was served a generous slice of blackberry with a mountain of vanilla ice cream. He immediately set about conquering it as he privately considered the answer to his question. Who would be more suitable to Kristina? God knows that he saw the flaws in Si's behavior.

He credited it to Mary's sparing the rod and Joe's inability to control either his wife or his son. The boy learned his behaviors from spending too much time in the bunkhouse and too little time mingling with town folks and business associates. Joe had long since given up on Si's training as a maitre d' in the restaurant, an education Joe thought necessary for Si to run the business some day. Still, Si might learn something yet.

After a long silence, Marlyss said, "Too bad about that position she wanted—I wonder about that English teacher of hers."

Aroused from his thoughts, Christian snapped, "What's he got to do with anything?"

"She applied to be his assistant."

"I didn't know that." A guarded jealousy entered his voice. "Did Kristina tell you that?"

"Actually Birdie mentioned it." She negotiated the waters of his need to control everything about their daughter. "I think Kristi would have preferred Birdie keep it to herself. She was embarrassed by the fact that he had turned her down. He had someone else for the job. I was just thinking that some other teacher might need…"

"Geoff Meyer is replacing Leif Sanders. He retired this year, did you know that?"

"Dear Leif. Surely he's too young…no, I guess he's not." The science teacher had been a favorite of hers, one who stood out in that crowd of academics for his authentic take on life, and his kindness. Then remembering her conversation with Kristi, commented, "Geoff Meyer, my, my."

Christian was calculating some solution in his head. "He'll be needing someone to assist him, I suspect. Maybe she has a chance there."

"Do you still see Dove?"

"His mother? Not often. Our paths don't cross so much these days. Occasional stock sale or feed auction is all."

"I thought you were an item," she smiled softly.

"She's not my type." His answer was gruffer than she expected.

"Pity. You're so well suited for each other—with your mutual interest in cattle herds and stock horses. You could use the distraction."

"From what?" Christian was annoyed at her probing into his life. He would reveal things in his own time, and not be teased out of them. "There's something else I want to tell you. I've been seeing a lot of Sofia Avila."

"Oh?" Marlyss thought of the bright exchange student from South America. She knew the girl, but not the woman who had returned to St. Clements the year Marlyss left Hawkes Ferry.

"I'm planning on marrying her."

"Does she know this?"

"Don't be so flippant. We've talked about it. But I don't want to steal the thunder from Kristi's plans. We'll wait until after their wedding."

"Ah. Now I see why Kristi's behavior is causing a problem. Maybe you should tie the knot with Sofia before you make plans for Kristi's wedding."

Christian shook his head. "Sofia's not ready yet."

"Not ready to give you that son?"

The remark was intended as a light tease, but Christian was livid. "Don't be cruel, Marlyss, it doesn't suit you. You've grown bitchier by the year, since you ran out on us."

"You kicked me out," she said evenly, as she took a sip of coffee.

Christian found the woman infuriating. "You killed my son," he sneered in a hostile whisper.

"You don't know that. I don't know that." Marlyss corrected. "It was a sexless speck, Christian. A cell. A zygote. Let it go and be happy for Sofia's desire to give you a son."

Her words were as unfeeling as they were inaccurate. He had no such agreement with Sofia, but he would die before admitting that to her. He virtually spit out retort, "You violated the sanctity of life—defied the will of God."

"God's will?" she said with more vigor than intended. "It was your will, Christian, not God's—and certainly not mine."

His pontification was extraordinary considering how he had forced himself on her. She was unprotected, never suspecting that she had to guard against the man she loved and trusted most. Yet in his mind, the marriage contract gave him rights over her body. Well, it didn't. And she proved him wrong, with her autonomous decision to abort the responsibility that she had already told him she didn't want.

"We're done here," she said, collecting her purse and standing up.

As Christian flagged the waitress, she started to walk away.

"Just a minute," he said, his voice easing as they turned out to the world. He left two twenties on the table and followed her out to her car.

Marlyss climbed into the car and started it up. The motor choked and spit before catching. She rolled down the window.

"You ought to get yourself better transport. Take care of yourself a little instead of worrying about how everyone else's life is going."

"Talk to your daughter, Christian. Maybe you'll learn something about her." She backed out of the parking spot then paused and added, "Maybe you'll learn something about love, too, and avoid repeating mistakes of the past."

He watched as the beat up Impala lugged onto the road and disappeared into the desert. His mistakes of the past? They were all hers, with the possible exception of marrying a beauty queen with a pretty face and no family or fortune to speak of. Back then she was full of love and laughter and compassion. She'd grown tough and cold in this new life of hers. He walked back to his own vehicle.

There was a time when he could depend on the softness of her comfort and her enduring love, as she depended on his strength and his money. Didn't have a need for any of it now, apparently. She acted as though she were detached from the effects of the world, responsible only to herself and for herself.

What about Kristina?

Well, he could take care of his own and leave her mother to heaven.

The hot afternoon sun beat down on Kristi as she filled the water trough. After a full grooming session, the mustang deserved the sweet grasses and alfalfa patch in the front pasture which Father had planted some years ago to test a new variety of feed. Nikki had taken to her grooming with pleasure, standing free in the shaded yard of the stables, her reins drooping to the ground, shaking her head with delight as the brushes worked down her haunches. Kristi let the horse to pasture when she was done and watched her take delight in the freedom as she raced around the two-acre plot.

Feeling grubby with sweat along the rim of her hat, Kristi returned to the cool shade of the stable yard. She removed the heavy hat, ready to tackle her biggest obstacle of the day, grooming the bay gelding. She had been working the bay all summer, as her father had advised. She hoped to surprise Si, and astonish his mother, in asserting full command of the horse by the time of their engagement party later in the month. The first action she had taken to establish the bay as her own was to toss out that fancy greenhorn name, Common Dancer, and call him Dandy. It was similar enough, although it evoked an attitude, like those greenhorns in pulp novels who came out west to lord it over common folk with their blue blood and highbrow manners. And just like those characters, Dandy couldn't hold a candle to the feral-born Nikki, whose instincts of the open west favored her endurance of the harsh, arid climate.

Earlier in the day, Kristi had tried to socialize the bay by letting him loose in the yard while she was tending to Nikki. He had pressed an assault of annoying passes to distract the mustang, causing her to twitch and turn nervously. Kristi finally tied him to a rail of the corral, on the other side of the yard. Now, with Nikki in the pasture, she moved the bay back to the grooming station, securing his rein to the rail—there was no letting him stay free to do as he pleased. With a clear view of Nikki running free, Kristi thought he might be distracted enough to yield to a quick grooming.

Instead, he whinnied in protest at his imprisonment. In a show of power, the horse nudged her arm, pushing her hand away, then pressed his flank against the fence to prevent her from brushing him. He started a campaign of whinnying, making such a ruckus in the yard that the foreman came to check up on them. As soon as the bay spotted John, he stopped his antics in anticipation that the man was going to take charge.

Kristi waved John off. "No. You're going to have to put up with me, you old bugger." She had to admit that she'd made few gains over the past four months. She had yet to take him up the trail or over the western rangeland. As he fought against the grooming, she considered being free of him altogether.

What she wanted to do was send him packing back to Befford Ranch. Even if Mary didn't want the horse, one of the cowhands would surely appreciate him with his instinct for cutting and driving stock. And the horse would pay more heed to the heavy-hand of a wrangler on his back. But returning Si's gift to his father's ranch would add tons to the mountain of speculation already circulating in the Befford clan about her intentions, adding to the hullabaloo already created by her postponing their engagement. The truth was, she didn't want a summer engagement party. She had always envisioned a gala event at Christmas, warm and romantic and full of the love of the season. What she didn't want was to louse up the rest of her summer, buried in planning that was aimed at wooing Si's mother any more than she wanted to be locked in the stable yard trying to win the respect of his resistant mount.

The last days of summer needed to be carefree and feckless, especially these days in which she was facing the last summer of youth, the final days of her freedom. Not that she had ever been free, exactly. Yet, with Si whisked off to New England by his family, she was getting exactly what she had wanted all along. The thought pleased her.

The antsy bay took advantage of her distracted mind to scuttle away from her. Stopped by the fence, he shuffled his back feet and scraped her boot, nearly knocking her over. Kristi steadied herself and approached his reins from the left. She moved him back to the corral, where she could work on his other flank, away from the tease of Nikki romping free in the pasture.

Kristi's biggest problem with a summer engagement was devoting the full month of August to Mary Befford, who had insisted on—and won—Father's blessing to oversee the project. She had certainly usurped Grandmother's role, yet Kristi saw no way to recover the situation. Grandmother, who had reluctantly agreed to go along with this plan, advised her that asking Mary to forfeit the role would set a tone between Kristi and Mary that would reverberate into disharmonies across the years. Apparently, Grandmother had not heard the discord that Mary had struck against Marlyss years before.

The horse seemed to settle as Kristi moved the brush across his back and down the haunches. Kristi debated on whether to let the bay loose with Nikki in the pasture when they were done. He hadn't deserved the treat, but was she being cruel to play favorites? What kind of a parent would she be? Sibling rivalry was a subject she knew little about. Si had rarely shared anything with his sisters. Maybe that was to be expected, given the difference between boys and girls growing up.

Still, he had difficulty sharing with her as well, which wouldn't be expected between a man and a woman who claimed to be in love. She mused on how Mary rated in the fair parent arena—and Joe, for that matter. Both of them favored Si above either of the girls, he was their heir apparent. Elena might be moving up the rank, though, engagement wise. Kristi smiled.

Si didn't seem any too concerned with her suggestion to delay. In fact, he took some pleasure in his role as the offended party, letting everyone know it was her idea to delay the event. It didn't seem to cost his family much grief, either. Within a week, Mary had whisked the whole family off to New England for an extended stay at the Delaney estate on Long Island.

Elena had let Kristi know that it was to be the idyllic setting for her own wedding in two years, when Ross was established in his law practice. Letting her thoughts flow with the ease of the brush, Kristi considered how elegant the wedding would be at such a place, with plants climbing along white trellises, and white gowns billowing under green arbors. Christmas would be the perfect time for them to announce the engagement, giving eighteen months to plan the complicated affair.

It struck her now, for the first time, that the August date had been driven by Mary's desire to reserve the Christmas season for Elena's announcement. Here she was, accommodating them all, to her own disadvantage. Pleasing others big time, Birdie's voice intruded. Kristi frowned. Yes, she was obliging, trying to fit in with the Beffords, to mollify their matron. The past few months, though, had altered her willingness to play the inoffensive future daughter-in-law.

Stepping back to assess her grooming job, Kristi was dismayed to see the tail still matted in spots, and the mane in need of more primping. But she'd had enough of the head tossings and attempted nips. She was done with the tail swatting and kowtowing to Befford blue-blood pretensions. When she loosened the reins, the horse reared up in protest of her control. She yanked on the reins pulling him back. "Stop that!"

The horse settled immediately. For once she had command of him.

"That horse needs to be taught some manners," a familiar voice called from the gate.

Kristi's heart leapt. She whirled around to find Geoff Meyer strolling toward her. She wanted to say the horse preferred men, but couldn't find her voice. Lost and found was all she could muster up in her mind.

He approached the bay from the left, and slapped his rump. The horse gave him an easy greeting. "Aren't you going to say hi?" Geoff asked her, smiling.

Shock mixed with memory, pleasure with pain of rejection, her senses electrified and robbed her of all rational thought. Kristi tried to conjure up appropriate civilities—but here she was, looking like a stable boy, her clothes filthy, stringy hair clinging to her sweating forehead and neck.

She pulled back, stunned. "Yes. Hello... Welcome back. You're here for..."

He swooped down and picked her up, kissing her with an eagerness that transcended time. She responded in like, with the hunger and desire of four lost years.

Fourteen

How long Truitt had stood at that railing, he did not know. The tumultuous force of the falls thundered into a basin half-hidden in rising mist that was washing over him, flooding him with a dreadful awe, overwhelming him with a power much greater than man. Not a whole man. Not a man at all—but a small boy holding fast to her hand, them rushing together in the black night under the elevated tracks of the city. He had been scared—of the dark, of the screeching metal above them, the chaotic crowds rushing past. The man at the falls was scared too, of something darker and deeper and more enduring.

Memory bit into the chill wind of his heart—his refusal to yield the only thing she desired from him—his love. A love he hoarded secretly for the Lost Mother and Father, the worthy parents she had etched from her pain, her disgrace, an idea of parent a boy could be proud of, could look up to. That boy—no orphan at all, but the bastard child of a seducer who took his own stepdaughter at seventeen. The shame, her shame, our shame.

His tears mixed with the mist. The unexpressed sob took flight.

"Mommy, what's wrong with that man?" A small voice stood close.

Heels scuttled by. "Hurry along, dear."

"But he's crying..." the voice faded.

There was no dignity left to help him rise to his full authority, to claim his victory, scholar, professor...Gone, all gone, in the blackest hour of his night.

He drove westward toward his Avalon, his eternal place of peace, outrunning the endless days of pages and papers and books never written. They held no meaning without her at home, without her love to harbor him, to celebrate his success...he hadn't even told her! Not on the phone, there's plenty of time. Fool, fool, fool.

He drove on until the explanations and excuses, the rationalizations and reasonings played over and over, always ending with blame, until the truth of his loss exhausted him. Then he pulled off the road to sleep. So the days passed, driving hard until he was spent, pulling off on deserted waysides, always avoiding the interstate and its link to the cities with their crowds of strangers.

Grief rose again with memory and drained his mind leaving him numb and defeated. He held onto her hand so tight—as they scurried along under the elevated trains rushing toward home—scared of the dark and darkness, the chaos and danger. Vulnerable. The city was too big, and not green at all. Auntie, Auntie are we all done? Can we go home now?

And the realization would descend upon him. Am I all alone now, Auntie/Mother? He cried without shame for all that was lost. The blackness of the night settled over his thoughts, so he drove again into the night, wanting to end the relentless memory, the pain, the roiling waters still crashing over him, still crushing, obliterating time and space and distance, all thought of her, of them.

And at the end of everything, when he could no longer distinguish hour or day or place, he stopped in front of a small chapel along the road, a wayside, where something rose up in him, strange and unfamiliar. A small ember glowed, ancient and forgotten, a memory long past, and with it, he heard her voice. Take my hand, Emery. It's all right now. You're safe.

Still in the car, Truitt fell into a deep, untroubled sleep.

Truitt awoke, cramped and stifled by the heat of a midday sun beating down on the car. The first thing he saw was the small white chapel in the midst of open prairie and the sign over the door, Wayfarer's Chapel. The second thing he saw was a grizzled beard that flowed from a weather beaten face, and curious eyes peering into the passenger window.

"Morning," it said.

Truitt was startled. He unfolded his body from the car and stretched to his full height. The stranger was five-ten to Truitt's six-one, looking like the half-starved hermits who lived in the mountain caves around the abbey at St. Amadour. He wore jeans with a tee-shirt that was stamped with a large peace sign, and around his neck he bandied a simple cross worked in leather, hung on a leather thong.

Truitt nodded a greeting, then walked around the back of the chapel to relieve himself. When he returned, the man stood in the same spot, with a large military duffle bag at his feet. Truitt wondered how long he had been sleeping in his car, and how long this fellow had waited for him to waken.

"Where're you headed?" The stranger asked, in a soft voice, his eyes scouring the prairie, which ran to the horizon in all directions. He had a kindly face and a humble manner like Leif Sanders, but Truitt saw that he was not nearly as old as the geologist.

Truitt had no idea where they were at the moment, and even less of an idea of where he had been headed. He certainly had no plan. Running away was the honest answer, but caution prevailed. The question implied a request that Truitt would deny, not being one to risk picking up strangers on the road. Yet considering the hard penitence of the past few days, the hours and days of playing tedious reruns without relief, the risk to his person was of little consequence compared to the dangers he faced from solitude.

"Just traveling. See the country a bit. Going westward, mostly."

"Funny to find this place, just traveling. Near a hundred miles to the interstate." The stranger seemed to be weighing his own risks. He looked toward the chapel. "Peaceful enough here, though."

Truitt didn't recall seeing anyone around the night before. "You been here long?"

"Came in last night. Didn't want to bother you. Actually, I was hoping you'd be sacked out till daybreak so's I could catch some shut-eye myself." He looked up at the sun which held near its zenith. "Though, I started wondering whether you was alive, or not."

"Good God!" Truitt said, surprised to hear his darkest thoughts expressed.

"Mind if I haul with you a bit?"

"Where are you going?" Truitt asked.

"Wherever road and opportunity lead. West works, for now."

Truitt popped open the car doors. "Do you know where we are?"

"Sure. And if you like these back roads, then I'm you're man."

"You can put the duffle in the backseat."

The stranger pulled two apples from his sack before tossing it in the back. "Figured you're hungry, like me."

Truitt was grateful. As they started down the road, he devoured it down to the core, seed and all, a risk he had never dared before.

They drove in companionable silence until the apples were eaten. As the sound of the tires strummed unevenly along the rough road top, the stranger chatted amiably about the bounty of the land that surrounded them.

"A lot of people don't like it here, flat and monotonous they say. But every bit of this country, America delivers. You know, like the words we learnt as kids, from sea to shining sea." He stayed with that thought a long while before adding, "You ever see a shining sea?"

Truitt admitted that he hadn't. The seas of his youth where stormy or hazy and always distant. And when he crossed the Atlantic on his way to Europe, it was a black mirror out someone else's window. The sea was not something that spoke to him, in a personal way.

The stranger carried on. "Sometimes the sea shines so bright and long and relentlessly that you want to roll over with it, wave upon wave, dive into it, become part of it."

The sentiment startled Truitt, who was pulled back to the sensation at the railing, the raw power of water spilling over the falls, feeling their draw, the impulse to jump into them. He glanced at the man beside him who was gazing out the passenger window.

He hummed quietly as the car rolled through a prairie teeming with wild grasses, occasionally dotted with tracts of agriculture, grains and bushy green plants. Large steel silos cut the horizon, were flanked by open rail cars waiting.

"Ever see anything so beautiful as the prairie stretching under these spacious skies?"

Truitt could have argued with the man, but kept his own counsel. Dipping and swelling like a ship, the car traveled the road through wind-swept grasses.

"Amber waves of grain," the stranger said, then sang a little. "Purple mountains majesty.... You ever see a purple mountain, Brother?"

"Can't say as I have," Truitt said. Green, brown and hazy were the three colors he associated with mountains.

"Alaska Range in summertime, rose and violet and purple, especially at the solstice when the sun nods at dusk then winks at dawn. Most beautiful sight I ever saw."

"You're from Alaska, then?"

"Nah. Took a freighter there once, from Seattle. You could say my work took me there—Look waves of grain." He pointed at the landscape filling both sides of the road, the crops were caught in a gentle wind, fences now lining the road. "Dakota. Bread basket to the world. Kind of a cliché, ain't it? Like the ocean, I guess, the Spirit moves through the grasses—as it moves the human heart."

"What is it you do, exactly?" Truitt was growing restless with the inane chatter.

"You could say I minister to lost souls."

"So where are you headed now?"

"I travel where the Spirit moves me."

Truitt wondered how the spirits met his daily needs.

"How about you? What's your calling?"

The question caught Truitt off guard. It was the first time he had thought of school in weeks. Why was he still moving west? He should be back in Delaware preparing to return to Idaho. A panic gripped him. "What's the date today?"

"Don't rightly know," the stranger answered, then continued humming.

Niagara was how long ago—four, five days? The trail from New York to Virginia to Washington was blurred in his mind like a bad dream. How long had he been gone?

The stranger had stopped humming, and regarded Truitt with cool eyes. Responding to the change in Truitt's mood, he said, "You miss something? Or, are you like the White Rabbit, perennially late for someone else's gig?"

Truitt felt an impulse to open up. He heard her again. *You're safe now, Emery.* Yet caution prevailed. "I just need to know the date. Hope it's not August already. I have a commitment mid-month."

"Don't know, sorry." The stranger said, pondering his words for a few minutes. "Commitments are good, though—when they're true. Shows a connection to life I hadn't pegged you for. Probably near town."

"Probably? You don't know."

"Can't rightly say. Stay away from towns myself, if I can."

"You're joking. How do you eat?" Truitt was growing annoyed with the man's lack of responsibility. "Where do you sleep?"

"God's good to me, I'll say that. The earth is my bed, the land serves up its bounty, if you know how to reap it."

"You do this travel thing hand to mouth? No funding at all? No family paying you to stay away?"

The stranger turned cold eyes on Truitt, who had glanced over at him. Truitt felt a shiver move up his spine. With the forked beard and cold eyes, he could be the devil incarnate. Was he after Truitt's sorry soul? Ridiculous, he chided himself.

"Didn't say that, did I?" The man turned his attention back to the road. "But I'll tell you a truth. Wandering's to atone for my sins."

"How's that?"

"Jesus said turn the other cheek, Brother. But I obeyed The Man instead. Killed for it. Just doing my duty, he said. But God forgive me, I killed for it, and now I atone for Him, one soul at a time."

Truitt was growing anxious, traveling down the endless road. He had a weird feeling about the stranger. Was he going to be killed in the middle of nowhere, a limbo at the edge of the earth?

"Where are we?" He asked again, more urgently.

"There's a crossroad in another mile or two. Takes us to a gas station and a diner."

It was less than a mile, and as he turned, Truitt spotted the water tower—a mirage rising from the heated pavement—long before the rooftops of the small settlement came into view. The gas station was a two-pump service bay sitting in front of a general store. While Truitt filled the car with gas, the stranger headed across the road toward a small store front with a red neon sign that said Diner. He left his duffle in the back, which irritated Truitt. Inside the store, Truitt paid for the gas and bought food enough to cover several more days on the road, mostly juices and packages of crackers and granola. He thought about the stranger.

From the clerk, he discovered that it was already the eighth of August, and Wheatville was in North Dakota, more west than east. No, they didn't have any maps, sold out. In answer to his further questions, she was less certain, but her brother told him that Butte was a day's drive west, and Des Moines a day's drive east.

Stowing the bag of food into his trunk, Truitt reasoned that he did not have time to return to Delaware now. In another week, he needed to be sitting in the faculty dining hall, attending Mudd's kick-off staff meeting. He moved the car to a parking space in front of the diner and went in. The stranger was seated at a table near the rear of the place, which was little more than a galley with several small tables lining the wall opposite the counter seating.

"I ordered the meatloaf. Cook assures me it's as good as the last time. Hope you like it too." He smiled, shoving a ten dollar bill across the table. "Gas money. Just so's you know, I can. And I thank-you, Brother."

Truitt felt better after eating a solid meal. The meat loaf was satisfying, and the stranger had paid for that too. They returned to the main road and continued west until the Missouri River blocked further progress and they were obliged to turn north toward the interstate, which they followed west into Montana. Once he had a handle on where they were, Truitt felt better about his passenger too.

"You still taking your time or answering to the Man now?"

"I've got time still." Truitt had no desire to rush back to school ahead of his report date.

"Lots of pretty scenery, if we stay on the Interstate. The Yellowstone's mighty scenic all the way up to its source. We'll be near the mountains by nightfall."

There would be mountains enough for him in Hawkes Ferry. "Let's stick to the back roads."

The stranger directed Truitt into the heart of Montana's big sky country. The green edge of the river disappeared into a prairie land that was half desert, hot and arid, with sparse vegetation. Where the wind caught the loose soil, it whirled up dust devils. The stranger talked about ancient sea beds and dinosaurs mixed with tales of early settlers running away from marauding Indians.

It was a hellish land in some ways, Truitt agreed.

Then the stranger fell silent for a good while, resting his head on the back of the seat. His eyes closed, and soon he was asleep.

For the first time, Truitt thought about school, his lack of preparedness for the new semester. He had thought of nothing else for weeks but the past and his loss. He hadn't thought of school since he left it in June. The idea unnerved him. He couldn't recall the state in which he had left things, what had been prepared—probably nothing. What he had brought home for the summer sat in his valise in the trunk of the car. Trying to recall the unfinished work on his desk conjured up the image of his den, that night Bill called and the chaos that ensued, catapulting him to the mortuary, the coffin with her frail body lying in repose. The grief tumbled down on him once again.

"You got to let that go, Brother," the stranger said quietly with his eyes still closed. "The burden you carry. Got to let others in, share your load. The heart yearns for the glory of God, for His love."

"What do you know about God's glory?" Truitt asked, taking offense at the intrusion. "I thought you sold out to The Man, you said. Who is that, anyhow?"

The stranger nodded. "I've seen the Devil. Stared him down. Seen my own reflection in his eyes, my own black heart."

Truitt felt the cold eyes brush across him. He shivered. The man might have traded his soul, Truitt thought, if he believed in such things.

"That old devil rises up when you turn your eye from Him, your Source and Redeemer...."

"Where is it you're going, then?" Truitt cut him off, being in no mood for a sermon from a satanic pastor.

"As far as I can with you."

It was a non-answer, like all the others. "West, you mean? I'm going as far as Boise, then I head south."

"Suits me fine."

Late in the afternoon they had reached a land of grassy knolls and streamlets, cattle ponds and grazing lands. Truitt guessed they were still a few hours from Butte, although he had never traveled in this region before. As dusk deepened, the stranger suggested they camp out under the sky. He guided Truitt toward a bluff that overlooked a river, then down a dirt road which led to the bank below. They settled near a copse of trees. The stranger built a campfire, taking care to clear all the brush and surround the pit with river rock. Truitt offered up dinner from the stash he had purchased earlier, to which the stranger added two apples from his sack.

The night sky was alive with stars and, like Sanders, the stranger seemed to know them all. Truitt felt the danger lurking all around the open camp with the howling of coyotes and the rooting of wild critters in the dry brush around them. Truitt worried about wolves and bears, although he'd heard that they had been wiped out in the region, years before. When he voiced his concerns, the stranger just laughed. When the stranger unrolled a blanket to bed for the night, Truitt retreated to the car.

The stranger was already up by the break of day. He was sitting on a rock, eating another apple when Truitt woke. After tending to his needs, Truitt broke out the granola bars and juice. They ate in silence and cleaned the camp before heading out.

On the road again, Truitt was surprised to find out that in ten miles they were already back at the interstate. He would have liked more of the back roads, but was now willing to surrender to civilization and slough off his traveling companion. In retrospect, Truitt considered that aside from a few weird moments, and the intense nature of the man's eyes, he hadn't regretted giving him a ride, but he was growing weary of the inane chatter.

At the interstate, the stranger had a different idea. "If your goal is south to Idaho or Utah..."

Truitt assured him it was.

"Then there's a shorter way to our purpose, if you still like the back roads."

"I thought you were going west?"

"And so I am. But we're here, aren't we? And I'll be hauling off shortly. That way," he pointed down a county road.

The road trekked across the foothills, flanking a stream and then crossing it, traversing canyons and cresting ridges, then sloping down again into grazing lands. At an unmarked crossroad, the stranger told Truitt to turn. The county road had been in poor repair, but at least the ride was smooth. This road was pocked with the ruts of many winters, untended except for an occasional pothole that was filled with gravel.

"Are you sure this connects to a southerly route?" Truitt asked.

"Yep. You got to trust in the spirit that guides, Brother."

The azure sky was clear and bright when they had set out, but the trail through the foothills brought them to a different climate. Large black thunderheads were accumulating over the ridge ahead of them, dragging rain squalls in their wake. A sense of foreboding was building in Truitt. Why had he trusted the stranger to lead him on the unfamiliar path?

After crossing a stream via a rough wooden bridge, the blacktop gave way to gravel, forcing Truitt to slow down the car.

"County don't maintain this leg of the road. No sense in it. Keep going—blacktop's ahead."

The road narrowed ahead of them cutting a cleft through the ridge. It appeared to be blocked.

"What the heck is that?" Truitt asked, but as they drew close, he could distinguish the mounted cowboys from moving cattle. The animals were stirred up by the building storm, filling the air with anxious moans and the evasive stench of a stockyard. The cowboys worked to herd them up the road.

Truitt had come to a standstill.

"Just press on," the stranger advised, "They're used to it."

What? Was he an expert cowboy now? "I don't want to hit one." Truitt paced the rear of the herd.

"Got to work your way through," the stranger said. "They expect it."

The cowboys paid little attention to the car. But as Truitt inched forward in fits and starts, he could sense the irritation to cattle and man alike. He was jittery himself. Each jolt of the car unnerved the animals huddled around it. They complained loudly, eyes rising full of fear, snouts pressing against haunches, the cowboys urging the herd forward.

A bolt of lightning flashed across the ridge above them setting a panic the cowboys worked to contain. In a minute the thunder roared, and the static air was saturated by the downpour.

A cowboy near them loomed like the devil, whistled sharply and shouted, "Get that damned car out of the way!"

"I don't want to hit one!" Truitt shouted back. His hands were frozen to the wheel, every muscle in his arms and shoulders awake to the task of pressing forward through the herd of moving animals.

"Be one with them, Son, part of the herd." The stranger spoke softly. "Urge your way through."

All Truitt could think of was the narrowness of the opening through which they all squeezed, the storm, and the knowledge of flash floods that rolled through canyons sweeping cattle and cars and humans away.

"You've got to let go, Brother. Connect to the spirit. You're a steer now. Open your heart and embrace the herd."

As the stranger spoke, Truitt felt himself open up to the rhythm and flow of the moving animals, the gees and clicks of the cowboys who seemed now to work him through the herd. In a minute, he was ahead of the herd and free. As the road forked, he followed the stranger's lead, up the slope and out of the canyon.

At the top of the ridge, the road forked again, gravel top in both directions, east and south. The stranger said, "You can let me off here."

Truitt's heart was still pounding. All he could see was hills and rangeland all around them with a range of mountains in the far distance. He spotted no structure or landmark where the stranger might be headed. The stranger had already opened the door and was hauling out his knapsack and duffel bag from behind his seat.

"Where in God's green earth are we?" Truitt said in exasperation. He didn't want to be dumped in the middle of nowhere.

"God isn't out there somewhere, Son. He's in here—" the stranger thumbed his chest. "In our hearts. We need to open ourselves up to Him, or we perish. She knew this. God would not abandon her. We are all connected. We are all a reflection of His Glory."

"Wait." Truitt demanded. "Where are you going?"

"Trust in God, Brother. He'll lead you to salvation straight down that road." He pointed east.

"I want to go south. What's that way?" Truitt asked of the other road.

"My next mission."

"Why wouldn't I take that road, then and take you a bit further?"

"Blacktop's that way," he pointed east again, "In nine-ten mile. God Bless, Brother, and thanks for helping me."

Truitt reluctantly followed the man's directions, not sure if the voice he listened to belonged to God or the devil.

Fifteen

Kristi shed the blue shirt and denim jeans in favor of the frilly pink rodeo shirt and complementary brown jeans. She was being silly, really. It was only an afternoon's ride, no more meaning than if she were meeting Birdie up at Jake's place. But it wasn't Birdie but Geoff who would be in the stable at ten waiting to saddle up. She pulled her hair back into a low pony tail, to accommodate the wide brim of her hat.

Geoff had wanted to ride the trail out to Jake's, but Kristi needed to avoid that trail with him, for a while at least, given it's previous association with their past relationship. She decided they'd take the trail down the bluff around the back of the school and over to Fish Camp. She had asked Tessa to pack a lunch at breakfast. That's when the housekeeper had weighed in on the shirt and jeans as "not soft enough for the occasion," in her I'm-not-saying-a-thing voice.

Kristi reluctantly ascended the stairs to change. It was only a ride. The jeans would be far more practical than anything frilly—and the shirt much cooler in a midday sun. The ride would leave her as sweaty and grimy as she was in the stable yard grooming the horses. Why should she care about dressing up, anyhow? Her future belonged to

Si now, and there was no room for further complication on that end. A cloud of doubt suddenly shadowed her anticipation of spending the afternoon with Geoff.

How lucky she was, that Si was safely stowed, for the moment, at the Delaney estate on Long Island. Not that she would hide Geoff's attentions from Si. It was Si's presence, rather, that she feared would muddy the renewal of an acquaintance with Geoff. Si would make things so much more complicated than they needed to be. Just exactly why, she dared not pursue. Yet, it was vital to find her bearings on the territory of her relationship with Geoff, before adding Si to the mixture.

On learning that Geoff was in town, Father had asked him to dinner straight away. Grandmother was gone, but Sofia made four at the table. Geoff had regaled them with stories about backpacking in the Sierra Nevada Mountains of California—which, he assured them, was not so much a range of individual mountains like the Rockies, but a single slab of granite that ran in jagged peaks north to south, with an enormous pie-shaped wedge that formed the Yosemite. He talked of rock hunting in Arizona and New Mexico and meeting up with the Navajos and Zuni that Jake Redtree traded with.

He talked about earth and rocks and mantle and plates and earthquakes, and so many topics that Kristi could hardly keep up. Father seemed to appreciate the conversation and Sofia listened with attention, asking questions to spur him on. Kristi wished she had something clever to ask about volcanoes, just to show she was interested in his passion. Mostly, though, she was interested in hearing the sound of his voice and the optimism with which he looked at life and the future. What would it be like to share a future with him? She was ashamed of the thought.

Sofia had introduced the topic of Women's Issues, and then elicited from Geoff some of his experiences on the coast. He had stories, too, about the instigation of programs and courses at Berkeley for "the ladies." He talked about bonfires and bra burnings, and women who hated men, but admitted that many of his female students were feminine enough to make pleasant company on field trips, but could wield their own picks and shovels in the dirt.

It was at dinner that Christian had given Geoff an open invitation to the stables. Geoff called the day before to set up a time with Kristi. Luckily she had scheduled her work session with Sofia for the next afternoon and would be free for Geoff today. She wondered, though, if Geoff intended to use the stables only at her disposal. That would be a problem when Si returned to town.

Without saying a word, Kristi led them out the front pastures to the trail along the bluff. She lured Geoff with promises of wildlife and a refreshing ride along the rim of the canyon. He grinned but said nothing.

Over the river canyon, a hawk soared on the updrafts seeming to glide upstream against the current. Antelope grazed on the far rim, and the horses moved steadily along the trail until the grazing lands opened up beyond the school sports fields. Geoff dismounted to open the gate into the grazing land. They galloped across the open land until Geoff came to rest in the fields behind the staff bungalows known as bachelor's row.

"Want to check out my digs?" He asked Kristi, presenting a key.

Kristi wondered what he was up to, but agreed. Geoff hobbled the horses near the bungalow and stretched the barbed wire fence allowing Kristi through first. She caught sight of Professor Truitt's bungalow next door. His little car was still in the carport behind the house wearing the dust of summer. He hadn't returned yet. She felt discouraged, turning her attention back to Geoff.

He opened the front door with some ceremony as he welcomed her inside. As with all the faculty housing, it was modest but fully furnished. But the place was otherwise empty.

"You haven't moved in yet," Kristi said.

"Plan on it this weekend. Wanted to eke out the last days of freedom before I hunker down to responsibility." He laughed. Then took her on the grand tour.

"Sitting room or salon, or whatever you want to call it. Small den. Quaint. Kitchen, bathroom." He jiggled the toilet and flushed it. "Works. That's a good sign. And Ah! The bedroom."

He glanced at her. Kristi understood that he was testing her reaction. She gave him none.

"Looks like you have a job ahead of you." She entered the room and checked the closet for linens. "Sheets are in here. Place smells like pine cleaner—clean and fresh."

"Maybe I could get you to help me move in? There's a dinner in it for you."

"Who's fixing it?"

"The Steakhouse."

"Hmm." She thought about Truitt's place next door. If she were helping Geoff move in next week, she would have easy access to the professor to pursue her goal of nailing that TA position. Earlier in the summer, she had met Tad Martin at the dry goods store. From him, she had learned that he had been offered the job, but had turned it down. In addition, she had discovered from the student employment office that Professor Truitt had yet to hire anyone for the position.

"It could be done." She smiled at him and headed out the door to the horses.

They rode across the grazing lands that filled the canyon between town and the river. At Fish Camp, they watered the horses, surveying the old ferry crossing which was marked on the other side of the river by a rutted road that led to what was now the upper reaches of the wilderness area.

Upstream a gravel road led to more grazing lands. They crossed the steppe and headed back toward town. Kristi and Birdie had followed the progress of a giant nest in the craw of a half-dead dogwood in a deserted pasture of sweet grass, whose fences had long given up to the ravages of weather and wildlife. In May, they had caught sight of four chicks, ferruginous hawks. The parents kept close by, ready to attack intruders, and the girls knew to keep their distance.

By late July, the nest was empty with the hawks hanging close by in the tops of surrounding cottonwoods that lined the creek bed. And now, as she brought Geoff to see them, the nest was empty with no hawks to be seen. White tail deer lay in the grass under the shade of the trees, watching them carefully. Suddenly two grouse flushed up out of the grass and moved away from the horses' advance.

They stopped for lunch at the way station. The dilapidated buildings, especially the barn and stable, provided ample shade from the midday sun. Geoff hobbled the horses while Kristi set out a blanket and cloth in the grass and pulled sandwiches and fruit from the saddle bag. They had filled their canteens at the river.

Geoff stretched on the ground, leaning his head on his arm, and watched Kristi finish her peach. She carefully packed the trash back into the bag, and started to get up. He grabbed her arm and pulled her down on him. She didn't object, but gave in to the heady lure of his kisses, answering back until her body was warm with desire.

She sat up. "We've got to stop this. You are so devilishly charming."

"Then why stop?" He pulled her back down, she willingly returned to his side, putting a slight gap between their bodies.

"You were a Greek god to me back then. I was so young."

"Yeah." He gently rocked the toe of her boot with his foot. "I was crazy about you too. We were both so...."

"I was seventeen. You told me I was dangerous then. Do you remember?"

"Did I?" The rocking stopped, and he leaned toward her, his head shading hers from the sun.

She guessed he was trying to read her face. Probably trying to assess how naïve she still might be. He must have decided she wasn't, for he turned to lie on his back and read the sky instead. "I hope you didn't say anything to your father."

"Of course not. I was a good little girl. You were counting on that."

"It wasn't like that at all. You were—are very, very attractive. Do you know that? Say, you don't think I was using you?"

"You never called after that, or wrote. I never heard from you again. I don't know what I thought."

He rolled over and kissed her again, long and tenderly in a way that made her wish the sky would go on forever, and Long Island would sink into the sea.

"Kristi, I am so sorry. Maybe things can be different now."

Kristi could not wipe the sweet memory of Geoff's kisses from her mind, try as she may. They hummed through her with a melodious timbre that brought a lightness to her day and filled her with anticipation of seeing him again. In Sofia's office, as she typed up the book lists, she could not help but wonder what Geoff's take on the list of women writers would be. He seemed to disdain some of the women that Sofia mentioned, but overall he had a generally respectful attitude toward her gender.

A decidedly gentle and warm respect. She smiled. Something that Kristi experienced from few men, now that she thought about it. Then the specter of Si would rise up, with his boasting and possessive ways and the lightness would take on weight and shadows and darken her mood. So the morning went until Julie, Sofia's teaching assistant, showed up at eleven. Then, it was all Professor Avila and her new program, which Julie had little to do with. The mask of business matters stilled her heart.

Kristi worked on the special task force for Professor Avila, with Amy and Birdie, as a student volunteer in the development of the new Women's Studies program. During the summer, Kristi worked in the office two days a week, Amy came in one afternoon a week, working around her summer job, while Birdie was doing her internship with the newspaper. When Professor Avila arrived at noon, Julie commanded her attention for the first hour, then left for the day.

When they were alone, Sofia mentioned bumping into Geoff in the faculty lounge. They ate lunch together. "He certainly admires you," Sofia said. "He said you went riding together, yesterday?"

"We rode out to the way station and had a picnic." Kristi was working on the bibliography and didn't look up, but an involuntary smile accompanied the memory.

Sofia went about her own work, working in a conversation about the postponed engagement. Kristi wondered what had brought this on. As she shuffled through the collection of scraps piled in front of her—Sofia often jotted her references on scraps of paper while she read—she wondered if Father had put her teacher up to it. He hadn't mentioned any concerns to her. Suddenly she realized that it didn't matter why. She needed to air her own feelings about the situation to someone, given Grandmother and Birdie were both out of pocket for the time being.

"I do feel bad about it," Kristi said. She typed out the last three references then pulled the page from the platen. "But Si was going to Mexico for most of July, camping in Sonora with the guys. He wasn't going to be around." She clipped the pages together and handed them to Sofia. She hadn't finished, but thought better of letting Sofia know her true feelings about Si's mother.

As Sofia looked over the work, Kristi was reminded of another thing. "Besides, August was never actually my pick. Summer doesn't suit me at all for a formal party. I was going along to please everyone else."

Sofia stuffed the bibliography into the manila folder. "We'll begin making these copies tomorrow. Do you have the changes I made to the outline?"

Kristi pulled out the edited pages. "Next?"

Sofia nodded, then smiled. "So you aren't getting cold feet?"

Kristi put a clean page in the typewriter and started in. Of course she had growing doubts about Si, who wouldn't? What had felt so certain last winter, when she had promised an engagement after his graduation, had faltered in late spring with the approaching event, and Si's increased tendencies to shirk personal responsibility—like the weekend trip to Elko.

She typed the first page of the outline. "Christmas is a much better time to throw an engagement party, don't you think?"

"Perhaps. But I sense something else is going on. Perhaps you are afraid to tell your father about your doubts because you'll disappoint him?"

Kristi was annoyed that Sofia persisted in trying to pierce her veil of privacy, but she wouldn't play coy. She thought of rough edges and tobacco stained kisses stinking of stale beer, of being alone on Friday nights while the boys traipsed across the state line in search of poker games, slot machines and who knows what else. The future stretched darkly ahead of them. The light and possibilities presented by the return of Geoff Meyer was too painful to consider. She was bereft.

"I don't think it's my father I'm afraid of disappointing, but myself. I made a commitment to Si, and I intend to live up to my word."

"Your word?"

"We don't need another scandal to feed the denizens of the territory. Grandmother has been through enough. Father too." Even if it would knock Mary Befford off her high and mighty pedestal.

Sofia started to respond then reconsidered. As Kristi went back to her typing, Sofia seemed to bury herself in her writing. After a few minutes, she put aside her pen and tablet. "It's close to three. We should get ready for the meeting."

"I have time to finish this page."

"Stop there." Sofia commanded.

Kristi put the work aside and retrieved her notebook for the meeting.

Sofia hadn't moved. "Kristi, I hear what you say. I see how you behave. You are an honorable young woman. But I think you've confused a promise to try out a bond of unity with the marriage vow itself. The marriage is the commitment. The engagement is a promise to try out that relationship, to explore your self with another, to see if the union fits your individuality—and his—as well as that entity you form together. This business of narrowing down the field to a single suitor is the beginning, not the final commitment."

"I suppose you think that includes sex in the trial run," Kristi said with some disgust. Everyone was a little too interested in a subject that was her own business alone.

"Not as a matter of course, no. It depends on the couple. But that too is a marker in the period of exploration. If one wants to explore and the other doesn't, what does that mean to the progress of the union?"

Sofia respected her stand. Kristi was relieved.

"There's another set of values to consider here. Your commitment to Kristi, to yourself. It's more critical than your commitment to another person. Because if you fail yourself, you can never be content, and your discontent will cast a shadow over your marriage and your family. This cannot be advantageous."

"Okay, then, I am committed to myself, to my word. If I fail to live up to the promise I've made, I will feel like a liar and a cheat. I will be most unhappy." She wondered if Geoff's sunshine could pierce that dark shadow.

Sofia sighed. "And what does this duty have to do with love?"

Amy Gaites let herself in after rapping on the door. The team met for an hour, working out the schedule of tasks that needed to be completed before the faculty review at the end of the fall. Several times they rued the absence of Birdie, whose creative insights always popped them into a different and more exciting space than either Amy or Kristi could manage.

Sofia did not direct the action, she let the girls work out the issues that represented the student's point of view. In addition, though, Sofia was hoping for help in writing the teaching materials from work based on the textbooks. That meant a lot of reading and intensive seminars for discussion and analysis before the writing. Of course, this task was not due until mid-semester in the spring, when the course would be subject to the tough review of a reticent male faculty.

After the meeting ended and Amy left, Kristi wanted to broach Sofia on a topic concerning her schedule.

"Before we speak of that, I'd like to finish our previous discussion on love and marriage. You have a commitment to yourself, but you also have a responsibility to yourself, and to others. You must carefully weigh all the factors to come to the right decision. Right now, you are focused on your family—your grandmother and father—and how they would be affected. But you must also consider how the other family would be affected, and how involved with them you expect to be. Beyond all this, is the responsibility to your future family, the children yet unborn. Then, there is the responsibility to yourself, your own well-being."

As Sofia spoke, Kristi sensed that Sofia was revealing a deeper part of herself. Kristi didn't know much about her life outside of the school and the few years she spent in their home as an exchange student.

"Don't rush into any decisions. Take time to think and explore. Give yourself time to see if there truly is only this one option for you." Sofia relaxed into her chair. "Now, something about your schedule this fall?"

"Maybe it fits into commitments for myself." Kristi reasoned. "I don't know how much time I can commit to this project this term. I applied for a teaching assistant position with Professor Truitt."

"I see. Well how delightful. I never thought Dr. Truitt would choose a woman, quite frankly. Bravo for him!"

Kristi hadn't expected such support. "He hasn't exactly chosen me—he hadn't hired anyone for the job when he left town."

"You'd like me to recommend you, then? Of course! My goodness, I think you are industrious enough to serve two masters, Kristi. And of course, Dr. Truitt will take precedence over this work. Perhaps, though, we can find a way to make use of the unique position you will be in." She winked and smiled.

That evening Kristi felt a sense of relief having been so honest with Sofia. She felt more confident in going after Professor Truitt's position. Sofia had made her feel fully qualified as well as desirable for the job of teaching assistant. She felt less guilty, too, about deferring the engagement to Si. She had taken responsibility, she now saw, to meet her own needs. Christmas belonged to her as much as it did to Elena Befford. She sent warm prayers to the whole Befford clan, wishing them a delightful visit on Long Island. She couldn't think of a better place for all of them, at this time.

Geoff Meyer joined them at dinner again, on Thursday evening. Planned by Anne Day, it was to be a party of eight, but the Beffords had cancelled, on account of them still being in New York. With an uneven setting, Christian's mother had begged off as well, preferring to remain at the lake through Labor Day weekend. At four settings, Christian found the group a little too intimate, not broad enough for general conversation to be of much interest. Yet with Meyer in the mix, it was not intimate enough for family talk.

The Beffords' absence was unfortunate in another sense, since Christian was hoping to temper Kristina's rapt attention to Meyer, and introduce the new professor to the reality of things between his daughter and young Befford. Although the kids had postponed the event, he was given to believe, by Sofia, that it was a timing thing, a matter of having the gala during the season of romance.

He was hoping that once Meyer observed the obvious intimacy between Kristina and Si, he would figure out what's what, and take the right attitude. No one wanted to chase him off, and as cattlemen, they should all get along decently. Now, with the Beffords' absence, it would be Christian doing the watching. His eyes were opening to the growing intimacy between the two young people at the table. He had scoffed at Marlyss when she suggested a thing between the two of them. But after their dinner together earlier in the week, Sofia had said something similar. Now he could see in the way his daughter's eyes sparkled as Meyer spoke, her smile, the way she hung on every word he said. This delight she showed was nothing like her intimate responses to Si. There was indeed something more between them than he was privy to.

Christian poured the wine as Meyer entertained them again with his travels to study rocks and crevices in the earth's crust. Christian wasn't too interested in the details of geology, so he veered the conversation toward the more familiar ground of cattle breeding, which at least was a shared interest. Geoff turned with the conversation, asking a lot of questions about the innovations Day Enterprises had cut in the field. They talked about his mother's spreads in Idaho and Montana, and her continued interest in competition.

Sofia asked if Geoff and his mother would be attending the Cattleman's Gala.

"Well I've avoided the event for the past six years while I was at Berkeley. But that might be more difficult now, seeing as how I'm actually in the state." Geoff laughed and winked at Kristi. "Mother has a retinue of guests lined up. I think she has plans to stick me with the Cabrillo sisters from New Mexico. I'm supposed to bring a second escort with me. She thinks the college is littered with available bachelors."

"Sofia has agreed to accompany us, this year," Christian smiled at her across the table. "We'll be lodging at Befford's place up near the Lodge."

Sofia guided the conversation toward the start of school, and asked whether Geoff was settling in to his new position.

"I've been focused on preparations for my classes. But I'll undoubtedly need some help."

"You are entitled to a teaching assistant," Christian said. "Surely someone told you?"

"Well, yes. I was thinking that Kristi would like to do that." He glanced at her.

Kristina did not jump at the opportunity, which surprised Christian.

"Well, I don't think it's possible. I'm in the Humanities Department."

"But you can do office work? Isn't that the primary task?"

Sofia spoke up. "Your teaching assistant will be selected from among your senior students, professor. There are administrative tasks, yes. But also this student will be asked to tutor and help you in research as well."

Kristina nodded her head in agreement. They seemed to have worked this all out before the issue arose. Christian wondered what was going on. Of course, he was pleased to see Kristina take to Sofia so well. But he couldn't help but wonder what they might be up to. He was glad to see that Kristina's sudden distancing perplexed Meyer, causing the excitement between them to subside, but he was sure it was momentary.

The evening broke off rather quickly after that. After their guests had departed, Christian told his daughter that he had bumped into Joe Befford at Martin's Dry Goods. Apparently the only Beffords who remained in New York were Mary and her two daughters. Joe and Si had returned the day before.

"You haven't heard from young Befford, have you?"

To her credit, Kristina looked concerned. No, she hadn't heard a word.

"Joe was friendly enough, but kind of cool, you might say. You wouldn't have any idea of why, would you?"

She seemed as surprised as he was. Perhaps, though, not as concerned as she might have been.

A shadow had hovered above Kristi on Friday, a mood that she couldn't shake. As she worked through her day, her mind played a devilish game of tormenting her first with images of a crestfallen Geoff and secondly of a rejected Si. The fact that she had disappointed Geoff in his expectation of having her as his teaching assistant was apparent by his constrained goodbye at the door. Of course, he could hardly take her in his arms with Father and Sofia hanging about. Still, his effluviant manner was suddenly contained.

Then the news about Si Befford being in town was distressing in so many ways. The fact that he hadn't called on his return opened the door to so many reasons why, she didn't know what to pursue. She hadn't heard from him since he left, not a phone call or a post card, nothing.

And she hadn't missed him, either. At first she was too busy with the new program, helping Sofia build the foundational materials—well, supporting her with office work, really. Then Geoff showed up. She had barely given Si a thought since then. Yet, if she did not hear from him by the end of the weekend, she would take the bull by the horns and force a decent discussion about their plans for the future.

On Saturday morning, after breakfast, she was getting dressed, the back doorbell rang. Tessa came up the stairs and announced, "The professor's here." Kristi had no doubt who she meant. She climbed into her blue jeans and, rejecting the tee shirt she had selected, found an alternative with a lace trim in summery colors.

"Ready to ride?" He said as she greeted him. Tessa had already placed a cup of coffee in his hand. "John's saddling up for us."

"Where?"

"It's a surprise."

Kristi might have held back if she weren't so excited to see him. When he led them out the front pastures instead of through the corral she could at least put her mind to rest that this wasn't another ploy to get her to Indian Spring. They took the same route as previously, along the bluff. As they reached the sports field, Geoff guided them toward the road that separated the college campus from the Steakhouse, and led directly to the bungalows on Bachelor's row.

Kristi spotted a pick-up truck parked on the lawn in front of Geoff's place. It was filled with boxes and odd bits of furniture. "Is that yours?"

"It's my transportation today. My car's up at the Rolling J," referring to his mother's spread in the Lehigh valley.

"So what's back at my place?"

"Nothing. I hiked it over there. What?" He said, to the face she made of disbelief. "Hey! I spent six years in Berkeley hoofing it all around town."

"So how are you getting back? On foot?"

"Unless someone gives me a lift." He smiled and winked. When they dismounted, Geoff led the horses to the back of the house, where the grasses stood outside the range, ungrazed and plentiful.

Geoff unloaded the truck while Kristi took charge of the kitchen. The college crew had left nothing untouched, and the place sparkled with a fresh smell of pine cleaner and a hint of bleach. Even the stove had been disassembled for a good scrubbing. Of course, she didn't know how much Professor Sanders ever used the stove, but he had been in the house for as long as she could remember, permanently fixing in her mind his face as the definition for bachelor. After asking Geoff his preferences in where things might be stored, she went about fixing up the kitchen to accommodate how she might want it for cooking and cleaning the dishes.

He was carting boxes into the bedroom when she was done. But he pointed her to the sitting room and suggested she fill the bookcases from the boxes of books stacked on the floor. He had a motley collection of Louis L'Amour western novels, paperbacks mostly but hardbacks, too, not all of which were tattered and worn. There were two boxes of textbooks or references on geology including a whole slew focused on different ages in the geologic time scale like precambrian or paleocene, things that reminded her of dinosaurs and prehistoric man rather than rocks. One box alone was dedicated to books on volcanoes and earthquakes. Under the stack of books was a collection of dusty rocks, not clean and polished, but still crusted with dirt which dusted the bottom of the box.

"What do you want to do with all these old rocks?"

"What?" He came into the room and spied the contents of the box. "Hey! I wondered what happened to these." He picked up one. "This, my dear, is a sample of the earth's mantle. I picked it up right here, in Idaho." He described the trip for her. He was fifteen when he had made the discovery of the core rocks and launched his life's work in geology. Kristi held the dull-surfaced rock in her hand, surprised at how blunt and uninteresting it seemed.

With the books lined neatly on the shelves and the rocks placed in a prominent spot on the mantle place, she took a break in the open with a glass of water. Leaning against the fender of the truck, she was facing Professor Truitt's house. He wasn't yet back from his trip east. She had heard that his aunt had died. The administration sent flowers. She wondered if he would ever return. She considered how dull the year might be, without his classes to look forward to. She thought of their last meeting. It had been ghastly.

She had been arrogant and, to some degree, she acted the spoiled child he always saw her as. Sofia had helped her understand this by explaining what a professor might be looking for in a candidate. By now she had prepared a better offense, which was not to be offensive at all, but to work within the boundaries that the professor would set for the relationship.

Kristi was also discovering that she must be persistent in defining her value as an assistant, something no one else ever had questioned before. It was essential for her to refrain from arguing with him over the way she thought or acted. It was funny how she had never had problems with any of this before, for she was liked universally, and always seemed to fit in nicely. The specter of Si flitted across her mind. Until now, that is. She vowed to let the professor define how she would provide support to him.

When they were done, Geoff told her that he wanted to take her to dinner. At first she objected, but he insisted. At the ranch, he asked John to drive him back home, and promised to pick her up at seven after they'd both had a chance to clean up.

As they walked into the steakhouse, Kristi was embarrassed to find that Joe Befford was playing maitre d' for the evening. He asked after Geoff's family, showing keen interest in his mother's new bull. To Kristi, Joe adopted a businesslike smile. "Sorry to have missed your soiree the other night, Kristina. We had just gotten in and would have made sorry company for you all. "As her father had noted, there was a decided coolness about his manner toward her.

He took keen interest in finding them the appropriate seating.

Geoff struck the right posture for the occasion, when he said "I'm rewarding Miss Day for her enormous help today." Kristi was glad to hear him request a table front and center with a good view of the bar and its promised entertainment.

On Monday morning, Kristi drove out to Befford Ranch. There was no one at the house or in the stables, but she learned from the foreman that Si was at winter camp working with the boys on annual maintenance. That alone was odd, for Si rarely helped out unless it was driving or branding cattle. Winter camp was thirty miles from town, out past Salmon Creek Road. It was late morning by the time she got there.

She slowed down when she spotted Shorty and another hand mending the fence along the road. "He's up at the windmill," he called out. She waved in response and cut across the sagebrush track that was little more than wagon ruts. The windmill stood on the far side of the ridge, where it caught the wind that swept through the gully from the west. Si's truck was parked at the base of the metal tower.

Si was sitting on the ground, pulling the guts from the pump, in the process of oiling them down. At the sound of her Rover, he glanced up then returned to his work as if it were Shorty or Slim coming up.

Be responsible—Kristi coached herself with Sofia's words. He clearly was annoyed at something, although too many reasons and rationalizations clouded her mind. She could not fathom what his problem was now, or what it might have been when he arrived in town last week and didn't call her.

"Mighty hot day to be working out in the sun," she said warmly.

Si finished the gear shaft and wiped down the pulley, biding his time with long careful strokes that would ordinarily be executed in a single swipe. The wind was hot and dry, and her throat was swelling with it. She retrieved her canteen from her Rover and offered him a drink.

Si wiped his hands on a rag and paid too much attention to his handiwork, before taking a swig from his own jug of water. Getting up, he swaggered to the bed of the truck barely glancing at her. It was his way of registering his anger. Kristi was in no hurry herself. She didn't think he'd be so unneighborly, as to leave her standing there in the dust, without saying a word.

He threw the oily rag in the open bed of the truck. "What do you want?" He made a job of rearranging tools and motor parts already neatly contained in the bed of the truck.

"Geoff Meyer is back in town." She was testing the waters.

"Yeah, I heard." He loaded his tools from repairing the pump into the truck. Then he added softly, "Sorry to hear about it."

"You've been home a while. How come you didn't call me?"

Then he paid attention to her. He turned on her, with a look of half hopeful contempt, and railed, "Where do things stand between us, Kristi? First you cancel the engagement, then you're gallivanting all over the territory with big-shot Professor Meyer."

"Whoa. Wait a minute. You agreed to postpone the engagement because you were going to be in Mexico all month. As I recall, you couldn't give up your camping trip to help me plan things."

"My mother had a handle on things. In fact, she's quite pissed that you called it off. Do you know how much trouble she had already gone to?"

"Phone calls and appointments she had set up without my participation? Yes, I am quite aware of what your mother was doing." Kristi's ire was rising, but she swallowed it. "We were expecting you for dinner. Geoff was keen on reconnecting with you, especially."

"I'm sure he wasn't. It's my father he's interested in." He turned to face her in full fury. "Why are you here? Because from my point of view, you're holding all the cards. Deal or get out of the game!"

She was not going to react to that anger. She turned into the wind for a moment, taking another long sip of water. Then turned back to face him. "Si, we need to set a new date for the engagement party. I was thinking…"

"As I recall, girl, you cancelled the engagement."

"Postponed, Si. Postponed. I wanted a holiday engagement party and your mother was forcing August on us. August. When you want to be on the range playing cowboy, for crying out loud. You know the last thing you want to be doing, at this time of year, is donning a tux."

Si was leaning on his truck hood gazing into the distance. He appeared to be ignoring her, but she saw a glint of truth flash across his eye when she mentioned the tuxedo.

"What about all the rumors that you've been riding all over the territory with Meyer? Sly saw you two at Fish Camp, nuzzling up to each other plain as can be."

"The fact that it was plainly out in the open says how innocent it all was. I resent your network of spies watching me. If you're going to go out of town all the time, you'll just have to trust me." Kristi was bordering on the edge of deceit.

"And him strutting all around on the gelding. My gift to you."

"If he's a gift, then he's mine. My friends will always be welcome to choose their mount in my stable. If you can't see your way clear to accept that, you'd better take him back."

"Friend? Is that what you call it?"

"He's your friend, too, Si. We all grew up together, riding in your dad's drives."

"He wasn't no friend to me. The big bully. Wrestling me to the ground, pretending to brand me with everyone else looking on and laughing."

Kristi had forgotten all about the incident. Si was seven years old and acting like a prize bull, bullying his sisters and her. Geoff had been older and was already taking shape as an adult. He sought to teach Si a lesson, but got himself into trouble, instead.

"A man's got pride, you know." Si was still nursing that wound. "So, you and he aren't a number now? You didn't cancel because he was coming back?"

"I most certainly did not do that. I wouldn't have had any reason to do so. He's a lot older. He's been teaching for six years already." She was hoping that Si could see how many years lay between their ages.

"Yeah. I know." He opened the door and hauled into the front seat. "You'd better go first. That track is in need of some stabilization."

She got into the Rover and started it up.

"I'll be in touch."

Kristi waved and started down the track.

They should have talked, but she spent most of the time assuaging his anger, or more likely her guilt. Everything ended up in the wrong place, and she didn't know how to right it.

Truitt filled up at a small station in a place west of the park. The clamor of excited visitors around him was infectious, an alluring call to spend his last few days wandering the natural wonderland promised beyond the river stone gates. So many times in the past few years, Sanders had tried to tempt him with the natural mystery and geologic wonder of Yellowstone. Approaching the tollbooth, Truitt was stuck behind a large recreational vehicle. At the tollgate, they were separated into two lanes. In his little car, Truitt broke free from the campers and dashed ahead of the crowd as if he were bent on some finish line somewhere past a post marker.

The landscape was cluttered with giant boulders, like those around Hawkes Ferry, but the land was rich with high grasses and wildflowers, with pine trees cropping up in distant vistas. Traffic slowed as the road cut around a large black wall of obsidian, its sleek black surface glinting in the sun. Truitt worked his way around vehicles pulling off the road, drivers dis-engorging with cameras in hand. The diversion left him ahead of the pack again, until he was caught by a jam, traffic crawling at a snail's pace around tight bends created by cuts through sedimentary rock. The sun was decidedly hotter here than it had been in town. He shed the jacket he had put on to ward off the morning chill.

Truitt now considered the wisdom of allowing himself the diversion of a national park. The clutter of city crowds and clog of vehicles hadn't been part of Sanders' stories. He wasn't sure where he was at the moment, or where the road might lead. To guide him, he only had Sanders' praises, and his friend's idealized accounts of following the Snake northeast to the park, the tales of camping beside a large lake under a full moon, whose visage sliced orange across rippling waters of an early autumn. His passage through the gate seemed to Truitt an adventure that would reverse that route, following the Snake southwest, leading him to Hawkes Ferry and the fall term at St. Clements.

As the car crawled through the red rocks, Truitt wondered why it was called yellow stone. He rolled at a snail's pace through short rifts and stubby valleys. The hot sun creating an oven inside the small car. When the traffic stopped altogether, he vigorously rolled down the front windows to the still air. Near a bend in the road ahead, he spotted the rounded dome of a forest service hat, in the midst of a cluster of summer-clad visitors blocking the oncoming lane, armed with cameras. Abandoned vehicles littered both sides of the road.

Truitt finally broke free of the line as the ranger coaxed the lane of traffic with a steady wave of his hand. Suddenly, the camper in front of Truitt veered off the road into a spot on the grassy shoulder. The driver jumped out, camera in hand, and rushed out of sight around a large boulder. Once past the rock, Truitt saw the vista that had caused the traffic to jam. A herd of bison was making its way across a broad grassy valley, grazing and wandering, taking little notice of the interruption to man's progress or presence.

"Keep it slow, sir." A second ranger, posted near the boulder, urged him on. "But keep it moving."

Truitt glanced at him and nodded. When he looked back to the road, his vision was blocked by the broad forehead and glaring eyes of a large bison—its tonnage aimed at the car's hood and windshield. Assured of a collision, Truitt braked, against the chanting ranger. "Keep it moving, sir. Keep it moving." The bull stood his ground.

Truitt froze.

Work as one with the herd, an inner voice advised. The bull snorted menacingly. Suddenly the animal veered off the blacktop into a group of bison cows and calves, half-hidden in the high grasses of a wallow on the edge of the road.

It was incomprehensible to Truitt that these creatures were allowed free range—maybe fifty or sixty animals—without fences to contain them, clogging the public road and impairing traffic. The cattle herds that ranged around the campus were restrained from the roads and populations by barbed wire fences.

Irritating logic dissipated into confusion. The national park was a wildlife refuge. Did he seriously think that nature should be contained, boxed up for the pleasure of man?

Confusion was sublimed by wonder, then awe. The greatness of the place rose in him. Overwhelmed by the immensity of its purpose—and the extant population of a near-extinct species, Truitt's heart rose, and the tears fell again—not from grief this time, but from something greater than life, recognition of the terrible awe of God's glory.

Suddenly, it appeared all around him. He felt it. The sacristy of the earth captured in Moran's celebrated painting—one he had seen on a student trip to the nation's capitol—a vision from oils on canvas, Yellowstone as cathedral, its peaks towering toward heaven, naves and altars carved from its valleys, trees and massive boulders rising like icons to God's magnificence. It was a sanctuary. It was Eden, whose edifice and towers were sculpted out of rock by the forces of nature, reaching across the inter mountain divide, spanning across the land, even to the sagebrush steppes, a place where now he longed to return.

Truitt followed the road to a village where he was able to get his bearings from a park map posted in the parking lot. At the local deli, he bought a sandwich and a drink and ate as he drove. The park was much larger than he had expected. As the sun dipped into shadows of the forest, he discovered that there were few accommodations, and none to be had at all without reservations.

Following directions the ranger had given him to the lake, he found himself lost, ending in a tranquil forest unlittered by tourists. Where the road forked, a sign pointed him toward the headwaters of the Snake.

A small parking area marked the viewpoint, but Truitt bypassed it altogether, to run a course downstream with the waters as they gushed through dense forest.

As the stream grew, he passed through the south gate of the park and rolled down the road cut through the Grand Tetons, winding with the river from Jackson to Idaho Falls. In exhaustion, he found a cheap motel on the interstate and slept the few hours until dawn. At a nearby truck stop, he had his first sound meal in a week. Home lay a few hours off, and he cut across the state to Mountain Home, then southwest toward Hawkes Ferry.

Sixteen

The day before the faculty was to report to school, Geoff called on Kristi early and suggested another morning ride along the bluff. Instead of following the path along the bluff, however, when they reached the grazing land behind the sporting fields, Geoff took an unexpected detour along the road by the restaurant, heading toward his bungalow.

"I have a few things to clear up," he explained, as he reined the horses to a makeshift rail on the sweet grass between the two houses.

Kristi nodded agreeably and stood idly by the palomino, as she gazed at Professor Truitt's place, thinking of his prolonged absence. Once again she wondered if he would return at all. Her hopes would be dashed, and the upcoming school year would lose the luster of its appeal.

"I thought you'd want to help me," Geoff, who had entered the house, called back to her.

"Do what?" she asked, following him through the front door.

It had only been three days since she helped him unpack, but the place looked as if it had been trounced by a herd of crazed steers. Clothes were tossed on the chairs and sofa of the front room, while a cup of coffee sat stale and cold on the table. Plastic glasses were scattered about. His den served as a dumping ground for his papers and books.

"I have to get this paperwork finished up before tomorrow's meetings," he explained. "I was hoping you'd help me straighten things out. It'll only take a few minutes."

More like a week, she thought, yet cheerfully asked, "How can I help? I know almost nothing about geology."

"I was thinking you could help me straighten things up a bit," he grinned impishly. "I'll never be able to concentrate, with everything upside-down like it is."

Kristi glanced down the hall into the bathroom, then the bedroom. Both were strewn with discarded clothing—tee shirts, jeans, socks and shoes. A cardboard box of underclothes remained on the dresser, where he had left it the day he moved in, now half-empty as if he were using it instead of the dresser.

The underwear—undershorts worn and tossed on the floor for someone else to pick up—embarrassed her, not only for the lack of propriety, but also for the intimacy it suggested between them—an intimacy Geoff still desired. The tacit suggestion to Kristi was as clear as his desire to dip into Indian spring, or as Si's increasing pressure for sex. Resisting Geoff's advances would be harder to defend, if it were not for her pending—and well anticipated—engagement to Si.

Giving herself to Geoff at seventeen had been a mistake. Although it was something she could not erase, she had no intention of repeating that particular mistake. She would live up to her vow of chastity—to wait for the right man, and to wait until her wedding night. Maybe that man was Si, maybe it was Geoff. At the moment, neither of them felt right, yet both felt entitled to have her. Perhaps the measure of a good man, the right man, would be the respect he showed toward her decision, toward that vow she made at nineteen, regardless of what she'd done at seventeen. She shut the bedroom and bathroom doors on the subject of underwear and ardor.

Kristi decided to help him out by cleaning the kitchen. The dirty dishes and empty food packages seemed less objectionable to her than the dirty laundry, even with crumbs scattered across every surface. She cleared trash from the counters and table, and stacked the dishes in the sink. She wiped down the surfaces with soap and water, then filled the basin and washed the dishes.

"Maybe we can have some coffee?" Geoff called out.

As she made the coffee, she couldn't help compare this real Geoff with the white knight who had swept her off her feet. His personal appearance always trumped that of Si, who always worked to look as if he'd just gotten off the range. Si's personal space was another thing altogether, though, orderly and neat—a trait Kristi had attributed to his mother's continual fussing over him. Perhaps Geoff's mother also ordered his life. But if that was true, what had he done for the years he was in California, when he was far away from her? She surprised herself by asking him outright, as she set the cup of coffee on his desk.

Grinning, he took her hand, kissing her palm. "There's always a handful of babes on campus fighting over the chance to do your laundry or fix you a good meal."

She was sorry she asked, but was compelled to finish the game. "Maybe you can hire someone from the campus cleaning crew to help out," Kristi sipped her coffee. She had no intention of being one of those babes. Perhaps this is how it was to be with him. His affable and carefree manner, presented to the world-at-large, made possible by the little woman behind the scenes, doing laundry and fixing meals. She was beginning to see that being pursued by Geoff was one thing, letting him catch her was quite another.

He shuffled through the piles of papers on his desk, complaining how she wasn't going to be his assistant.

Kristi wanted to tell him that she had applied for a TA position with Professor Truitt, but since the professor had not selected her—yet—she decided against it. She was pretty sure of the position, though. No one else had applied for it. She had checked with the admin office the day before, and the professor had yet to report in. She considered that although she might be the only candidate, Professor Truitt still held reservations about her, not just because she was a woman—although that was a problem too. Before they could work together, the air between them needed to be cleared.

"You could just help me get this started today, couldn't you? Like you can label the folders and I'll hand you the papers to put into them."

She shook her head, smiling. "You're hopeless. Give me the folders and the marking pen." She wrote the names that he gave her as he called them out. Then stuffed the folder with the appropriate pages. Occasionally she suggested changes to his instructions.

"Class rosters," she repeated. "Wouldn't it be better if you put the rosters into separate folders, labeled for each class?"

"Why? I only use them for administrative record keeping at the beginning and end of the term. It's easier to keep them all together."

"Okay. But let's see who is in your senior lab class."

"Is that ethical if you're not my TA?" He pulled out the page and showed it to her.

"You'll find your TA candidate there." She pointed to two names. "Both Sly Checci and Eugene Macdonald are excellent choices. I think that Mac—that's what we call him—might be more reliable, though. But you should probably interview both."

A car door slammed. Kristi's heart jumped, thinking it might be Professor Truitt.

"I think we'd better think of getting the horses back to the ranch. The day's getting hotter, and they've been without shade for a couple of hours. We can drive back to finish up, if we need to."

As he flipped through the remaining pages, Kristi was already out the front door.

Truitt approached his bungalow, noticing a new half-ton pickup had taken residence next door where Sanders' derelict Jeep had once stood. He was going to miss the old professor. Sanders had been the perfect neighbor, quiet in his ways, willing to leave a man to his solitude, but just as ready to share lively conversation and a meal at the Steakhouse.

In the side yard between the two houses, a couple of horses were tied to a makeshift fencing rail, grazing on the brown summer grass. Sanders had mentioned family connections in cattle ranching. Truitt doubted, though, that the man had moved his own horses to the campus, since there was no place to shelter them.

As he approached the animals, one of them raised its head and pronounced a loud protest. He patted the neck of the other one, a palomino, as Kristina Day emerged from the front door of the neighboring bungalow.

"Professor Truitt, welcome home."

The new professor followed her out the door.

"Good afternoon, Miss Day. I'm surprised to see you here. Your horse, I presume?"

"Both of them, actually. I don't believe you've met Geoff Meyer."

As they shook hands, Truitt tried to remember what Sanders had said about Kristina Day and the new man. Whatever it was, he speculated the relationship was deeper than Sanders inferred, dangerously close to crossing the student-teacher boundary, which Truitt held sacrosanct.

Meyer was a tall, lean man, with the ruddy complexion of someone who spent most of his time outdoors, not unlike Leif Sanders. He had the sun-dried skin common to most of the denizens of the region. Rubbing his own chin, Truitt remembered his own neglected appearance.

"I like it," Miss Day smiled. She had been studying him too closely. "It makes you look distinguished."

"Hardly. A few weeks of the road needs scraping off."

Meyer began to ask him about the college and his field of study, but Miss Day cut him short. "We need to get the horses back. Are you ready to go?"

"Almost. Got two more files to finish." He winked and smiled at Truitt, then withdrew.

"Geoff is an old family friend," she explained, as if she had read Truitt's mind. "My father volunteered my services to help him settle in."

"It's none of my business, really."

"I was sorry to hear about your aunt's death. Were you close?"

Truitt didn't want to discuss his aunt with her. There was too much confusion about her memory, too much ambiguity in his thoughts about this place. A western outpost, he used to call it. At the moment, it was the closest offering he had for home. He didn't want to talk about that either. "Yes. Thank-you."

She had something else on her mind.

"Professor Truitt. I still want to be your TA. I saw Tad Martin last month in his father's store. He said he wasn't taking the position. I'm assuming that, since you've been gone a couple of months that you haven't had time to talk to anyone else."

Meyer bounded out of the front door. "Ready, Kristi."

Meyer loosened the reins of the palomino from the rail and gave her a boost into the saddle, then stepped around to mount the bay.

Truitt patted the palomino's neck and said quietly, "I'll think about it."

Meyer turned back to him and said, "Say, Truitt why don't you join us at the Steakhouse tonight?"

He took in the two riders and their mounts. "I think I'll pass."

"Come on, man. We've hardly had a chance to talk. You can't tell me that you have any food in your larder. Five o'clock and we'll make it an early night."

The man's enthusiasm was contagious. There was a bit of Sanders about him. Truitt realized he still longed for company, and there was an echo of something else.

Be one with them, Son, part of the herd.

"All right," Truitt said waving them off.

Truitt spent the afternoon cleaning up from his trip, trying to avoid the three boxes stacked in his den and the insistent light on his answering machine. The air was stifling in the small house. He opened all the windows and left both front and back doors ajar in the hopes that even a hot wind might whip up to replace the closed in air.

In the shower, he considered Kristina Day. There were several compelling reasons for not hiring her as his assistant. His whole idea of the position was based on his own experience working for Dr. Conner at Columbia. There, assistants were assigned teaching responsibilities for the general requirements classes in reading analysis and composition. Of course, St. Clements was a four-year institution, with no graduate school.

Dr. Conner was a noted linguist and, as his assistant, Truitt accompanied him to the coffee houses and jazz bars of upper Manhattan, providing the professor with a virtual Tower of Babel to research his latest book. Truitt worked long hours in his office, as well as his home. He worked well beyond the hours covered by his pay. Even as he remembered the elderly professor, Truitt missed the camaraderie that they shared until Truitt decided to take his master's in medieval studies. They would be friends today, Truitt was sure, if the old man hadn't died while he was in Europe.

Toweling dry, Truitt considered further that the relationship had worked because Truitt was unattached and readily available to meet Conner's needs. And he was wholly committed to the position, making himself available when the need arose. It was those attributes that he now sought in his own assistant. He thought he had found them with Martin. Apparently he had misread the student's commitment.

Truitt gazed into the mirror assessing the effect of his newly acquired facial hair. The beard would never be full and square as the one sported by Wolfe Haug. Yet shaving it off today would emphasize the boyish looks by leaving his skin scraped and nicked like an under ripe strawberry. Remembering the positive effect it had on Miss Day, he realized that it might add a few years, make him look his age for once.

He trimmed it, grooming it close to his face, thinking of Miss Day's persistence in going after the position. It was a most inappropriate job for a woman. The sequestered work sessions prohibited him from considering a female. Long hours, ready availability, these were conditions that would raise eyebrows. No, he couldn't see a woman fitting into that vision at all.

Satisfied with his appearance—a new face to match his new outlook on life—he went to work assessing his starting position for the fall term which would begin the next day in faculty meetings. The house was less claustrophobic, but the air was still hot and unmoving. He dumped the contents of his valise on the desk and sorted it into piles.

He had forgotten all about getting back to the lawyer, about the appointment set up, and speculated that more than one phone call might be from that office. He set aside the personal papers, notes and other material he had taken at the Cloisters. The visit to the museum seemed now part of a remote past.

He was obliged to address the three boxes that he had abandoned in his den. They had been carefully packed to provide him enough resources to create course materials for his fall classes. Originally he had drawn two core requirements courses, Freshman Comp and second year Introduction to Literature, a small price to pay for the privilege of spending a full year devoted to classes in his field of study. With Temple coming on board with only a master's degree, the freshman course was reassigned. Mudd bestowed on Truitt the sought-after senior seminar for English majors, Theory and Criticism – Chaucer to Johnson.

Last spring Truitt had been delighted at his luck. None of the courses was new to Truitt, with the exception of Mudd's class, so he would be working off the general syllabus for each class that had been filed with the department chair. He intended to follow the guidelines offered by Mudd in his syllabus. But the actual material would be revised to include topics of more contemporary issues, revised views of critical papers, and the like, to make his lectures more appealing to the students, and to himself. Additionally, this approach prevented students from anticipating exams or from tempting the students to rely on the work of those who had gone before.

The task was daunting. What should have taken at least six weeks, must now be done in as many days. Even if he could write up new lecture notes and the related handouts, he could not possibly hope to get it done in time for the first class. A second pair of hands could be typing and copying, while he continued to write up the lectures. The image of Kristina Day rose in his mind, capable of doing the office work, willing to be of use to him.

There must be another way. Perhaps he had one or two applications waiting for him, maybe a hire in the offing. Surely, then Mrs. Rowan wouldn't mind helping him out, just for a couple of days. On that happy note, he set out to meet his new neighbor at the Steakhouse.

"Good evening, Professor. Nice to have you back." Nora Caldwell smiled in welcome. "The usual seat?"

"I'll handle it, Nora," Joe Befford who was making a rare appearance as the host, intruded. "The others are waiting."

As he led Truitt to a booth in the corner window, Befford offered his condolences. Truitt was heartened by the welcome he received from the restaurant staff, bolstering his impression of finding a home of sorts in the small western town.

Befford stopped at a sizeable circular booth where Meyer was seated in the middle, surrounded by Kristina Day and Sofia Avila. The professor offered her condolences as Truitt scooted into the booth next to Miss Day, who had made room for him. The seating might have been awkward if the booth that been smaller and if Avila intended to stay for dinner, which she did not. She was meeting Christian Day for dinner,

As drinks had already been served to the group, Befford took Truitt's order before leaving them to their conversation. Meyer and Avila seemed to be finishing out an argument on Avila's new program. Miss Day filled him in on the details of the argument, which had obviously been conducted over the past week. Meyer was standing firm against a program designed specifically for women.

Avila's response was passionate, her eyes flared with delight as she responded to him. Yet Truitt saw that she was not angry or even disturbed at her opponent. Her passion was a natural response to life. Far from trying to lure Meyer to support her view, Avila seemed to enjoy the argument itself.

This was confirmed by Miss Day who watched the two with a smirk, then half-whispered to him, "Geoff has had enough of women's programs at Berkeley."

"I heard that. It's not the programs at the university that have informed my opinion. It's the twenty-nine years of being the only son—only child—of Dove Meyer, cattlewoman extraordinaire. My mother needs no encouragement to be more liberated than she already is. How about something for the guys—like issues for men's lib?"

Avila laughed, and patted his arm, "Pobrecito! I will not deny your feelings. Your mother is an exceptionally strong woman, yes. But you must admit, in general, that the deficiency is with woman. Men have always been in charge. As you have your mother, so I have my father, a man who raised four children with the traditional view of his authority, granted by God alone. But with his youngest, seeing the world from a much different place—with the loss of his wife—he finds another way. And I am much better for it."

The waitress arrived with Truitt's scotch. Geoff took the opportunity to change the subject by ordering the house special. He encouraged Truitt to order the same thing. Kristi ordered a petite portion of the steak dinner.

"Professor Avila," Truitt said, "How is the program coming along?"

She told him about the current state that the curriculum was in, and the help her girls had given to her over the summer, with a special emphasis on Kristi's skills. She knew that Kristi had applied for his TA position, then, and was advocating for her.

"Next week we will have a meeting with the faculty interested in developing some pieces of the program. I have heard back from everyone except you. I am most anxious that you join the committee."

The suggestion didn't seem as appalling to Truitt at the moment as it had last June.

"I learned lots from the females at Berkeley, who were indoctrinated into that program," Geoff said helpfully, then he smirked, "and many more who were avoiding it."

"I'm sure you can." Sofia gave him a sly look. "So, Professor Truitt, you have driven back in a new car, it seems? How was your drive back?"

Truitt surprised himself by describing his trip west across the Dakotas and Montana, then through Yellowstone, admitting that it was his first trip through the park. He mentioned the stranger, as well, and the cattle drive. The telling put him in mind of one of Chaucer's pilgrims.

"I've never heard you tell stories before," Kristi said, obviously enjoying herself.

"A hitch-hiker?" Professor Avila said with the admonition, "That is an experience a woman could never have—driving alone across the country and picking up a stranger."

"Not even another woman?" Geoff asked.

"That's dangerous too," Kristi added, "To hitch a ride with a stranger."

The waitress delivered the dinners and informed Avila that Christian was waiting for her at a table in the back. A shadow crossed the professor's face, she stood up, placed a bill on the table to cover her drink, and went to find her dinner date.

"I wonder why he didn't just come to get her?" Kristi said.

Truitt ate with relish being far hungrier than he had anticipated. He enjoyed the company and the meal. The world appeared to have shifted in some indefinable way. Perhaps the world was changing for Sofia Avila—her relationship with Christian Day had certainly advanced since he last saw her, a fact that might soften her outlook, taking the hunger off the edges of past goals. Kristina Day no longer seemed so young to him. The effect of Meyer coming on board seemed to change her attitude. Truitt could not think where Si Befford fit into her picture anymore, if he still did. This evening, among the casual friendliness of the group, Truitt could see himself in a position to work with Sofia Avila on some parts of their shared curricula.

He was reminded of Sanders' observations about Kristi's natural ease with people. That trait could complement his own aloof nature, often interpreted as arrogance by others. Working with her—as she supported some administrative aspects of his work—would also be possible to envision under the right circumstances.

As they were leaving the restaurant, Truitt turned down the offer of a ride back to the bungalow. "I need the walk."

"I'll hoof it back with you," Geoff said. "Let me hit the head first."

Truitt stood awkwardly outside the front door with Miss Day. Neither of them spoke. Then, as if to fill the silence, he said, "Miss Day, if you are still interested in an interview for the TA position, come to my office Thursday. Around ten?"

"It seems that chivalry is quite dead," Sofia said softly as Christian finished the last of his wine. As they shared dinner Sofia had been content with light conversation, listening to his day and talking about hers. In short, she allowed the dinner to serve as a comfortable distance between the act and her discussion of how it affected her. Sofia Delores Margarita Avila was not used to being summoned like a common servant.

"What?"

Sofia shook her head, cupping the glass of red wine in her hands. "You summoned me to dinner. The waitress? Really, Christian."

"Oh, that." Finished with his plate, he gently nudged it away and mopped his lip with the napkin. "Befford was telling me about their trip back east. I think he was hinting at something, giving me a warning about the kids."

"And you could not come to the table to get me when you were done? You had to send someone after me?"

The bus boy had cleared the table as the waitress descended upon them with a pot of coffee. "Dessert?"

"I was thinking of the chocolate mousse," Sofia said.

"Fine," Christian said to the waitress. "I'll take the strawberry-rhubarb pie with ice cream."

When they were alone again, Sofia returned to the subject of lapsed manners. "I'm not used to being sent for, Christian, as if I were one of your employees."

"You were locked in a conversation with Meyer. I didn't want to look as if I were hounding you. Besides, I needed a drink."

"Yet your summons intruded upon the conversation in a most haughty manner, where an interruption by your presence would have been welcomed by all." Sofia stirred cream into her coffee.

He sipped his coffee with purpose, expecting her to carry on. Sofia regarded him critically. "You know, Christian, these are my friends. And as I offer to your friends the greatest of respect, so I expect your conduct to be."

"Friends? Kristina is now part of your circle? She's my daughter, for God's sake."

"You don't want me to be friends with her?"

"Of course I do. That's not the point. You can't expect me to change my relationship with her just because she is in your circle."

The waitress served the desserts and refilled the coffee cups.

Sofia tended to her mousse for a few minutes.

"You know, Christian, whether you approve of him or not, Emery Truitt is my colleague, and good breeding requires me to give him that respect at least. Beyond that, though, he is a brilliant academic who has much to offer us in medieval culture and literature."

Christian sighed. "So Dean Withers would have us all believe."

His tone told her that he didn't agree with the dean's opinion—or with hers.

"It may interest you to know," she said, "That I am counting on Dr. Truitt to help recruit other collaborators. Many of my colleagues are holding out, waiting for the effort to fail."

He was annoyed and surprised. "How's he going to do that?"

"Perhaps you think he is incapable of influencing others? He may not be well liked, but he is universally respected."

"I've never heard that." Christian shoved his empty plate to the side.

As she finished her dessert, Sofia watched a pantomime proceed in the parking lot, as the two professors walked Kristi to her Rover.

Professor Truitt had been most congenial that evening, telling a delightful story of his trip back to school. Perhaps he was not such a loner as everyone suspected. In the past, she had rarely engaged him in personal conversation. Or perhaps something else had altered the way he considered the world.

Pulling her thoughts back to the table, and to Christian, she said, "I want to know why you are so set against Professor Truitt."

Christian studied the coffee in his cup, a collage of feeling crossed his face. "Why is he hanging around Kristina? What does he want with her?"

"It's not what he wants with her. It's what she wants from him. It was Geoff that invited him to join us tonight, though, not Kristi."

Christian looked into his coffee cup. "Marlyss was of the opinion that he had turned her down for the TA position."

"I see. You already know about that. Yet, this cannot be the heart of your dislike for him. You've never been kind where he is concerned."

"Now I have to be kind to him, to please you?" A hard edge developed in his tone.

Sofia softened. "So how does he offend you?"

"He can't be trusted, that's all. I can't tell you anymore. It's confidential. You do recall he was put on probation a few years back?"

"Ciertamente. Dr. Walter accused him of teaching heresy. But the good doctor was as ignorant as his son concerning the literature of Britain and France during the twelfth and thirteenth centuries."

"For God's sake, the man was teaching freshmen and sophomores about pagan cults and goddesses. Kristina was in that class."

"Pete Walter didn't want to attend college at St. Clements, under his father's watchful eye, which is how he felt with his father on the board."

"He was right. Walter resigned as soon as his boy transferred. Tell me, how did you come by this information? It was supposed to be confidential."

"Julie Howard was dating the boy. She didn't have much sympathy for him. Made a full report of the event in French class. Evidently, he exaggerated the lesson to make Truitt's transgression seem intentional and careless. His purpose was not to malign anyone but to raise a campaign against St. Clements so he could attend the state university."

"Yes, that was obvious to everyone. But the fact is, that Truitt was teaching outside the curriculum and counter to the interests of the school."

"Yet the professor to this day does not know that you were behind those charges. He holds Kristi responsible, still, for raising the flag and reporting the issue to you."

"Now why would he do that?" He frowned.

Sofia didn't know and said so. But she suspected more lay behind Christian's dislike of the man than he was now revealing. His evasions, though, were unsettling to her. She sensed a primal issue at work in it, something that could make all the difference in her own happiness. And that was a treasure she was not willing to hand over to anyone else's control. A mystery that might be tolerated between friends—for pleasant conversation and shared dinners do not require deep understanding of the other—could not be tolerated in a spouse. In that relationship, Sofia would require an open heart and mind.

"Sorry, Professor, no can do." Mrs. Rowan, Dr. Mudd's secretary explained to Truitt as she continued typing. "Everyone's tied up this week. The staff is glad to help out where the need is greatest." She finally looked up, ripping the page from her typewriter. "But Associates have the TA allotment, and you're expected to hire someone. The students need the work, you know."

She fed a blank sheet of paper into the machine and continued typing.

"Yes, I've been gone."

She stopped and looked up at him. "Tsk. Yes, A sad thing too. I'm so sorry." And then as if she remembered something she added, "You did get the flowers, didn't you? Listen, in a couple of weeks we'll have time to breathe and…"

"Classes start next week."

She went back to her work. "Surely you won't need to have everything done by then?"

"I need handouts done for the students."

"Try Millie Hardy then, in the Admin Office, she always has plenty of students working this time of year."

The admin staff worked in the admin office on the first floor of the Humanities building, adjacent to the lobby. He checked his mailbox and found it empty except for a note to see Mrs. Hardy. Inside the office, she was supervising the use of the copy machine, which she abandoned immediately on his arrival.

He asked about clerical support.

"I'm sorry Dr. Truitt. I've got only two students this fall, and they don't report in till Wednesday next." She pointed to an empty worktable stacked with requests for typing and copying. "Already have them pretty much queued up till October."

"You left this note in my mail box?"

"Box was full-up by the end of July." She disappeared and returned with a basket overflowing with packages and letters. There were a handful of telephone messages on top.

"This fellow was insistent on speaking to you," she picked up a message. "Ridell. Called twice, even though I tell him that I can't do a thing, if the teachers don't keep me informed of their whereabouts." She shot Truitt a suspicious glance. "Then had his gal keep it up, too, for the past six weeks. Seems nobody could find you. This Bill Wahl wants you to call as soon as you get in.

Truitt carted the basket up to his office. His mail consisted of a few literary journals and college newsletters, responses on his submission to university presses, and a handwritten envelope from Willema Rutherton. He opened that first and skimmed her note and enclosed outline of her prescription for submitting with success at the Journal. She noted that he did not have to change his topic, he merely had to expand it to include an audience of wider interest than one interested only in the twelfth century church.

Interesting. The manuscript belonged with the other material still boxed in his den. He put it aside, along with the stack of messages from Bill and Ferd Ridell. No doubt, his answering machine at home was filled with similar calls. The whole trip to Delaware—the funeral, the conversations with Bill, the visits to the lawyer—was a blur. He couldn't remember how he had left things. He took off looking for answers to the chaos forced on him and ended up back at school where order reigned. He was aware, though, that he had removed Nell's car from the state without any proof of ownership, leaving himself in a sort of limbo as to its fate, since he could neither sell it nor register it should he opt to sell his own car instead. He was also keenly aware of a trust fund, something he had shown no curiosity about, even as it seemed to intrigue everyone else, including Willema.

For the moment, he would have to put all this to one side and focus on the departmental and college level welcome-back meetings that filled the day. He grabbed a notebook and headed for the Fine Arts auditorium where President Gerhart kicked off the session, giving a broad overview of the institution's goals for the year. Surprisingly, Avila's program got top billing. The college obviously had great hope for its immediate success. Even though it was not to start until the following autumn, there had been a measurable rise in applications from potential female students, many of them past the age of incoming freshmen. Dean Smithers, who headed curriculum and programs, spoke next emphasizing the need to pull together, that he expected full faculty support for Avila's effort, and hoped that those recruited to assist in the development or collaboration of courses would not shun their academic responsibilities. Everyone was aware that few of the staff outside of the Humanities Department would be asked to take a role. To that end, there was a general shuffling from the direction of prominent Humanities faculty such as Edmund Smythe, Cecil Durham and Bob Phillips.

Mike Temple, who had stuck to Truitt like glue since meeting him in the plaza, made an audible tsk, whispering, "I hope she doesn't ask me to help. I have enough on my plate."

Truitt said nothing, but thought that Avila had more sense than that. Temple had been broadly hinting for a copy of Truitt's notes and handouts for his freshman comp class. Apparently, he had accumulated a stack from others who had taught the course over the years. Truitt didn't mind, and agreed to do it. Yet, the request demonstrated, to him, a lack of preparation, and perhaps a certain lack of ambition, to ask, at this late date, for material he needed to have organized two months ago.

The rest of his colleagues left Truitt nothing to complain about. Mudd had been genuinely concerned about not hearing from him. Ralston and Brooks shared concern for Truitt's welfare, and Smythe was obsequious in his expression of condolences. When chatter was building up for a celebratory adjournment to the Steakhouse, Truitt begged off. He hiked down to the local market and bought a bag of staples, then obtained a large bottle of scotch from the supplier. At the end of the day, Truitt was glad to retreat to the solace of his bungalow.

The next morning, Truitt hauled the three boxes in his den back to his college office. They contained all of the material he would need for preparing the handouts for next Wednesday's classes. He made piles on the worktable in his office for his three fall preps. The textbooks remained in two of the boxes. The third box contained his work on the Joachim series, to which he added the letter he had just received from Willema.

At nine o'clock, he prepared for the interview with Kristina Day. The folder he expected to find in his filing cabinet was missing. He was not surprised, given his state of mind when he left in June. He assumed that it was in his cabinet somewhere, or his desk drawer, both of which he riffled through to no avail.

In the top left drawer, usually reserved for papers of a sensitive nature, he found an unlabeled manila folder with handwritten pages outlining his thoughts on the position, with a draft version of the job description, primarily addressing clerical support. The version he gave to Martin the week following finals included tutoring and research tasks as well. He finally discovered the handwritten original for that later description in the folder he kept for secretarial support. It was marked with Mrs. Rowan's initials, indicating it had been typed by her office and delivered back to him, along with the original.

Truitt remembered giving Martin the full job description and only now realized that he must have given him the only typed copy and its folder. He had been so sure that Martin would accept the job. How confused everything was. And how hasty he had been, in his hurry to retain Martin before Miss Day could discover that no offer had been extended before her interview. Truitt realized that Martin must be in possession of the missing job description and folder.

There was no time to type up a new description. Yet, that might work to his advantage. Although he was desperate for clerical help at the moment, by October he would be able to find the right kind of student, one better suited to his needs—one that fit his vision of a proper assistant. He had a fleeting sense of remorse, it was a bit unfair, perhaps exploitive. The draft version of the job description was suited for this purpose. He justified his decision, realizing that she hardly needed the job, and rationalizing she would find it boring after a few weeks.

"This isn't the job description that I applied for." Miss Day scanned through the revision of the description he had typed up in the faculty workroom. "It excludes tutoring and research."

"There's a great deal of administrative work to be done in the next week or two," Truitt said, trying to distract her from the omission. He pointed to the material piled on the worktable and the boxes sitting underneath. "If this all gets done, then we'll get to the other tasks. First things first."

She was clearly disappointed. She pulled out another, more complete job description.

"Where did you get that?"

"It's the general job description for a TA. Admin gave it to me last spring when I was first interested in the position."

"Well, you must understand that each professor has his own set of requirements."

"Of course. I'd like to see the full job description."

"To see if the job is worth your effort?" Suddenly, Truitt felt his plan might backfire.

"Not at all. I want the position," she said. "But when I'm doing the clerical work, I'll also be learning the way you work—how you think and organize stuff. If I know how I will have to apply the knowledge later, I can build the right threads in my mind. It's the way I remember things."

"Remembering? I won't be testing you." Truitt found some humor in her notion.

"I know. But while I am typing and sorting and filing, I am also organizing the information in my brain. If I know what you'll expect from me later, I'll organize things to support your needs instead of my own."

Truitt wasn't quite sure of her logic—if it were rational at all. "You understand that I haven't had a chance to work up the rest of it yet."

"But you had written a job request for Tad Martin? You must have had something in mind when you defined the position for him."

"You seem to know a lot about how the admin office works. You couldn't have been a TA before," Truitt said.

"That's right. I've helped a few of the teachers, though, here and there. And, before you think I have special privileges, I'm not the only one. In high school, seniors are expected to perform thirty hours of community service each term. I worked in the school office—with several other students. Occasionally, we were asked to help out in the College Admin office, as well."

"No doubt it helped that the board president was your father," Truitt couldn't help pointing out.

"More importantly, Professor, it might help you that I have plenty of office experience—including sitting in for my father's secretary when she goes on vacation."

Embarrassed that he had dipped into a pettiness he vowed to avoid, he gave her the handwritten job description. "We can make a copy of it."

"I can type it up before noon."

There was another matter that he needed to discuss, something more personal and less direct than the job description. "Let's go for a cup of coffee, shall we?"

Kristi accompanied the professor to the faculty lounge. He was in no hurry to put her to work, which bothered her. She knew he had no other candidates—Mrs. Hardy had told her that—and the professor was in straits to get materials ready for the following Wednesday. Although she had offered to start immediately, Professor Truitt was still reluctant to take her on.

The faculty hall was empty when they settled into comfortable seats, setting their cups on a coffee table that formed conversation nook. Taking the divan, the professor gestured her to take the armchair. He worked to keep the conversation light, which was difficult for him, as he was no expert at small talk. Each word labored to shape a particular point, like one of his lectures. He was going on about ground rules and boundaries but mentioned nothing specific that Kristi could identify as some past offense she might have incurred on her part.

"Trust, Miss Day, is a critical asset in developing a close working relationship," he seemed satisfied that he had finally come to his point. He was perched on the edge of the sofa, like a tightly wound talking parrot.

She didn't understand what he was getting to at all. However, she did have her own issue to clear up. "Professor, I have always held you in the highest esteem. I have never found fault with anything you've taught us. I've never had a reason to speak against you. Ever."

He seemed startled by the proclamation, then settled back into the sofa on which he was seated.

"I have so much to learn from you. Despite what has happened in the past, you have been one of my favorite teachers. I want to work with you," Kristi said.

As a few more teachers straggled in, sensitive conversation became difficult. Then Geoff showed up, all enthused to see her in the faculty room. She sent him away, but by that time, Professor Truitt was draining his cup.

"I'll want you to start right away."

"I'm prepared for that."

"This afternoon and all day tomorrow?"

"Yes."

"Then you need to get the paperwork from Mrs. Hardy. You need to fill it out for my signature and get it back in before you can start. Can you get that done before one?"

Back in his office Truitt could not believe that he had surrendered the opportunity to set things clear with Miss Day. He was unable to clearly articulate his expectations of her role, not to mention, the boundaries of their working relationship. He had failed to note his respect for the lines between student and teacher, and his need that it never be crossed. She had disarmed him with her openness. He had no idea she admired him, in fact, he would have thought the opposite. But she had addressed that as well, hadn't she? Ever.

Miss Day had dispatched the paperwork as promised and shown up at one o'clock, ready to work. Where he had expected to guide her through the sorting and organizing of his class materials, she anticipated his desires so well, that he was inclined to let her work until she had a question for him.

By four fifteen, she had sorted through all the course material from the three boxes, created sets of file folders to manage the subjects through the term, organized space in his cabinets to hold the new folders, and had typed student handouts for two of the classes. All evening he worked up notes on the third course. He marked up lists of books for her to create bibliographies for each course, and revised his lecture notes for Wednesday's session of the sophomore lit class. It was enough work, in fact, to carry any one through two full days.

When Miss Day had finished by three-thirty the next day, she asked if she could help with some development work he was doing for the sophomore class. He denied her request and sent her home early again.

Seventeen

On Saturday morning, Kristi was in the stable yard grooming Nikki, waiting for her father to return with the bay gelding, having gone out earlier with the foreman to check fencing along the southern pastures. Geoff was due at ten to go riding. Kristi wondered if she should let him ride her father's prize mount. Certainly Geoff wouldn't want to wait out Father's return. Kristi had discovered this vein of impatience growing as she came to know him better. Another trait he shared in common with Si Befford.

She was relieved when she spied the two riders approaching the corral. They split up at the gate with John heading east back into the rangelands. Father came on through to the stable yard and dismounted. "I suppose you're going out with Meyer this morning?"

She nodded. "Around ten."

Lifting the horse's right fetlock to inspect his hoof and shoe, he said. "Get Meyer to watch this leg. He's been acting a little gimpy down toward the bluff. Favoring it—seemed all right coming back, though." He released the leg, patting the horse's haunch." Maybe some arthritis setting in. Hope not."

Kristi made a mental note to watch the bay during their ride.

Father led the horse across the yard and released him into the front pasture, returning to help her saddle up Nikki. "Be sure that you see to him after your ride."

At that moment, Nikki was following the progress of her stable mate with some envy, turning her head against Kristi's attempt to bridle her.

Father grabbed the horse's mane to steady her head while Kristi worked quickly.

"Could use another mustang from the auction," he said, "Especially if Meyer intends to ride from here on a regular basis. Heard it was a lousy year for the Codys. Might be a way to help them out. You up to checking that out while I'm gone?"

Thinking of her growing responsibilities, Kristi didn't jump at the added task. Her father glanced at her with some scrutiny. "Maybe I can get Geoff to go out with me."

She tied Nikki to the fence post and tossed the saddle blanket onto the horse's back. Christian hoisted the saddle off the fence and settled it on the blanket. "Heard from Si since they returned?" He asked in an off-handed way.

"Not exactly. I did go out to see him, though—he was at winter camp."

Father grunted his displeasure in her going out there alone. "He say anything?"

Kristi raised the stirrups to cinch the saddle, glad that he had refrained from the usual fatherly warnings about transient cowboys and loose women.

Father was more focused on the state of affairs with Si Befford. "He didn't like hearing about you and Meyer, I'll bet?"

Kristi tugged at the cinch strap and secured it. "He told you that?" She turned to face him.

"Didn't have to." He tugged at the strap, finding too much play for his comfort. "You've been seen with Meyer all over town. Folks can't help but notice that his attentions please you."

He gave another tug to the cinch, then stepped back to face her. "Exactly what are your intentions concerning young Befford?"

Kristi was perplexed at being called out by her father. "Why haven't you said anything before this?"

"Didn't know it was a problem before Befford gave me an earful the other night."

Kristi walked Nikki to the pasture gate and loosened her to join the bay.

"Seems that Mary was doing a little match-making of her own in New York." Father helped as she cleaned up the gear. "Trying to set him up with a Delaney cousin. Joe didn't say how much Si might have liked it. I reckon the fact that the boy came home with his old man—instead of staying on with his mother and sisters—might suggest something."

"Sure. He missed the range." Kristi said. As they mounted the brushes back on the tack house board, she offered her side of things. "So he comes home to a slew of rumors and goes off to pout down-range. Typical. Why didn't he just call and ask me about it?"

Then in a rush of sudden anger, she added, "Si Befford has no call setting his spies on me, while he dallies with some frou-frou Miss back east."

"Is that it, you think?" His voice was heavy with irony. "Thing is, I see the same thing without wanting to see it. It's obvious to everyone. Coffee?"

Kristi latched the shed door and followed her father to the house.

"What I need to know is, what you are going to do about that bay?"

Kristi was confused at this sudden turn of topic. "The bay? What should I do with him?" They were approaching the kitchen door.

"A month ago, you were of a mind to return him to Befford Ranch." He held the kitchen door open for her.

A fresh pot of coffee stood on the stove. Tessa was running the vacuum somewhere on the second floor. Kristi took two cups from the cupboard and filled them with coffee, setting one in front of her father who was sitting at the kitchen table. She sat across from him.

"He's yours," Father said, "But he's a gift intended for a Befford gal, the one that Si's going to marry. A skilled cutter belongs at the ranch, working with livestock. If you aren't the one joining the herd as Si's intended, then the horse needs to be returned. Pronto. Is all I'm saying."

Kristi was annoyed at having to explain herself. "I haven't cut anything off with Si, Father. We have simply postponed things for a few months."

Her father leaned back in the chair, looking into his cup. "I'm saying, is all. If you're no longer taking up with Befford—well, no one could blame you. That young buck has a lot of growing up to do."

He leaned forward, setting his mug on the table. "I was always hoping you'd settle him down. But he's a hard nut to crack, for sure."

Kristi was relieved to hear him validate her feelings on the matter.

"Thing is, Kristina," he caught her attention and held it. "If Meyer is more to your liking... Well, that's okay by me. And your grandmother, too, I'm sure."

Kristi was speechless, taken aback by his further meddling into her life.

He laughed suddenly. "Your mother would be pleased—that's for sure."

"I know," Kristi admitted. Yet, her own heart was hardly turned toward the same direction as her family. Geoff's return to Hawkes Ferry had unleashed a secret passion for Geoff, one that she had nurtured for years. The everyday reality of his presence, however, had done much to dampen any lingering ardor. The funny thing was, Geoff didn't seem to notice her diminishing regard for him.

"Just saying," her father concluded. As he stood up, he grabbed his cup and headed toward the sink. "I'll be leaving tomorrow afternoon for Sacramento. Your grandmother's not due back till Tuesday after next. Think you can hold down the fort?"

Kristi rose to refill her cup. "Of course. I'll be available to Tessa and John—who will be running the show as always. You need a ride to the airfield tomorrow?"

"Sure." Then, almost as an afterthought, he said, "By the way, Sofia tells me you've taken a position with Emery Truitt to be his assistant."

Kristi was embarrassed that he had to hear the news from someone else. She should have told him about it herself.

"I wouldn't become too friendly," he warned. "He's not like us, Kristina. You know nothing about the man."

"I'm only his assistant, Father, a lowly student in his eyes, not a peer. I expect that the position will be a boost to my record."

He opened the back door. "You don't need a fancy degree, Kristina, to make a successful home for a rancher—or a professor."

Kristi was startled by his last word. Then she realized he meant Geoff Meyer.

Why did he still harbor such ill will against Professor Truitt?

Kristi got up and refilled her cup and returned to the table, keeping an ear out for Geoff's truck in the yard.

She wrestled with the mess her father had just created for her. Just as the rosy color was fading from her inner lens, and she was seeing Geoff in a truer light, Father had placed him in the center of the family portrait. It was easy to see why he was an appropriate replacement gene-pool-wise for Christian Day's progeny. Geoff was another aristocrat cowboy, a stallion with pedigree. The Meyers were old, pioneer stock with solid connections to big sky country, family strung all the way from Canada to Texas. Like Si, Geoff was born in the saddle and bred on the range. Geoff would surely endow his sons with all the right values—and through her, connect them to the Hawke-Day clan.

Geoff was appealing to her beyond that. Comfortable in his own skin, he had no need to swagger down the street in order to draw attention of the ladies. He didn't find the need to bluster and boast in the company of men. And he didn't use vulgar language, chew tobacco, or brag about his trips across the state line. Well, there were those "babes" in Berkeley, but that was an isolated comment, one that she had not heard repeated. Geoff went better with dinner and respectable company, something her father surely appreciated.

Yet, for her tastes, he was as self-centered as Si, using wit and charm to win the support of others, and draw the attention of the ladies with a Texas-style drawl he learned at his mother's knee. Every story turned on his adventures, his opportunities, his dreams, and his needs. In fact, Geoff had asked little about her plans or dreams for the future. And almost nothing of her personal tastes and preferences.

In all fairness, she countered, Geoff might be keeping distance knowing that Kristi was committed to another. She sipped her coffee. She chuckled. His actions hardly supported that contention—she was thinking of the picnic, when they had dallied by the river in a stand of trees. The memory of that kiss caused her cheeks to flush, even now—weeks later. She soared, then crashed at the very thought of Si's spies—her supposed friends—eyeing the heat of their passion, of her own hungry response. She shook off the image.

In the end, she understood that Geoff was far more interested in Kristi coming to know him, rather than any interest he had in coming to know her. Her relationship with Geoff was no more equitable than the one she had with Si. And both men wanted Christian Day in the family tree more than either wanted his daughter. It would be awful to end up with either one.

And why should her life be thus constrained between two unsavory choices? Look at Sofia Avila, a brilliant professor, sophisticated, well traveled, with an admirable career. Why shouldn't Kristi be inspired to follow a similar path? She enjoyed the discipline of mind that academics offered. She enjoyed the tasks of research, of reading and writing, of creating premises around which sound arguments could be built. In fact, she found that arguing through an idea brought her to a new understanding of the world—no matter how lame Professor Truitt found her work to be. It was this rational application of her mind that attracted her to the TA position in the first place.

For the most part, though, she realized that the academic life called for some autonomy and a considerable amount of isolation, prolonged withdrawals from social endeavors. This was less appealing. Sofia had accumulated a world full of knowledge in her travels and studies, yet she had no family, no children to share that with. The trips home to Argentina to visit the families of her brothers and sister seemed too much like borrowing other people's lives. Perhaps this was not a goal for Kristi.

Maybe she just needed a worthier man to support, like an academic, but not Geoff. Someone more reflective and serious about his work. Someone who would share his work with her, who would value her contribution, and her views. Someone to grow with. Someone as committed to Kristi Day as she was committed to him. There was no one in her acquaintance—no one in the entire region—who could fill that bill.

Professor Truitt's face popped into her thoughts jolting her out of reverie.

Impossible. The idea was as dangerous to her peace of mind, as it was alluringly exotic. She smiled at the thought. How enraged her father would be. She would be free at last to choose her own destiny. What a thrill, to shock her friends and all those who thought they knew her so well. Why, the man was an arrogant elitist. Birdie would be hurt—then irate that she hadn't seen it coming. How stunned the community would be that she had chosen an easterner.

And how scandalized the professor would be to see her playing with his life in this careless way. That sobered her. She had no call to toy with the professor's good name. As improbable as it was impossible, Professor Truitt's behavior did not lend itself to a girl's foolish fantasies—nor should it.

Geoff's truck pulled into the yard.

Now there was an idol worthy of adoration, she thought with irony.

As she washed her cup and placed it in the rack next to her father's, the specter of Professor Truitt rose again, in his new beard and jeans, looking the very image of a western hero, like one of us. She smiled in defiance of Father's cautionary words.

She went into the yard to greet Geoff.

Kristina Day had so exceeded his expectations, that Truitt spent the entire day Saturday creating more work for her to do. In order to keep her distracted from the tutoring and research aspects of the job, he needed to occupy her with typing up his notes, copying them and organizing them into folders. Until she could prove herself capable of reflecting his own thinking—and he doubted she ever would—he would keep her busy with administrative tasks. He certainly did not want her let loose on his students.

His preparations were interrupted with a phone call from Bill Wahl in Delaware.

"Emery, been worried about you. Couldn't figure where you'd gotten off to."

Truitt apologized for disappearing without a word, but said nothing about the nature of his trip or where he'd been.

"I've kept an eye on the house. Hope you don't mind. Been bringing the mail in, checking the temp and all. Ridell's been calling around, too—he's anxious to speak with you. Do you think you'll be back any time soon?"

Truitt had not given the house in Delaware another thought, once he was free of its claustrophobic memories. He was glad to hear that Bill had been keeping an eye on things. "Not until the Christmas holiday, I'm afraid. School starts next week. I'll be hunkered down till midterms."

"That's too bad. Wouldn't mind seeing you sooner." He sounded disappointed. "If there's anything I can do for you. I can continue to check up on the house, if you like. Pick up the mail. That sort of thing."

"Yes. I'd appreciate that. Also, I haven't been able to register Nell's car yet. I need the ownership papers. You'll find them in her desk...."

"I know where she kept them. I'll get them into the mail on Monday."

Truitt gave him the college address, requesting that all forwarded mail be forwarded in plain envelopes. He promised to do a better job of keeping in touch.

Not too long after Bill's call ended, the lawyer Ridell called.

"Wahl told me that I could catch you at home. Don't you believe in returning phone calls? I must have left half a dozen." His tone was curt and rude, not the friendly banter Truitt had expected.

Truitt apologized, but offered no explanation. The lawyer proceeded to bring him up to date on the probate process and to admonish him for contacting Nell's family without his advice. Truitt should have informed the lawyer's office of his intention to visit the Dodsons in Washington. Something about the terms of agreement when the trust fund was set up. The lawyer's wrath tapped out as Truitt made no response. He finally ended by declaring that—as the old lady was still ignorant of her grandson's existence—no harm had been done in the long run.

Ridell updated him on the details of the fund distribution. Nell could count on twenty to thirty thousand a year, depending on the financial markets. Congressman Dodson, the eldest son, turned out to be a wise steward of the family's fortune, investing for long-term stability. The amount quoted was staggering to Truitt, as it amounted to half of Nell's annual salary. When he commented that he didn't see where the money went, the lawyer said it had paid for his education, the private schools he attended, and the university costs.

Agreeing to retain Wahl to manage the estate, and to meet with the lawyer in December, Truitt ended the conversation with haste. For a good while, he remained seated by the phone, staring into the past. There was never any evidence of a fortune in the wings. On her meager salary, every new dress was a triumph of economy and thrift, she saved up for months to buy. She had been like an angel, who had no need of worldly gain. The extra income was kept for his benefit alone—his education and his future. Most likely, it had funded the term in Europe.

And how had he rewarded her? With delays, in returning home

on holidays, and postponing trips never taken. She had offered more than once to pay for his ticket home. He always denied her, thinking of what she might be sacrificing for his bit of pleasure. Now he was left to think of the pleasure he could have sacrificed to return to her early.

And what use had he of that money now? It would have covered those sporadic visits home—the plane rides he couldn't afford—that he had desired for the past few years. But now, there was no Nell to visit, anymore. No Nell to fill up the holes created by his investigation into the past, nor to relieve the devastation wrought by her death.

Nothing the lawyer said would change anything about his life right now. No matter how much income there was, Truitt was still charted on the same course, the need to mark time in the Associate position to build up his name and respectability. And for the time being, that position was at St. Clements in Hawkes Ferry.

And that position came packaged with a teaching assistant, Kristina Day, who now needed work to do. Truitt turned to the papers typed by Miss Day the previous day. She had done exemplary work, leaving clean pages without a trace of error. Her level of professionalism far exceeded what he expected from a student, much less the college admin staff, whose idea of updating pages came through the application of correction fluid and retyping over outdated information, leaving changes smudgy and hard to read. Truitt had made a mistake giving her a trial run with pages he had not yet updated from his changed lectures. They would have to be retyped when he finished updating his lecture notes.

Through the morning, Truitt set up a stack of typing requests, which had grown to eight pages. By Monday, he hoped to have added the lecture notes from at least one of the core classes, if not both. She would not be handling material for the seminar class, Theory and Criticism, because she would be one of seven students in the class. Truitt thought the suggestion most inappropriate—to give one student the advantage over others by giving her access to the lecture notes—especially given Miss Day's self-prescribed method of learning.

By Sunday Truitt had finished most of the revised lecture notes for his sophomore class, when he heard a car pull up in front of his place. Shortly there was a rap on the door, followed by the familiar greeting of his former neighbor, Leif Sanders. Truitt was delighted to see him, but offered his regrets that he was too busy to visit for long.

Leif held up a bottle of scotch. "No problem. I assumed you needed some bolstering. A fine single malt from the coast."

When Truitt fussed in the sitting room to make space for the visitor, Sanders said, "Sit down and get back to work. I know where the glasses are."

After retrieving tumblers from the living room cabinet, Sanders headed toward the refrigerator. "Any ice?... Got it."

Sanders handed Truitt his drink and dragged a kitchen chair into the den. "Rumor has it, you've taken on Kristina Day as your teaching assistant."

"You've been checking up on me?" Truitt smiled.

"Nope. Meyer told me. Didn't believe it. I came by to see for myself."

"Where did you run into Meyer?"

"Didn't see him. Talked to him on the phone. We have a meeting tomorrow, going over the lab. So I thought I'd come down a day early and bother you."

"Staying in the dorm?"

"Freshman floor. Lots of fun. I scare the little buggers to death." Sanders laughed. Then he sobered. "How did things go this summer? You get any of my messages?"

Truitt pointed to the light on his answering machine. "I just got back on Tuesday. Been snowed under."

Sanders turned his attention toward the piece that Truitt was working on. "And what's this? Why are you copying everything from your notebook to a clean sheet of paper?"

"I'm transcribing my illegible notes, so the TA can read them."

"Give her the original notes with your mark-ups. That's what you pay her for."

"My hen-scratchings are almost illegible. I don't want her to be wasting time by typing the same page over and over, as she cleans up her misreadings."

"So you're wasting your valuable time making a clean copy?" Sanders chortled unpleasantly. "You are a dunderhead, Emery Truitt, even if you are the best academic at St. Clements. Kristina Day is a competent assistant. She's honed her craft at the forge of Day Industries playing girl Friday. I can't vouch for her knowledge of your field, but her command of English grammar and usage is not to be questioned. She did an excellent job proof reading my textbook. Even surprised me with practical suggestions on how to present the material, even though she knows little about geology. She understands people."

"So you have said before." Truitt frowned. "Wait. You've never told me that she helped you on that book."

"It was unofficial. I didn't pay her. Actually, she volunteered—for the experience, she said."

Sanders sighed as he sat by, watching Truitt recopy the pages. "I don't suppose there's any hope of your joining me for dinner?"

"Good lord no. I have to have this stack ready tomorrow morning, or Miss Day will have nothing to do."

"I don't know. She could be developing a plan for tutoring your lower-class students."

Exactly what Truitt was trying to avoid, but he needn't tell Sanders that.

"Do you mind?" Sanders asked, picking up the pile of finished pages. He thumbed through them, then slapped them down on the table and guffawed. "Give her the marked-up sheets, man. She'll figure it out."

Truitt copied on with no comment.

Sanders sat back into the chair and sighed again. "I wanted to hear all about your summer—and regale you with my adventures in the woods by the river."

Truitt finally set the pen down having finished the first set of lecture notes.

He turned his chair to give his old neighbor the satisfaction of his attention. "So what kind of fish tales have you assembled over the summer?"

Truitt took his first sip of the scotch. "Nice, thanks,"

"Face it old man," Sanders said. "You'd rather be writing an article on that monk of yours, than creating busy work for Kristina Day. Give the girl a chance! What's to lose?"

"What if she's not up to the task? Then I'm even further behind."

Sanders laughed. "Why you arrogant son-of-a-gun. I'll bet you've never given her anything but an A in any course you've taught her."

"She earned every one of them." It ruffled Truitt to recognize that he had joined the category of teachers whom he had accused of appeasing the board president. "Anyhow, what makes you so sure of that?"

"Because I know Kristina Day. She'd never accept anything less than an A from any teacher in any course. Her father was the same way. Bull-headed to the end. He had sponsored a weekend to Yellowstone for the entire class, just because he missed a question on the midterm, regarding the concept of continental divide. He insisted on studying the physical evidence."

"They could afford it," Truitt said in a sour tone. It jolted him to realize that he could do the same thing now. "What about the other students? I don't want to turn Miss Day loose on them until I'm sure of her competence."

It was only an excuse, he knew. His words sounded shallow, even to his own ear. If Martin were his TA, then Truitt wouldn't have hesitated. Yet, Martin scored no higher on tests that she did. He did concede, however, that Martin had been the more serious student, focusing on issues of a higher nature—or so he had believed.

"Test her," Sanders said. "See where she falls short. My money says she'll blow you away. But don't believe me. Ask her for her plan—she'll give you one, don't worry. You can supervise her through questions and suggestions. Like Plato."

"Socrates."

Thinking of the philosopher brought Truitt to his senses. This lack of trust was no way to treat a student who was about to graduate. He was treating her like an underclassman. Had he granted her any space to grow with the subject since the heresy incident in her sophomore year? Suddenly, Truitt wanted Sanders to be right. If Martin were his TA, he'd leave Martin to struggle with the raw material.

"Oh I give up! Let's go have dinner," Truitt said.

"Now you're talking," Sanders grinned. "You won't be sorry—in either case."

They left together to enjoy an evening of swapping tales at the Steakhouse.

On the following morning, Miss Day happily complied with his request that she retype the work she had done on Friday, without comment. She finished that work by mid morning, then set about typing up his lecture notes as he completed them. In between, she organized and filed the papers scattered around his desk, adding continuous updates to his bibliography from the new texts she found in the three boxes as well as from the resources she found in his notes. On this master bibliography, she made notes on the courses the books supported, with the intention of recreating bibliographies for the two core classes. He had not expected her to engage in such autonomous tasks, but bit his tongue and let her continue as Sanders had prescribed.

On the first day of each of the core classes, he asked her to be on hand for an introduction to the students and to pass out the materials. He had decided that she should remain in the sophomore lit class in order to establish rapport with students, who she would be tutoring. If she did well here, he would invite her to participate in the survey class, as well. Sanders was right about her competence. She had taken both classes from him, and he knew full well her excellent abilities in that domain. She sat in the back of the room taking notes. She was available to the students after class, referring to her notes as she answered their questions. Truitt was satisfied that she was trying at least to repeat his teachings and instructions.

Gradually they slipped into an easy relationship. Truitt worked on updating the core class material for the new crop of students, while Miss Day worked in tandem, to organize his notes and keep his files in order. She dutifully recorded the students' concerns and comments, reporting back to him in detail. She suggested some changes to the student handouts. Then, she offered to create a few more handouts, if he were willing to share the additional material with them. He couldn't have dreamt up a better administrator to support him.

It amazed Truitt that with all her help, Miss Day never took the slightest advantage of her position to lord it over her fellow students in the senior seminar course. Nor did she try to gain prior knowledge of the lessons or the discussions, which would have placed him in a delicate situation. The difficulty he had anticipated in the beginning had not materialized. She was content to be as any other student and liked nothing more than to be considered one of the crowd. Miss Day seemed most comfortable assimilating into the group with little to distinguish her.

Oddly, this was the singular trait that had discouraged him from considering her at all in the beginning. So focused on the wants and needs of others, she never seemed to have a thought of her own. Yet, this was the exact trait that invited the trust of the other students, that gave her such easy commerce with people, and that rendered her an excellent choice for his TA.

"I heard from Jake that you and Geoff Meyer are an item now." Birdie Caldwell said as Kristi sipped her coffee. They had met up for the first time in their senior English seminar class. The last time they spoke, Kristi had informed her friend that she was postponing her engagement.

As Kristi had never spoken of their past relationship to Birdie, she needn't explain the wild passion with Geoff that had already cooled. "We were out at Jake's last weekend. Checking on a mustang at the Codys that Father is interested in obtaining. Since Geoff moved back here, he's riding out of our stables. You could say that he subbed for you this summer on the trail. He's not as much fun, though."

Birdie studied her with open skepticism. "So what's happening with Si?"

"He spends a lot of his time out on the south range, I guess. I haven't heard much from him since he returned from New York." Kristi talked about her summer and Si's absence, not omitting the tension growing between her and Mary Befford. "But tell me what you've been up to. Your internship must have been an exciting experience for you."

Birdie needed only the encouragement to jump into the details of her summer job spent with a mid-sized newspaper in Clark County, whose largest population base was in Las Vegas. The circulation of the paper was targeted at the populace wedged in between the fast-growing urban center and outpost character of the rural environment. Birdie called it schizophrenic, an idea adopted from two local reporters she was assigned to tag.

"You'll be jazzed to know that they took a keen interest in your mother's mission when I told them about it. They plan a series of articles on lost girls of the strip. My idea! They've invited me to contribute. I thought I could do a couple of interviews…."

"How did she take it?" Kristi was concerned that her father would disapprove. Any negative publicity would reflect badly on the family and the company. And such a story—on the underside of Vegas life that was served by the mission—would not be positive.

"I introduced them first, silly! She was all over it. She started talking about some foundation she's trying to set up and everything."

Kristi tried to smile. She was not jealous of her friend's growing relationship with her mother, but she felt so left out of Marlyss Day's life.

As always, Birdie read her mind. "We need to go down there during the holidays, don't you think?"

"Don't forget, I'm committed to Professor Truitt for the term. I don't know what that means for the holidays. Besides, Father has already been making plans with Joe Befford."

"So you are still involved with Si?"

"Since things have cooled between us, I have set my mind to focus on the TA position and graduation. I'm putting men on a back burner."

Birdie raised her eyebrows with a little grin that signaled she didn't think so.

They were already collecting their things to head out toward the Humanities Building for Birdie's afternoon class. "I don't know, creative writing is so dull this term. I'm the only female, and I have no one to commiserate with. Durham is such a dud, he makes Truitt look exhilarating by comparison. Do you think our senior seminar is going to be all discussions like today? Or does he have a dull lecture up his sleeve?"

Kristi didn't reply.

"No matter. The only thing real for me this term is Sofia's task force."

"I'll see you in the morning, then. Raring to go on Women's Issues."

The student task force for the new program on women's issues reconvened for the first time two weeks into the term. Sofia Avila welcomed her team back and launched into the goals for that term. Simply stated, the group was to work on the five key issues holding women back in the twentieth century. It was a talented group though hardly one representing broad experience—namely, Kristina Day, Amy Gaites and Birdie Caldwell. None of the girls had ever lived on her own, but that was a general profile of coeds at St. Clements.

Birdie's experience was probably the most useful for the task force, having been raised in two worlds, and in each by female guardians who shared a common vision for her destiny. Amy had the narrowest view, the only child of two devoted parents, her father was a farmer and her mother worked as a nurse's aide in the Sunset Home at Rupert to afford the education she wanted for Amy. Kristina had a privileged background but was raised with a strong sense of community and charity, but her mother's abdication of family and her strong relationship with her grandmother gave her a cross-generation view of the plight of women.

With this group, Sofia expected to refine the more universal material that she had developed from observing other programs. Eventually she wanted the program to appeal across gender boundaries. It was critical to take a balanced view that did not demonize men, as she had observed of other programs. This was essential not only because it would alienate her primary sponsor, but also because—as one of two girls in a family dominated by brothers—she knew too much about the pain and dreams of her siblings to dismiss them all with the singular epithet, male chauvinist pig.

Motherhood was the first subject she would tackle.

"Motherhood is the natural state of women. I don't see why it's a problem." Amy was agitated.

"It's an issue," Birdie said, smiling at Sofia. "It's not necessarily a problem, but it could be one. That's why we're discussing it! It's an issue because women are primarily responsible for reproduction: the breeding, feeding and rearing of the next generation."

"All I'm saying is, what else did God put us on earth for? Yes, it's our responsibility."

Sofia was not surprised at Amy's view.

"Men do play a role," Kristi said, glancing askance at Sofia. "Protectors and providers, so the offspring are kept in relative safety and comfort."

Birdie hooted. "Not in my world, they don't. I got all my rearing from Gran and my aunts. Not a male in sight."

"What about Jake, your uncle? He's always been around for you and Gran," Amy pointed out.

"Jake's a pretty cool uncle, I have to admit." Birdie responded, then looked at Sofia directly. "But he's never been responsible for me like Gran who is my guardian."

"What about the Caldwell sisters?" Amy was becoming irritated.

"They are my father's sisters," Birdie again directed her response to Sofia, then turned to her friend. "As you well know, Amy Gaites. Gran sent me to live with them because they are in town and close to school. But Gran didn't have to let me. She is my guardian."

Sofia got out of her seat and went to the board armed with chalk. "So let's continue with the idea of Motherhood as an issue with its pros and cons." She made note of Amy's comment on the natural laws, and a second note on Birdie's comment of obligation.

"Jake has taught me plenty, though." Birdie leaped in with a conciliatory tone. "I agree that he'd be the first to defend my honor and all. He's been a tremendous help in showing me how men justify their actions, you know, how they sort things through."

Sofia made note of the responsibilities so far attributed to men.

Amy wasn't going to give up easily. "You're an exceptional case, Birdie. In regular families, the father is responsible. So what is the key issue for women?"

Seeing a feud brewing between the girls, Sofia quickly added another note on men and responsibilities.

"Just get preggers, Amy," Birdie said, with an edge to her tone. "Without the loving support of that wedding ring. Just you see who's going to be responsible for that offspring. You are, Girl. One-hundred-percent. That's the breeding part. Men, for all their grandiose promises, do not honestly want to be saddled with a parcel of kids. Women have no choice."

Amy was indignant. "Sure they do. They can choose to wait."

"I can't agree, Birdie," Kristina Day stepped in, trying to maintain peace between the two friends. "Lots of fathers step up. My father, for instance. Mr. Gaites, Mr. Befford. We could go through a list of faculty members...."

"Let's not," Sofia said. "I've made note of your comment, Kristina. Now for...."

"A responsible girl would wait until she's married," Amy asserted with self-righteous authority.

In the girl's insistence, Sofia heard the self-righteous authority of one who had taken the reverend's Chastity Pledge. She sighed and added the comment to her list.

Birdie showed disgust toward Amy's naiveté. "I suppose your intended will wait until the wedding night."

Amy nodded, "As a matter of fact. And Mac does want kids. Five of them." She smiled coyly.

Sofia chided the girls for getting off track, looking to Kristina for some help to curb the tension.

"Si wants children too," Kristina said cheerfully.

"So is he going to come off the range to change diapers and feed them, while you go on to the office?" Birdie said in an ironic tone.

"Well, not so much children, I guess, as sons. He's had enough of girls with two sisters." Kristi reconsidered.

"And his mother," Birdie muttered.

Kristi ignored her and continued. "He's like my father, I guess, who still expects to have a son to pass the business on to."

Sofia lurched. Turning quickly to the board in order to hide her reaction, she jotted down Birdie's observation on men and children, taking time, to let the shock of the news dissipate. She would deal with that later.

"Well, Birdie," Amy said in a tone meant to pacify their relations. "I think you are right about some men. I know that Professor Meyer has no intention of producing offspring."

"What makes you so well informed on his private life?" Birdie asked with a side-glance at Kristi, who blushed.

"Mac is his TA."

Kristi was now annoyed, at what it was hard to discern. "He'd hardly be discussing anything so personal with you and Mac. You must have misunderstood something. He was probably reacting to your notion of five kids."

"I didn't misunderstand a thing. He said no kids at all. Actually he said he didn't want any rug rats messing up his life. He wants to travel the country—maybe it was the world—doing geology stuff. His dream is to travel across the land with a wife beside him, like a desert nomad making home in tents wherever they land. She'd be a helpmate, like the Bible says—only they'll be producing papers instead of kids."

Sofia made note of Amy's implication, that kids kept a man tied down, musing that they might be an impediment against women's progress as well. She also found some amusement in the fact that Geoff Meyer might be showing true colors in the unguarded relationship with his TA. She was amused that Christian—who had lately been campaigning heavily for Geoff as a replacement to Si in Kristi's affections—was as blind to his shortcomings as he had been to Si's.

"Isn't that quaint?" Birdie noted with a smirk. "A traveling caravan complete with its own domestic service and unpaid assistant, too."

After the meeting had ended, Sofia copied the notes off the board, merging the ideas with her initial list. Although they had never diverged from responsibility issues, she was able to rearrange the discussion into broader ideas that needed further exploring. Amy volunteered to type up the material on the board and distribute it back to the group. Each of them would further articulate the issues, adding illustrations that would appeal to local and contemporary interests.

As she reached the topic of men and children, she paused to reflect on Kristi's words, that her father expects to have a son. The girl had been looking directly at her, as if for confirmation. Christian had never broached the subject of children with her. She thought that he had understood, with his unflinching support of her program and her goals. How could he expect the program to be successful, if she were to be shackled—breeding, feeding and rearing—his progeny at Day Ranch? She had believed that Kristina was enough for him. Indeed, on more than one occasion he had agreed it was a pity to see opportunity wasted for her sister Belle, who had produced six babies before her thirtieth birthday. She had read his show of sympathy as compassion, a sign that he was truly a soul mate for her. And everything that followed seemed to validate her presumption.

She thought he knew her position. At thirty-eight, she had no intention of changing her mind. They needed to clear up this misunderstanding before the relationship could advance another step.

Kristi was dissatisfied with the first meeting of the task force. Working with Truitt later that afternoon, she asked how he viewed motherhood as an issue for women.

He was working on his lecture notes for October, half mindful of her question, showing little interest in the topic. "What do you think?"

"I guess... Since it's the natural law of God, given to Eve in the Garden, it assuredly isn't an issue at all. It's the way things are."

Truitt put down his pen and looked up at her. "And for a woman who can't see it as a natural law?"

"What do you mean? Who wouldn't see it? It's in Genesis."

"True. My own mother was a believer in the Good Book."

"I thought your mother died when you were an infant."

"Well, yes. My aunt also believed in the Good Book. She, however, did not—Take your own mother, for instance. Better example. She left you in the care of your father and grandmother. Do you find her unnatural?"

Kristi felt the blood rush to her face. "No, I don't think she's unnatural."

He looked as if he had regretted his callous assessment.

Kristi tried a new tack. "Let me ask you this, Professor. Do you think children are forced onto men—I guess you'd say trapped—by women?"

The professor coughed in embarrassment. After a short reflection, he asked, "This is part of your work for the task force on women's issues?"

"Motherhood is one of the issues, yes."

He glanced up at her. "Every child needs a father." His response was sharp and cool. Then he turned back to his work.

"And a mother," Kristi offered gently, taking up her station.

Neither response answered her question at all.

Eighteen

Kristi adapted well to her tutoring duties, developing a quick rapport with the sophomore students. She offered ready assistance on their perception of lectures to interpretation of assigned readings. She held discussion groups and encouraged participation in class discussions. Professor Truitt was appreciative for the positive effect she had on the students and on his schedule.

Within weeks, she found herself increasingly defending the professor against complaints. Dana Gilbert, in particular, accused Professor Truitt of being biased against the female students. Kristi had attended every class since the beginning of the term and had observed no such thing. She had noticed, in fact, a decline in the professor's proclivity toward favoritism. He had adopted a conscientious sensitivity to pursue balance. Kristi attributed this, in part, to his involvement with the faculty team for the new program in women's issues. Had his aunt's untimely death given the professor new insights about women and equality?

Further investigation into student opinion revealed that a general bias against the professor stemmed from the women's dorm where it was "common knowledge" that he preferred his male students. The basis of the accusation was laid at the feet of the two Resident Assistants. Both had declared majors in English, but changed fields rather than suffer Professor Truitt as their advisor.

Kristi tried to coach Dana Gilbert in hopes that she would give the professor a chance, but the girl said sharply, "You've got to defend him—you're his TA."

How would the professor ever be able to get away from this if students kept the past stories alive? She realized that she could not subvert the wave of opinion against him. Yet she felt duty bound to at least caution him of impending trouble, a subject she broached in their next weekly review. He asked if she had noted anything in particular that might offend the students in any of his classes.

"Not at all—nothing like... before." She felt awkward.

He chuckled at her response. "You needn't be so shy about it."

He admitted to past failures, and added, that as these things take years to die down, he was willing to accept his fate of playing the "draconian male" of the English Department. He dismissed the subject and seemingly the meeting in a single gesture, by rising out of his chair and heading for the door.

He stopped abruptly and turned back to face her. "This isn't for common knowledge, you understand?"

She agreed.

"I'll admit to you that I've never been totally at ease in female company." He grimaced, returning to his desk. He reclaimed his seat. "The truth is, I haven't run across many women who were rational or showed much interest in the world around them."

He shuffled some papers on his desk, then sighed involuntarily. Glancing at her with a timid expression, he added, "My aunt's a rare specimen, you see. I've yet to meet another woman who is so stoical, so well informed, so... perfect as she... was."

Kristi felt his loss.

He shook his head. "Most females are...Well, more emotional, you see."

"As you've told me before," Kristi said with irritation.

"Did I?"

He seemed genuinely surprised, she noted, even though the ensuing argument was etched into her own memory.

"It's not so much a bias, you understand," he said in a conciliatory tone, "as a general lack of exposure to female company. Until university, my world for all practical purposes existed in the company of men. I had little exposure to the social niceties offered by female companionship. In short, I don't do small talk well."

"But you do. You use it all the time with the male students. You talk about the weather, sports, how the teams are doing."

"That's something one would hardly say to a woman, I think."

"Why not, if it puts everyone on equal terms?"

"It's the inference."

"Inference?"

"Of drawing someone into idle conversation. Then where does it go?"

"Where does it go with the males? It's the same thing."

"No, it's not." His reply was curt.

Kristi backed off that topic. "You might try being more equal in the way you address the students. You use surnames to address males, but every female is Miss or Missus. Why not address everyone equally?"

"It would hardly be in good form to reference females by their surnames! I'm surprised at you, Miss Day, of all people, suggesting such a lapse of etiquette."

"Professor, if education is to be equal between the sexes, then we must all be seen as equals in your eyes," she asserted. After a short silence, she said, "How about using our Christian names then? Like calling me Kristi."

"And blur the line between student and teacher? Certainly not." The idea seemed to scandalize him.

Kristi sighed. "Your objections, Professor, are so illogical."

Later that week, in the midst of reading essays, Kristi paused to observe the professor working at his desk with his back to her. Often she had tried to imagine him in a picture, his long arms draped around an adoring female. She couldn't make the image work. Who could fit his ideal of woman? Birdie Caldwell's face popped up—a perfect match to his rational aloofness. Resistant to Kristi's designs, though, Birdie leaped out of the frame like a cartoon frog hopping out of harm's way.

When the professor took a break from his writing, Kristi ventured a question. "Professor, did you never have a special girl?"

"What an impertinent question, Miss Day." His tone was sharp and forbidding. "The position of assistant does not entitle you to the revelation of your professor's dark secrets."

She saw that he was teasing her. "I was trying to understand your position better."

"The lesson I took from my admittedly limited exposure to females, is an affirmation that the Greeks were right in their depiction of unattached females. That is, either as sirens or sorceresses set out to trap wandering heroes."

Kristi made special note of his terminology, intent to research these Greek women.

"Of course, I was very young back then," he said, "and far too fond of Homer."

"And on that you condemn the whole female race?"

He seemed to assess her in a new way. "I'm not saying that it's right, Miss Day. It's just the way it is."

In the library, Kristi looked up siren and sorceress but found nothing useful to help her understand what those words, or symbols, said about the women in the Professor Truitt's life. The librarian suggested she read Homer, and in particular, the Odyssey. As if she had the time this year!

As she drove home, though, Kristi formed a different notion altogether. The source may be from the Greeks, but weren't these also representations of females in the male psyche, as well? What a man wanted in a woman, perhaps. That didn't exactly fit the professor's profile. Yet it did raise an interesting issue for discussion with Sofia's team. If a man is tempted by his own desires, why is the woman at fault?

The more Kristi mulled over the professor's words of sirens and sorceresses, the clearer she saw the shy, reclusive student that dwelt within him. Had he been splintered psychically by some unfortunate experience of his youth? Or were his hopes dashed against the rocks of desire? Were the siren and the sorceress the same person from his past, or two different players on different stages? What power had shredded his psychic body across a craggy bluff before throwing it into the sea?

Whatever the truth, Kristi felt her own heart rush to heal the sorrow of this needy boy who had somehow been abandoned to a world of wily women. Kristi pitied him like she would a great hawk injured on the range or an orphaned cub. In the past month, she had grown to see in Professor Truitt's aloofness, not the cold rationalist, but the boy longing to be fulfilled.

By Halloween, Truitt was finally done writing up the lecture notes for the term, revising the exams, and completing other miscellaneous tasks for all of his classes. He could finally settle into addressing Willema's recommendations for revising his submissions to the Journal. Simply put, she felt that he should expand his subject to be inclusive of women.

Truitt's objective in publishing, however, was to bring to light the work of a Cistercian monk from Calabria in the Italian peninsula. Truitt would make the case, over time, that Abbott Joachim's treatise on the Trinity not only had provided the trigger for radical change in the twelfth century Church but also laid the way for the Inquisition and spawned the Reformation four centuries later. At the age of twenty-four, Truitt had concluded that this would be his life's work.

Willema was asking him to dissipate the focus of that topic, to expand his premise so as to appeal to women. Although it had been through her connections that he had been invited to study the manuscripts at St. Amadour, he felt no obligation to humor her request. She had sent him there to further her study on the manuscripts from Eleanor's court at Poitiers, the proving ground for secular and profane arts of the culture of love and courtly manners. Truitt had no interest in such things, especially at the age of twenty-two, when his interests in Arthurian lore were giving over to more serious study, such as politics and religion, as they influenced the high Middle Ages.

While the transformation of Arthur from pagan king to hero-king of Christian mythology still intrigued Truitt, it was not a topic for serious scholarship. He would find no respectability—nor earn a name for himself—by joining the pack of graduates chasing a topic formed by myth and speculation. Serious scholarship demanded references, research, source materials and rational argumentation.

During the twelfth and thirteenth centuries, the noble women of France held a good deal of land and its attendant political power. But by the middle of the fourteenth century, the Church had acquired enough of its own power to exclude them from succession, and ensured that they were denied political legitimacy.

Under holy writ, then, freethinking wives and daughters were confined to the castles of their lords, locked in towers, or shut away in nunneries, effectively eradicating female political power and will, rendering the individual woman of no interest to the biographers or historians. What the Church could not achieve by suppression or banishment, the Inquisitor pursued through witch-hunts.

The sunny afternoon had slipped quickly into twilight, the crisp autumn air giving over to damp chill. Truitt turned on the heater and flipped on the desk light. He could hear the excited chirps and squeals of Halloween revelers down the street. The din of giggling rose with joyful shouts, as a group came up his walk. There was a rap on his front door. In accordance with the informal rules of the occasion, he had left his porch unlit in order to discourage trick or treaters. Nevertheless, he answered the door anyway.

A half-sized witch with a green face peered up from under an enormous hat, a small ghost emerged from the billowy black robe. A pony-tailed cowgirl, in a red felt vest and skirt, appeared behind them.

"Trick or treat!" they cried. Before he could utter a mild chastisement, three bags were raised in hopeful expectation.

"What's this then?" Truitt felt a surge of delight, sweeping him back to the falling darkness on his first Halloween outing with Nell.

Gordon Sims stepped into view. "Sorry, Truitt. I told them that you weren't home, then Pammy saw the light come on. Come along, girls, the professor is busy."

"Wait," Truitt said, leaving the door ajar. He fetched some coins from a jar he kept in the bedroom, tossing a couple into each bag.

The little ghost giggled excitedly. "Oh boy!"

"Thanks, Truitt," Sims said, in a tone of gratitude Truitt rarely heard from him. "Thank the professor, girls."

The choir of voices sang their appreciation.

"The wife's got a pot of cider brewing. We've invited a few of the faculty over. You are most welcome to join us."

Truitt declined the invitation and the group moved on.

It had been his second invitation for the evening. Kristina Day asked if he would like to join them at Day Ranch for her grandmother's annual party, "In costume or not, as you prefer." Although Truitt had declined, Geoff Meyer dropped by anyway, apparently commissioned to bring him along. Truitt wanted nothing more than to return to his writing, after having to put it off for so long. So, he declined a second time.

As he reviewed his work, reading the article six months later with fresh eyes, he was struck by the narrow vision of his thesis, which was overstated. His tone was defensive, as if he were defending it in a court of law. Maybe he was, with Willema serving as judge and jury. But hammering on the righteousness of Joachim's work was not the way to win his editor's approval.

He took distance from the piece, assessing it as objectively as he could. Here was the author standing as the lone hero of Truth, carving a unique path through the woods, wresting critics and skeptics in his pursuit of the Holy Grail. How arrogant he had been. The world did not exist to serve the solitary knight, however holy his cause.

Wasn't that the lesson he learned at St. Amadour under Brother Guillaume's deft hand? Through daily prayer and meditation, Truitt had come to understand that the true path to glory was a life of service—to the brothers in Christ, to his family and community back home, to the broader community of man. The path of the knight might lead to fame and glorification of his person, but the path of the monk led to eternal bliss. His community now was the world of letters, the global university, peopled by women as well as men. It was his duty to find a way in which to draw women into his field, as well as reach out to all students.

If Truitt could succeed, he would be making it up to Nell in some way, offering up to her an education she was denied. It would begin to heal the black hole left by her death, and to atone for the wounds inflicted on her by his own flesh and blood, his father. Could he find a new horizon to fulfill his ambition, without losing his intention or his passion? Could he make room for genuine feminist inquiry?

Still, he saw no way to do it.

A small jazz combo livened up the front salon of the Day house, while Mrs. Day served up her famous mulled wine from an antique vessel that her grandmother had carried around the horn as the family resettled into the bustling Irish-friendly city of San Francisco. The glass cups had been added later and carried with them the stigma of Prohibition style tea parties and illicit liquor, so folks said, enjoying every nugget served up on the infamy of their local hero, Clement Hawke.

There was a tub of water on the patio full of apples. Kids young and old took a turn at bobbing for them. Festive orange lights blinked from the shrubbery and a black cauldron of dried ice created a shroud of mystery at the front door, which was draped in spidery fish-line web spun by several inert pipe-cleaner spiders, each the size of a baseball.

With both Si and Geoff appearing for the party, Kristi felt safer behind her black cat apron and a row of hot appetizers than she would be volleying between two camps of rivals. Si's group was posted on the back patio, near the beer keg, while Geoff worked the crowd from the college. Kristi was glad for once, that Professor Truitt had turned down the invitation. She didn't need the complication of others observing her behavior around him, especially after so much speculation had been served up in her friendliness to Geoff Meyer. His staying away also saved her the onerous task of keeping him out of her father's way. He had shown a little too much interest in Professor Truitt's attendance.

Kristi took a tray of food to set on the bar in the salon which was being manned by Mac. He and Amy had decided to work the party as part of the catering crew. Birdie signed up as well, working in the kitchen with Tessa, which was the assignment she preferred.

Amy was carrying a tray out to the boys on the back patio when Kristi intercepted her. "I'll take that. See if Mac needs a sandwich or something. He looks famished."

Si was entertaining the group with stories of his exploits on the east coast. When Kristi appeared, the boys showed their gratitude with light teasing, kidding Si for abandoning her all summer.

Si took the opportunity to pull Kristi aside. Making a wise crack about Geoff stalking her. She glanced and saw Geoff out on the patio talking to one of his senior students, who was also a close friend of Si. "What's the deal? Are you two a thing or not?"

"We've already discussed this, Si. And since the beginning of September I've seen even less of Geoff. We're all in school now."

"So, I suppose he's taking you to the Gala?" Si said with resentment in his voice.

"Why do you assume that? As a matter of fact, I'm going with my folks. You've probably heard that Father is taking Sofia Avila, since we are staying at your family's lodge."

Si stood awkwardly studying the ground. Then said, "You care to go with me, then?"

"Why, yes, I would. Thank-you." She was pleased to be asked by him, as a matter of fact. Her public appearance with Si should quell a lot of gossip and put to rest her father's latest plans for her future. "I'm wearing last year's gown, though. It might cause your mother some distress."

He was grinning, apparently pleased that she said yes. "She'll get over it. Say, I'll be working the range through Friday, so I won't be able to leave till Saturday morning. Early."

"That suits my schedule better." The gala occurred the second weekend of December, just before school broke for the holidays. It was midterm week, and she was glad not to have to ask Professor Truitt for time off. "We can drive up together, if you want."

"Sure." He smiled, returning to his group, while she returned to her other guests.

Truitt waited in his office for his TA, since she would need to use the office for reading the essays while he attended Avila's faculty team meeting. He had been working on the article, trying to meet Willema's requirements while avoiding damage to his work. Miss Day soon showed up, and he was off to the meeting.

The entire meeting was focused on placating the extreme views of Cecil Durham—who had been dead set against the program from the start. Avila was bending to accommodate Durham, yet the man shifted ground as soon as an accord might have been reached. His obstinacy was driving Avila further away from a reasonable compromise, which meant a skewing of the western canon to address the missing view of women. The meeting had ended on a sour note.

The contention of the meeting put Truitt in a mind unsympathetic to Willema's request for his own topic. Yet he knew now, more than ever, that the editor was right, and his success lay in the direction of appealing to a wider audience, feminists included.

Opening the door to his office, he found Miss Day sitting at his desk, reading.

She looked up in surprise, with some embarrassment. "I finished the essays." She stood up, still grasping Willema's letter.

"Did you find it interesting?" He tried to take a severe tone, but found he was interested in her response.

She blushed. "Well, you understand that I have no point of reference for the context. I can only guess what you meant, from our medieval class and from Professor Avila's French class."

"I see," he said.

As he moved forward, she abandoned his space.

"It's a minor story in the epic wash of medieval history," he said. "At least it was history."

She picked up on his tone. "Didn't the meeting go well? Sofia thought it might, if Professor Durham were willing to come on board."

"He did come, but to agitate, it seems, not to help."

"Oh dear."

"On the matter of my article...." Truitt explained the dilemma caused by Dr. Rutherton's position. "The rising fortune of woman, which peaked in the eleventh century, had been extinguished by ecclesiastical reform in the thirteenth. And as I said, Joachim was a minor figure in the vast drama that included hundreds of more prominent figures."

"What about the court of Eleanor and her daughters?"

"She died at the end of the twelfth century. Within a hundred years, women had become marginalized."

"What about the paper Amy wrote? Couldn't you do something with the Romance? Educating warrior knights to be suitable visitors in a lady's parlor, or something like that."

"The works of Eleanor's court were written by men, for the most part, under the direction of Eleanor and her daughter. At best we have a masquerade of reality, like the Romance itself, in a way. Besides, all hope fueled by the court at Poitiers for educating a new kind of knight had vanished by the time Chaucer created his Tales. The secret words of the romans courtier were translated in the tart apologies of old hags like the wife of Bath. He chopped up the courtly rituals into fodder for satire, like the exaggerated longings of saucy wenches like the Miller's daughter."

Miss Day glanced at the Willema's letter, discouraged. "But, still—you must see some value in teaching women, Professor, or you wouldn't still be here. You can bring the whole era alive for us."

He sat in his chair. "Miss Day, I am thoroughly against changing the canon just to satisfy the whims of females—who have an endless need to find everything palatable." To his own ears he sounded as immoveable as he had found Durham an hour before.

"So, we are to remain forever standing outside the candy shop looking in? Is that it?"

"What's this?" The evocation of childhood made him smile.

"Are we to be outsiders forever, banned from the pages of history written by men?"

"Come, now, aren't you being a bit dramatic?"

"Not at all. The absolute power of the Church over women's lives back then has become tyranny by tradition. Men own education." She took the chair in front of his desk. "It can't be ours too, unless we see ourselves in it."

She did have a point, but he was still not willing to sacrifice Truth to accommodate special interests. Yet, hadn't he gone around this pole before? He leaned on the desk and folded his hands. "So, what would you have me do about it?"

She smiled, as if she had been waiting for him all along to ask. "A new kind of knight was emerging, you said. And in your preliminary notes there," she leaned across his desk and extracted a sheet of notes she had earmarked for the discussion.

"You've written, 'Joachim saw the Church hierarchy dissolving, replaced by a society of new men, a new order of freedom guided, not by clerics, but by Spirit.' Why not new knights for Joachim's New Age?

And didn't Joan of Arc figure in here somewhere? Wasn't she also a new woman speaking to God directly?"

"Miss Day! What you are suggesting would require highly imaginative speculation on known scholarship. Devoid of historic foundation, I might add."

"Men write what they see, as they believe. Just read the Bible. No one in his right mind believes that a man who was swallowed by a whale could be coughed up again whole three days later. What was the real story?"

Truitt frowned. Her example was a stretch.

Kristi waved the letter from Willema. "This is what your editor seems to be asking for. 'Risk reaching beyond what is known. Conjecture what might also be true.' Those are her words."

Truitt gave up, tired of an argument that seemed to run in circles without ever settling. They worked on the essays for class, and he had to admit to himself that she was a good reader. Her comments revealed an understanding of the finer nuances of the writer's intention, even when the subject lacked focus on paper. Perhaps because of this he was willing to admit that she also might be right about Joachim's work on the new age.

Later, when she was gone, Truitt gave his imagination play, speculating on what women in the French court might have thought of the Calabrian monk. He considered the possibility of what they might have known, from that vista in the center of Western Christendom, the crossroads between the Italian peninsula and Santiago de Compostela, the cultural center for nobles from the British Isles to Jerusalem. Taking cues from the controversies sparked by the monk's followers, and the flagrant flaunting of the Church by the feminist courts of southern France, Truitt saw potential avenues for further research.

He had dispatched Willema's unwieldy request in one new paragraph, suggesting the possibility that Joachim's influence restored a sense of renewal in a European society decimated by the black plague, led to rebellious acts against an increasingly corrupt clergy, and encouraged man—and woman—to unshackle themselves from the tyranny of the Church. Then Truitt returned to the main business of his own thesis.

Within two weeks, the article was ready to re-submit to the Journal. A celebration was in order, Meyer insisted. The three of them went to the Steakhouse where Avila was waiting for them. Truitt would not have thought the occasion a cause for celebration, but Miss Day did, and she managed a little party. Even Christian Day joined them toward the dinner hour, unexpectedly picking up the check. Truitt was uncomfortable with his gesture but didn't make a fuss. Surprisingly, the board president was congenial to him, if in an impersonal way.

Thanksgiving being only a week away, they shared notes on how they would spend the holiday. Meyer had an excursion planned to the Newport Caldera in Oregon. The Days were hosting family at the ranch. Sofia was increasingly included in family gatherings. Truitt declared that he would be traveling up to Sanders cabin in the north wilderness. That evoked some teasing from Meyer, who could not picture Truitt trekking in the wild.

The trip up to the cabin was slow and treacherous in places. The roads were crowded, and the pace was slow, due to snowdrifts and packed blacktops all the way up the mountain. The highway was narrow as it wound toward the river. In the failing light, Truitt was not sure if he had passed his cutoff when he caught the reflection of light off of chrome. A shadowy form emerged onto the road to flag him down. It was his old friend.

"I thought I'd better come down to meet you," Sanders said, as he waved off the driver of a truck parked on the roadside. He jumped into Truitt's car. "My neighbor's on his way to town. Nice fellow—he volunteered to sit here with me till you showed. I assured him how exacting you are about time...." Sanders chatted all the way up the mountain.

With two bedrooms, the cabin was nearly twice the size of the bungalows in Hawkes Ferry. They settled in to a comfortable visit, taking walks, drinking scotch and chatting long into the night. With no work to accomplish, Truitt allowed himself to adapt the rhythm of Sanders' world. When his host set out for fishing or hunting, though, Truitt stayed in the cabin reading the few books he carted along.

Thanksgiving dinner was modest, a roasted chicken with potatoes from a box and gravy from a can, with cranberry jelly and frozen rolls. Truitt didn't complain, recalling holidays with Nell, her hand deft in the kitchen. He missed her, the serene joy with which she filled their home. He was glad to have Sanders share stories of a boyhood tortured by three sisters, living on a homestead in the rangelands near Magic Mountain.

Eventually Sanders wandered onto the topic of Kristina Day and how she was faring as Truitt's TA. He wondered if Truitt's predictions had been realized.

"You were right to scold me. Miss Day has proven to be a most excellent assistant, all the way around." He was not reticent to tell his friend about the girl's many accomplishments, her ability to anticipate and deliver, whether for him or his students. Perhaps it was the scotch, or the comfort of the cabin, or perhaps Sanders' keen interest in his affairs, but Truitt found himself speaking of Miss Day with a warmth and tenderness that he hadn't realized he felt. And he did so without reservation, with no sense of alarm. "She is an adequate scholar, as well. Has a real nose for research and assumption. In fact, I am indebted to her for helping me over a hurdle with my article."

"Rejected again?"

"Let's keep our fingers crossed," Truitt said, helping himself to another taste of the scotch.

Back at school, Truitt was aware of new feelings for Miss Day. He had talked too much about her to Sanders, for now he looked forward to their meetings with anticipation instead of the dread he once felt. He encouraged her to talk, allowing her to chatter about her holiday at first. Gradually she was sharing her feelings and opinions on the men in her life, namely Meyer and Befford.

It seemed that Befford was not a thing of the past as he had believed, but very much in the present. Instead of being in the front seat of her life, Meyer had taken a back seat. She made note of their assets and their failings comparing one to another as if she were choosing between two dresses. He asked if she had to make the choice now, and she laughed. No, of course not. Then, her chatter wandered in the direction of academics and graduate schools, and she asked what he thought of her pursuing a career like Professor Avila.

He was confused. The growing ease with which she shared her stories about Befford and Meyer were beginning to alarm him. In fact, he was distressed about them, though he couldn't say why. Finally, he decided that it was not appropriate, given his association with Meyer, for her to be discussing such things with him. She seemed offended, but agreed that it might be in poor form.

It was nearing the Christmas holiday. Mid-terms were coming up. Miss Day threw her full support behind the project and together they created a process which was smooth sailing for the students as well as for themselves.

In the mail one day, he received a notice from the Journal. Kristi was working at the table in his office when he announced to her the good news. Holding up the letter, he said. "It's been accepted. She finally accepted my work."

Kristi immediately joined him, wanting to see the letter for herself.

He could not suppress his joy, and thanked her for helping him to succeed.

"Oh, Professor! I'm so happy!" With that, she threw her hands around his neck and kissed him.

He put his hands on her shoulders to hold her at bay. Instead, he encircled her in his arms, drawing her close, returning her kiss with his own burning desire. Something shifted deep, in his very core, giving way to an irresistible force, an avalanche of joy.

A rap at the door, then Meyer stuck his head in. "Want to go for a drink?"

Truitt's spirit crashed. He stood speechless, horrified. Already she was moving away, running to Meyer. What had he done? The barrier had been crossed. He was full of shame. What had Meyer seen?

"Not ready yet," she said to Meyer, collecting her things. "I'll finish up on Monday," she said, hurrying out the door. Then she was gone. Meyer remained.

"Coming, old man?" He was searching Truitt's face as if looking for an explanation.

"No. No, not tonight. Have these tests to work over."

After Meyer left, Truitt locked the door. What had he been thinking? Well... he hadn't been thinking at all. He had allowed himself to cross that line—to become one of those teachers who preyed on the young females who held them in trust. He had brought shame on Miss Day. Why else would she have fled?

Truitt could not bear to recall the warmth, the openness, the union he felt with her just moments ago. In searching for the cause of his infamy, he thought of her gesture. She had started it, hadn't she? She'd embraced him—kissed him.

Tell yourself that. Convince yourself—and then you are no better than the rake who defamed your mother, the despoiler who brought shame onto that worthy woman.

Her gesture had been meant as a trifle. It was what she did, wasn't it? A sign of fondness he had witnessed on any number of occasions. It was her way, to buss a cheek in recognition or encouragement—not an invitation, for God's sake.

He had turned it into something else altogether, hadn't he? Something raw and hungry and uncontrolled.

Miss Day. Kristina Day.

Meyer.

How could he ever face them again?

Nineteen

It was just a hug, Kristi reasoned, a celebration of his good fortune, but he hadn't seen it that way at all. There they were, locked somewhere between heaven and hell when Geoff Meyer suddenly flung the door open. It was the worst possible humiliation for her. And the sly look on Geoff's face—the hurt look in his eyes—revealed an understanding of how-things-were. Only they weren't, were they? The professor broke off. Her head began to spin. All she could do was to flee from the room.

When Geoff caught up with her in the plaza, she had begged off dinner with a growing headache. She'd gone home, then. With Father already gone to the Beffords' cabin and Tessa at her sister's for the weekend, the house was empty. She went directly to her bedroom. She nursed the memory of her terrible joy, the longing in that moment of something old and familiar and now lost forever.

She played the scene over and over in her mind with chords of reproach and humiliation alternating in the background. She'd thrown herself at him. How could she after all that talk of sirens and sorceresses? She'd lived up to his worst expectations of women.

She cried and chastised herself and found no peace in memories of working together. In the end, she had a few hours of fitful sleep, leaving her drained and exhausted by morning. At four, Kristi roused herself from bed, and was packed and ready for Si when he arrived just after six.

"You're awfully quiet," Si said, after they had been on the road a while.

"Sorry I'm not better company. I keep dozing off."

"I expected to see you last night at the restaurant. Meyer said you'd gone home."

"I had to pack," Kristi said. "Were you working?"

"Not at the restaurant. Thought I'd find you there and have a drink with you guys."

Kristi found the inquiry oddly polite. He was acting the part of a gentleman. Coming to attention, she glanced over at him with some interest. "So how was Thanksgiving in New York?"

He responded with pleasure, recalling events at the Delaney estate, blending summer with Thanksgiving. He talked of the Delaney family and the assortment of people collected by the Delaneys. Yet he made no mention of any particular cousin. Kristi laid back and closed her eyes again, not caring to unearth any deceptions. Si chatted on about the parties and summer yachting and how impressed he was with the racing stable kept by a neighbor close-by.

Somehow he managed to work in Elena's wedding plans, "Announcing their engagement over the holidays."

The statement jogged Kristi awake. She restrained from an open reaction, noting that he hadn't seen the smirk on her face. She took no satisfaction in knowing how right she had been about his mother's plans. There were bigger storms to ride. She felt herself slide back into the seas of remorse—dark, cold and numbing.

"I owe you an apology...." he said after a while.

That woke her up.

"For the way I was last August—you know, at the windmill. I was being selfish, expecting you to wait at home all summer while I screwed around. But, god! You can't imagine how it feels—it's so liberating! To be free of books and papers, classes and all that crap. Just wait until next summer. You'll see."

She did see. She had seen it all along. It was one of the obstacles that kept Si from ranking out as the perfect man for her, no matter how suited he was to marry into the Day family. She ran his profile against the professor's, in an unconscious way, which brought forth all the admirable qualities of that good man, and all the reasons he could not suit her father's aspirations. She sighed in regret, then pounced on the random thoughts racing around her brain. Why should the professor have to suit anybody? She wasn't looking to him for that reason. He was an excellent mentor. That's what she needed.

"I could eat a horse," Si said, pulling into the drive of the roadhouse where they were to have breakfast.

Before Kristi could collect her coat and purse, he had hopped out of the car, and dashed around to open the car door for her—another demonstration of his vastly improved manners. Inside, Si packed away a ranch house breakfast, while Kristi could barely down one egg and a single slice of toast. She pushed her plate away and watched as he ate with gusto. She saw in his newly acquired manners the invisible hand of an unnamed Delaney cousin.

On the last leg of the road trip, Si chatted with enthusiasm about his work on the ranch, his father's ideas for his future, and how he intended to turn his father around on cattle breeding. By the time they arrived at the cabin, she knew a whole lot about the new Si, and saw that the distance between them had widened even further. He had no love of learning or books, not even his mother's woeful collection of first editions. He had no patience for the care and deliberation she gave to her writing, and especially no desire to see her excel in her studies.

In considering the cause of this vast improvement of his manners and civil discourse, she had to look no further than his two recent trips to Long Island and his absence from Kristi. In the spirit of Queen

Eleanor's court, the unnamed Delaney cousin had, no doubt, taken the rough-hewn western cowboy on as a project. Kristi considered why a female in this day and age—especially one educated in the best schools of New England—would be interested enough to take him on.

Such thinking led her to realize other significant changes in his behavior. Absent was the annoying, clawing hands-on stuff that she disliked. He hadn't attempted to foist wet kisses on her—in fact, he hadn't tried to kiss her at all. During the past four hours, he had not even tried to touch her, or to challenge her resolve on chastity before marriage. Even more remarkable was the absence of a wad of chew, and the sweet smell of wet tobacco mingling with beer or whiskey on his breath.

She didn't understand what it all meant, to him, to her, to where they were going. She wouldn't call attention to her own motives by complimenting him now, which would certainly initiate a discussion she no longer wanted to have with him.

Sofia wandered around the Beffords' lodge vexed at the turn of events. The whole idea seemed romantic when Christian invited her to the Cattleman's Gala weekend, staying with the Beffords at their mountain cabin. Despite the nomenclature, the house was the size of a small hotel, built with an eye toward art collecting and intellectual withdrawal, both of which eluded the Befford clan as far as she could tell.

The library was well appointed but filled with first editions of the book-of-the-month best sellers. The small concession to intellect was a recent edition of the Encyclopedia Britannica—with thirty volumes—and a leather bound collection of selected master works of the western canon. Sofia noticed that neither El Cid nor Don Quixote took place among the volumes including Shakespeare, Austen, Dickens and the New England Transcendentalists. The art provided better fare. Sofia enjoyed the next hour walking among the bronze Remingtons, the western paintings of Charles Russell and Indian drawings by George Caitlin, before she surrendered to boredom.

Christian had deserted her again for the day. She learned too late that the anticipated Gala weekend was arranged around activities that separated the men from the women. Tradition had the men folk gathering in neighboring barns and stables drooling over innovative operations and machinery for reaping, seeding, hauling, milking, branding or almost anything else that a rancher or farmer could do in these wide-open spaces. Womenfolk gathered around their needles to gossip, quilt, embroider or embroil as the mood suited. After lunch, they would retire to their rooms to prepare—all primping and preening—for the men folk to return. How positively Victorian!

After breakfast, as soon as the men left, Mary Befford disappeared, inviting the senator's wife to a private chat. Mary's sister, Pamela, was also in attendance, but preferred the company of her four children, and soon excused herself to join them in the rumpus room.

For all her prominence as a senator's wife, Mrs. Delaney—Leanne—proved to be a small-minded woman. Leanne showed little interest in Sofia once she learned Sofia was foreign born. Indeed, Sofia felt her standing slip in the woman's eyes, as the day progressed. She held little esteem for teachers, and was appalled at the notion that Sofia took an active role in touting women's liberation.

During dinner, Sofia felt the disdain of unfriendly eyes that had marked her as Christian's paramour. There was no doubt about whose hand had planted and watered that seed of disregard. Under such scrutiny, Sofia held her head high and demonstrated genuine interest in the senator and his constituents. She promoted Christian's interests, as a wife might feel entitled to. On several occasions, she smiled directly at Leanne Delaney and invited her into the conversation.

When dinner ended, and the men retreated to Befford's den for a cigar, Sofia retired to her room. At least she could get some work done on the program. The evening had offered up fresh examples as illustrations of challenges that contemporary women faced.

Christian came by later, bringing her a nightcap. He wanted to visit a while, sharing the success of his day. What she had seen as a pleasant holiday for them, he had seen as an opportunity to conduct business. He was hoping to be selected, by the senator, to serve on a panel for land management. He was also working on several prospective customers. Sofia listened with polite interest, waiting for the opportunity to share her own day. However, he stopped speaking mid-sentence and declared that he was exhausted.

"I need to get out early in the morning before breakfast, I'm afraid," he said.

"And your plans do not include me, then?"

He stooped over to kiss her goodnight. "You'll be wanting to pretty yourself up for the ball. The women will want to get to know you. And remember, tomorrow night I'm putting you on display. You'll make me proud."

At ten-thirty, when Si's truck rolled into the front drive, Mary came downstairs, followed by Pamela and three of her children. Sofia had been waiting in the library, anxious for Kristi's company.

Mary gave the girl a brief hug, "Kristina. You're looking well."

Sofia thought she looked frightful. If she didn't know Kristi any better, she would think Kristi had been up all night.

As the attention of the group shifted to Si, Kristi asked about her room.

"You'll be in Harriette's room."

"We're sharing," the eldest of Pamela's girls told her.

"I was sure you wouldn't mind," Mary added quickly. "Sandra's disappointed that she can't go tonight. I thought she could help you dress."

"Fifteen should be old enough," the girl said, sizing herself up to Kristi's height. "I'm taller than she is."

Kristi headed toward the stairs dragging her garment bag.

"Let me help," Sofia said, following with her overnight bag.

When they reached the room, Sofia asked Kristi if she were ill.

"I've had a frightful headache is all," she said making room for her bag in the closet. She opened her suitcase on the ottoman and removed her jewelry and make-up.

"How was the trip up with Si? Did everything go all right?"

"I'm afraid I wasn't much company for him. He was a perfect gentleman about it though." She chuckled, "Believe it or not."

Sofia smiled. "Distance makes the heart grow fonder, I believe. He hasn't spent any time with you recently. He probably misses you."

"I think it's more than that," Kristi said. "Did father tell you about the Delaney cousin?"

"I don't believe so...."

A knock on the door, Si called out, "Kristi."

She opened the door.

"I'm going out now to catch up with the fellows. I'll see you at six, all dressed up proper, and ready to go. Maybe you should take a nap or something."

"I'll be fine."

His comment was a hint to Sofia that Kristi was in need of a lie-down. "Do you want me to make excuses for you at lunch?"

"No. I'll be down eventually. But I would appreciate some time, if you don't mind. What room are you assigned to?"

"The rose-colored one on the guest wing."

"Near Father, I hope."

"Fairly close. We're separated by the Delaneys and the Peters."

The lunch was already served when Kristi arrived looking somewhat refreshed, but she still looked unwell. Mary introduced her to Mrs. Delaney, who immediately began to ask questions, even before the poor girl was settled at the table. She asked about her family, her education, and her plans for the future, all topics that were impertinent but allowed by Mary Befford for the entertainment of her illustrious guest. In fact, her attitude was not so much curiosity but of one who has a purpose. She was interviewing Kristi for what reason, Sofia could not understand. She expanded her questions to include Christian's business and his dealings with customers as well as his political affiliations. Sofia was offended at the nature of such questions, and demands the woman made upon Kristi to answer them. She wanted to speak out and defend her student, but that would have undermined Kristi's status in Mary Befford's house.

After lunch, Sofia accepted Kristi's offer to show her the grounds that surrounded the cabin. She was relieved that the others had declined.

"What did you think of Mrs. Delaney?" Sofia ventured.

"I found her a little rude, if you want the truth. Those questions about Father's business and associates. As if I were the one to ask about that. Mary knows his business far more than I do. I'm sure she's gossiped all about it—and other things. I was offended by her treatment of you, too. Who does she think she is?"

"I've been looking forward to your company. It's not been a fun holiday for me. Luckily I brought my work along. At least she provides substantial material on the issue of women's attitude toward other women. Does she have any daughters, I wonder?"

"Not that I know of. I've only met Ross—the same time you did. I had the sense he had a brother."

"I haven't seen much of your father, either. I was hoping this would be a romantic interlude of sorts. A way to see him in a different light, among his closest friends. In his milieu, as it were."

"Poor Sofia!" Kristi consoled her with upbeat humor. "You've been moved into the castle now, I guess."

Sofia smiled as her heart sank. There was much truth to the facetious comment that Birdie Caldwell made in class, on the destiny of medieval women entrapped by marriage.

As they rounded the cabin back to the side door, Sofia asked how Kristi's work with Truitt was progressing, expecting a report of improvement as Truitt now must realize how reliable and worthy Kristi was.

The question was innocent enough, but Kristi's reaction was instant, a short gasp of breath, turning pale, the girl withdrew quickly, shouting back a promise to visit her room later.

Sofia stood outside the door as it shut soundly against the jamb. That Kristi was deeply affected by her words pointed Sofia in the direction of what might ail her. Neither Si Befford nor Geoff Meyer had caused that kind of grief. It was Professor Truitt, and although Sofia might speculate on the reasons for such deep feeling, she couldn't know the truth of it until Monday when she could interview Geoff Meyer, who undoubtedly held part of the answer.

Kristi rushed into the house and up the stairs praying that Sandra was not in the room. It was murderous to have to share a room today of all days when her heart was near to breaking. What had she done?

Not until facing Sofia—with the horrible specter of Professor Truitt's disgust frowning on her—did she realize the full impact of her offense. For at that moment, when her heart hung between heaven and hell, she understood that here was the one perfect man for her. And yet it could never be. A man who would never love the siren—Jezebel, Circe, Morgan la Fay all rolled into one. And as if to prove him right, here she played with the affections of another man, one who feels entitled to her affections. More damned than Eve was her own blighted heart.

What had she done? All those months of hard work and devoted effort on her part to gain his respect, not only for her work but for her person as well. Building trust day by day. She wanted him to move beyond the schoolgirl persona he had cast her in, and to recognize the scholar she wanted to be—to see her as he saw Martin, who didn't care a whit about scholarship or academia.

All thrown away in one careless gesture!

Si presented Kristi with a corsage just before they left the house. Father and Joe Befford were on hand, glad to witness a patching up of sorts between the two. Mary was still in her room primping with the other ladies, although Mrs. Delaney had made an appearance, no doubt to assess the quality of the gentleman's manners as well as the degree of attachment that might exist between Si and his old friend.

At dinner, Si had eschewed the Befford table opting instead to sit with his new-found friends, the cattle breeders from Elko. The three other couples were widely mismatched, in Kristi's opinion. One couple seemed to be engaged—at least the girl wore an ostentatious diamond that she kept admiring while the men chatted. The other two girls were dressed in lavish gowns that more properly belonged on stage than at dinner in The Lodge. Neither was groomed in a manner that suited the dresses or the occasion, and through the conversation Kristi gathered they had been picked up as last minute dates at the Casino. The girls did not speak among themselves.

Kristi was utterly bored. It was a relief to have Sofia approach her and request a chat. They headed toward the powder room. On opening the door, Kristi heard her name. Mary Befford was commenting on Kristi's gown as being horridly out of date. Mrs. Peters commented how lovely it looked given Kristi's blue eyes, and sapphire in winter is never trite. Mrs. Delaney sympathized with Mary's opinion. The group of ladies was in the powder room, out of sight from the entry. Sofia pulled Kristi back out of the door and found a quieter retreat.

"That horrid woman," Sofia said.

"Mary? Or Mrs. Delaney?" Kristi asked with a smile.

"Both! Leanne Delaney thinks I am too Latino to bother with. And Mary.... Mary.... I cannot even put into words how betrayed I feel at those hands!"

"I realize that you must feel betrayed by her, in light of Mrs. Delaney's bias, but has she done something else to offend you?"

Sofia's angry speech resorted to half-Spanish as she tried to describe the slight she felt from Mary's behavior. "She has not insulted my face, yet the manner that she treats with Christian is most unforgivable!"

"Oh. That." The relationship between Mary and her father had always been acerbic, with a cool graciousness that she now recognized as cloaked hostility—at least on Mary's side. Father continually deferred to her small rebuffs and chastisements, and Kristi had always believed his behavior was aimed at maintaining a civil deportment with his best friend's disagreeable wife. The conversation with her mother in Vegas had given Kristi a totally different take on their history. Now, she was acutely aware of Mary's meanness, and how often she shot him with poisonous barbs and spiteful leers. While it was not her place to tell Sofia this history, Kristi was not going to let her teacher be strung up for Mary's entertainment.

"I'm sure Mary is attempting to make you feel unwelcome—an outsider—and not just to support her new friend."

"It's working," Sofia said. "But she won't win."

"Ask Father to tell you the truth about his relationship with Mary. It might explain a lot."

"And you won't tell me, of course. Loyalty to your Father." Sofia said with compassion.

"I won't tell you because neither one of them has told me. What I know is simply gossip." They headed back to the dining room. "But if he won't tell you, I promise to give you the gossip."

Si was gone when Kristi returned to the table. She scanned the tables scattered around the ballroom.

"Gone outside with Cherry," Don from Elko said. Cherry was his date. He held his fingers up to his mouth to mime a cigarette. Kristi suspected there was more to it than that, since every table accommodated guests with smoking with matches and ashtrays.

"So you the old girlfriend?" Don asked. "Your Daddy is Day Enterprises? Si said we might have a little chat. Maybe be invited to Hawkes Ferry for cocktails or something?"

The man was of an age with Professor Truitt, but had slicked-back hair and wore a large gold ring on his right hand. He had the manners of a field hand and was openly flirting with her. She wondered how the professor would feel about a man who would try to pick up his friend's girl while on a date with someone else. What was the term for a male siren? Or did the rules not apply in reverse?

"I'm sorry, I am not in the habit of inviting people home with whom I have no acquaintance. You'll have to work through Si in order to gain access to Day Enterprises."

"Befford works for Day Enterprises?" One of the other men intruded.

"No. But he can invite you to Befford Ranch, and perhaps my father will show up as well. Then you can be properly acquainted."

Don stood up and gestured for her hand. "Why don't you just introduce us now?"

Kristi sat firm, well aware that all the eyes at the table were on her. "No, I won't. I'm a literature student and have nothing to do with my father's business. Since we are not well acquainted, I couldn't honestly represent your character. But you are welcome to introduce yourself."

Don frowned and sat down. Cherry came back to the table grinning with satisfaction. Si followed her into the room but detoured to his dad's table. He talked momentarily with Mr. Befford and then Kristi's father. Both men glanced at Si's table and shook their heads to decline, then sent Si packing.

"Well, I guess that settles that, gentlemen," Kristi said.

Si returned with less exuberance than he had displayed earlier in the evening. Kristi had to admit she felt a little set up, but then rationalized that Si was not exploiting her. The men at the table chided Si on his failure and Don leered at Kristi from time to time as he talked of advances he wanted to make in his business, if only he had the right kind of help.

Kristi noted with some apprehension that the men at her table were shedding their manners as they drank, and the girls were becoming freer in their comments, as well as the vulgar language. Si didn't seem to notice. Occasionally, Kristi reminded him that his mother or Mrs. Delaney seemed to be interested in what was happening at their table. That would have some effect. Clearly, though, Si was out of his league at this table, and Kristi suspected his father had told him that.

From time to time, Kristi glanced at the Befford table, checking on how well Sofia was getting on. The professor was uncharacteristically quiet. The general company of cattlemen did not lend themselves to intellectual conversation and academic wit such as Kristi had experienced with the professors in their Friday night gatherings at the Steakhouse. Even Professor Truitt had taken to joining them regularly.

Cowboys were used to controlling their herds and the range they rode on. They tended not to control themselves that much. And although Kristi chided herself for the generalization—she could think of a dozen cowboys who were as roughshod and brash as the men at this table, including Si Befford. They took turns riding the bronco of ego until one or the other got knocked off. It was a tiring evening.

Kristi longed for a quieter, more inward looking man, like the professor—even Sofia was of that ilk. They controlled the classroom and their area of study, which could be compared to the herd and the range, she guessed. But the very nature of that control caused them to look inward, to discipline the self, rather than control others outwardly. Even Geoff didn't try to control, so much as manipulate.

"So, Kristi Day," Don said, "are you ready for a little circle around the floor with me?"

The dinner tables were quickly emptying, and people were moving toward the second ballroom on the lower level. Cherry had excused herself with the other two women to seek out the powder room. Kristi excused herself and followed them out. Instead of heading with the crowd, she went around to the small powder room that she and Sofia had found earlier.

To her dismay, Mary Befford and Mrs. Delaney had also taken the same evasive action. Unfortunately, the size of the room offered no way for Kristi to hide her entrance.

They were deep into discussion about the upcoming wedding, about which Mary had yet to inform Kristi. They were speaking of candidates for Elena's attendants. Mrs. Delaney offered a few names. Mary invited Kristi into the conversation by explaining to her guest about the postponed engagement of Kristi and Si.

"Of course, if they had gotten engaged, Si wouldn't have been free to date Tricia, would he?"

"Certainly not. My niece is the paragon of propriety."

"Leanne's niece, Tricia Winslow, will be one of Elena's bridesmaids," Mary told Kristi as she dabbed her freshly painted lips.

The women showed no sign of irony or insincerity.

Mrs. Delaney added her thoughts. "And it's lucky for you, Kristi, that Tricia is in Florence with my sister and her family. Otherwise, she'd be on Si's arm tonight instead."

Kristi smiled. "Oh yes! I've heard all about her. She's done a fantastic job with Si, to rub the range off his manners. He's such the gentleman these days."

Mary was as surprised at the news that Si had talked about Tricia to Kristi, as Mrs. Delaney was pleased at the apparent accolades he poured on her niece.

"She graduated cum laude from Bryn Mawr in June."

Kristi responded with enthusiasm. "Such a good match, both graduating at the same time. Si and I thought it would be downright fun to spend the weekend with you all. You know, reliving happy times."

She was almost relieved when the door closed between them. She had wished to God, though, that Si had said something, and saved all of them the trouble of pretending to like each other.

Kristi made a short job of packing up her things the next morning. Sandra, finding Kristi quite boring, moved back into the rumpus room with her siblings. So Kristi was able to sort things without intrusion. Although the pervasive sense of disaster that had loomed since Friday night was lessening, a dark cloud still lingered. The previous evening had provided much fodder for thought, as she navigated through Si's ambitions and his deceptions, through Mary's finagling and Mrs. Delaney's manipulations. Rather than seeing things as an all-out disaster, Kristi conceded she was simply lost in the dark forest of her own discontent.

Somehow she had to overcome her error, regain the professor's respect, his admiration for her work, and win his trust again. Kristi felt her whole future was dependent on getting past this incident, coming back into balance with her feelings and her rational mind. All of this could occur if the professor were to see that she was not interested in pursuing him. And it was true that the delay of their engagement had sent Si flying off in new directions, which, oddly enough, made him more attractive to her. Yet, it was hardly the scale of her rising attraction to the professor. Things were becoming complicated. Her plan to use Si as the backdrop for getting back on track with the professor was hitting quick sand.

As soon as she and Si were on the road heading home, Kristi asked, "So, who's this Tricia Winslow?"

Si was startled. "Who told you about her?"

"People talk." Kristi was nonchalant. "You didn't think you could keep it a secret, did you?"

"I told my mother to keep it to herself."

It surprised Kristi that Mary would betray her little man. She wasn't going to fuel that fire. "My father said something about it, actually. Heard it from your father."

Si looked worried. "Yes. She's in school with Elena."

"So you'll be walking down the aisle with her next Christmas, I suppose."

He turned to look at her. "What? I've only met her a couple of times. Who said that?"

"Elena's wedding. You're both attendants."

"Oh, that." He was relieved.

"When did you connect?"

"Her mother is Leanne Delaney's sister. They were in the party on Long Island last August," he said. Then added with less vigor, "She was there at Thanksgiving, as well."

"I heard that you invited her this weekend, but she was in Paris with her parents."

"Florence," he corrected her. Then he was irritated. "If you want to know the truth, I was pretty hurt when you postponed the engagement, Kristina. Kind of lost face with a lot of the guys, you know. But you got to give it to Trish. She defended you. She pointed out how you must've felt with me gone all summer."

"Smart girl," Kristi said.

"She's incredible, Kristi. You'd really like her. She's the smartest gal I know, including you. Graduated with honors from one of the best schools in the east."

Kristi discovered that she had majored in some kind of literature, and was accepted to graduate school at Fordham, a really big deal to Si.

"Of course, she's not as beautiful as you are, no blonde hair or anything. Her eyes are darker."

Kristi wondered if he meant the concession as a compliment.

"I know I've been selfish, taking off all summer, but you'll want to do the same thing. You want to enjoy your senior year like I did. Going out with different guys—Meyer, for instance."

Kristi took it all in, the tone of his voice, his enthusiasm for the girl, his willingness to delay their future. Her backup plan for the future was shattered, as it should be, she chided herself. She saw how she had been setting up Si to use him, exploit him. She was a little ashamed of herself. That would not be the way to win back Truitt's respect.

Si was still extolling the praises of Trish when he said, "You know we shouldn't even be thinking about getting engaged for a while. Maybe it's better to wait a couple of years, plan things out like Mac and Amy. Get settled in life a little, build a savings account, buy property, that kind of stuff. As Trish says, 'What's the hurry?' We should all have a little fun before taking on all those obligations of marriage and family."

Kristi was thinking of the fun Trish and Si might have had already. "You mean like sowing all those wild oats of yours?"

"What about Meyer?" he snapped back. Then just as quick added, "He's a good head, Kristi. I know that you like him. You've been talking about the future with him."

"I'll admit that Geoff has ideas, but we are worlds apart as far as our vision of the future. I was seriously intent on getting engaged at Christmas, as I told you last summer. But maybe you're right about waiting. You want to see if this deal with Trish is the real thing," and Kristi saw that it was, "I need time to adjust to this news. I have Father to consider. Let's just try to enjoy each other's company through the holidays. Is that fair?"

"Agreed," Si replied with a smile.

He, too, was relieved that the postponing of their future would also result in putting off the moment when their fathers must be reckoned with. Beyond that, Kristi had another motive for pretending to get back together with Si. Geoff Meyer's attentions would no doubt cool, and she was sure he'd get the word back to his neighbor and friend, Professor Truitt.

Meanwhile, she needed a strategy to get through the upcoming week working alongside the professor reviewing and grading midterms, an activity that would necessarily throw them uncomfortably close together. Kristi needed to navigate the waters with Truitt, with a more pleasant demeanor, of course, as required by her position in tutoring students. She remembered Miss Trout, the old lady who used to head up the Easter charity at chapel. Not one of Kristi's favorites.

A woman of few words, she attended strictly to the task before her, shared little of herself, and took no trouble to ease the discomfort of a young helper. Kristi had complained about the old lady's meanness. Grandmother wisely responded, "No one is ever wasted by the Lord, Kristina. There is a purpose to everyone who graces your life."

Let Miss Trout be her model now, for the deportment Kristi needed in order to get through the upcoming week with Professor Truitt. Focus on the task at hand. Share few thoughts, offer no opinions. *And be compassionate*, Mother might add.

Twenty

The flight out of Boise rocked on the eastern draft off the mountains all the way to Chicago, making reading impossible. Truitt closed his eyes and longed for the desensitizing narcosis of sleep, which had eluded him for the past week.

In the wake of the egregious error he had made, in handling the heartfelt reaction of his assistant, Truitt had been determined to take academic distance as they worked through midterm week up to the Christmas break. He had been supportive, attentive to her musings while moving her forward through the week's challenges.

As painful as it had been for Truitt, Miss Day worked in silence. She spoke only when necessary to obtain information or clarify a point. She was moving herself forward without his coaching. Their weekly review of the students whom she tutored had been as cool and rational as if he were sorting out some departmental business with Durham or Sims. There had been no animosity on her part, as he had expected. She had been coolly pleasant and dreadfully detached.

So, she had recognized her mistake and was correcting course—as she should. After all, Truitt was not the sort of man one treated like a pal, hugging and kissing at a moment's notice. It had been most inappropriate on her part, a naïve gesture sprung from a too open heart. It might have gone unnoticed had it not been for the intrusion of Meyer—that look of confusion on his face.

The airplane rocked disruptively in a brewing storm. A child wailed in the back of the cabin while groups of passengers broke out into excited chatter. The flight attendant announced the delay of the meal service. Truitt dismissed the distraction, the early summer storm hardly worthy of his notice. He closed his eyes and settled his thoughts into the quiet he forged through years of discipline and practice.

His office had been extraordinarily quiet too, all week, while she sat at the worktable absorbed in her tasks, and he likewise at his desk. Communications between them remained tolerable, with some effort, as they focused on shared goals. Yet the hours seemed to drag on only to end too soon. She would say goodnight and vanish with still nothing acknowledged or resolved. But of course, it was resolved. They were student and teacher, as they had always been and nothing more.

Her incessant chatter had ceased at last, a fact that should have brought him some peace. She no longer inundated him with bulletins on Avila's progress with the program, or opinions of various relatives and friends on inane topics concerning school, church and town. He had been glad for its demise. He grew tired of her praises of Meyer's wit and charm. She was sure to let him know—even in the scarcity of commentary that week—that she had reacquainted herself with Befford's attributes at a weekend gathering at the family's mountain lodge. He had been half-fearful that she would drown him in stories of the fellow's prowess and bullishness, his heroic deeds on the cattle range. But on such matters she held her tongue.

Truth be known, neither man was worthy of her. Each had, no doubt, held high hopes for acquiring the vast Hawke-Day fortune through an alliance with its heiress, a daughter too willing to please her father by choosing the "right" husband.

Now Truitt was being shrewish, for Meyer was clearly the better man, and for Truitt's sake, the better choice. For with Befford, he had little hope of retaining any connection to her after she was done with school. With Meyer Truitt could entertain some hope of acquaintanceship with the couple. But there was always the chance that *hope* itself would become a casualty, should Meyer with his fickle nature choose to move on from St. Clements. She would never move with him. Or would she?

The images haunted him as the plane rocked him like a cradle into fitful slumber. The winds of fate tossed him one way and the other, casting hope against expectation, foiling any suit he might attempt for her hand. Ghouls... wraiths... Raif....

He woke suddenly. *The blatant greed of his brother, slamming the door in his face.* Anger turned to sorrow then to despair. What could a man who had no wit or charm do to win their hearts? Without name or family, without fame or fortune?

What could Truitt do to enter that Kingdom, the place of those who belong?

"Thanks for driving up here to pick me up," Truitt said as he climbed into Bill Wahl's car. "I should have booked a rental earlier in the season."

"No need, Emery. You can depend on me."

"That's kind, but not for two weeks. By the way, I'm sorry about Christmas."

"Not to worry. Business first. If you get a job back here, there will be plenty of opportunities in the future."

Truitt had called Willema's office earlier in the week, as much a reaction against his uncontrolled responses to Miss Day as to his desire to finally move on. She had pounced on the opportunity and insisted that he join the family for Christmas in their country home. That meant dealing with Caroline and her brother, not to mention her parents, who were unknown to him. It also meant rearranging his plans to spend Christmas with Bill at his club. Yet the trip might be worth something. Caroline's father, Charles Rutherton, was well connected to academia in New England. Willema had inferred that it was Charles that she wanted Truitt to see.

"I took the mutual fund statements to the lawyer, like you asked. Ferd didn't know anything about them either."

Several weeks before Bill had told him about the statements from the mutual fund, which suggested a sizeable amount of money had been invested by Nell outside of the funds that Bill managed for her. Bill had been surprised at the independence she had shown. "There might be other investments. You need to have a thorough look through all her papers and books. I hope you will make time for that."

Truitt acknowledged the request, and then added, "I'll need to rent a car to go upstate. The airport agencies were fully booked for the holiday. Do you have any suggestions?"

"Those airport places charge too much. I'll set you up with a car from my agency. We'll go tomorrow."

"On Saturday?" Truitt asked doubtfully.

"They owe me a few favors."

It was after ten when Bill dropped Truitt at the cottage in Sycamore Falls.

Truitt thanked him for the ride. "I'd invite you in, but...."

"You're tuckered. I'll give you a ring in the morning."

The cottage was comfortably warm against the stinging cold of the wet weather outside. Bill had prepared for Truitt's arrival by turning up the water tank and furnace, allowing the rooms to be heated comfortably. Truitt was grateful even as he resisted the man's presence, which he considered somewhat intrusive.

He turned on the small electric wall heater in his bedroom and unpacked his bag. In the kitchen, he found the half-full bottle of scotch that he had opened the previous year. Pouring a glass, he settled into the wooden chair in the sitting room and glanced around the once familiar room. Nell's absence cast a strange dimness on things, making Truitt feel even more remote from the world around him.

The loss he felt now was not as intense as it had been, when each room still echoed with her presence. But it was now deeper felt, knowing that she would never again cross the threshold into the living room, rosy-cheeked from the heat over the stove, with little bits of gossip from her day in the library. Her laughter was gone. The heart of his home was reduced to a mere memory, its hearth stone gone cold.

Dear Emery. Dear, dear boy. She would say from the kitchen, mixing up something warm and comforting while he complained of a slight he'd taken at school, or the lack of esteem he had among the other boys with their leather cases and fine fountain pens. In later years, it would be the club memberships and late model cars, always a lack, some need on his part. For she had never been enough, and here he was still in need. But what he needed now was her person, her presence—the comforting warmth of her smile. *Dear, dear boy.*

The memory of her words, her voice, sang from the corners of the room. As he took in the desk, the still-unread books, the apron draped over the door waiting, her specter raised again, the heart and soul of the place. *Heart, hearth....* The goddess of the place, she was. The power of her love. Those noble knights were drawn to ladies who would fuel the fires of their hearts.

Woman as Hearth. Woman as power of Love.

The sentiment startled him, even as he instantly recognized its truth, for as far as he might roam, he had always returned here—to her hearth, to the heart of his own blood. He thought of the worlds they had not shared, and memories without her seemed meaningless. For his life felt whole only when he returned to her welcoming arms. Only then did he feel part of something greater than himself.

He closed his eyes, willing her to be there. Her image rose momentarily but dissipated, blending into another, younger face, a single sensation, the unfulfilled desire of yearning. Startled at the vision, he opened his eyes welcoming the shadows in the room. *You're home now, Emery.*

He stood up quickly to dissipate the apparition. The medieval monks had been right to warn of the devastating power of women, of the enigmatic rose culture and the riddle that consumed a man's loyalty that turned his heart from chapel pew to lady's bed. How quickly a man could be swayed by engaging eyes and a gentle heart. He had seen how easy it was done, how delightfully easy to stray. He was afraid of her—of what she could do if he would ever let go.

On Christmas Eve, Truitt made his way up the Hudson River valley toward the Rutherton family estate. The road cut through wooded hills and open fields, bordered by the white fences of gentlemen's farms. He expected the Rutherton place to be of this ilk, having been in the family since the seventeenth century. The land and the people were steeped in the history of the country, through eras of colonization, revolution and expansion, the very culture of the new nation etched by Ruthertons and their neighbors, its literature and music and art of little interest out in the open ranges of the west.

Small villages dotted the landscape with festive lights, an idyllic scene from an old greeting card. Today, as he traveled through the countryside in a late model sedan, for the first time Truitt felt as if he belonged in the picture, one of those native sons. Two days earlier in the lawyer's office, he had learned that his mother's estate was worth considerably more than anyone had anticipated.

In addition to the two accounts Bill had reported to him, Truitt discovered three additional accounts from paperwork Nell had tucked away in a book he found stacked in the pile beside her desk. Apparently not all of them had been unread. Her interest in investments had been keen in recent years. She had taken it on as a hobby of sorts, Bill Wahl had told him, to fill her time. Bill was sincere in his appreciation for Truitt's good fortune. Bill did admit, thought, to being saddened at Nell's lack of trust in him. Truitt tried to ease the older man's disappointment.

"You knew her, Bill. It was just another topic she could dive into, a new adventure to read up on. You whetted her appetite and she wanted to delve into it. Live it, apparently."

"She certainly got the hang of it, I'll say." Bill said.

It was mid-afternoon by the time Truitt crossed through the stone pillars that marked the entrance to the Rutherton property. The manor house was perched on a knoll in the distance facing west, across a low divide filled with fenced pastures and scattered woods. Trees in the final throes of defoliation lay bare against a slate gray sky. The stone edifice of the house took shape as he approached as columns emerged from the silhouette and defined a veranda on the western face.

In the courtyard, Chuck Rutherton directed Truitt toward a parking area near the detached garage. Chuck had been Truitt's roommate in graduate school. It was through him that Caroline had entered Truitt's life. Two young children were scampering around the gravel walk on onto the grass between the house and garage.

"Welcome to the old homestead," Chuck called out. "Glad Willa could talk you into coming up. They've all gone to town, I'm afraid. I've been elected bellman."

He stooped to pick up the bag Truitt drew from the trunk, leading the way to the front entry through an arbor defined by once green vines dying back for the season.

"Dreary, isn't it?" Chuck said. "Father is looking forward to showing the place off to you. He's proud of it. I have to warn you, he'll bore you with it and family history, if you let him. Thinks we're all dying to return here someday to run it."

"I'll come back and run it." One of the children opened the door, having entered the house through a back way. Chuck introduced her as Magdalene—Maggie, she said—and the other was William. There was some confusion among them as to what Truitt should be called. Little William said, "Shall we call you uncle?"

"Certainly not, you little rascal," his father said. "You can call him Dr. Truitt—or Professor, if you want to be chummy."

The housekeeper approached from a side hall.

"Mrs. Lenehan will show you to your room. Drinks will be served in the sitting room—down that hall—at five. We're doing things a bit early so the kids can open presents before bed. We'll hold dinner till eight."

"I wish I could eat dinner at eight," the little girl complained to no one in particular. Addressing Truitt she said, "I'm almost ten."

Her father smiled. "All right, Maggie. Let the professor freshen up."

The room was in a wing with a balustrade and reading nook that overlooked a salon that Mrs. Lenehan identified as a sitting room. Bordered by glass doors that opened to a veranda overlooking the river, the open room allowed the Christmas tree to sweep up into the second story space.

Truitt's room proved to be a generous suite with a private bath and sitting area, which the housekeeper had supplied with a pot of hot tea and plate of cookies. She asked if he wanted for anything else, before leaving him to unpack his things.

Truitt would have preferred a long walk before cleaning up from hours spent on the road. Instead, he attended to his belongings, which included a coat and tie for dinner, as Willema had instructed. The Ruthertons retained their customs in the country, with drinks generally at six-thirty and dinner at eight—apparently accommodating anxious children on Christmas Eve with drinks at five rather than six-thirty.

The ladies returned from the village by three. Caroline came up immediately to see him. "Aunt Willa is anxious to see you," she reported after throwing her arms around him in a gesture of welcome. His acceptance had apparently signaled to her a turn in their relationship, something he was not entirely comfortable with. He returned the hug briefly then held her at bay. "Have you met father yet?"

"Only your brother—and his children, of course."

"And what did you think? Did you ever believe Chuck could produce such darling little things? Its Adrienne's doing, really. She's a doll." Caroline gazed keenly, taking in his face and sighed. "Well, I'd better go dress for dinner. Drinks at five?"

At the appointed time, Truitt showed up in the sitting room to find it occupied by the two children and their mother. "Hello, Dr. Truitt.

I'm Adrienne, Charles' wife." She referred to her father-in-law as Dr. Rutherton, and like Caroline, she referred to Willema as Willa.

Maggie asserted herself when her mother ran out of small talk. "Auntie Cay says you live out with the Indians and cowboys. Do you have a cattle ranch and horses?"

"Do you wear your guns all the time? We saw it on TV." Little William joined in.

Truitt described as best he could, the state of affairs for the Native Americans he had as students. He knew surprisingly little about how they lived, but he could assess how that select group thought about things. He said little about the cowboys, whom the children obviously saw as heroes. No point in letting them down.

Willema came into the room, adding to the discussion on her arrival. She offered Truitt a welcoming hug before turning the children from the romance of the West to the bravery of the knights around King Arthur's roundtable. The turn had brought him to those early Christmases with Nell feeding him the fantasies that would spark his life and his lifelong yearning for a Camelot of his own.

Dr. Rutherton made his entry with Caroline and Chuck. After introductions, Dr. Rutherton offered his condolences for Nell's death.

"You knew her then?"

Dr. Rutherton glanced at Willema and then responded, "Yes. Willa first brought her here, thirty, thirty-five years ago. She was a courageous girl then, I thought. And she proved herself to be a steadfast woman. She did right by you, given the circumstances. A fine woman, I'd say—now."

The children offered welcome distraction, with grandfather and grandaunt showering them with attention and praises without shame. Caroline chatted comfortably with Adrienne, about shops in town.

Truitt did not know what to make of this imposed intimacy with Willema Rutherton's family. He had expected something much different, much more formal to match the suit and tie, the subtle insinuations and coded messages that ride the top of guests milling in the front salon—like a faculty gathering at Day Ranch. What he was now privy to was the inner family doings he had witnessed as a day student visiting the estates of schoolmates—namely, Chas Greenstone and Trevor Steed. But it wasn't exactly like that, either. He was an honored guest, held in some regard by the family, welcomed in his own right. He had the sense that he belonged here, somehow.

Adrienne soon corralled the children into the kitchen for their dinner. Caroline and Chuck bandied about adolescent insults while Willa looked on amused.

"As you see, Emery, my children have never grown up. Either that, or they find much enjoyment in tormenting me." Dr. Rutherton said as he motioned an offer to refill Truitt's glass. "I hear you're an Associate now at that college out west. Good work. Willa tells me that you'll be published this spring in her journal."

"June issue," Willema chimed in, turning to join them.

"Willa puts a little too much faith in her own work," Dr. Rutherton said, smiling. His children were not the only ones who liked to vex and poke at each other. "The work I've seen of yours, published in venues with less acclaim, has not gone unnoticed—in my circle at least. That piece on Arthur's roundtable in *Medieval Times*, for example.

"You may not realize this, son," Dr. Rutherton cast a look of triumph at his sister, "I have some influence in my sister's world of medieval minds, governor's boards and the like. I think Willa will agree that, while limited, your curriculum vitae is not insignificant."

Willema did agree. Once satisfied that she had succeeded in connecting Truitt to her brother, she seemed less interested in their conversation and wandered away.

"Your time with the academics at St. Amadour speaks highly of your intentions," Rutherton said to Truitt. "It's a different life altogether, isn't it? Did you find things difficult there?"

Truitt relaxed into a favorite topic. "Not at all. I rather enjoyed the...."

"It's time for presents, everybody," Maggie's vibrant voice trumpeted the news as the rest of the company came into the room.

The adults settled into their seats while Adrienne engulfed them with a mountain of packages wrapped in holiday paper and ribbons. A great deal of delight ensued as the children ripped through their gifts. Maggie opened each one with exaggerated joy, pausing briefly for commentary, finding enjoyment in new clothes, colorful bracelets and a new chest for her doll clothes. William, on the other hand, tossed aside the clothing, and dove into mechanical superheroes that resembled armed vehicles.

"That's my boy," Chuck beamed.

His wife chided their son with, "You're wearing this to church tomorrow, whether you like it or not."

Gifts were then passed around among the adults. Caroline and Adrienne were explaining the gift giving tradition of their drawing names among the adults.

"Otherwise it all just becomes too much," Adrienne added.

Willema presented Truitt a large red box wrapped with a white bow. Inside was a woolen plaid robe with his initials embroidered on it. He was surprised and touched, but embarrassed that he had brought nothing in return, not even a gift for the house.

Willema watched him unwrap it. "Nell had asked me to get it for you on my trip to Edinburgh last year. I never had the chance to give it to her," she added with marked sadness.

Caroline handed him another package. "And this is from us—from the family."

It was a leather portfolio, large enough to hold a hundred-page manuscript. His name and title were inscribed on the front in gold letters.

"Congratulations of sorts, for your Associate—and a Christmas gift—combined," Caroline added.

The children rushed to see the gift and withdrew a little disappointed that it looked no different from one that grandfather or Auntie Willa might carry.

The wrapping was cleared as the children said their goodnights.

Mrs. Lenehan served a crown roast dinner on Christmas settings in the oversized dining room. Conversation turned on the season, events in town that had been attended and tasks that needed tending during the family's short stay at the estate. They returned to the sitting room for dessert and coffee where they discussed the next day's activities and topics of a lesser nature. Truitt listened with an open heart, not quite believing how easily he had stepped onto the ladder that would bring him to his highest goals.

The younger Ruthertons parted shortly after their return from church, as they were to spend the day with Adrienne's family. As Chuck had promised, his father gave Truitt a tour of the grounds. They walked along the dirt paths, then the stepping stones that circled the trout pond, finally meandering down to the stables. Along the way, he pointed out the features of the estate, adding little bits of family history. The tenants' housing had long ago been leased to families, who raised their own food. No longer used for hunting, the wood had been designated a conservation area, although the grounds man still lived in the caretaker's cottage.

"He keeps up the stables, as well, and manages the day workers we take on. We used to have a full-time crew out here, when my father was alive. He lived on the place and could keep an eye on things. I've only recently moved back, but I doubt that I will take on the onerous task of managing the laborers."

At a vista point, he directed Truitt's attention back toward the house. "The original structure was built in 1734. Although a considerable remodeling had been done in 1848, the left wing was only added this century, in the twenties, when the current guest rooms were built. The original rooms were turned into servants' quarters. By the next decade, only the housekeeper and cook remained. Today, only the housekeeper remains in residence, along with her husband, a general handy-man."

They ambled around the other side of the lake and up to the top of the bluff. Another vista point was marked by a stone shelter, overlooking the river.

"I lost my wife last year—my companion and dearest friend of forty years. Believe me, I know what you're feeling, Emery, with the loss of your mother. We all knew how close you were."

"I was sorry to hear of your loss, as well," Truitt offered.

"I've tried to emulate my father, a great philanthropist, as you know. I've done some good in my time." He sat on a bench in the stone shelter. "However, in one particular instance, I have been extraordinarily cruel. I was driven, by jealousy and arrogance, to ignore a wrongdoing. And my interference contributed to a grave injustice."

Truitt listened respectfully, wondering why the man seemed bent on unburdening so much private business to a stranger.

"My sister and I were of similar minds and disposition, learning Christian virtues at our father's knee. Yet, she bested me in his eyes, by bringing into our home a frightened young girl who had been most cruelly treated, and denied the safety of her own home. Your mother."

Truitt grew anxious, not wanting to have this man discuss the private business of his own family.

"I was a young fool, then, quick to deny that any girl who found herself pregnant could be innocent of the deed. I was blinded by a false reverence in law, and in the esteemed position of a popular senator. I was also jealous of my father's generosity on her—your—behalf. And, angry at Willema's blind devotion to an ignorant girl devoid of a moral compass." He stared at the river vista. "She left us last Christmas, you know. Heart attack. Fifty-seven on her last birthday. As beautiful on the day she died, as on the day we met."

For a moment, Truitt was startled, until he realized that Rutherton was talking about his wife.

"She told me that I was wrong. She sensed the girl's inner spirit, the soul that dwelt in the midst of all that squalor."

"My mother was a remarkable woman. I am only learning now how much she sacrificed on my behalf."

"This home should have always been open to her—to you. You were baptized in the church we attended this morning. Willa held you over the fount in her own christening gown. She stood as your godmother, did you know that? And she has watched over your lives since, like a mother hen." Rutherton seemed older now, sitting on the stony bench, his skin taking on an ashen hue, his mind lost momentarily to the view.

Truitt allowed his own thoughts to bend to the river which was marking the holiday as well with one or two pleasure boats, an unhurried scape without commerce. The place invited reflection of higher thoughts untied to memory and loss.

As if he could read Truitt's mind, Rutherton quietly reflected, "Your mother is gone now, and we can make no amends on her account. But we can make things right with her progeny. Willa wants you to think of our home as yours, as well. Charles and Caroline are both in agreement. They are very fond of you."

"Another generation of philanthropy?" Truitt said with some reserve.

"Perhaps—one can hope. But I think it's more banal that that. Charles means to make amends for some slight he inflicted on you—when you were at school together, was it? And Caroline—well, she thinks she fancies you. I wouldn't take it too much to heart, though. She fancies a lot of men, but finds no satisfaction in any, least of all the man she married five years ago. They've recently divorced."

A chill wind was rising off the river. Dr. Rutherton stood up and led Truitt back to the house. "Yesterday I mentioned my position with the association. I have access to information regarding open positions, before the official postings. Willa seems to think you'd be interested in moving to New England, if the right position were available."

"My ultimate goal would be to teach medieval studies in a prestigious school. I see New England as offering the best opportunities. I've only just received my Associate, though. I believe I'll need a few years in that position before anyone would consider my credentials."

"And why would you believe that?"

"You know that it's a competitive field. There are more graduates every year than positions for them to fill."

"Interesting perspective. Cautious. Yet, you might be interested if there is something in the nearer term—like next summer?"

"A permanent position you mean, at the Associate level?"

"I know of a position that might be coming up locally. It's too soon yet to talk about it. But could you be available by mid-summer?"

"As long as I can give St. Clements a term's notice, yes, I can be available."

"Of course," the old man smiled and ambled along.

Since they were down to a party of four, Willema arranged a cold supper for dinner, spread on the sideboard, which allowed the housekeeper and her husband to spend the holiday with nearby relatives.

Caroline was in a bright mood. "What do you think of our little kingdom here, Emery? Isn't it the most delightful place to visit? But you certainly wouldn't want to live here. Too dull."

"Don't be too sure, Caroline," Dr. Rutherton said. "I doubt that Emery has your taste for night life in the city. I sensed that he actually enjoyed our little stroll around the grounds."

"I enjoyed the walk," Truitt said, "even as cold as it was."

"Walk as often as you want, then," Dr. Rutherton said. "Explore the place."

"Yes," Caroline agreed, "But leave me out of it, until April—or possibly May."

"The brisk air would do you well, Caroline," Willema smiled, "your mind and your body."

"I'll stick to my creature comforts, thanks. I'll take my walks in town through the shops."

"You'd better watch out for this one, Emery. She's likely to run her next husband into bankruptcy," Dr. Rutherton took a sip of wine.

"Daddy. That's not fair. I do not spend excessively. Ask Willa."

"You could use with some sensible restraint, dear," Willema answered. "You should not have abandoned the Jaguar, at the very least. Money does not...."

"... Grow on trees, I know. But I'm working now."

"As assistant editor to Willa?" Dr. Rutherton said, with the final word, "That's a hobby, not a proper job."

After dinner, Dr. Rutherton retired to his study. Willema invited Truitt and Caroline to her study, to look at the proofs for the next issue of the Journal. Truitt's article made the cover story. Caroline was pleased with the job she had done on his behalf, and Truitt complimented her work. Willema opened a bottle of cognac and poured two glasses, for Truitt and Caroline. She invited Truitt to enjoy her collections, and promptly wished them both goodnight.

Caroline acted as a guide through Willema's modern addition to the collection of their ancestors. She admitted she knew little about the older volumes, which covered works on jurisprudence and government that preceded her birth. Caroline proved most familiar with the novels and collections of poetry. She had, in recent months, taken an interest in Willa's reference collection, the dictionaries, etymological treatises, publishing guides and scholarly criticism on medieval literature and letters.

Truitt was absorbed in the library, pointing out classical works in French and Latin, as well as English, all of which Caroline had little interest. She seemed to take more interest in his person. He tried to distract her with a number of books that might provide material for sequels to his article. She feigned a precursory interest.

Soon he found what her real interest had been all along. He had taken a seat on the sofa—reading passages to spur her interest in his paper—when she pushed the book aside and offered herself instead.

The dimmed lighting of the room and the enticing effect of the cognac drew Truitt's desire closer to hers. What she started, he embellished, returning her kiss, his heart searching for a spark of desire that could forge a future with her, in this house, with her family. Yet, nothing but gratitude rose—and a sincere desire to please, to reciprocate for all the kindness they had shown to him since his arrival. He found in Caroline nothing to quicken the latent desire that burned inside him for someone else.

He gently pulled away. "You're a delightful woman, Caroline. You're warm and witty. You always bring light into any room. You make people happy."

"You didn't always see things in that light," she teased, running her fingers through his hair.

He caught her wrist, gently returning it to her lap. "I was young back then, with no knowledge of women. And you were already so experienced. I thought you would chew me to pieces."

She laughed. "And what about you? Operating on some academic super-ego back then. We're both adults now. No one will interrupt us here. That's why Willa left us alone with the cognac."

She raised her face to kiss him again.

He stood up, giving particular attention to the book he was holding—he had been reading to her an excerpt from C. S. Lewis, Allegory of Love. Replacing the book on its shelf, he said, "You've been around the world. Married. Divorced. I haven't actually progressed at all in that direction."

"Surely, there are girls out there." She was hurt by the rejection.

"Students."

"Let me guess—your sensibilities don't allow trans-generational affairs with girls half your age. Or adulterous affairs with faculty wives, I would guess."

He shook his head.

"A pity. So your super-ego is still on?"

"Caroline, I value your friendship. But I don't love you."

"And what does love have to do with it?" She was genuinely surprised at his remark. "We make a terrific team, don't we?"

"A team?" He mulled over the concept. "Perhaps. I might have agreed with your assertion last summer at Columbia—at the restaurant. Now, however—things have changed."

"Have they now?" She followed the contour of his face, and then set her gaze on his eyes to delve deep, trying no doubt to ferret out his soul. "I see."

She released him as she stood up. "I hope she's as worthy of you as I am, dear boy. Goodnight, Emery." And she was gone.

Truitt poured another cognac and settled back into the sofa, taking in the grandeur of the room. A place fit for a king. He could sense that his dreams for the future, his Camelot, was easily in reach now. He sipped slowly from the crystal as subtle refractions of amber light danced off the collections of books and art that filled the room. Truitt reflected on the grandeur of the house and its surrounding park. He considered the world that was opening up to him, a world he had longed to be a part of since boyhood. Yet there was now a different type of yearning calling to him, one that would not be fulfilled without Kristina.

The sun-drenched day was chilled, with winds blowing from the north Pacific. Even in Las Vegas, Sofia had to don a full-length woolen overcoat, hat and gloves. She was headed toward Caesar's casino, to meet Birdie Caldwell for lunch.

Sofia and Christian had flown down on New Year's Eve for festivities. The trip was planned as an intimate getaway for just the two of them, after she had endured the entire holiday season in the company of the Beffords and their expanding family. She had earned the holiday. But her relationship with Christian had not advanced as she had hoped. He was perhaps being a little too gallant and gentlemanly, when she would have preferred an escalation of intimacy. Las Vegas had done nothing to help her. There were parties arranged with other friends, a breakfast and dinner. All meant to show her off, no doubt. Today, Christian had deserted her early for a six-hour session with his southwestern sales staff.

Sofia crossed the Strip heading toward the casino where she was going to meet Birdie Caldwell for lunch. It was not so much a meeting with her student, as an opportunity to meet Birdie's Aunt Joni, a woman who loomed large in Birdie's stories on family and tradition. Joni seemed to break all the traditions—or at least the preconceptions people have about traditional Native American women. A blackjack dealer at a major casino, she served as a role model to her niece, was entrenched in her family and cultural traditions, yet lived comfortably in the world she found herself in. Sofia saw in her a paragon of a modern woman, someone who certainly was worthy of contributing to her course in women's issues.

Sofia met up with Birdie in the lobby of the casino. They ordered coffee in the restaurant where Joni was to join them for lunch. A striking woman with long stylishly-cut auburn hair approached the table. Sofia saw instantly her strong family resemblance to Birdie. As Joni took the seat next to her niece, Sofia noted that the difference in their ages was no more than ten years or so.

They had a delightful lunch. Joni was as well spoken as her niece. She had a quick mind for assessing her own experiences in terms of what might be useful for Sofia's course. Before they were finished, Joni had promised to visit Sofia and the school on her next visit to her mother who lived on the reservation southwest of the school.

"By the way, I have a load of clothes in the car for Marlyss, the mission," Joni told her niece. She handed Birdie her car keys. "You can load them into your car. Leave the key with Stan at the parking kiosk."

They finished lunch within the hour and parted ways, after Sofia had obtained a promise from Joni to participate at least peripherally in her research. Birdie asked Sofia if she wanted to tag along to the mission to deliver the clothes. Lunch had ended quickly and Christian would be tied up for another two hours, at least. Sofia accepted the offer with some pleasure. It would be useful to meet with Marlyss at the present time, when so many questions lay unanswered. At the very least, she would like to see how Marlyss was handling herself in her new life. That too would be instructive for the development of her women's course.

When Sofia and Birdie entered the mission they were caught up at once in the busy occupation of the place. Marlyss was huddled with a teenage girl giving instructions on the sorting and folding of clothing donations. Several other girls were employed in various other tasks scattered around the open area that seemed to Sofia much like a warehouse of sorts. Even before Birdie could announce their arrival, Marlyss looked toward the door and offered them a bright smile. Giving final instructions to her helper, she abandoned the table and greeted Birdie with a generous hug. Spying Sofia, she registered her surprise and her delight, giving her a grand welcome.

Birdie mentioned her cargo of clothes and took one of the girls to fetch the boxes from her car. Marlyss took Sofia to the kitchen and prepared a pot of tea while chatting about the support Birdie's family—on both sides, the Redtrees and the Caldwells—offered to the mission. As they settled into conversation, Marlyss asked about Sofia's program, she mentioned Kristi's enthusiasm. Gradually Sofia came round to the subject of her growing relationship with Christian, which she supposed that Kristina had apprised her mother of. Marlyss admitted to knowing about the Gala event, the stay at Befford Lodge, and Mary's rude behavior to Sofia.

"At least that's the way Kristi saw it," Marlyss said, refilling the tea cups.

Sofia assented that Mary's behavior was odd indeed. She was glad to hear the note of compassion from Christian's ex-wife, something she had no hope to expect.

"You poor dear! How on earth did you survive the whole season with Mary constantly at your side? I think she must have been since Christian and Joe are rarely separated. She must be insufferable about her aristocratic connections now that Elena is engaged to that senator's boy."

"She hasn't been any too kind to Kristina, either." Sofia said. As she had suspected, the girl had not written to her mother about the slights that she herself had received at Mary's hand. "Mary is set against me now, which is hard to understand since we have always been friendly before—at church, at school functions. Now she seems intent on humiliating me in as many polite ways as she can."

"By *before*, do you mean before Christian showed particular interest in you?" Marlyss asked. When Sofia grinned, Marlyss added, "Not to worry. You'll regain her good will again when—*if*—you let go of Christian. He's the one she's out to destroy."

"But why should she be so determined to destroy him? Certainly she understands the bond he has with her husband?"

"That's a discussion you must take up with Christian. Don't be disappointed, though, if he won't answer it."

"That will be difficult. Christian won't tolerate a word against her. I've tried to indicate how toxic she can be but he can't see her ill behavior."

"He *won't* see it."

Sofia felt the layers of meaning in her response. "Is this why you left?"

Marlyss smiled as she shook her head. "I'm not that frivolous, regardless of what townsfolk might think. The issue was far more serious than that." She studied the cup then drained it. "More?"

Sofia shook her head. "You're not going to tell me, are you?"

"No, I won't. This is something you must learn from Christian. You must have faith in him, no matter how you feel about what he tells you. He's a decent man, Sofia. He needs the support of a good woman—and I think you're that woman."

Sofia was relieved to still have the support of her old ally. Birdie came into the kitchen looking for them, indicating that she needed to get back to her newspaper work. It was already a quarter of two. Sofia stood and offered Marlyss a hug and thanks for her generosity. "I hope you don't feel that your trip was wasted, coming out here to find something that I won't give you."

"You can't. I understand." At the door, Sofia glanced around the mission and saw the hope fostered for the salvation of women. She and Marlyss were in the same game, flanking the herd from different positions, all with the same goal. She admired this woman. "You are doing a tremendous job here, I think. Kristina is proud of you. And if you will allow it—so am I."

"You have a special place in my heart, Sofia. Always. And thanks, Birdie. You two can come back anytime, as Birdie well knows."

When Sofia arrived back at the hotel, she found Christian in the suite where he had been pacing impatiently for the past ten minutes, he said, checking his watch as she opened the door.

His meeting had finished earlier than planned and he was anxious to be off. "I'd like to be home before dark, now that I can be," he said coolly.

Sofia hurried to finish up her bags, explaining, "Birdie had to drop a bag of clothes at the mission. She asked me along."

"You went to see Marlyss? Why?" he asked with some annoyance.

"You would have preferred me to refuse, as if I held some grievance against Kristina's mother? Well, I don't. And if you object to this, you should have made it clear to me earlier that Marlyss was off-limits."

He was surprised at the fierceness of her tone. "I didn't know you were interested in going over there. It's hardly a gathering place for academics."

As she gathered her last belongings into her purse, he rang for the bellman, and ordered the car be brought around.

"Besides," he smiled indulgently as he set the receiver in the cradle, "I doubt if such heavy-handedness would have stopped you. It probably would have spurred you on."

Sofia was glad to hear a slight levity in his voice, but things seemed cooler between them. Was he annoyed that she was not back when he was, or was he annoyed that she had gone to see Marlyss? She had less interest in sorting out his sensitivities at the moment. She had other issues to pursue with him.

The car was waiting when they arrived in the lobby, with the bellboy loading their bags into the trunk. "I hope you enjoyed your stay, Mr. Day." The bell captain said, opening the door for Sofia.

When they settled into the limousine, and the driver had raised the privacy window, Sofia sought to smooth things out by inquiring after Christian's meeting, but he did not want to discuss the details of his business with her. Soon she resorted to a light hearted chatter about Birdie, Joni, and finally the mission and Marlyss' warm reception of her.

Christian frowned. He wasn't going to make this easy for her. Finally she simply asked, "Why did you get divorced?"

"What is this, a test?" he said. "You didn't ask her?"

"Yes, I did but she would tell me nothing. She felt it more appropriate that I should learn from you. Presumably I should learn only what you wish me to. She's very kind, you know. Most divorced women wouldn't hesitate to list every offence of a cast-off spouse."

"Marlyss is not like that," he said.

"She's always been kind to me. It's more than that, though, isn't it? She still loves you."

He disregarded the sentiment then signaled the driver to drop open the privacy window. Christian instructed his man to contact the air strip. "Be sure Frank has the jet ready when we arrive. I'd like to be in the air in the next hour."

The driver saluted as the window closed again.

"I suspect you still love her, too," Sofia said softly. It wasn't an accusation, only an acknowledgement of the way things were.

Christian was annoyed. "She's the mother of my child, Sofia. You may find it hard to understand, but I will probably always...We will always have Kristina between us. Do you object to that?"

"I wonder that you divorced her at all."

"What's this about, Sofia? Did she tell you something? Is there some question you need to ask of me?"

Sofia did not think it would be easy, but she also did not expect Christian's attitude to be anything other than the openness they had shared since getting together last Christmas. "If we are looking at marriage now, then I have a right to know how the game is played with you—your rules. And yes, I do need to know why you would have divorced a woman you still love."

"That's an odd thing to say—*my* rules?" He considered her words briefly, then answered directly. "Well... don't sneak off and get an abortion...period. *That's* how the game is played with me."

Abortion. Sofia hadn't expected this. She knew how Christian felt about the sanctity of life. Yet, Marlyss also valued love above all other Christian virtues. She too revered the sanctity of human life. Sofia couldn't reconcile the act with the person.

"She destroyed my son, if you want to know. Discarded the seed as if it were worthless garbage." His mood darkened. Then, as if he remembered where he was, and with whom, he brushed the whole matter aside with a smile. "But it's not important anymore."

"Because you have me?" Sofia said, feeling his need for a son was still strong and alive. It was the perfect moment to have the conversation they needed to have. "Listen, Christian...."

"It wasn't the abortion," he snapped suddenly, as if he would lose her in the silence. "It was the betrayal. A man and a woman marry on certain precepts of trust and faith. She breached that trust and lost my faith, by aborting my seed."

It was an odd way to think of a son, a child—even the unborn. Yet there were more weighty things to be curious about than his diction. "Why would a married woman, kind and loving—as good a mother as Marlyss is to Kristi—why would she abort the baby that she is carrying?"

Christian derailed the question as they reached the airport. He gave much attention to overseeing the baggage and repeating instructions to his driver, who would be returning to the branch office of Day Enterprises.

After boarding the company jet, and settling into their seats, drinks and sandwiches were served by the crewmember. When he finally disappeared into the cockpit with the pilot, Sofia returned to her quest.

"More important to me than Marlyss' motive for an abortion is your reaction to it—that you would cast her aside for this transgression, as if you were a king from the Bible."

Christian clenched his teeth in a grimace of exercising his patience with the topic. The plane lifted off the field and with a rocking motion settled into an air trough that moved them swiftly forward.

"Sofia, what Marlyss did was no small transgression. She violated the will of God. She deserved to be cast aside."

Sofia would not be cowed by him. "Come now, Christian. The will of God? We have evolved since those days. Look at your own business. You waste seed in your breeding operations testing to improve cowherds. Yet look also at Nature herself, God, wasting millions of seeds for each individual to sprout."

"Are you comparing animals and plants to the sanctity of human life?"

"I'm saying that the loss of one seed is not of any significance. It's not as if you couldn't produce another child later. God has little to do with it."

"Is this what your Papist religion teaches you? That God doesn't care?"

"Certainly not, the pope is forever intruding into the bedrooms of upright Catholics. I am not a devoted practitioner of my faith, as you know, since I attend chapel with you every Sunday."

"Most Sundays."

"I am a humanist, Christian. I am concerned more about the sanctity of the human condition than the worship of a sperm cell. So one attempt at pregnancy was lost. Try again, when the lady is more willing."

"It's not that simple. Marlyss didn't want another baby."

"Then the whole situation is curious to me. Why didn't she just protect herself? On the point of conception, at least in this country, women hold all the power, don't they? It's the ultimate power that we have. That's why you are upset."

The plane was droning along through the drafts above the basin and range contours heading toward the airfield near Hawkes Ferry.

Sofia mused aloud. "All she needed to do was protect herself from getting pregnant in the first place. Marlyss is a smart woman. She must have been using something—did it fail? She's been able to prevent other pregnancies—or Kristi wouldn't be an only child."

"Look, it wasn't that way at all. She didn't need to take any protection, okay? There was never a threat of an unplanned pregnancy with me."

"With you? What does this mean—that she was carrying someone else's child?" Sofia heard the inherent lack of logic in her own statement. It was Christian who seemed to carry the pain of loss, not Marlyss.

"I'm impotent, Sofia," he said, his voice dropped to a raspy whisper. "I should have told you sooner. I was always waiting for the right time, the right mood."

She heard his words but couldn't grasp their meaning. Her mind sprung into confusion with the topic swirling into half formed ideas. "Well... Then how could... You said your seed... What about Kristina—where did she come from?"

"You're a smart woman, Sofia. Use your imagination. How do you think Kristina came out?" Christian showed no appetite for delving any deeper.

Seed. Livestock. Breeding. "Oh." She was shocked, putting herself into a much different scenario than she had heretofore. That reticence of his to press her for sexual concord, she had attributed to an exaggerated—no, a dramatic—sense of nobility. She started to laugh at herself, but choked it off, realizing how hurtful it would seem.

Christian watched her with growing detachment. "At least you are kind enough not to laugh out loud as Mary had."

"Mary Befford?" she was further confused. The little scene she had painted around this relationship was fraying at the edges.

"Years ago. Before Marlyss. I was too young to know how mean girls could be. And too stupid to keep my pants on."

"Ah. This is the power that she holds over you. Yet, this is not common knowledge—as I'd expect with Mary sitting on the golden egg."

"Joe would cut her off in a second if she used that knowledge."

The bond between the two men ran through their lives from birth, yet it ran much deeper than Sofia had understood. Mary had wanted

Christian but got Joe. What a loss that must have been to her. Joe was a fine, reliable provider but had none of Christian's zest for life. Maybe that, too, was better understood.

Sofia wasn't buying into Joe as the great Protector of womankind, either. "Yet he can sit by and watch Mary skewer worthier women like Marlyss or Kristina, who is worth a hundred of Mary's selfish daughters." She was surprised at her own vitriol toward another woman.

They sat in silence, draining their glasses and turned away from each other to watch the ground rise up to meet the plane, landing on the snow crusted field. Nearby, the tower of Day Enterprises could be seen. The heart of Christian's home, his worth and his self-worth lay with the business inside that tower. And to preserve it and his legacy, he needed a son.

The flight crew loaded the bags into Christian's Rover, and they headed home.

Settling behind the wheel, Christian took charge again.

"I think it is poetic justice that Si has come back to Kristina. Don't you? That cupcake of his back in New York hasn't worked out so well. A genteel lady rocked out of her comfort zone by the rough and ready ways of a true caballero." The statement was mean-hearted and robbed Kristina of the respect she deserved.

Sofia voiced her disagreement. "Kristina needs a man who is equal to her mind and intellectual curiosity, to her praiseworthy values and gentle nature. Si Befford is not this man."

"If you're meaning to hook her up with Meyer, look again. He seems to have faded from the picture altogether, if Christmas is any measure. I was open to accepting him. I told her so. But she knows that the kind of man she needs is one who will match her in fortune and name. I don't think Meyer could live up to that. She'll be happy with a cowboy, mark my words, and I'll make a full-fledged aggie out of him before I'm done, despite his father's objections." Christian was enjoying the resurgence of Kristi's romance and his own victory at recapturing control. Suddenly, he came round to Sofia's role in things. "You need to keep out of that business, Little Lady, and let things develop as they should."

Sofia frowned at his tyranny, but a light opened onto the other topic. "I understand now. Si is the son you've been deprived of."

His silence was all the confirmation she needed. Her fancy led her to envision their future together, a lifetime of holidays and gala occasions bleeding away in the company of drab women and pretentious caterwauling, spearheaded by Mary Befford.

She put aside her growing resentment for the woman, and returned to the subject of Kristina. With her natural optimism, her voice brightened, she said, "It's odd that you wouldn't consider any other single males at the college. Those more suited to Kristi's creative gifts."

"I might have, years ago. But Kristi's never been keen on any of the boys her own age. Her interest in Meyer this summer showed me that I'd have to change my spots on this, if Si became history. I haven't done too shoddy a job, eh?"

As they moved along the highway, Sofia watched the snow-covered fields fly by, allowing the visions and hopes to settle into a comfortable space between them. Then she risked, "What about Emery Truitt?"

Christian's face froze, all warmth lost to the rising anger. "That son-of-a-bitch. He's not worthy enough to step across our threshold, much less bear the standard of Day Enterprises. He's not like us, you know. He could never match up to the legacy of Clement Hawke."

"You've said that before," Sofia said, retaining a temperate mood. "He bears an invisible mark that, for some clandestine reason, is known only to the board of St. Clements College."

"Known only to me." Christian growled back. "You do hang onto things, don't you? For crissakes, Sofia, the boy was bastard-born, his mother a little tart who got caught playing around with the big boys. Then she blackmailed the senator who screwed her, riding free for the next twenty years on that booty."

"Until she died this summer." The picture was not pretty. But instead of letting him distract her with the unworthiness of the mother—which she could scarcely believe—she kept her eye on the son. "Yet, it seems to me, that Professor Truitt neither looks nor acts as if he had much money at all."

"Spent it all on herself, no doubt, as perverse as she was. Do you see why he is not appropriate for Kristina? Would you sentence her to a life of public defamation?"

"From an unfeeling man like you are showing yourself to be at the moment?" Sofia tossed back at him. "Honestly, Christian, I've never seen you act so unkindly toward anyone. You accuse the man of the sins of his mother. Your lack of charity on his part is incongruous with the generous heart I have come to love and revere. Where is that open heart that has backed me all the way to the president, who has been the avid sponsor of the women's program? Where is your charity for this misguided girl and her babe?"

"I hired him, didn't I?" Christian said, mollified a bit by her passion. "But, being kind doesn't require me to sacrifice my daughter to the winds."

Sofia agreed, pursuing another curious term he had used. "Why did you say she was perverse?"

"Did I?" He thought for a moment.

"You said...."

"Ah, yes. She should have aborted the thing! The senator had paid for a holiday in Europe, so that she would have a safe procedure. She was seventeen, for crissakes! She should have taken the money and set herself up in a new life. Instead, she keeps the money, has the baby and goes after him for more. Some low-life attorneys then nail him for the long term."

"And you know all this from his curriculum vitae?"

"Of course not. I owed a political chit to a senator who got us the extensions on the land deals in the Jarbidge range. An intermediary needed to find a place for the boy out of the political boiling pot. They were afraid that he would stay in the East, keeping things hot for the family. That atmosphere has cleared, though, since his old lady died."

"His aunt? She was the...."

"His mother. She was his mother. You see how undependable he is? An arrogant, lying bastard."

They had arrived at her place. As he pulled into the drive, she asked, "So why does this story eat at you any more than any other hard luck tale?"

"Why?" He turned to her with fury in his eyes. "That unwanted bastard son lived, and my rightful heir was destroyed. Don't you see? I may be impotent, but I can still be a father."

Christian carried Sofia's bags into the cold house. As she circled the front room to turn on the lights and heat, she offered him a drink.

"No, no. I'd better go."

His tone was cold, and she felt him take distance, something that she could not afford to let happen. "Run away, you mean. You've no appointments to rush off to. We need to settle things between us."

"What's to settle? You've no stake in who Kristina marries."

"You're wrong about that on several levels—but that's not what I meant. We need to finish this conversation—the whole thing, while it is open, on the table."

"Got any sour mash?" He shed his scarf, tossed his hat and coat on the sofa, and settled beside them.

She poured two glasses of the whiskey, diluting hers with ice. Then she chose the easy chair, instead of perching next to him on the sofa.

"We've been dating for six months. I've always felt a particular bond with you, a closeness I've felt only toward my father and my brother. I've had no other man, you know that. You and Marlyss have both been important to me and I was crushed when your marriage fell apart. I did not want to choose between you, yet, when it seemed that you were looking for another wife, when Marlyss had left the picture, my feelings for you grew. I thought that you might consider me suitable. You've been a most desirable suitor, kind, generous and seemingly devoted to my ambitions, my life."

"I have, Sofia." He leaned toward her and touched her knee. "I hope we will create something very special."

"Special, yes. But you must realize I am no longer the young schoolgirl from Argentina who needs your protection. As our hearts have opened to each other, I have most sincerely hoped for more—much more."

"And you will have it all. Everything in my power...."

"But you tell me now that you have no power to give me what I want. I am thirty-six years old, Christian. I have saved myself for my husband, for you. I have focused on my career and my work. I have put aside all personal joy and satisfaction on that account."

He sat back to take her in, looking alarmed. He searched her face, looking for some clue to her meaning, another meaning, that is, one that did not end in rejection.

"Our relationship has been based on meeting *your* needs—on my fitting into your life, enduring your friends and associates. But this issue of which I speak, this is about me. I want a full relationship with a man, Christian. I am a healthy woman with natural desires."

His face turned red, and his shoulders sagged. "You want sex, you mean."

As soon as he gave voice to the thought, his voice filled with urgency. "You do see that a child is possible, don't you, Sofia? Even desirable. Yes, I want a son, Sofia—I want you to bear my son."

"And I see this is what you want. But I want the real relationship—the one that can satisfy me as a woman. I want a partner to love and to revere, as I will be loved and revered in return. And I want that man to walk the road alongside me, not a man who intends to always lead, directing me to his places, the places I don't wish to go."

She paused, softening her face and quietly delivering the blow he would not abide. "In the end, Christian, there is no room for children on my path. I do not want to bear a son—or any child—for you, or for anyone else."

He was stunned as a wounded animal. "Sofia...."

She had never been so callous to another human being. Yet her words spoke the truth of her heart. "I am so sorry, Christian. I love you, but not enough. You need to find the woman who can give you what you need."

"No. No." He stood, faltering. Then as if he could not be in her company any longer, he collected his things.

Sofia stood with him. She turned away from his face, from the specter of his now swollen eyes wet with tears. She reached for his arm, but he brushed it away.

Then Christian fled without another word.

Sofia watched as he drove away. She was not proud of what she had done, yet everything had moved so fast. She had little to reprimand in herself. She had been swift about it. Knowing it was the kindest thing she could do. The advice she had so coolly dispensed to Kristina regarding commitment and responsibility, had backwashed into her own life. It was much easier to dispense that advice than it was now to experience its effect.

Twenty-One

Kristi sat at her dressing table staring at the pale face reflected in the mirror. School resumed the next day, leaving her no time to restore her usual cheer. She felt robbed of all optimism for the future. All the pretense and animated interest in the affairs of others had taken their toll on her goodwill this holiday season.

Christmas had been ghastly. The Beffords had invaded for Christmas dinner, with Elena attached to Ross and showing off her engagement ring. As they had planned on the drive home from the Gala in November, Kristi and Si continued the sham of their "reignited" courtship, offering themselves up for some ribbing and ridicule from their parents. Ross and Elena were held in esteem as the ideal couple, with much urging for Si and Kristi to take notice of "how it's done." Si accommodated them by increasing his affection towards Kristi. For her part, Kristi played along with wan smiles while doubling her effort to help Grandmother get dinner on the table.

Elena's formal engagement party was to be held on New Year's Day in "The Club" on Long Island, hosted by Senator Delaney and his wife. Joe and Mary spent the best part of the evening urging Father's attendance along with Kristi. Anne had received her own invitation as well. Sofia had not been invited, nor included in Father's invitation. That evening Mary went out of her way to demote Sofia's status to outsider, with references of "her people" and "her faith." Mary made it clear that Sofia would not feel welcome in the company on Long Island.

Finally, Father made it clear that none of them would be in attendance at the New Year's event. The Beffords left soon after. Si joined them, almost as pleased as Mary, that Kristi was not going to Long Island with them.

All the time she spent with Si that week, her heart ached for another, for what she couldn't have. Her conscience served up spoonfuls of remorse for betraying a relationship that was so important to her, a man whom she had worked so hard to impress.

As a student, not a lover. Kristi reprimanded the image in the mirror reflected back on her. The whole charade with Si had been for the professor's account, a role played to convince him that she was not interested in him, something to carry her through graduation, so he would not dismiss her as his assistant. It would have worked out well, she was convinced.

But, alas, it was not to be. Just ten minutes ago, Si had arrived unannounced, fresh off the plane from New York, anxious to tell Kristi before seeing anyone else. In a hurry to cut her off from all hope, and extinguish all obligations and commitments tying him to her. He was now betrothed to Trish Winslow. Kristi took the news stoically. Apparently Trish had changed her mind about all that freedom to roam and find herself.

Si told her that they had become secretly engaged on New Year's Day after the big event at "The Club." He begged her not to mention a word. He hadn't told his parents, and he wasn't sure he would until the marriage had taken place.

What? No lavish engagement party? Kristi had said lightheartedly, although she hardly felt that way. Her own plans at dissemblance were disintegrating with his every word.

"I'm tired of all the fuss Mom makes about things. Trish wants to elope, in fact. Thinks it will be spontaneous and fun. Freeing, she said. So you will, won't you? Keep it a secret?"

Kristi nodded, sympathizing with his views. It was probably a smart idea, given Mary's obsession with pageantry and form—and control—over harmony and goodwill. She was actually pleased to see Si break away to such a profound degree. Trish, it seemed, meant more to him than his mother, something Kristi could never achieve, even if she had wanted to.

Kristi leaned toward the mirror to examine the darkening circles under her eyes. She pulled at one eye lid then the other. She still felt heavy with the burden of her blunder three weeks past. That scene in Professor Truitt's office haunted her like a persistent nightmare. The days since had offered little to restore her spirit, filled as they were with bad company and empty hours. Tomorrow she would have to face him again. She covered her face with her hands, drawn and distraught, unable to muster up even a slight feeling of hope.

Since the moment he realized that he loved Kristina Day, Truitt could not remove her from his mind. He wanted to see her, talk to her, laugh with her—and yes, he wanted to fall off the precipice of her lips and lose himself in her irresistible charm. But such thoughts were useless. Yet, the harder he tried to eradicate them, the quicker some new thread of memory would find its way through the morass and hook him again.

He wanted nothing more than to see her. As he drove back home from the airport, a two-hour trip, a whirlwind of thought pinned him in the vortex of his heart. He tried to move away, remind himself of tasks to do in the morning, but the threads would lead back to Kristina Day, and he would long again to see her. When he thought of starting his lectures for the next semester, she would be laughing at the typewriter, fingers dancing, bells clinging, and he would long to hear her voice.

It was no use. He could not keep her as his assistant. The very thought of holding her, as he once had, set him into a fit of angst. He couldn't keep working with her in the tight confines of his office. She needed to go. And the kindest thing would be to tell her now, today. He decided at that moment to stop by her house. It was the right thing to do. He would see her that very day—and of course talk sense into her about this whole TA business. Even if her father or Befford were to answer the door, neither would deter him from his purpose. He needed to see her. But it was not a man who opened the front door.

It was Anne Day, Kristina's grandmother. "Good afternoon, Professor. Won't you come in?"

Cautiously he stepped over the threshold, not prepared to address this kindly person. Glancing down the hall, he half-expected to encounter the bullish form of Christian Day barreling down on him. "Is your granddaughter...Is Kristina in? I have some business...."

"Certainly." She escorted him into the front salon. "Make yourself comfortable. I'm putting the kettle on for some tea. Would you care for a cup? Or perhaps you'd like coffee?"

"Tea sounds fine."

"I'll get Kristina for you, then."

She withdrew, in which direction Truitt couldn't tell. But it was no more than a minute before Kristina came into the room, her face full of concern. He stood up.

"Professor Truitt," she said, her face lighting up in the gesture of welcome.

"Kristina, I need to talk to you...."

The smile vanished, and she considered him oddly.

"That is, with you... Are you busy? If so, I can come back." He was ready to flee. "We might take this up later... tomorrow...."

"No. Not busy at all. Please. Sit down. Tessa is bringing some tea." The concern returned to her face.

He didn't mean to alarm her. Things were coming out a bit rough. He scanned the foyer and then looked out to the patio. Before taking a seat again, he said, "No one else is here? I mean company or such?"

She moved into the room and sat on the sofa. "My father's gone to

Las Vegas for the weekend. He'll be home this evening. Is this about work? I've finished the midterm essays. They're above average. I'll go get them, if you like."

"No. Well, not just yet." He got up and walked around the room. "It's just that—well... I think I should find a new TA."

The light drained from her face. The apprehension returned. "Oh, professor, please. I made a terrible mistake. I am so very sorry. It won't happen again."

"You're sorry?"

"I know what horrid things you must think about me, but please...."

The housekeeper made her presence known. She set a tray with teacups and slices of cake on the coffee table.

"Oh Kristina. It's not you at all." Truitt dropped his voice. He got out of his chair and came to her side. "It's me. It's how I feel about you. And I can't go on working so close—so dreadfully close—to you day after day... knowing how I feel... knowing that your heart belongs to someone else."

She stared at him in shock. "You called me Kristina."

He stepped back from her, knowing that despite his urge to embrace her, to taste her kiss, he had no right to touch her at all. If it weren't for Befford—if it weren't for school and teachers and students and the chasm that divided them—Truitt knew exactly what he would do.

She shook her head, then turned her face from his view. He realized she was crying. "There is no one else. Si's just told me that he's engaged. It wasn't working between us anymore."

Truitt was elated at the news, but concerned for her sorrow.

"I've been so foolish," she said.

He was helpless in her pain. She needed solitude to work through the disappointment. Yet he couldn't move. "Shall I leave?"

"No. I'd like you to stay, if you don't mind." She turned to him. "I want to be with you more than anyone else in the world."

He faltered for a moment then touched her arm. Within a moment they were clasped in each other's arms. He awoke again to her inviting warmth. That spark reignited in him, taking him past the hunger and longing, the elevation of his soul with another forging a new kind of power within him. And he knew she felt it too.

The distant ring of the telephone lured them back to the room. Kristi pulled him to settle beside her on the sofa. The cooling tea still waited for drinking. As they sipped from delicate cups, they declared their love for each other, and shared their tales of loss and longing. They laughed and talked.

Eventually, Truitt came back to the purpose of his visit. "We need to do something about your TA position. I mean, we can hardly carry on like this." He chuckled self-consciously.

"I've done some thinking about that," Kristi admitted. "I see no reason for you to take on anyone else. It would double your workload, while depriving me of meeting my goals for the future."

Truitt shifted uncomfortably. "I don't see how we can keep going on in the office as if we mean nothing to each other."

"We have done it for a while, haven't we?"

"For only one week, a devilishly difficult week. I was so focused on ignoring you that I could scarcely concentrate on my work. Not to mention how distracted I was at your efforts to take distance from me."

"Yet we were both focused on the same higher purpose, weren't we? The students," she added to the question in his eyes.

"Have you forgotten that you are one of my students? It will be difficult enough to retain objectivity in that class."

"I'm not quitting the class. Besides, Martin's been your favorite for three years. There's no reason that should change."

Truitt flushed. "You're joking, aren't you? That was before I realized he had no interest in graduate school."

"Still, you favor him in the class, but, I think that should continue. Until, of course, you come across another student who is headed to grad school. Then it will be reasonable to gradually shift interest away from Tad."

"No one in the senior seminar has declared an interest in grad school this year, sorry to say."

"She's declaring it now. I've been checking into programs since Thanksgiving."

"I don't believe it. You'd actually have to leave Hawkes Ferry to do that."

"Tch. Tch. Is that any way to coach a student with such high aspirations? No wonder Martin begged off."

"He didn't beg off—and we shouldn't be talking about this subject, anyhow. Part of the problem of working together, would be establishing the appropriateness of discussion topics. See? It isn't that simple. But there's something that I need to tell you. I am considering a position back east for the next school year."

"Where?"

"Nothing's been firmed up. New England, most likely upper state New York."

"A medieval program? That would be awkward, if I were to be accepted to the same school.

"Probably not medieval lit. I have to confess that I wanted to escape this place. I couldn't bear to watch you throw away everything on Befford—your mind, your good nature, your joy."

"And I want to be worthy of you."

"Worthy of me? By acquiring a master's degree in medieval lit? I won't say that I don't like the idea. You are as good a candidate as any of my students. Yet, you don't need anything else to be dear to me."

Truitt cupped her chin in his hand and kissed her. Kristina stroked his hand and then his cheek, both of them surrendering to the moment, unmindful of time or place or any mischief looming to knock them off course.

The ruckus rumbling through the house reverberated unheard by them, until a blast of cold vitriol called their attention to Christian Day lumbering into the room.

"You!" Christian shouted at Truitt with the suppressed venom of seven years. "You bastard. How dare you come sniffing around my house like an alley cat."

Truitt stood immediately and Kristina rose with him, grasping his arm protectively.

"And you," Christian spat at his daughter. "Acting like a common tart while Befford's away. Is this your idea of fidelity? You're as fickle as a slut these days. What the hell has come over you?"

He charged to the drinks cabinet and poured whiskey into a tall tumbler, downing a large swallow.

"Father...." Kristina left Truitt's side. "We need to talk about..."

"About that business with Meyer? And no sooner do I come on board with that decision than you're back to Befford. Now this—this...."

As Kristina moved back to shield Truitt, he placed his hand on her shoulder, and grasped her hand. The action set Christian Day off with a torrent of names and grievances he had suffered from the girl and her mother.

"If you'll let me explain...." Kristina said, meeting the man's mighty wrath with an unwarranted gentility.

"There's nothing to explain here. I have eyes, don't I?" Her father growled.

The man was oblivious to reason as long as he ranted. He took another swallow of the drink and turned his attention back to Truitt. "And *you*. I'll have your head for this. Crossing the line. Consorting with students. That's a dismissible offense," he sneered.

Kristina stiffened. "Then you'll have to go after Geoff first, I think. He's been far more familiar with me than the professor has."

Her defense further enraged her father. He aimed all his discord at Truitt. "You *no-name* bastard! I warned you, Kristina, that he wasn't one of us. His mother actually...."

"Si is engaged to Trish Winslow," Kristina blurted out as she stepped forward to block Truitt from the full force of her father's words.

"What?" Christian finally addressed his daughter. His face contorted from a sneer to puzzlement. "*Who?*"

"The Delaney cousin. Joe talked to you about her."

Truitt stepped forward to stand beside her, giving her arm an encouraging squeeze as she sought to volley her father's anger with quiet reason.

"We broke up months ago, if you want the truth. Everything faded after his graduation. He wanted to keep it quiet for a while...we were reluctant to deliver the final blow because.... Quite frankly, because you and Joe were so set on a marriage between us."

"And Meyer? Was he a passing fancy too?"

"I had a crush on Geoff long before Si was a player, when I was in high school. Things warmed up between us while Si was in Mexico, I admit, but already that relationship was fading. And I discovered that my feelings for Geoff were simply the remnants of that teenage crush. It didn't take long for it to fade."

Christian scowled at her and headed for a refill. "Women! And all those layers of emotions to sort out. So what do you call that recent business with Befford at the Gala—and over the holidays—a reprisal?"

Kristina glanced over her shoulder at Truitt, then sat down on the sofa. "It was a ruse, a sham."

Truitt was surprised at her response. He pivoted to the back of the sofa still facing Christian, but unsure of what this revelation meant.

Her father eyed the two of them with visible disgust. "Why would you do that?"

Kristina's body stiffened. She glanced back at Truitt. "Because I didn't want the professor to think I was a *siren*."

Truitt almost laughed audibly from relief. So this was how she intended to move through the next few months?

"A *what?*" Her father snarled, looking from Kristina to Truitt.

"A tart," she said evenly in a quiet voice.

"You call my daughter a... Why you no-name bastard. Does she even know about the base beginnings of the high and mighty professor?"

"Father."

"It's not yet been discussed." Truitt shrugged off its importance, although he could see that it meant a great deal to Christian Day.

"Let me enlighten you, Daughter-of-mine, about the Truitt family line. His mother was a gold-digger putting the screws to the john who impregnated her—"

"Sir. This is not tolerable," Truitt said, stepping around the sofa to address Christian Day head on.

The man mocked him derisively. "So what are you going to do? Punch my lights out? Why don't you tell her, then? Tell her that you're a lowlife fortune hunter following the smell of money, just like your old lady."

Truitt turned to Kristi. "I'd better leave. We can...."

"No," she cried, rushing forward to stand by him. "I'll have you here by my side. There's nothing shameful in what your parents are or were. As you well know," she addressed the last comment to her father.

There was more. "Everything is always about you, Father, isn't it? And for you. I never loved Si, and if he were to tell the truth—which he rarely does—he would admit that he has never loved me. Talk about fortune hunters! That's all Si cared about, Day Enterprises merged with his Befford Ranches. The great inland empire. The carrot you have dangled in front of him for the past five years."

"He's like a son to me." Christian countered. "He's the closest thing..."

"I never loved Si, Father. Get over it! What I did was all for you, your dreams and desires, and if you were looking with your heart instead of your ego, you would have seen what has been so obvious to everyone else."

"And that business with Geoff was my aching heart crying out for recognition of some other, satisfying life. The love of a good man. But it was never Geoff that my heart longed for. It was—I wanted Emery Truitt."

Christian reddened and then turned as if to refill his drink, yet

Truitt thought he was making a strategic retreat from his daughter's anger.

"If you're going to fix yourself another whiskey, Father, you might as well fix us some scotch while you are pouring."

Reluctantly, he fixed the drinks and handed them to Kristina. "No ice," he warned then poured his own.

Kristina took the glasses as a peace offering, no doubt, and handed one to Truitt. He set it down on the coffee table with the tea serving, as he addressed her in response to Christian's accusations. "My mother was very dear to me, Kristina. She was a single mother, yes, but she sacrificed everything to keep me from the devastating poverty she grew up in."

They had returned to the sofa while Christian settled into the wingtip chair opposite them. He was showing the effects of the whiskey, but Truitt was not convinced the eagle's talons had been dulled, in any way.

"Great sob story," Christian scoffed.

"She wasn't the trollop you suggest, Sir. She was his stepdaughter, his seventeen-year-old *ward*, and he betrayed her. Yes, while her own mother—his legal wife—was pregnant with his other son."

He turned to Kristina now, "I never knew there was any money until this summer when I went back for her funeral."

"Your aunt's funeral?"

"The boy can't keep his stories straight," Christian criticized.

"The woman I believed to be my aunt was actually my mother. Something else I learned this summer. I'm still not used to the idea. *All that money*. We lived like paupers. Don't get me wrong. She created a wonderful life despite apparent lack. She was my anchor. I always thought of that cottage as my harbor from the world. She was a unique woman. And I've never met another woman like her—until I came to know you, your heart." As Truitt spoke, his voice softened. He sought to evoke for Kristina an image of how wonderful Nell was.

"What happened to all the money?" Christian barked, breaking the mood.

"Spent on my education. Investments." Truitt responded. Then to Kristina he said, "It doesn't amount to anything like the fortune you are used to, but it's not a pittance. It's enough to maintain a comfortable home in a college town."

Christian bolted to a stand. "Get out of here, you bastard. You'll never have her hand in marriage." His voice echoed off the glass doors leading to the patio and reverberated down the long empty hall.

Anne Day came bustling into the room carrying a tray with an ice bucket and several mixers for the drinks cabinet. "What are you bellowing about Christian? Tessa and I could hear you all the way into the kitchen. Have you no manners? Especially with a guest in the house." She set the tray on the cabinet.

"No guest. An interloper! Get out of my house, you thief!" Christian urged Truitt to leave, pointing to the door.

Truitt squeezed Kristina's hand, then rose to go.

"I apologize for my son's behavior, Professor. Please stay seated. You are Kristina's guest."

"Mother! You go too far...." Christian moaned, dropping back into his chair.

"I have indulged you too much, Christian," Anne said, placing herself between her son and her granddaughter. "I have tried to compensate for the shortcomings of your father, but there has been no mending of the scars he laid on you, emotional and physical. These old wounds grow from those inflicted on him as a child in the harsh mountain home of his youth. From father to son, from generation to generation. They must end here. Three generations lost in pain. That is enough. I will not see you destroy Kristina's happiness as you have destroyed your own."

Anne poured a cup of tea for herself from the cold pot. "Dr. Truitt, I should have stood up for you months ago, when I first suspected the leanings of Kristina's heart. I have wrongly believed that a man's home is his castle and I have let Christian rule this castle—my home—since his father's death."

She then looked at her son. "But this is my castle and Kristina's as well. My father built this home as a homestead for the Hawke family, all future generations. That is why it sits in trust. None of us has a right to bar any invitation that has been extended. As the professor is Kristina's guest, he is most welcome. As far as I am concerned, his gentility and good manners will always be welcome in *my* home."

With that, Christian left the room without a word. In a moment the door to his den was slammed. Anne withdrew then with a second apology. "I do hope you will be a frequent visitor, Professor."

After she left, Truitt said to Kristina, "I was hoping for tentative truce with your father."

With a half-hearted smile, she said, "He'll sulk for a while. But he'll come round. You've given him a lot to think about. You've exploded some of his dearest preconceptions. Now he has to figure out what to do with all the pieces. He's not a bad man, you know. He's just had some crazy thing against you. I may be starting to figure him out."

The first few weeks of Truitt's return to school were sharply enhanced by the presence of Kristina Day. There were weekly dinners at Day Ranch, and occasional excursions to regional attractions he had taken little interest in, before. They took trips to her favorite ski resorts, while snow favored that sport. As winter melted and the days grew warmer she introduced him to long day hikes up the Wood River, and Magic Mountain. There were the lava beds, the sand dunes and the expansive canyon of the Snake as it turned north and west to the Columbia. He learned the place names and began to feel a part of her land and her life.

Working together had improved as the term progressed, the muscles of self-restraint were exercised to the fullest. Their common goal of serving the higher good—the students—above their personal desires was a winning strategy that he had to thank Kristina for. They hovered over the development of the students, as the great hawks nurtured their nests in the bluffs above the river. The process fed their growing relationship as well, bringing them closer to purpose and heart.

Gradually, Kristina's bid for graduate school did displace Martin in Truitt's focus, but no one seemed to notice. By that time, the collective group of seniors was already in graduation mode. Martin, in particular, was distracted by new responsibilities at the dry goods store, as well as his wedding plans. Kristina had been correct about that, too. Truitt enjoyed Martin's mind and still played to him in class, a maneuver unnoticed by anyone else.

Few suspected the nature of their relationship, especially once Kristina opened up about graduate schools in medieval studies. There were exceptions. Geoff had guessed long before even Truitt understood. Sofia had wished it to be so, even at the cost of her standing with Christian Day. And Birdie had to be enlisted by Kristina as a matter of faith. As much as Truitt had resented this antagonistic student, he grew to admire her independence and her tenacity for uncovering the truth. She was a truthsayer, one not given to hyperbole or prefabrication. She was a true friend to Kristi. For that alone Truitt found his heart opening to her.

The position in upper state New York had opened up and Dr. Rutherton set him up in two interviews. His work preceded him, and the interviews were nothing more than a chance for the faculty to meet Truitt and see how they could work with him. As he suspected, there was no medieval program. Truitt was the top candidate for the school primarily because he had experience in setting up a program. The small Catholic college was impressed with his connection to St. Amadour, and that had clinched his nomination to the post. Dr. Rutherton was quite pleased, and true to his word, offered Truitt residence at the family estate, which Truitt accepted, for the initial move, anyhow.

Kristina took the news with stalwart objectivity. She refused to be concerned at his parting in June. Instead, she doubled her efforts in applying for graduate school programs which could bring her closer to his position. Of course, any such position would hardly be open to her until the following year. Truitt thought that she might visit him in Tivoli knowing how well she would fit in with the Rutherton clan. Even Caroline, who had moved her attentions to a recently arrived Belgian count could not help but be swayed by Kristina's charm. Yet even with his newfound joy, Truitt began to worry about walking away and leaving Kristina behind.

One day in passing, Sofia revealed her sympathy for Truitt's predicament, offering to keep Kristi working to the bone on the new program, leaving her little time to miss his presence. The new program was in the final stages of planning, but there was much to do to prepare the course work for its first class next fall. Avila anticipated Kristi's unfettered mind to take charge of the student volunteers over the summer. In all, Truitt had come to learn that Avila was not the femme fatal that he had always cast her as. Although she was no longer a frequent guest at the Day house, she occasionally appeared at Mrs. Day's table when Christian was away.

In the last week of his tenure at St. Clements, Truitt joined a party Kristina had arranged to picnic on Jackson's Bench. After Geoff joined them in the corral at Day Ranch, they saddled the horses and headed up the steppe toward Jake's ranch, where they were to meet up with the horse trainer and his niece, Birdie.

Setting out early in the morning, they reached the back pasture of the ranch before noon. The lunch Tessa had packed was carried in small packets spread across the saddlebags of the three riders. The path took them along a bluff above the river canyon, through rocky terrain and across the open rangeland above Day Ranch.

They chatted easily about the end of the term and what lay in store for each during the summer months. Geoff was relentless in teasing Truitt about Kristi and she took it all in good humor. He commented on Kristi's loss of the great inland empire, the dissolution of the Day-Befford partnership. "And what's going on with old Si, anyhow? Don't see him around anymore."

Kristi pulled up her horse, to wait for him to catch up, then fell in with him. They rode behind Truitt. "He's run off with Trish Winslow to some tropical playground—Martinique, I think it was. Mary Befford is scandalized."

"That's the kind of thing I'd picture him doing. Makes you wonder about the little lady, doesn't it?" Geoff said smugly.

"What do you mean?" Kristi asked.

Taking interest in the direction of their conversation, Truitt turned back to join them. "Martinique is known for its clothing optional recreation," Truitt jumped in.

"Well, he never did like the idea of chastity anyhow," Kristina said with aplomb.

"Oh ho!" Meyer called out, then galloped off mischievously.

"Oh no, you don't!" Kristina shouted, chasing after him. "Geoff! Stop! Come back here."

He led them toward a rocky point positioned above the bluff overhang known as Jackson's Bench. Truitt took up the rear, and as he approached, Kristi was dismounting while Geoff stayed amount. They were looking into the roiling water of a small hot spring hidden in the rocky terrain.

Geoff was finishing his comments to Kristina with "...does he know?"

Kristina glanced briefly at Truitt, then said harshly, "Thanks a bunch, Geoff."

"Know what?" Truitt asked. Taking in the vista, the pool, Geoff's teasing tone and Kristina's obvious discomfort, he thought he could guess.

"Got to go see Jake." Meyer took off again, heading further up the steppe.

"What's this all about?" Truitt asked gently. She had known Meyer for years, and he knew they had a significant relationship, no doubt born of a special bond. It would fit Meyer's sense of fair play to have everything out in the open. "You and Meyer were here together?"

He dismounted and joined her at the water's edge.

"Not recently, you understand. Years ago. When I was seventeen. Before Si and all that."

"And it bothered Meyer to know that you came here with Befford?"

"No. I didn't. That's what bothered Si so much. I wanted to wait until after the wedding. He didn't."

"He didn't like the idea of your chastity. I see."

She turned away from him and stood on a rock near the water's edge. "Back then, Geoff had my heart and soul. I was going into my senior year. I thought I was so mature. My mother was gone by then. I felt so old and so responsible. What I did was stupid—very naïve. I never considered the risks. I was so very, very lucky." She gazed into the steam rising from the water as if she saw the specter of her past.

Truitt thought he knew how it might have been for her. He thought then of another girl at seventeen, of one who had been led to ruin by placing her trust in a man who should have been guiding her judgment, not exploiting her youth.

She walked to the head of the pool and looked down, the steam barely rising to the top of the rock surround.

"I realized what an enormous risk it was the next fall, when a friend from school—she was only sixteen—had ended up pregnant after agreeing to meet a boy up here. She was ostracized by everyone and forced to marry the boy, someone she never loved. How easy it is to please yourself for the moment. The years drag by afterwards for those who get caught."

She finally settled down on a rocky ledge over the pool. Only then did she dare to glance at his face. "I vowed after that to remain chaste until the day of my marriage. Reverend Smythe's drive to maintain the innocence of all the girls at school with his chastity vow helped. Truly, though, Si made it easy for me to keep the vow."

"I thought he was against it?" Truitt joined her on the ledge.

She laughed momentarily, then said, "The truth is, I had no desire to touch him or to be touched by him as long as he smelled of beer and tasted of chew. His bedside manner is not too inviting."

"You weren't in love with him," Truitt said.

"No, I never had been. I thought that love would grow with the years and shared lives."

Truitt sat next to her, taking her hand. "And if you had been in love with him? Would it have made any difference?"

"To the vow you mean?" She thought about his question for a moment. "No. I don't think it would have. For one thing, I wasn't about to repeat that same mistake, no matter how smitten I thought I might be."

"And now. Do you feel the same way?"

She glanced up at him. He took her hand and searched for the answer in her eyes.

Just then they heard the pounding of hooves rushing up the trail. Geoff Meyer called out, "Hah! I knew they'd still be here!"

He pulled his mount up to the rocky ledge that bound the pool. "Are we going to picnic on the bench or are you guys going to spend the night here?"

Birdie and Jake approached more cautiously. Kristina jumped from the ledge back onto the terrain and pulled Truitt down with her.

Geoff and Birdie rode on while Jake paused to say, "We'll be waiting on that lunch out yonder, in the meadow." He followed the others.

"We'd better go," Kristina said starting toward their horses.

Truitt pulled her back. "Wait. You haven't answered my question." He drew her close and as if by tacit agreement, they kissed again.

Kristi was the first to let go, but she held fast to his hand. "My thought is, Professor. I've waited this long—through thick and thin. It's been good discipline. And you have to admit, it's saved me from unnecessary complication."

He glanced up the trail the others had left.

"A mistake, I agree. I hope that you can appreciate that." she kissed his cheek. "I never really knew the depth of my love until you kissed me in your office that day."

He pulled her close again. "At that very moment? And, what about this very moment? How do you feel now?"

"Like I am going to die if we don't get moving, because I sure as heck am not going to repeat that mistake *here*, even with the man I love—even as my whole being yearns to."

"And mine," he admitted, taking one last kiss. "But I can wait. After all, heaven is best served with the joy of anticipation."

About the Author

Jo Guasasco Meador was born in San Francisco at the end of World War II. She has written nonfiction, memoir, poetry, and fiction through clerical and data jobs over the years while pursuing her lifelong avocation to be a writer. She holds a master of fine arts degree from the Northwest Institute of Literary Arts on Whidbey Island, where she lives with her ever patient and stalwart husband of thirty years.